"You have plenty of reason to be worried," Sean reminded Emily.

"Don't make this into a worst-case scenario." Emily continued to hold his hand, and he felt the tension in her grip.

"Seriously, Emily, you *do* need a bodyguard."

"I agree, and the job is yours."

He'd expected an argument but was glad that she'd decided to be rational. He glanced toward the dining room. The snowstorm raged outside the windows. "I could do with another bowl of chili."

"Me, too."

Before she hopped down the step to the floor, she went up on tiptoe and gave him a kiss on the forehead. It was nothing special, the kind of small affection a wife might regularly bestow on her husband. The utter simplicity blew him away.

Before she could turn her back and skip off into the dining room, he caught her hand and gave a tug. She was in his arms. When her body pressed against his, they were joined together the way they were supposed to be.

Then he kissed her.

ROCKY MOUNTAIN THREAT

USA TODAY Bestselling Author

CASSIE MILES

&

CINDI MYERS

2 Thrilling Stories

Mountain Blizzard
and *Snowbound Suspicion*

ISBN-13: 978-1-335-74496-8

Rocky Mountain Threat

Copyright © 2022 by Harlequin Enterprises ULC

Mountain Blizzard
First published in 2017. This edition published in 2022.
Copyright © 2017 by Kay Bergstrom

Snowbound Suspicion
First published in 2019. This edition published in 2022.
Copyright © 2019 by Cynthia Myers

Recycling programs
for this product may
not exist in your area.

For questions and comments about the quality of this book, please contact us at CustomerService@Harlequin.com.

Harlequin Enterprises ULC
22 Adelaide St. West, 41st Floor
Toronto, Ontario M5H 4E3, Canada
www.Harlequin.com

Printed in U.S.A.

CONTENTS

Cassie Miles, a *USA TODAY* bestselling author, lives in Colorado. After raising two daughters and cooking tons of macaroni and cheese for her family, Cassie is trying to be more adventurous in her culinary efforts. She's discovered that almost anything tastes better with wine. When she's not plotting Harlequin Intrigue books, Cassie likes to hang out at the Denver Botanic Gardens near her high-rise home.

Books by Cassie Miles

Harlequin Intrigue

Mountain Retreat
Colorado Wildfire
Mountain Bodyguard
Mountain Shelter
Mountain Blizzard
Frozen Memories

The Girl Who Wouldn't Stay Dead
The Girl Who Couldn't Forget
The Final Secret
Witness on the Run
Cold Case Colorado

Visit the Author Profile page
at Harlequin.com for more titles.

MOUNTAIN BLIZZARD

Cassie Miles

For Nafina, who will always be my screen saver and, as always, to Rick.

Prologue

The double-deck luxury yacht rolled over a Pacific wave just outside San Francisco Bay as Emily Peterson wobbled down a nearly vertical staircase on her four-inch stilettos. Her short, tight, sparkly disguise gave her a new respect for the gaggle of party girls she'd hidden among to sneak on board. Somehow those ladies managed to walk on these stilts without falling and to keep their nipples covered in spite of ridiculously low-cut dresses.

Her plan for tonight was to locate James Wynter's private computer and load the data onto a flash drive. She'd slipped away from the gala birthday party for one of Wynter Corporation's top executives. The guests had been raucous as they guzzled champagne and admired their view of the Golden Gate Bridge against the night sky. Some had complained about having to surrender their cell phones, and Emily had agreed. It would have been useful to snap photos of high-ranking political types getting cozy with Wynter's thugs.

Belowdecks, she went to the second door on the right. She'd been told this was James Wynter's office. The polished brass knob turned easily in her hand. No need to pick the lock.

Pulse racing, she entered. The desk lamp was off, but moonlight through the porthole was enough to let her see the open laptop. In a matter of minutes, she could transfer Wynter's data to her flash drive, and she'd finally have the evidence she needed for her human trafficking article.

Before she reached the desk, she heard angry voices in the corridor. She backed away from the desk and ducked into a closet with a louvered door. Desperately, she prayed for them to pass by the office and go to a different room.

No such luck.

The office door crashed open. One of the men fell into the office on his hands and knees while others laughed. Another guy turned on the lamp. Light spread across the desktop and spilled onto the floor.

Her pulse thundered in her ears, but Emily stayed utterly silent. She dared not make a sound. If Wynter's men found her, she was terrified of what they'd do.

Carefully, she stepped out of her red stilettos and went into a crouch. Through the slats in the door, she could see the shoes and legs of four men. The man who had fallen kept apologizing again and again, begging the others to believe him.

She recognized the voice of one of his tormentors: Frankie Wynter, the youngest son of James Wynter. Though she couldn't exactly tell what was going on, she thought Frankie was pushing the man who was so very sorry while the others laughed.

There was a clunk as the man who was being pushed flopped into the swivel chair behind the desk. From this angle, she saw only the back sides of the three men. One of them rocked back on his heel, cracked his knuckles and then lunged forward. She heard the slap, flesh against flesh.

They hit him again. What could she do? How could she stop them? She hated being silent while someone else suffered. Each blow made her cringe. If her ex-husband had been here, he could have made a difference, would have done the right thing. But she was on her own and utterly without backup. Should she speak up? Did she dare?

The beating stopped.

"Shut up," Frankie roared at the man in the chair. "Crying like a little girl, you make me sick."

"Let me talk. Please. I need to see the kids."

"Don't beg."

Emily saw the gleam of silver as Frankie drew his gun. Terror gripped her heart. The other two men flanked him. They murmured something about waiting for his father.

Frankie opened the center drawer on the desk and took out a silencer. "I can do what needs to be done."

"But your father—"

"He's always telling me to step up." He finished attaching the silencer to his handgun. "That's what I'm going to do."

He fired point-blank, then fired again.

When Frankie stepped away, she saw the dead man in the chair. His suit jacket was thrown open. The front of his shirt was slick with blood.

Emily pinched her lips closed to keep from crying out. She should have done something. A man was dead, and she hadn't reached out, hadn't helped him.

"We're already out at sea," Frankie said. "International waters. A good place to dump a body."

"I'll get something to carry him in."

He glanced toward the closet…

Chapter 1

Colorado
Six weeks later

He'd been down this road before. Though Sean Timmons was pretty sure that he'd never actually been to Hazelwood Ranch, there was something familiar about the long, snow-packed drive bordered on either side by wood fences. He parked his cherry-red Jeep Wrangler between a snow-covered pickup truck and a snowy white lump that was the size of a four-door sedan. Peering through his windshield, he saw a large two-story house with a wraparound porch. It looked like somebody had tried to shovel his or her way out, but the wind and new snow had all but erased the path leading to the front door.

Weather forecasters had been gleefully predicting the

first blizzard of the Colorado ski season, and it looked like they were right for a change. Sean was glad he wouldn't have to make the drive back to Denver tonight. He hadn't formally accepted this assignment, but he didn't see why he wouldn't.

Hazel Hopkins from Hazelwood Ranch had called his office at TST Security yesterday and said she needed a bodyguard for at least a week, possibly longer. He wouldn't be protecting Hazel but a "friend" of hers. She was vague about the threat, but he gathered that her "friend" had offended someone with a story she'd written. The situation didn't seem too dangerous. Panic words, such as *narcotics*, *crime lord* and *homicidal ax murderer*, had been absent from her conversation.

Hazel had refused to give her "friend's" name, which wasn't all that unusual. The wealthy folk who lived near Aspen were often cagey about their identities. That was okay with him. The money transfer for Hazel's retainer had cleared, and that was really all Sean needed to know. Still, he'd been curious enough to look up Hazelwood Ranch on the internet, where he'd learned that the ranch was a small operation with only twenty-five to fifty head of cattle. Hazel, the owner, was a small but healthy-looking woman with short silver hair. No clues about the identity of her "friend." If he had to guess, he'd say that the person he'd be guarding was an aging movie star who'd written one of those tell-all books and was now regretting her candor.

Soon enough he'd know the truth. He zipped his parka, slapped on a knit cap and put on heavy-duty gloves. It wasn't far to the front porch, but the snow was already higher than his ankles. Fat, wet flakes swirled around him as he left his Jeep and slogged along the remnants of a pathway to the front door.

On the porch, the Adirondack chairs and a hanging swing were covered with giant scoops of drifted snow. He stomped his boots and punched the bell under the porch lamp. Hazel Hopkins opened the door and ushered him into a warmly lighted foyer with a sweeping wrought-iron staircase and a matching chandelier with lights that glimmered like candles.

"Glad you made it, Sean." Her voice was husky. When he looked down into her lively turquoise eyes, he suspected that a lot of wild living had gone into creating her raspy tone. Though she wore jeans on the bottom, her top was kimono-style with a fire-breathing dragon embroidered on each shoulder. He had the impression that he'd met her before.

She stuck out her tiny hand. "I'm Hazel Hopkins."

Compared with hers, his hand looked as big as a grizzly bear's paw. Sean was six feet, three inches tall, and this little woman made him feel like a hulking giant.

"Hang your jacket on the rack and take off your wet boots," she said. "You're running late. It's almost dark."

"The snow slowed me down."

"I was worried."

Parallel lines creased her forehead, and he noticed that she glanced surreptitiously toward a shotgun in the corner of the entryway. Gently he asked, "Have there been threats?"

"I had a more practical concern. I was worried that you wouldn't be able to find the ranch and you couldn't reach us by phone. Something's wrong with my landline, and the blizzard is disrupting the cell phone signal."

He sat on a bench by the door to take off his wet boots.

Without pausing for breath, she continued. "You know how they always say that the weather doesn't affect your service on the cell phone or the Wi-Fi? Well, I'm here to tell you that's a lie, a bold-faced lie. Every time we have a serious snowstorm, I have a problem."

The heels on her pixie-size boots clicked on the terracotta floor between area rugs as she darted toward him, grabbed his boots and carried them to a drying mat under the coat hooks. She braced her fists on her hips and stared at him. "You're exactly how I remembered."

Aha, they had met before. He stood and adjusted the tail of his beige suede shirt to hide the holster he wore on his hip. "This may sound strange…" he said. "Have I ever been here?"

"I don't think so. But Hazelwood Ranch is the backdrop for many, many photos. The kids came here often."

Her explanation raised more questions. Backdrop for what? What kids? Why would he have seen the photos? "Maybe you could remind me—"

She reached up to pat his cheek. "I'm glad that you're still clean-shaven. I don't like the scruffy beard trend. I'll bet you picked up your grooming habits in the FBI."

"Plus, my mom was a good teacher."

"Not according to the photo on your TST Security website," she said. "Your brother, Dylan, has a ponytail."

"He's kind of a wild card. His specialties are electronics and cybersecurity."

"And your specialty is working with law enforcement and figuring out the crimes. I believe your third partner, Mason Steele, is what you boys call the 'muscle' in the group."

"I guess you checked me out."

"I have, indeed."

He took a long look at her, hoping to jog his brain. His mind was blank. Nothing came through. His gaze focused on her necklace, a long string of etched silver, black onyx and turquoise beads. He knew that necklace…and the matching bracelet coiled around her wrist.

Shaking his head, he inhaled deeply. A particular aroma came to him. The scent of roasted peppers, onions, chili and cinnamon mingled with honey and fresh corn bread. He couldn't explain this odor, but his lungs had been craving it. Nothing else was nearly as sweet or as spicy delicious. Nothing else would satisfy this newly awakened appetite.

His eyelids closed as a high-definition picture appeared in his mind. He saw a woman—young, fresh and beautiful. A blue jersey shift outlined her slender curves, and she'd covered the front with a ruffled white apron. Her long, sleek brown hair cascaded down her back, almost to her waist. She held a wooden spoon toward him, offering a taste of her homemade chili.

He had always wanted more than a taste. He wanted everything with her, the whole enchilada. But he couldn't have her. Their time was over.

He gazed down into her eyes…*her turquoise eyes!*

"You remember," Hazel said, "the wedding."

That Saturday in June, six and a half years ago, was a blur of color and taste and music and silence. His eyelids snapped open. "I recall the divorce a whole lot better."

These were dangerous memories, warning bells. He should run, get the hell out of there. Instead, he followed his nose down a shadowy hallway. Stiff-legged, he marched through the dining room into the bright, warm kitchen where the aroma of chili was thick.

Two pans of golden corn bread rested near the sink on the large center island with a dark marble countertop. She stood at the stove with her back toward him, stirring a heavy cast-iron pot. She wore jeans that outlined her long legs and tight, round bottom. On top, she had on a striped sweater. Over her shoulder, she said, "Hazel, did I hear the doorbell?"

The small, silver-haired woman beside him growled a warning. "You should turn around slowly, dear."

Sean gripped the edge of the marble countertop, unsure of how he was going to feel when he faced her. Every single day since their divorce five years ago—after only a year and a half of marriage—he had imagined her. Sometimes he remembered the sweet warmth of her body beside him in their bed. Other times he saw her from afar and reveled in coming closer and closer. Usually, he imagined her naked with her dark chestnut hair spilling across her olive skin.

Her hair! He stared at her back and shoulders. She'd chopped off her lush, silky hair.

"Emily," he said.

She whirled. Clearly surprised, she wielded her wooden spoon like a knife she might plunge into his chest. "Sean."

Her turquoise eyes were huge, outlined with thick, dark lashes. Her mouth was a thin, tight line. Her dark brows pulled down, and he immediately recognized her expression, a look he'd seen often while they were married. She was furious. What the hell did she have to be angry about? He was the one who had driven through a blizzard.

He stepped away from the counter, not needing the support. The anger surging through his veins gave him the strength of ten. "I don't know what kind of sick game you two ladies are playing, but it's not funny. I'm leaving."

"Good." She stuck out her jaw and took a step toward him. "I don't want you hanging around."

"Then why call me up here? I had a verbal contract, an agreement." TST had a strict no-refund policy, but this was a special circumstance. He'd pay back the retainer from his own pocket. "Forget it. I'll give your money back."

"What money?" Emily's upper lip curled in a sneer that she probably thought was terrifying. Yeah, right, as terrifying as a bunny wiggling its nose.

"You hired me."

"Not me." Emily threw her spoon back into the chili pot. "Aunt Hazel, what have you done?"

The silver-haired woman with dragons on her shoulders had maneuvered her way around so she was standing at the far end of the center island with both of them on the other side. "When you two got married, I always thought you were a perfect match."

"You were the only one," Emily said.

Unfortunately, that was true. Sean and Emily were both born and raised in Colorado, but they had met in San Francisco. She was a student at University of California in Berkeley, majoring in English and appearing at least once a week at local poetry slams. At one of these open-mike events, he saw her.

She'd been dancing around on a small stage wearing

a long gypsy skirt. Her wild hair was snatched up on her head with dozens of ribbons. He'd been impressed when she rhymed "appetite" and "morning light" and "coprolite," which was a technical word for fossilized poop. He would have stayed and talked to her, but he'd been undercover, rooting out a drug dealer at the slam venue. Sean had been in the FBI.

When they told people they were getting married, their opposite lifestyles—Bohemian chick versus federal agent—were the first thing people pointed to as a reason it would never work. The next issue was an age difference. She was nineteen, and he was twenty-seven. Eight years wasn't really all that much, but her youthful immaturity stood in stark contrast to his orderly, responsible lifestyle.

"If you'd asked me at the time," Aunt Hazel said, "I'd have advised you to live together before marriage."

Sean hadn't wanted to take that chance. He had hoped the bonds of marriage would help him control his butterfly. "It was a mistake," he said.

Emily responded with a snort.

"You don't think so?" he asked.

"Are you still here? You were in such a rush to get away from me."

His contrary streak kicked in. He sure as hell wasn't going to let her think that she was chasing him out the door. Very slowly and deliberately, he pulled out a stool and took a seat at the center island opposite the stove top. He turned away from Emily.

"Aunt Hazel," he said, "you still haven't told us why you hired me as a bodyguard."

"You? A bodyguard?" Emily sputtered. "You're not a fed anymore?"

"Do you care?"

"Why should I?"

"What are you doing now?" he asked.

"Writing."

"Poetry?" He scoffed.

She exhaled an eager gasp as she tilted her head and leaned toward him. Her turquoise eyes flashed. Her face, framed by wisps of brown hair, was flushed beneath the natural olive tint. He remembered her spirit and her enthusiasm, and he knew that she wanted to tell him something. The words were poised at the tip of her tongue, straining to jump out.

And he wanted to hear them. He wanted to share with her, to listen to her stories and to feel the waves of excitement that radiated from her. Emily had always thrown herself wholeheartedly into whatever she was attempting to do. It was part of her charm. No doubt she had some project that was insanely ambitious.

With a scowl, she raised her hand, palm out, to hold him away from her. "Just go."

"Such drama," Aunt Hazel said. "The two of you are impossible. It's called communication, and it's not all that difficult. Sean, you're going to sit there and I'm going to tell you what our girl has been up to."

"I don't have to listen to this," Emily said.

"If I'm not explaining properly, feel free to jump in," Hazel said. "First of all, Emily doesn't write poems anymore. After the divorce, she changed her focus to journalism."

"Totally impractical," he muttered. "With all the newspapers going out of business, nobody makes a living as a journalist."

"I do all right."

Her voice was proud, and there was a strut in her step as she strolled from one end of the island to the other. Watching her long, slender legs and the way her hips swayed was a treat. He felt himself being drawn into her orbit. She'd always had the power to mesmerize him.

"Fine," he muttered. "Tell me about your big deal success in journalism."

"Right after the divorce, I got a job writing for the *Daily Californian*, Berkeley's student newspaper. I learned investigative techniques, and I blogged. And I started doing articles for online magazines. I have a regular bimonthly piece in a national publication, and they pay very nicely."

"For articles about eye shadow and shoes?"

"Hard-hitting news." She slammed her fist on the marble island. "I witnessed a murder."

"Which is why I called you," Aunt Hazel said. "Emily's life is in danger."

This was just crazy enough to be possible. "Have you received threats?"

"Death threats," she said.

His feet were rooted to the kitchen floor. He didn't want to stay...but he couldn't leave her here unprotected.

Chapter 2

Emily couldn't look away from him. Fascinated, she watched as a muscle in Sean's jaw twitched, his brow lowered and his eyes turned as black as polished obsidian. He was outrageously masculine.

With a nearly imperceptible shrug, his muscles tensed, but his frame didn't contract. He seemed to get bigger. His fingers coiled into fists, ready to lash out. He was prepared to defend her against anything and everything. His aggressive stance told her that he'd take on an army to keep her from harm.

When she thought about it, his new occupation as a bodyguard made sense. Sean had always been a protector, whether it was keeping a bully away from his sweet-but-nerdy brother or rescuing a stray dog by stopping four lanes of traffic on a busy highway. If Sean had been hiding in that louvered closet instead of her, he would have saved the man she now could identify as Roger Patrone.

Sean reached toward her. She yanked her arm away. She didn't dare allow him to get too close. No matter how much she wanted his embrace, that wasn't going to happen. This man had been the love of her life. Ending their marriage was the most difficult thing she'd ever done, and she couldn't bear going through that soul-wrenching pain again.

"Did you report the murder to the police?" he asked.

"Of course," she said, "and to your former FBI bosses. Specifically, I had several chats with Special Agent Greg Levine. I'm surprised he didn't call and tell you."

"Levine is still stationed in San Francisco," he said. "Is that where the crime took place?"

"Yes."

"In the city?"

"Just beyond the Golden Gate Bridge."

"In open waters," he said. "A good place to dump a body."

It was a bit disturbing that his FBI-trained brain and Freddie Wynter's nefarious instincts drew exactly the same conclusion. *Maybe you need to think like a criminal to catch one.* "As it turned out, the ocean wasn't such a great dump site. The victim washed up on Baker Beach five days later."

"The waiting must have been rough on you," he said. "It's no fun to report a murder when the body goes missing."

Definitely not fun when the investigating officer was buddy-buddy with her ex-husband. She'd asked Greg not to blab to Sean, but she'd expected him to ignore her request. Those guys stuck together. The only time Sean had lied to her when they were married was when he was covering up for a fellow fed.

She wondered if Sean's departure from the FBI had been due to negative circumstances. Had Mr. Perfect screwed up? Gotten himself fired? "Why did you leave the FBI?"

"It was time."

"Cryptic," she snapped.

"It's true."

God forbid he give her a meaningful explanation! Leaving the FBI must have been traumatic for him. Sean was born to be a fed. He could have been a poster boy with his black hair neatly barbered and his chin clean-shaven and his beige chamois suede shirt looking like it had come fresh from the dry cleaner's. He'd been proud to be a special agent. Would he confide in her if they'd fired him? "You can be so damn annoying."

"Is that so?"

"I hate when you put off a perfectly rational query with a macho statement that doesn't really tell me anything, like a man's got to do what a man's got to do."

"I don't expect you to understand."

"Mission accomplished."

Hostility vibrated around him. A red flush climbed his throat. Oh yeah, he was angry. Hot and angry. They could have put him on the porch and melted the blizzard.

"I'll leave," he said.

"Not in this storm," Aunt Hazel said. "The two of you need to calm down. Have some chili. Try to be civil."

Emily stepped away from the stove, folded her arms

at her waist and watched with a sidelong gaze as Sean and her aunt dished up bowls of chili and cut off slabs of corn bread. Sean managed to squash his anger and transform into a pleasant dinner guest. She could have matched his politeness with a cold veneer of her own, but she preferred to say nothing.

There had been a time—long ago when she and Sean were first dating—when she was known for her candor. Every word from her lips was truth. She had been 100 percent frank and open.

Those days were gone.

She'd glimpsed the ugliness, heard the cries of the hopeless, learned that life wasn't always good and people weren't always kind. She'd lost her innocence.

And Hazel was correct. She'd gotten herself into trouble from the Wynters. Though she didn't want to be, she was terrified. Almost anything could set off her fear…an unexpected phone call, the slam of a door, a car that followed too closely. She hadn't gotten a good night's sleep since that night in James Wynter's closet.

The only reason she hadn't disintegrated into a quivering mass of nerves was simple: Wynter and his men didn't know her identity. Her FBI contact had told her that they knew there was a witness to the murder, but didn't know who. It was only a matter of time before they found out who she was and came after her. *Tell him. Tell Sean. Let him be your bodyguard.*

Her aunt asked, "Emily, can I get you something to drink?"

Hazel and Sean had already sprinkled grated cheddar on top of their chili bowls and added a spoonful of sour cream. They were headed to the adjoining dining room.

What would it hurt to have dinner with him? The

more she looked at him, the more she saw hints of his former self, her husband, the gentleman, the broad-shouldered man who had stolen her heart. She remembered the first time they were introduced when he'd tried to shake hands and she gave him a hug. They'd always been opposites and always attracted.

"I'm not hungry," Emily said.

"There's no reason to be so stubborn," Hazel scolded. "I've hired you a bodyguard. Let the man do his job."

"I don't want a bodyguard."

She glared at Sean, standing so straight and tall like a knight in shining armor. She was drawn to his strength. At the same time, he ticked her off. She wanted to tip him over like an extra-large tin can.

Edging closer to the kitchen windows, she pushed aside the curtain and peered outside. Day had faded into dusk, and the snow was coming down hard and fast. The blizzard wasn't going to let up; he'd be here all night. She'd be spending the night under the same roof with him? *This could be a problem, a big one.*

"I've got a question for you," he said as he strolled past her and set his chili bowl on a woven place mat. "What kind of murder would trigger an FBI investigation?"

"The man who pulled the trigger is Frankie Wynter."

He startled. "The son of James Wynter?"

She'd said too much. The best move now was to retreat. She stretched and yawned. "I'm tired, Aunt Hazel. I think I'll go up to my room."

Without waiting for a response, she pivoted and ran from the kitchen. In the foyer, she paused to put Hazel's rifle in the closet. It was dangerous to leave that thing out. Then she charged up the staircase, taking two steps at a time. In her bedroom, she turned on the lamp and flopped onto her back on the queen-size bed with the handmade crazy quilt.

Memory showed her the picture of Roger Patrone sprawled back in the swivel chair with his necktie askew and his shirt covered in blood. When they came toward the closet, looking for something to wrap around poor Roger, she'd expected to be the next victim. She'd held tightly to the doorknob, hoping they'd think it was locked.

There had been no need to hold the knob. Frankie told them to get the plastic shower curtain from the bathroom. Blood wouldn't seep through. His quick orders had made her think that he might have pulled this stunt before. Other bodies might have gone over the railing of his daddy's double-decker yacht. Other murders might have been committed.

She stood, lurched toward the door, pivoted and went back to the bed. Trapped in her room like a child, she had no escape from memory. Her chest tightened. It felt like a giant fist was squeezing her lungs, and she couldn't get enough oxygen. She sat up straight. She was hot and cold at the same time. Her head was dizzy. Her breath came in frantic gasps.

With a moan, she leaned forward, put her head between her knees and told herself to inhale through her nose and exhale through her mouth. Breathe deeply and slowly. Wasn't working—her throat was too tight. Was she having a panic attack? She didn't know; she'd never had this feeling before.

The door to her bedroom opened. Sean stepped inside as though he didn't need to ask her permission and had every right to be there. She would have yelled at him, but she couldn't catch her breath. Her pulse fluttered madly.

He crossed the carpet and sat beside her on the bed. His arm wrapped around her shoulders. His masculine aroma, a combination of soap, cedar forest and sweat, permeated her senses as she leaned her head against his shoulder.

Her hands clutched in a knot against her breast, but she felt her heart rate beginning to slow down. She was regaining control of herself. Somehow she'd find a way to handle the fear. And she'd set things right.

Gently, he rocked back and forth. "Better?"

"Much." She took a huge gulp of air.

"Do you want to talk about what happened?"

"I already did. I told your buddy, Agent Levine."

"Number one, he's not my buddy. Number two, why didn't he offer to put you in witness protection?"

"I turned it down," she said.

"Emily, do you know how dangerous Frankie Wynter is?"

"I've been researching Wynter Corp for over a year," she said. "Their smuggling operations, gambling and money laundering are nasty crimes, but the real evil comes from human trafficking. Last year, the port authorities seized a boxcar container with over seventy women and children crammed inside. Twelve were dead."

"And Wynter Corp managed to wriggle out from under the charges."

"The paperwork vanished." That was one of the bits of evidence she'd hoped to get from James Wynter's computer. "There was no indication of the sender or the destination where these people were to be delivered. All they could say was that they were promised jobs."

"This kind of investigation is best left to the cops."

She separated from him and rose to her feet. "I know what I'm doing."

"I'm not discounting your ability," he said. "You might be the best investigative reporter of all time, but you don't have the contacts. Not like the FBI. They've got undercover people everywhere. Not to mention their access to advanced weaponry and surveillance equipment."

"I understand all that." He wasn't telling her anything she hadn't already figured out for herself.

"You're a witness to a crime. That's it—that's all she wrote."

She braced herself against the dresser and looked into the large mirror on the wall. Her reflection showed her fear in the tension around her eyes and her blanched complexion. Sean—ever the opposite—seemed calm and balanced.

"Can I tell you the truth?" she asked.

"That would be best."

She made eye contact with his reflection in the mirror. "I didn't actually witness the shooting. I saw Frankie with the gun in his hand. He screwed on a silencer. I heard the gunshot, and I saw the bullet holes... and the blood. But I didn't actually witness Frankie pointing the gun and pulling the trigger."

"Minor point," he said. "A good prosecutor can connect those dots."

"The body that washed ashore five days later was too badly nibbled by fishes for identification." She splayed her fingers on the dresser and stared down at them. "I was kind of hoping he was someone else, someone who jumped off the Golden Gate Bridge, but Agent Levine matched his DNA."

"To what?"

"I'd given a description to a sketch artist and identified the victim from a mug sheet photo. His name was Roger Patrone."

He shrugged. "I don't know him."

"He was thirty-five, only a couple of years older than you, and made his living with a small-time gambling operation in a cheesy strip joint. Convicted of fraud, he served three years."

"You've done your homework."

"Never married, no kids, he was orphaned when he was nine and grew up with a family in Chinatown. He speaks the language, eats the food, knows the customs and has a reputation as a negotiator for Wynter."

"Roger sounds like a useful individual," Sean said. "I'm guessing the old man wasn't too happy about this murder."

"Yeah, well, blood is still thicker than water. The FBI brought Frankie in for questioning, but one of the other guys in Wynter Corp confessed to killing Patrone and claimed self-defense. He took the fall for the boss's son."

Sean left the bed and came up behind her. His chest wasn't actually touching her back, but if she moved one step, she'd be in his arms.

In a measured tone, he said, "You're telling me that Frankie's not in custody."

"No, he's not."

"And he knows there's a witness."

"Yes."

"Did you write about the murder?"

"Agent Levine asked me not to." But she had written many articles about the evil-doing of Wynter Corporation.

"Does Frankie have your name?"

"No," she said. "I write under an alias, three different aliases, in fact. And I have two dummy blogs. Since my communication with these publications is via the internet, nobody even knows what I look like."

"Smart."

"Thank you." Her reflection smiled at his. *So far, so good.* She might make it through the night with no more explanation than that. There was more to tell, but she didn't want to get involved with Sean. Not again.

He continued. "And you're also smart to have left Frankie and the other thugs behind in San Francisco. Hazelwood Ranch seems like a safe place to stay until this all dies down."

Unfortunately, she hadn't come to visit Aunt Hazel for safety reasons. Her gaze flickered across the surface of the mirror. She didn't want to tell him.

He leaned closer, whispered in her ear. "What is it, Emily? What do you want to say?"

The words came tumbling out. "Frankie is here in Colorado. The Wynter family has a gated compound over near Aspen. I didn't come here to give up on my investigation. I need to go deeper."

He grasped her upper arms. "Leave this to the police."

From downstairs, there was a scream.

Chapter 3

"Aunt Hazel!"

Though Emily's immediate reaction was to run toward the sound of the scream, Sean only allowed her to take two steps before he grabbed her around the middle and yanked her so hard that her feet left the floor. This was why he'd been hired.

He dragged her across the bedroom. There was only one thought in his mind: get her to safety. In the attached bathroom, he set her down beside a claw-foot tub.

"Stay here," he ordered as he drew his gun. "Keep quiet."

"The hell I will."

Though he hated to waste time with explanation, she needed to know what was going on. He spoke in a no-nonsense tone. "If there's been a break-in, they're after you. If you turn yourself in, we have no leverage.

For your Aunt Hazel's safety, you need to avoid being taken captive."

"Okay, help her." Her face flushed red with fear and anger. Her eyes were wild. She pushed at his shoulder with both hands. "Hurry!"

Moving fast, he crossed to her closed bedroom door. He wished he was wearing boots instead of just socks. If he had to go outside, his feet would turn to ice. He paused at the door and mentally ran through the layout of the house. From the upstairs landing, he could see the front door. He'd know if someone had broken in that way.

Sean was confident in his ability to handle one intruder, maybe two. But Frankie Wynter had a lot of thugs at his disposal, and they were loyal; one guy was willing to face a murder rap for the boss's son. One— or two or more—of them might be standing outside her bedroom door right now.

But he didn't hear anything. Outside, the snow rattled against the windows. The wind whistled. From downstairs, he heard shuffling noises. A heavy fist rapping at the door? A muffled shout. Sean turned the knob, pulled the door open and braced the gun in his hands, ready to shoot.

There was no one on the upstairs landing.

Emily dashed to his side. "Let me help. Please!"

He'd told her to stay back and she chose to ignore him. Emily was turning into a problem. "Is that tub in the bathroom made of cast iron?"

"It's antique. Now is not the time for a home tour."

"Get inside the tub and stay there." At least, she wouldn't be hit by a stray bullet.

"I'm coming with you."

Was she trying to drive him crazy or was this stubborn, infuriating behavior just a part of her natural personality? He couldn't exactly remember. He'd had damn good reasons for divorcing this woman. "No time to argue. Just accept the fact that I know what I'm doing."

"I need a gun."

"What you need is to listen to me."

"Please, Sean! You always carry two guns. Give one to me."

He pulled the Glock from his ankle holster and slapped it into her hand. "Do you remember how to use this?"

She recited the rules he'd taught her one golden afternoon six years ago in Big Sur. "Aim and don't close my eyes. No traditional safety on a Glock, so keep my finger off the trigger until I'm ready. Squeeze—don't yank."

"You've got the basics."

He'd treated their lessons like a game and had never insisted that she take his weapon from the combination safe when he was on assignment and she was alone at home. While he was working undercover, he'd worried about her safety, worried that she'd be hurt and it would be his fault. There was a strange irony in the fact that she'd put herself in ten times more danger than he could imagine.

He peered through the open bedroom door onto the upstairs landing where an overhead light shone down on the southwestern decor that dominated the house: a Navajo rug, a rugged side table and a cactus in an earthenware pot. A long hallway led to other bedrooms. The front edge of the landing was a graceful black wrought-iron staircase overlooking the foyer and chandelier by the front door.

Sean peered over the railing.

A menacing silence rose to greet him. He didn't like the way this was going. Emily's aunt wasn't the type of woman who cowered in silence. He gestured for Emily to stay upstairs while he descended.

At the foot of the staircase, he caught a glimpse of flying kimono dragons when Hazel raced across the foyer and skidded to a stop right in front of him.

She glared. "Where the heck is my rifle?"

Looking down from the landing, Emily said, "I moved it to the front closet."

"I had my gun right by the door," she said to Sean. "Emily shouldn't have moved it. Out of sight, out of mind."

The women in this family simply didn't grasp what it took to be cautious and safe. They needed ten bodyguards apiece. He rushed Hazel up the stairs, where she hugged Emily. The two of them commiserated as though the threat were over and done with. Had they forgotten that there might be an intruder?

"Hazel," he barked, "why did you scream?"

"I heard something outside and looked through the window. A fat lot of good it did, the snow's coming down so hard I couldn't see ten feet. But I caught a glimmer…headlights. I went toward the front door for a better look. At the exact same time, I heard somebody crashing against the back door like they were trying to bust it down. That's when I screamed."

Sean figured that five minutes had passed since they'd heard Hazel's cry for help. "After you screamed, what did you do?"

"I hid."

"Smart," he said. "You didn't reveal your hiding spot until you saw me."

She nodded, and her short silver hair bounced.

"Did you see the intruder? Did he make a noise? Was there more than one?"

"Well, my hearing isn't what it once was, but I'm pretty sure there was only one voice. And I guarantee that nobody made enough noise to tear down the back door."

As Sean herded Emily and her aunt into Emily's bedroom, he tallied up the possible ways to break into the house. In addition to front and back door and many windows, there was likely an entrance to a root cellar or basement. The best way to limit access to the two women was to keep them upstairs. Unfortunately, it also meant they had no escape.

From Emily's bedroom, he peered through the window to the area where the cars were parked. He squinted. "I can see the outline of a truck."

"So?"

"Do you recognize it?" *Is that Frankie Wynter's truck?*

"We're in the mountains, Sean. Every other person drives a truck."

A coating of snow had already covered the truck bed; he couldn't tell if anybody had been riding in back. But the vehicle showed that someone else was on the property, even if there hadn't been other noises from downstairs.

He gave Emily a tight smile. "Stay here with Hazel. Take care of her."

"What are you going to do?"

"I'll check the doors and other points of access."

Her terse nod was a match for his smile. They were both putting on brave faces and tamping down the kind of tension that might cause your hand to tremble or your teeth to chatter. When she rested her hand against his chest, he was reminded of the early days in their marriage when she'd say goodbye before he left on assignment.

"Be careful, Sean."

He tore his gaze away from her turquoise eyes and her rose petal lips. Her trust made him feel strong and brave, even if he wasn't facing a real dragon. He was girding his loins, like a knight protecting his castle. In the old days, they would have kissed.

"I should come with you," Aunt Hazel said. "You need someone to watch your six."

"Stay here," he growled.

Emily hooked her arm around her aunt's waist. "We might as well do what he says. Sean can be a teensy bit rigid when it comes to obeying orders."

"My, my, my." Hazel adjusted the embroidered dragons on her shoulders. "Isn't that just like a fed?"

Hey, lady, you're the one who called me. And he was done playing their games. As far as he was concerned, they'd had their last warning. He refused to stand here and explain again why they shouldn't throw themselves into the line of fire when there was a possible intruder. He made a quick pivot and descended the staircase with the intention of searching the main floor.

The house was large but not so massive that he'd get lost. First, he would determine if an intruder was inside. The front door hadn't been opened. The door to a long, barrack-type wing where ranch hands might sleep during a busy season was locked, and the same was true for the basement door and the back door that opened onto a wide porch. Though it had a dead bolt, the back door lock was flimsy, easily blasted through with a couple of gunshots. As far as he could tell, no weapons had been fired.

When he pushed open the back door, a torrent of glistening snow swept inside. The area near the rear porch was trampled with many prints in the snow. Was it one person or several? He couldn't tell, but Hazel's story was true. She'd heard someone back here.

As he closed the rear door and relocked it, he heard Emily call his name. Her voice was steady, strong and unafraid. Weapon raised, he rushed toward the front of the house. The door was opening. A man in a brown parka with fur around the hood plodded inside.

Though he didn't look like much of a threat, Sean wasn't taking any chances. "Freeze."

"I sure as hell will if I don't close this door."

As the man in the parka turned to shut the front door, Hazel came down the staircase. "It's okay, Sean. This is my neighbor, Willis. He was a deputy sheriff until he retired a couple of years ago."

"I was worried, Hazel." As he shoved off his hood, unzipped the parka and stomped his snowmobile boots, puddles of melted snow appeared on the terra-cotta tile floor. "Couldn't reach you on the phone, so I decided to come over here and check before I went to bed. Hi, Emily."

"Hey, Willis."

"Take off those boots." Hazel pointed to the bench by the door. "Are you hungry? Emily made a big pot of chili."

He sat and grinned at Sean and Emily. His face was ruddy and wet. A few errant flakes of snow still clung to his thick mustache. "And who's this young fella with the Glock?"

"Sean Timmons of TST Security." He shook the older man's meaty hand. "I'm Emily's bodyguard."

Willis was clearly intrigued. Why did Emily need protection? What other kind of security work did Sean do? He pushed the strands of wet gray hair off his forehead and straightened his mustache before he asked, "You hiring?"

"Part time," Sean said. "I can always use a man with experience as a deputy sheriff."

"Seventeen years," Willis said. "And I still work with the volunteer fire brigade and mountain search and rescue."

"Plus you've got your own little neighborhood watch." Sean had the feeling that Hazel got more attention from the retired deputy than the others in this area. "You have a key to the front door."

"That's right."

"Do you mind telling me why you banged on the back door and didn't let yourself in?"

"The back door is always unlocked, and it was a few less steps through the blizzard than the front. When I found it locked, I was pretty damn mad. I yanked at the handle to make sure it wasn't just stuck, and I might have let out a few choice swear words."

"Scared me half to death," Hazel said.

"I heard you scream." Willis looked down at the floor between his boots. He wore two pairs of wool socks. Both had seen better days. "And I felt like a jackass for scaring you."

She patted his cheek, halfway chiding and halfway flirting. "You're lucky I couldn't find my rifle."

While he explained that his keys were in the truck, and he had to tromp back out there to find the right ones, Hazel fussed over him. She was a touchy-feely person who hugged and patted and stroked. Sean noted her behavior and realized how similar it was to methods Emily used to calm him, mesmerize him and convince him to do whatever she wanted.

He glanced toward her. She sat on the fourth step, where she had a clear view of the others in the foyer. Her gaze flicked to the left, but he knew she'd been watching him. A hard woman to figure out. Was she angry or nervous? Independent or lonely?

Earlier tonight, she'd been on the verge of a panic attack. Her eyes had been wide with fear. Her muscles were so tightly clenched that she couldn't move, couldn't breathe. Scared to death, and he didn't blame her. James Wynter and his associates were undeniably dangerous.

A muscle in his jaw clenched. Why had she chosen to go after these violent criminals? And how did Levine justify leaving this witness unprotected? The FBI had been chasing Wynter for years, way before Sean was stationed in San Francisco. A chance to lock up Frankie Wynter would be a coup.

"Then it's settled," Hazel said. "Willis is sticking around for some chili and a couple of beers. You kids come into the dining room and join us."

"In a minute," Emily promised as she rose to her feet and motioned for Sean to come toward her.

She stayed on the first step, and he stood below her. They were almost eye level.

He asked, "Did you have something you wanted to say?"

"You did good tonight. I know that Hazel and I can be a handful, but you managed us. You were organized, quick. And when we thought we needed you, there you were, charging around the corner and yelling for Willis to freeze. You were…" She exhaled a sigh. "Impressive."

Her compliment made him leery. "It's what I do."

"Not that we actually needed your bodyguard skills." She caught hold of his hand and gave a squeeze. "This was a simple misunderstanding because of the blizzard."

"You have plenty of reason to be worried," he reminded her. "You mentioned the Wynter family compound near Aspen. Tonight it was Willis at the door. Tomorrow it might be Frankie Wynter."

"Don't make this into a worst-case scenario." She continued to hold his hand, and he felt the tension in her grip. "Tonight a neighbor came to pay a visit. That's all. And the blizzard is just snow. It's harmless. Kids play in it. Ever build a snowman?"

"Ever get caught in an avalanche?" He was keeping the tone light, but there was something important he needed to say. "Seriously, Emily, you need a bodyguard."

"I agree, and the job is yours."

He'd expected an argument but was glad that she'd decided to be rational. He glanced toward the dining room. "I could do with another bowl of chili."

"Me, too."

Before she hopped down the stair step to the floor, she went up on tiptoe and gave him a kiss on the forehead. It was nothing special, the kind of small affection a wife might regularly bestow on her husband. The utter simplicity blew him away.

Before she could turn her back and skip off into the dining room, he caught her hand and gave a tug. She was in his arms. When her body pressed against his, they were joined together the way they were supposed to be.

Then he kissed her.

Chapter 4

Emily hadn't intended to seduce him. That little kiss on his forehead was meant to be friendly. If she'd known she was lighting the fuse to a passionate response, she never would have gotten within ten feet of him. *Not true. I'm lying to myself.* From the moment she'd seen him, sensual memories had been taunting from the back of her mind. It was only a matter of time before that undercurrent would become manifest.

Their marriage was over, but she never had stopped imagining Sean as her lover. Nobody kissed her the way he did. The pressure of his mouth against hers was familiar and perfect. *Will he do that thing with his tongue? The thing where he parts my lips gently, and then he deepens the kiss. His tongue swoops and swirls. And there's a growling noise from the back of his throat, a vibration.*

She'd never been able to fully describe what he did to her and what sensations he unleashed. But he was doing it right now, right in this moment. *Oh yes, kiss me again.*

She almost swooned. *Swoon? No way!* She'd changed. No more the lady poet, she was a hard-bitten journalist, not the type of woman who collapsed in a dead faint after one kiss, definitely not.

But her grip on consciousness was slipping fast. Her knees began to buckle, and she clung to his shoulders to keep from slipping to the floor. Her hands slid down his chest. Even that move was sexy; through the smooth fabric of his beige chamois shirt, she fondled his hard but supple abs.

This out-of-control but very pleasurable attraction had to stop before she lost her willpower, her rationality…her very mind. Pushing with the flat of her palms against his chest, she forced a distance between them. "We can't do this."

"Sure we can." He slung his arm around her waist. "It's been a while, but I haven't forgotten how."

Tomorrow he'd thank her for not dissolving into a quivering blob of lust. Firmly, she said, "I can see that we're going to need ground rules."

He kissed the top of her head and took a step back. "You cut it."

"What?"

"Your hair, you cut it."

"Too much trouble." She fluffed her chin-length bob. "And getting rid of the Rapunzel curls makes me look more adult."

"Oh yeah, you're really grown up. How old are you now, twenty-one? Twenty-two?"

She didn't laugh at his lame attempt at humor. "I'm almost twenty-six."

Their eight-year age difference had always been an issue. When they first met, she'd just turned nineteen. They were married and divorced before she was twenty-one, and she'd always wondered if their relationship would have lasted longer if she'd been more mature. It was a familiar refrain. If I knew then what I know now, things would be different.

More likely, they never would have gotten together in the first place. Older and wiser, she would have taken one look at him and realized that he wasn't the sort of man who should be married.

"I like your new haircut," he said. "And you're right. We need some ground rules."

She gestured toward the dining room. "Should we eat chili while we talk?"

"That depends on how much you want your aunt and former deputy Willis to know."

Of course, he was right. She didn't want to spill potentially dangerous information about Wynter Corp into a casual conversation. Until now the only thing she'd told Aunt Hazel was that she'd witnessed a murder in San Francisco. She hadn't named the killer or the victim and certainly hadn't mentioned that the Wynter family had a place near Aspen.

Regret trickled through her. She probably shouldn't have come here. Though she'd been ultracautious in keeping her identity secret and her connection to Hazel was hard to trace, somebody might find out and come after them. If anything happened to Hazel…

Emily shuddered at the thought. "I don't want my aunt to get stuck in the middle of this."

"Agreed."

"Come with me."

She led him across the foyer to a living room that reflected Hazel's eclectic personality with a combination of classy and rustic. The terra-cotta floor and soft southwestern colors blended with painted barn wood on the walls. The high ceiling was open beam. The rugged, moss rock fireplace reminded Emily that her aunt was an outdoorswoman who herded cattle and tamed wild mustangs. But Hazel also had a small art collection, including two Georgia O'Keeffe watercolor paintings of flowers that hung on either side of the fireplace.

While Emily went behind the wet bar at the far end of the room, Sean studied the watercolor of a glowing pink-and-gold hydrangea. "Is this an original?"

"A gift from the artist," Emily said. "Hazel spent some time with O'Keeffe at Ghost Ranch in New Mexico."

"I keep forgetting how rich your family is. None of you are showy. It's all casual and comfortable and then I realize that you've got valuable artwork on the wall." He made his way across the room to the wet bar. "When I was driving up to this place, I had the feeling I'd seen it before. Did we come here for a visit?"

"I don't think so. Hazel was in Europe for most of the year and a half we were married." She peered through the glass door of the wine cellar refrigerator. "White wine or red?"

"How about beer?"

"You haven't changed." She opened the under-the-counter refrigerator and selected two bottles of craft beers with zombies on the labels. "You'll like this brand. It's dark."

He didn't question her selection, just grabbed the beer, tapped the neck against hers and took a swig. He licked his lips. "Good."

A dab of foam glistened at the corner of his mouth, and she was tempted to wipe the moisture off, better yet, to lick it.

"Ground rules," she said, reminding herself as much as him.

"First, I want to know why I have déjà vu about Hazelwood Ranch. Do you have any photo albums?"

She came out from behind the bar and shot him a glare. "If you don't mind, I'd rather not take a side trip down memory lane. We have more urgent concerns."

"You're the one who introduced family into the picture," he said. "I want to understand a few things about Hazel. How long has she lived here?"

"The ranch doesn't belong to our family. Hazel's late husband was the owner of this and many other properties near Aspen. He renamed this small ranch Hazelwood in honor of her. They always seemed so happy. Never had kids, though. He was older, in his fifties, when they got married."

She scanned the spines of books in a built-in shelf until she found a couple of photo albums. As she took them down and carried them to the coffee table in front of the sofa, she realized that she hadn't downloaded her own photos in months. Digital albums were nice, but she really preferred the old-fashioned way.

"I knew there'd be pictures," he said.

"Do you remember those journals I used to make? I'd take an old book with an interesting cover and replace the pages with my own sketches and poetry and photos."

"I remember." His voice was as soft as a caress.

"The Engagement Journal was the best present you ever gave me."

"What about the watch, the super-expensive, engraved wristwatch?"

"Also treasured."

She went back to the bar, snatched up her beer and returned to sit on the sofa beside him. "I'm an excellent present giver. It's a family trait."

"How are they, the Peterson family?"

"My oldest sister had a baby girl, which means I'm an aunt, and the other two are in grad school. Mom and Dad moved to Arizona, which they love." She took a taste of the zombie beer, which was, as she'd expected, excellent, and gave him a rueful smile. "I don't suppose Aunt Hazel told my mom that she was calling you."

"Your mom hated me."

Emily made a halfhearted attempt to downplay her mother's opinion. "You weren't their favorite."

Her parents had begged her to stay in college and wait to get married until she was older. Emily was her mom's baby, the youngest of four girls, the artistic one. When Emily's divorce came, Mom couldn't wait to say "I told you so."

"Toward the end," he said, "I thought she was beginning to come around."

"It was never about you personally," she said. "I was too young, and you were too old. And Mom didn't really like that you did dangerous undercover work in the FBI."

"And what does she think of your current profession?"

She took a long swallow of the dark beer. "Hates it."

"Does she know about the murder?"

"Oh God, no." She cringed. If her mother suspected that she was actually in danger, she'd have a fit.

Emily opened the older of the two albums. The photographs were arranged in chronological order with Emily and her sisters starting out small and getting bigger as they aged. Nostalgia welled up inside her. The Petersons were a good-looking family, wholesome and happy. In spite of what Sean thought, they weren't really rich. Sure, they had enough money to live well and take vacations and pay for school tuitions. But they weren't big spenders, and their home in an upscale urban neighborhood in Denver wasn't ostentatious.

Like her older sisters, she had tried to be what her parents wanted. They valued education, and when she told them she was considering becoming a teacher, they were thrilled. But Emily went to UC Berkeley and strayed from the path. She was a poet, a performance artist, an activist and a photographer. Her marriage and divorce to Sean had been just one more detour from the straight and narrow.

Aunt Hazel was more indulgent of Emily's free-spirited choices. Hazel approved of Sean. She'd invited him to be a bodyguard. Maybe she knew something Emily hadn't yet learned.

He stopped her hand as she was about to turn a page in the album. He pointed to a wintertime photo of her, wearing a white knit hat with a pom-pom and standing at the gate that separated Hazelwood Ranch from public lands. She couldn't have been more than five or six. Bundled up in her parka and jeans and boots, she appeared to be dancing with both hands in the air.

"This picture," he said. "You put a copy of this in the journal you gave me. I must have looked at it a hundred times. I never really noticed the outline of the hills and the curve in the road, but my subconscious must have absorbed the details. Seeing that photo is like being here."

His déjà vu was explained.

She asked, "What are we going to do to protect Hazel?"

"How does she feel about Willis? Do they have a little something going on?"

She and her aunt hadn't directly talked about who Hazel was dating, but Emily couldn't help noticing that Willis had stopped by for a visit every day. Sometimes twice a day. "Why do you ask?"

"We could hire Willis to be a bodyguard for Hazel. They might enjoy an excuse to spend more time together."

"That's not a bad idea," she said. "His performance tonight—tromping around in the snow looking for a house key—wasn't typical. Usually he's competent."

"I wouldn't want to throw him up against an army of thugs with automatic pistols," he said, "but that shouldn't be necessary. If you settle here and keep a low profile, there's no reason for Wynter to track you down. You're sure he doesn't know you're the witness?"

"I was careful, bought my plane tickets under a fake name, blocked and locked everything on my computer, threw away my phone so I couldn't be tracked."

"How did you learn to do all that?"

"Internet," she said. "I read a couple of how-to articles on disappearing yourself. Plus, I might have picked up a couple of hints when we were married."

"But you didn't like my undercover work." He leaned

back against the sofa pillows and sipped his beer. "You said when I took on a new identity, it was a lie."

At the time, she hadn't considered her criticism to be unreasonable. Any new bride would be upset if her husband said he was going to be out of touch for a week or two and couldn't tell her where he was going or what he was doing. She jabbed an accusing finger in his direction. "I had every right to interrogate you, every right to be angry when you wouldn't tell me what was going on."

His dark eyes narrowed, but he didn't look menacing. He was too handsome. "You could have just trusted me."

"Trust you? I hardly knew you."

"You were my wife."

It hadn't taken long for them to jump into old arguments. Was he purposely trying to provoke her? First he mentioned the age thing. Now he was playing the "trust me" card. Damn it, she didn't want to open old wounds. "Could we keep our focus on the present? Please?"

"Fine with me." He stretched out his long legs and rested his stocking feet on the coffee table. "You claim to have covered your tracks when you traveled and when you masked your identity."

"Claimed?" Her anger sparked.

"Can you prove that you're untraceable? Can anybody vouch for you?"

"Certainly not. The point of hiding my identity is to eliminate contacts."

"Just to be sure," he said, "I'll ask Dylan to do a computer search. If anybody can hack your identity or files, he can."

"It's not necessary, but go ahead." She was totally

confident in her abilities. "I've always liked your brother. How's he doing?"

"We keep him busy at TST doing computer stuff. You'll be shocked to hear that he's finally found a girlfriend who's as smart as he is. She's a neurosurgeon."

"I'm not surprised." The two brothers made a complementary pairing: Dylan was a genius, and Sean had street smarts.

"I'll use my FBI contacts, namely, Levine, to keep tabs on their investigation." He drained his beer and stood. "That should just about cover it."

"Cover what?"

"Ground rules," Sean said as he crossed the room toward the wet bar. "You and Hazel will be safe if you stay here and don't communicate with anybody. I'll need to take your cell phone."

"Not necessary," she said. "I'm aware that cell phones can be hacked and tracked. I only use untraceable burner phones."

"What about your computer?"

She swallowed hard. In the back of her mind, she knew her computer could be hacked long distance and used to track her down. There was no way she'd give up her computer. "All my documents are copied onto a flash drive."

"I need to disable the computer. No calling except on burner phones. No texting. No email. No meetings."

Anger and frustration bubbled up inside her. Though she hadn't finished her beer and didn't need a replacement, she followed him to the bar. She climbed up on a stool and peered down at him while he looked into the under-the-counter fridge. When he stood, she glared until he met her gaze.

To his credit, Sean didn't back down, even though she felt like she was shooting lightning bolts through her eye sockets. When she opened her mouth to speak, she was angry enough to breathe fire. "Your ground rules don't work for me."

He opened another zombie beer. "What's the problem?"

"If I can't use the internet, how can I work?"

"Dylan can probably hook up some kind of secure channel to communicate with your employer."

"What if I don't want to stay here?"

"I suppose I could move you to a safe house or hotel." He came around the bar and faced her. "What's really going on?"

"Nothing."

"You always said you hated lying and liars, but you're not leveling with me. If you don't tell me everything, I can't do my job."

The real, honest-to-God problem was simple: she hadn't given up on the Wynter investigation. One of the specific reasons she'd come to Colorado was to dig up evidence against Frankie. She swiveled around on the bar stool so she was facing away from him. "I don't want to bury my head in the sand."

"Explain."

"I want to know why Roger Patrone was murdered. And I want to stop the human trafficking from Asia."

He nodded. "We all want that."

"But I have leads to track down. If I could hook up with people from the Wynter compound and question them, I might get answers. Or I could break in and download the information on their computers. I might find evidence that would be useful to the FBI."

"Seriously?" He was skeptical. "You want to keep digging up dirt, poking the dragon?"

She shot back. "Well, that's what an investigative reporter does."

"This isn't a joke, Emily. You saw what happens to people who cross Frankie Wynter."

"They get shot and dumped."

Wynter's men could toss her body into a mountain cave, and she wouldn't be found for years. When she voiced her plan out loud, it sounded ridiculous. How could she expect to succeed in her investigation when the FBI had failed?

"If you want to take that kind of risk," he said, "that's your choice. But don't put Hazel in danger."

He was right. She shouldn't have come here, and she definitely shouldn't have talked to him. *Trust me? Fat chance.*

Their connection had already begun to unravel, which was probably for the best. He irritated her more than a mohair sweater on a sunny day. Her unwarranted attraction to him was a huge distraction from her work. She should tell him to go. She didn't need a bodyguard.

But Sean was strong and quick, well trained in assault and protection. He knew things about investigating and undercover work that she could only guess about. Her gut instincts told her she really did need him.

"Come with me," she said. "Back to San Francisco."

Chapter 5

At five o'clock the next morning, Sean stood at the window in the kitchen and opened the blinds so he could see outside while he was waiting for the coffeemaker to do its thing. He'd turned off the overhead light, and the cool blue shadows in the kitchen melted into the shimmer of moonlight off the unbroken snow. The blizzard had ended.

Soon the phones would be working. Lines of communication would be open. There would be nothing to block Emily's return trip to San Francisco. She'd decided that she needed to go back and dig into her investigation, and it didn't look like she was going to budge.

It was up to him whether he'd go with her as her bodyguard or not. His first reaction was to refuse. She had neither the resources nor the experience to delve into the criminal depths of Wynter Corp, and she was going to get into trouble, possibly lethal trouble. He needed to make her understand her limitations without insulting her skills.

Outside, the bare branches of aspen and fir trees bent and wavered in the wind. So cold. So lonely. A shiver went through him. Their divorce had been five years ago. He should be over it. But no. He missed her every single day. Seeing her again and hearing her voice, even if she was arguing with him most of the time, touched a part of him that he kept buried.

He still cared about Emily. Damn it, he couldn't let her go to California by herself. She needed protection, and nobody could keep her safe the way he could. He would die for her…but he preferred not to.

After she'd made her announcement in the living room, she outlined the plan. "Tomorrow morning, we'll catch a plane and be in San Francisco before late afternoon. There'll be time for you to have a little chat with Agent Levine and the other guys in that office. We'll talk to my contacts on the day after that."

He'd objected, as any sane person would, but she'd already made up her mind. She flounced into the dining room and ate chili with Hazel and Willis. The prime topic of their conversation being big snowstorms and their aftermath. The chat ended with Emily's announcement that she'd be going back to San Francisco as soon as the snow stopped because she had to get back to work.

During the night, he'd gone into her room to try talking sense into her. Before he could speak, she asked if he would accompany her. When he said no, she told him to leave.

Stubborn! How could a woman who looked so soft

and gentle be so obstinate? She was like a rosebush with roots planted deep—so strong and deep that she could halt the forward progress of a tank. How could he make her see reason? What sort of story could he tell her?

Finally, the coffeemaker was done. He poured a cup, straight black, for himself and one for her with a dash of milk, no sugar. Up the staircase, he was careful not to spill over the edge of the mugs. Twisting the door-knob on her bedroom took some maneuvering, but he got it open and slipped inside.

For a long moment, he stood there, watching her sleep in the dim light that penetrated around the edges of the blinds. A pale blue comforter was tucked up to her chin. Wisps of dark hair swept across on her fore-head. Her eyelashes made thick, dark crescents above her cheekbones, and her lips parted slightly. She was even more beautiful now than when they were married.

She claimed that she'd changed, and he recognized the difference in some ways. She was tougher, more direct. When he thought about her rationale for inves-tigating, he understood that she was asserting herself and building her career. Those practical concerns were in addition to the moral issues, like that need to get justice for the guy who was murdered and to right the wrongs committed by Wynter Corp. He crossed the room, placed the mugs on the bedside table and sat on the edge of her bed.

Slowly, she opened her eyes. "Has it stopped snow-ing?"

He nodded.

"Have you changed your mind?"

"Have you?"

She wiggled around until she was sitting up, still

keeping the comforter wrapped around her like a droopy cocoon. Fumbling in the nearly dark room, she turned on her bedside lamp and reached for the coffee. "I'd like a nip of caffeine before we start arguing again."

"No need to argue. I want to help with your investigation."

"I'd be a fool to turn you down."

Damn right, you would. His qualifications were outstanding. In addition to the FBI training at Quantico, he'd taken several workshops and classes on profiling. When he first signed on, his goal was to join the Behavioral Analysis Unit. But that was not to be. His psych tests showed that his traits were better suited to a different position. He was a natural for undercover work; namely, he had an innate ability to lie convincingly.

"Plus, I'm offering the services of my brother, the computer genius and hacker."

Suspicion flickered in her greenish-blue eyes. "I appreciate the offer, but what's the quid pro quo?"

"Listen to you." He grinned. "Awake for only a couple of minutes and already speaking Latin."

She turned to look at the clock and then groaned. "Five-fifteen in the morning. Why so early?"

"Couldn't sleep."

"So you thought you'd just march in here and make sure I didn't get a full eight hours."

"As if you need that much."

The way he remembered, she seldom got more than five hours. He often woke up to find her in the middle of some project or another. Emily was one of those people who bounced out of bed and was fully functional before she brushed her teeth.

"It's going to be a long day." She drank her coffee

and dramatically rolled her eyes. "Plane rides can be so very exhausting."

"Here's the deal," he said. "There aren't any direct flights from Aspen to San Francisco. You'll be routed through Denver first."

Watching him over the rim of her mug, she nodded agreement.

"Since we're already there, let's make a scheduled stop in Denver, spend the night and talk to Dylan. We'll still be investigating. Didn't you say you were looking for documents about imports and exports? He could hack in to Wynter Corp."

"Information obtained through illegal hacking can't be used for evidence."

"But you're not a cop," he said. "You don't have to follow legal protocols."

"True, and a hack could point me in the right direction. Dylan could also check company memos mentioning the murder victim. And, oh my God, accounting records." She came to an abrupt halt, set down her coffee and stared at him. "Why are you making this offer?"

"I want to help you with your new career."

Though he truly wished her well, helping her investigation wasn't the primary reason he'd suggested a stop in Denver. Sean wanted to derail her trip to San Francisco and keep her out of danger. As far as he was concerned, the world had enough investigative journalists. But there was only one Emily Peterson.

Her gaze narrowed. "Are you lying?"

He scoffed. "Why would I lie?"

"Turning my question into a different question isn't an answer." A slow smile lifted one corner of her mouth. "It's a technique that liars use."

"Believe whatever you want." He rose from her bed and placed his half-empty coffee mug on the bedside table. "I'm suggesting that you use Dylan because he's skilled, he has high-level contacts and he won't get caught."

She threw off the covers and went up on her knees. An overlarge plaid flannel top fell from her shoulders and hung all the way to her knees. The shirt looked familiar. He reached over and stroked the sleeve that she'd rolled up to the elbow. "Is this mine?"

"The top?" Unlike him, she was a terrible liar. "Why would I wear your jammies?"

"Supersoft flannel, gray Stewart plaid from L.L.Bean," he said. "I'm glad you kept it."

"I hardly ever wear flannel. But I was coming to Colorado and figured I might want something warm." She tossed her head, flipping her hair. "I forgot this belonged to you."

Another lie. He wondered if she'd been thinking of him when she packed her suitcase for this trip. Did she miss him? When she wore his clothing to bed, did she imagine his embrace?

He stepped up close to the bed and glided his arms around her, feeling the softness of the flannel plaid and her natural, sweet warmth. She'd been cozy in bed, wrapped in his pajamas that were way too big for her.

She cleared her throat. "What are you doing?"

"I'm holding you so you won't get cold."

He stroked her back, following the curve of her spine and the flare of her hips. With his hands still on the outside of the fabric, he cupped her full, round ass. Her body was incredible. She hadn't changed in the years they'd been apart. If anything, she was better, more firm and toned. He lifted her toward him, and she collapsed against his chest, gasping as though she'd been holding her breath.

"Ground rules," she choked out. "This is where we really need rules."

He lifted her chin, gazed into her face and waited until she opened her eyes. "You're supposed to be the spontaneous one, Emily. Let yourself go—follow your desires."

"I can't."

The note of desperation in her voice held him back. Though he longed to peel off the flannel top and drag her under the covers, he didn't want to hurt her. If she wanted a more controlled approach, he would comply.

"One kiss," he said, "on the mouth."

"Only one."

"And another on the neck, and another on your breast, and one more on…"

"Forget it! I should know better than to negotiate with you. There will be no kissing." She wriggled to get away from his grasp, but he wasn't letting go. "No touching. No hugging. No physical intimacy at all."

"You promised one," he reminded her.

"Fine."

She squinted her eyes closed and turned her face up to his. Her lips were stiff. And she was probably gritting her teeth. He'd still take the kiss. He knew what was behind her barriers. She still had feelings for him.

His kiss was slow and tender, almost chaste, until he began to nibble and suck on the fullness of her lower lip. His fingers unbuttoned the pajama top, and his hand slid inside. He traced a winding path across her torso

with his fingertips, and when he reached the underside
of her breast, she moaned.

"Oh, Sean." A shudder went through her. "I can't."

His hand stilled, but his mouth took full advantage
of her parted lips. His tongue plunged into the hot, slick
interior of her mouth.

She spoke again. "Don't stop."

She kissed him back. Her hand guided his to her
nipples, inviting him to fondle. Her longing was fierce,
unstoppable. Her body pressed hard against his.

And then it was over. She fell backward on the bed
and buried herself, even her face, under the covers. He
loved the way he affected her. As for the way she affected him? He couldn't ignore his palpitating heart
and his rock-hard erection. But his attraction was more
than that.

"About these ground rules," he said. "Don't tell me
there's no physical intimacy allowed. If I'm going to
be around you and not allowed to touch, I'll explode."

"You scare me," she said as she crawled out from
under the covers. "I don't want to fall in love with you
again."

Would it really be so bad? She kept talking about
how she had changed, but he was different, too. Not the
same undercover agent that he was five years ago, he
had learned tolerance, patience and respect.

Much of this shift in attitude came from his devel-
oping relationship with his brother; he was learning
how to be a team player. Sean still teased—that was a
big brother's prerogative—but he also could brush the
small irritations away. At TST Security, he didn't insist
on being the lead with every single job. He'd be nuts
to interfere with Dylan's computer expertise, and their

other partner, Mason Steele, was good at stepping in and taking charge.

His relationship with Emily was different. When they had been married, he might have been impatient. The way she kept prodding him about his work had been truly annoying. Why hadn't she been able to understand that undercover work meant he had to be secretive? If he kissed another woman while he was undercover, it didn't mean anything. How could it? In his mind, she was the perfect lover.

"First ground rule." He had to lay out parameters that allowed them to be together without hurting each other. "No falling in love."

"That's a good one," she said. "Write it down."

He sat at the small desk, found a sheet of notebook paper and a pen to jot down the first rule. "What about touching, kissing, licking, nibbling, sucking…" His voice trailed off as he visualized these activities. "I can't even say the words without needing to do it."

"I feel it, too, you know. We've always been amazing in bed, sexually compatible."

"Always."

In unison, they exhaled a regretful sigh.

"How about this?" she said. "No PDA."

Public display of affection? He wrote it down. "I can live with that."

She sat up on the bed and reached for her coffee mug again. After a sip, she proposed, "No physical contact unless I'm the one who initiates it."

He didn't like the way that sounded. "I need to have some kind of voice."

"You mean talking dirty?"

"Not necessarily. I might say something like I want

to touch your cheek." Illustrating, he glided his hand along the line of her jaw, and then he leaned closer. "I want to kiss your forehead."

When he kissed her lightly, she pushed his face away. "You can ask, but I have veto power. At any time, I can say no."

"So you have veto power and you can also initiate."

"Yes."

"What does that leave for me?" he asked as he returned to sit at the desk.

She cast him an evil smile. "Begging?"

"I'm not writing that down."

As far as he was concerned, their negotiation was taking a negative turn. The way she described it, she controlled all physical contact. She had all the power. No way would he be reduced to begging. There had to be another way to work it out.

As he doodled with the pen on the paper, he heard the ringtone from the cell phone in his pocket. "Finally we have communication from the outside world."

"Who is it?"

"The caller ID says Zebra929. So it has to be my brother. Dylan likes to play with the codes."

As soon as he answered, his brother said, "This is a secured call, bouncing the signal. It needs to be short."

"Shoot."

"I got a call from FBI Special Agent Levine out of San Francisco. Guess who he's trying to contact?"

"Emily Peterson," Sean said. A chill slithered down his spine. This was bad news.

"Whoa, are you psychic?"

"I'm looking right at her."

"Emily Peterson Timmons?"

Sean heard the amazement in his brother's tone.

"Emily the poet? Emily with the long hair? Your ex-wife?"

"What was the message from Levine?"

"He wanted to warn her. There's a leak in SFPD. Wynter might know her identity."

"Why did Levine call me?"

"He's grasping at straws," Dylan said. "None of her San Francisco contacts know where she went."

"What about her parents?"

"I asked the same question. The Petersons are out of the country."

Actually, that was good news. A threat to Emily could mean other people in her family might become targets for Wynter. Sean asked, "Did Levine mention an aunt in the mountains? A woman named Hazel?"

"Is that the Hazel Hopkins you took a contract with?"

Sean's pulse quickened. Not only had he received phone calls from Hazel, but he'd looked her up on the internet. It had taken nothing but a phone call for Levine to track him down. If Frankie Wynter figured out that connection, he might hack in to TST Security phones or computers. They could find Hazel. "How secure are our computers?"

"Very safe," Dylan said. "But anything can be hacked."

"Wipe any history concerning Hazel Hopkins."

"Okay. We should wrap up this call."

"Thanks, Zebra. I'll be flying back to Denver today with Emily. We need your skills."

He ended the call and looked toward her. No more fun and games. She was in serious danger.

Chapter 6

Emily watched Sean transformed from a sexy ex to the hard-core FBI agent she remembered from their marriage. His devilish grin became tight-lipped. Twin worry lines appeared between his eyebrows. His posture stiffened.

She didn't like the direction his phone call was taking. As soon as he ended the call, she asked, "Why were you talking to your brother about Hazel?"

"If you're in danger, so is your family."

"Not Hazel. Our last names aren't the same. Nobody knows we're related."

"Can you be one hundred percent sure of that?"

"Not really."

When she'd first started writing articles that might be controversial, she disguised her identity behind a couple of pseudonyms. She didn't want to accidentally embarrass her mom and dad or her sister in law school, and she liked being a lone crusader. Anonymous and brave, she dug behind the headlines to expose corruption.

One of her best articles dealt with a cheating handyman who overcharged and didn't do the work. Another exposed a phone scam that entrapped the unwary. This story about Wynter Corp was her first attempt to investigate serious crime.

She should have known better. A personal threat was bad enough, but she'd brought danger to her family. Her spirits crumbled as she sat on the bed listening to Sean's recap of the phone call with his brother. This was her fault, all her fault.

Moments ago, she'd been kissing her gorgeous ex-husband and had been almost happy. Now she felt like weeping or hiding under the covers and never coming out. Why couldn't the blizzard have lasted forever? The snow would have hidden her.

Trying to soothe herself, she rubbed the soft fabric of her sleeve between her thumb and forefinger. Despite what she'd told him, she hadn't worn this top by accident; she knew very well that it belonged to Sean. Cuddling up in his pajamas always gave her a feeling of warmth and safety. Sometimes she closed her eyes and pretended that she could still smell his scent even though the pajamas had been laundered a hundred times.

He sat beside her and took her hand. "Are you okay?"

"Not at all." She heard the vulnerability in her voice and hated it. "You probably want to tell me that I never should have done this article, that I'm a girlie girl and should stick with poetry."

He squeezed her hand. "As I recall, your poetry

wasn't all lollipops and sparkles. There was something about a fire giver and vultures that ate his liver."

"Prometheus," she remembered. "He started out trying to do the right thing, just like me. And then he was eternally damned by the gods. Is that my fate?"

"You made some mistakes, had some bad luck."

"I'm being a drama queen." She was well aware of that tendency and tried to tamp the over-the-top histrionics before she threw herself into full-on crazy mode. "Tell me I'm exaggerating."

"It's safe to say you're not really cursed by the gods," he said, "but don't underestimate the seriousness of this threat."

"I won't." Her lower lip trembled. She fought the tears that sloshed behind her eyelids. "Oh God, what should I do?"

"No crying." He held her chin and turned her face so they were eye to eye. "You told me you were an investigative journalist. Well, you need to start acting like somebody who stands behind her words and takes responsibility for her actions."

His dark gaze caught and held her attention. His calm demeanor steadied her. Still, she was confused. "I don't know how."

"You're not Prometheus, and you're not little Miss Sunshine the poetry girl. Think of yourself as a reporter who got into trouble. What should we do next?"

"Make sure my family is safe."

Her parents were currently out of the country, visiting friends in the South of France. She didn't need to worry about Mom and Dad. Her three sisters were back east, and the two who were still in school lived alone. It seemed unlikely that Wynter would hunt them down. Nonetheless, they should be warned. "I should call my sisters."

"I'm going to ask you to wait until we get to Denver," he said. "The signal from your phone might be traced, and Dylan has equipment that's extremely secure."

"What about you?" She pointed to his cell phone. "What about that call?"

"It originated from the TST Security offices behind strong, thick firewalls."

She sat beside him, struggling to think in spite of the static waves that sizzled and shivered inside her head. From outside her bedroom door, she heard her aunt chattering to Willis as they went downstairs. It was early, a little after six o'clock and not yet dawn, but they were both already awake. Did they sleep together last night? Emily smiled to herself. *Ironic!* The senior citizens were getting it on while she and Sean stayed in separate bedrooms.

"I need to talk to Hazel." She looked toward him for guidance. "How much should I tell her?"

"She already knows you've witnessed a murder, so it won't come as a big shock that she's in danger. Until this is over, I'd advise her to leave Hazelwood, maybe stay in a hotel in Aspen."

"I'm guessing that Willis might have an extra bedroom," she said. "And he would probably be a good protector."

"A former deputy," Sean said. "I'd trust him."

And she didn't think it would take much to convince Hazel to spend more time with Willis. Emily's eccentric aunt had never remarried after her husband had died fifteen years ago, but she had taken several live-in lov-

ers. Willis had always been a friend. Maybe it was time
for him to be something more.

She picked up her coffee mug from the bedside table
and drained it in a few gulps. Today was going to be
intense, and she'd need all the energy she could muster.
"After taking care of the family, what do I do?"

"It's up to you."

"The first thing that comes to mind is run and hide."
That was exactly what the old Emily would have done.
She would have hidden behind her big, strong husband.
But that wasn't her style, not anymore. "I want to take
responsibility. I'll go after the story."

He shrugged. "San Francisco, here we come."

With Sean at her side, she could handle the threat.
She could take down James Wynter and his son. What
she couldn't do was…forget. The blood spreading across
Roger Patrone's white shirt flashed in her mind. The
sounds of a beating and fading cries for help echoed in
her ears. She could never erase the memory of murder.

Over coffee in the kitchen, Emily convinced Hazel
that there was a real potential for danger and she ought
to move in with Willis. It didn't take much persuasion.
Hazel agreed almost immediately, and she was happy,
as perky as a chipmunk. Her energy and the afterglow
of excitement confirmed Emily's suspicion that her aunt
and Willis were more than friends.

Hazel dashed upstairs to her bedroom to pack a few
essentials, and Willis swaggered around the kitchen,
talking to Sean about how he should make sure Hazel
was safe and secure. Though Emily had a hard time
imagining Willis the kindhearted former deputy facing off with Wynter's thugs, she believed he was com-

petent. Plus, he had the advantage of experience. He knew how to handle the dangers of the mountains and to use the elements to his advantage. His plan was to take Hazel to a ski hut he'd built on the other side of Aspen. The hut was accessible only by snowmobile or cross-country skis.

"What about the blizzard?" she asked.

Willis squinted out the kitchen window at a brilliant splash of sunlight reflecting off a pristine snowbank. "The big storm gave up during the night. We only got twenty or so inches, probably not even enough to close down the airport in Aspen."

She'd lived in San Francisco for so long that she'd forgotten how dramatically Colorado weather could change. Yesterday was a blizzard. Today she could get sunburned from taking a walk outside.

The timer on the oven buzzed. Emily opened the door, and the scent of sweet baked goods rushed toward her. Hazel had popped in a frozen almond-flavored coffee cake to thaw. Not as good as fresh made but decent enough for a rushed breakfast.

Willis went upstairs to help Hazel, and Emily turned toward Sean. "We need plane reservations to Denver," she said. "I'll go ahead and make them."

"You shouldn't." He pointed out the obvious. "Just in case the bad guys have a way to track airline tickets, you ought to avoid using your real name."

"No problem." Her solution was sort of embarrassing, and she really didn't want to tell him. She placed the pan of coffee cake on a trivet on the counter and cut off a slab. With this breakfast in hand, she headed toward the exit from the kitchen. "I'm going to get packed, and then I'll call the airlines."

He blocked the exit. "I hope you aren't thinking about buying plane tickets with a fake ID and credit card. That kind of ploy can get you on the no-fly list."

"It's not exactly fake," she muttered. "Just out of date by about five and a half years."

As realization dawned, his eyes darkened. "The way I remember, you changed your name back to Peterson after the divorce."

"I did."

"Please don't tell me you're using your married name."

"The identity was just sitting there. I doctored an old driver's license and applied for a credit card as Emily Timmons, using my own Social Security number and my address in San Francisco. It works just fine."

"The no-fly list and fraud." Still blocking her way so she couldn't run, he glared at her. A muscle in his jaw twitched. "Anything else you want to tell me?"

"If I confess everything, we'll have nothing to discuss on the flight." She patted his cheek and slipped around him. "You can make the reservations."

"For today, you'll be Mrs. Timmons. And then no more."

"Don't count on it."

"What's that supposed to mean? Are you planning some kind of strange reconciliation that I don't know about?"

"This has nothing to do with you," she said coolly. "But I might need your name for fake identification."

With her almond cake in one hand and coffee in the other, she climbed the staircase and went to her bedroom. She sat at the small desk and activated one of her disposable phones. She couldn't wait until they got to Denver to contact her sisters. If Sean didn't like it, too bad. She really didn't think Wynter would go after them, but they deserved a heads-up. Michelle, who was in law school, asked how she could get in touch with Emily if she heard anything.

"You can't call me back."

"I know," Michelle said. "The phone you're using right now doesn't show up on my caller ID listing."

"Contact me through TST Security in Denver. I hired a bodyguard." Emily hoped to avoid mentioning her ex-husband. "They can get me a message."

"TST Security," Michelle repeated. "I'm looking them up on the internet right now. Found the website. Well, damn it, sis, here's an interesting coincidence. One of the owners of the aforementioned security firm happens to be Sean Timmons."

"I didn't call him."

"Really?" Michelle's tone dripped with sarcasm. "Do you want me to believe that he magically appeared when you were in trouble? Was he wearing a suit of armor and riding a white steed?"

"Aunt Hazel called him." Emily wanted to keep this conversation short. "And I don't have to justify my decisions to you or anybody else in the family."

"But justice will be served," said the future lawyer. "To tell the truth, Emily, I always liked Sean. I'm glad he's watching over you."

Emily avoided mentioning Sean to her other two sisters. Those calls ended quickly, and she jumped in the shower. Though she had time to wash and blow-dry her hair, she decided against it. Going out in the snow meant she'd be wearing a hat and squashing any cute styling.

She lathered up while her mind filled with speculation. No doubt, Michelle would blab to the rest of the family. And the questions would begin. *Would she get back together with him?* That seemed to be the query of the day. A few moments ago, Sean had asked about reconciliation.

Never going to happen. And her sisters should understand. Didn't they remember how devastated she'd been when she'd filed for divorce?

Their attitude about Sean had always been odd. When she first married him, the three sisters talked about how he was too old for her and his job was too dangerous for a stable relationship. In the divorce, however, the sister witches took Sean's side. They blamed her for being fickle and undependable when she should have been supportive. They told her to grow up. She couldn't always have things her own way.

Maybe true. Maybe she hadn't been the most understanding wife in the world. But he brought his own problems to the table: Being inflexible. Not taking her seriously. Concentrating too much on his work and not enough on his wife.

Wrapped in a towel after her shower, she padded into the bedroom and pulled out her luggage from under the bed. Since they were headed back to San Francisco, where she had clothes and toiletries at her apartment, she packed light. She tucked her three disposable cell phones in her carry-on. All data had already been downloaded off her de-activated computer.

She hid the flash drive in a specially designed black-and-silver pendant, which she wore on a heavy silver chain. A black cashmere sweater and designer jeans completed her outfit. Her practical boots and her parka were in the downstairs closet.

Before she left the bedroom, she checked her reflection in the mirror. *Not bad.* She didn't look as frazzled as she felt. Her hair was combed. Her lipstick properly applied. Her cheeks were flushed with nervous heat, but the high color might be attributed to too much blush.

Returning to San Francisco was the right thing to do, but she was sorely tempted to take off for a quickie Bahamas vacation with Sean. He owed her a trip. On their Paris honeymoon, he had held her hand in a sidewalk café and promised that every anniversary he would take her somewhere exciting. Their first anniversary rolled around and no trip. They couldn't get their schedules coordinated. And they argued about where to go. And when she told him to just forget it, he did.

What a brat she'd been! But at the time, she was too furious to make sense. She'd counted on Sean to be rational. That was his job. Somehow he should have known that even though she told him to forget it, he was supposed to lavish her with kisses and gifts until she changed her mind.

Their marriage had crumbled under the weight of hundreds of similar misunderstandings. Underneath it all, she wondered if they might actually be compatible. Certainly, there was nothing wrong with their sexual rapport. But could they talk? Was he too conservative? Were their worldviews similar? Was there any way, after the divorce, that she'd be willing to put her heart on the line and trust him? *I guess I'll find out.* While he was being her bodyguard and they were forced to be together, she had a second chance.

Chapter 7

Clearing the runway in Aspen took longer than expected, and their flight as Mr. and Mrs. Timmons didn't land at DIA until after four o'clock in the afternoon. Sean rented a car and drove toward the TST office, where Dylan had promised to meet them.

In the passenger seat, Emily shed her parka and changed from snow boots to a pair of ballet flats. She peeked out the window at the undeveloped fields near the airport. "It's crazy. The snow's already melted."

"Denver only got a couple of inches."

"And the sky is blue, and the sun is shining. Every time I come back to Colorado, I wonder why I ever left."

"You don't have family in Denver, anymore."

"Nope." She gave him a warm smile. "But you do. I'm looking forward to seeing Dylan."

When Emily was being cordial, there was no one

more charming. Her voice was as sweet as the sound of a meadowlark. Her intense blue-green eyes sparkled. Every movement she made was sheer grace. It was hard to keep his hands off her.

Sitting close beside her on the plane, inhaling her scent and watching her in glimpses, had affected him. He was going to need more than a flimsy set of relationship "ground rules" to maintain control.

Following the road signs, he merged onto I-70. His real problem would come tonight. Their flight to San Francisco was scheduled for tomorrow morning at about ten o'clock, which meant they'd be sleeping in the same place tonight. After the stop at TST, he intended to take her to his home, where the security was high and he could keep an eye on her. He had an extra bedroom. What he didn't have was willpower. When she was in bed, just down the hall, he would be tempted.

"Sean?"

He realized that she'd been talking while he wasn't listening. "Sorry, what did you say?"

"How did you name your company? I get that TST stands for your initials, Timmons, Timmons and your other partner, Mason Steele. But your logo is a four-leaf clover with three green leaves and one a faded red."

"At one time, there were four of us." Sean had told this story dozens of times, but his chest still tightened. Some scars never heal. This deep sadness would never go away. "We grew up together. Me and Dylan lived down the block from Mason and Matt Steele. Matt was my best friend. We were close in age, went to the same school, played on the same teams and went on double dates. When we were kids we pretended to be crime fighters."

"And when you grew up, you decided to fight crime for real."

"Not at first," he said. "We went to different colleges, followed our own separate ways. Matt joined the marines, and he liked the military life. That was why he couldn't be our best man. He was deployed, working his way up the chain of command."

There must have been a hint of doom in his tone, because Emily went very still. She listened intently.

He cleared his throat and continued. "About five years ago, Matt was killed in Afghanistan. His heroic actions rescued three other platoons, and he received a posthumous Purple Heart."

"I'm so sorry," she whispered.

"His death came right about the time our divorce was final. And I'd finished a sleazy undercover job where a good lawyer got the bad guys off with a slap on the wrist."

Remembering those dark days left a sour taste in his mouth. He'd just about given up. Life was a joke, not worth living. He went on an all-out binge, drugs and alcohol. Thanks to his undercover work, he was familiar with the filthy underbelly of the city, and he went there. He found rock bottom while seeking poisonous thrills that could wipe away his sorrow and regret and the senseless guilt that he was still alive while his friend was not. His judgment was off. He took stupid risks, landing in the hospital more than once. His path was leading straight to hell.

She reached across the console and touched his arm. "If I had known…"

"There was nothing you—or anybody else—could

do. I didn't ask for help, didn't want anybody holding my hand."

"How did you get better?"

"I came back to Colorado and got on a physical schedule of weight lifting and running ten miles a day. I visited places where Matt and I used to go." He paused. "This sounds cheesy, but I found peace. I quit mourning Matt's death and celebrated his life."

"Not cheesy at all," she said.

"Weak?"

"That's the last word I'd use to describe you."

"Anyway, I did a lot of wilderness camping. One morning, I crawled out of my tent, stared up into a clear blue sky and decided I wanted a future."

"TST Security?"

"I quit the FBI, contacted my two buds and set up the business. I'd like to think that Matt would approve. We don't take cases that we don't like. And there are times like now when we can actually do some good."

"Is that how you think of my investigation into Wynter Corp?" She brightened. "As something that could make a difference?"

"I guess I do feel that way."

He hadn't realized until this moment that he wanted Frankie Wynter to pay the price for murder. Plus, they might take down members of a powerful crime family, and that felt good.

Exiting the interstate, they were close enough to downtown Denver for him to point out changes in the city where she'd lived for so many years. Giant cranes loomed over new skyscrapers—tall office buildings and hotels to accommodate the tourists. New apartment buildings and condos had popped up on street corners, filling in spaces that seemed too small. Denver was thriving.

Sean applauded the growth. More people meant more business and more opportunity. But he missed the odd, eclectic neighborhoods that were being swallowed by gentrification. Like most Denver natives, he was stubbornly protective of his city.

He parked the rental car in a small six-car lot behind a three-story brick mansion near downtown. "We're here."

"Your office is in a renovated mansion." She beamed. "I can't believe you chose such a unique place."

"It's not unusual. This entire block is mansions that have been redone for businesses. We have the right half of the first floor. On the left side, there are three little offices—a life coach, a web designer and a woman who reads horoscopes. We all share the kitchen and the conference rooms upstairs."

"About the horoscope lady, what kind of conference meetings does she have?"

"Séances."

He opened the back door for her and held it while she entered an enclosed porch that was attached to the very modern kitchen with stainless steel appliances and a double-door refrigerator. It smelled like somebody had just microwaved a bag of popcorn.

"I love it," Emily said. "When you worked for the FBI, you never would have gone for a place like this."

"I've changed."

They went down the hallway to the spacious foyer with a grand staircase of carved oak and high ceilings. To the right, he stopped beside a door with an opaque glass window decorated with old-fashioned lettering for TST Security and their four-leaf clover logo. Using a keypad, Sean plugged in a code to open the door. Before he followed Emily inside, he touched the red leaf that represented Matt, as he always did.

Dylan greeted his former sister-in-law with enthusiasm, throwing his long arms around her for a big hug. He and Sean were the same height, but Dylan seemed taller because he was skinny. During his early years, Dylan was the epitome of a ninety-eight-pound weakling with oversize glasses and a permanent slouch. Sean had taken his little brother under his wing and got him working out. Under his baggy jeans and plaid flannel shirt, Dylan was ripped now.

They had two desks in the huge front office, but that wasn't where Dylan wanted to sit. He dragged her over to a brown leather sofa. On the coffee table in front of the sofa were snacks: popcorn, crackers and bottles of water.

She reached up to tuck a hank of brownish-blond hair behind his ear. "Almost as long as mine. I like the ponytail."

"I remember your super-long hair," he said.

"It was always such a mess."

"Not to me. It was beautiful. But I like this new look."

"Sorry to interrupt," Sean said, "but whenever you're done comparing stylists, there are some very bad men after Emily, and we need to take them out of the picture."

"Impatient," Dylan said as he pushed his horn-rimmed glasses up on his nose. He turned to Emily. "There's no need to be nervous in the TST office. It's one of the most secure spots in Denver. We've got bulletproof glass in the windows, sensors, surveillance cameras all around and sound-disabling technology so nobody can electronically eavesdrop."

"That's very reassuring." She opened a bottle of water and took a sip. "Can you make my computer un-hackable?"

"I can make it real hard to get in." Dylan pushed his glasses up again. "I've got an update."

"Another call from Agent Levine?" Sean guessed as he sat on the opposite end of the sofa from Emily.

"Levine isn't comment-worthy." Dylan plunked himself into a high-back swivel chair on wheels and paddled from a desk to the sofa. "I'm not insulting you, but the feds aren't real efficient."

"No offense taken," Sean said.

"This call was a few hours ago, a man's voice. He claimed to be an old friend from San Francisco. He identified himself as Jack Baxter. Sound familiar?"

"Not a bit," Sean responded. "Emily, do you know the name?"

"I don't think so."

Sitting on the big leather sofa with her hands in her lap and her ankles crossed, she looked nervous and somewhat overwhelmed. Dylan could be a lot to take; he tended to bounce around like an overeager puppy.

Also, Sean reminded himself, she was aware of the threat, the potential for danger. He directed his brother. "We need to focus here. What did Baxter want?"

"Supposedly, he was just thinking of you, his old pal. It seemed too coincidental for you to be contacted by a supposed friend on the same day Levine called." He shot a look at Emily. "He kept asking about you. Suspicious, right?"

Sean remained focused. "Did you track the call?"

"He claimed to be in San Francisco, and his cell phone had the 414 area code. But I triangulated the microwave signal." Dylan paused for effect. "He was calling from DIA."

Emily shot to her feet. "He's here? At the Denver airport?"

Dylan winced. "It gets worse. I ran a reverse lookup on the cell phone. It belongs to John Morelli."

"I know him," she said. "He works for Wynter."

"Bingo," Dylan said. "I've been doing a bit of preliminary hacking on Wynter. And Morelli is vice president in charge of communication."

"That's right," Emily said. "I interviewed him for my first article on Wynter Corp. He's the only person I spoke to in person."

"Which might be why he was sent to Denver to find you," Sean said. "When you met with him, did you use the Timmons alias?"

She shook her head. "Timmons is only for travel and the one credit card. I use another alias for my articles and interviews."

"How did Wynter make the connection between us?"

Dylan rolled toward him on the swivel chair. "Remember how I said the feds were idiots? Well, I think Wynter had their phones tapped. When Levine called here, looking for you, I told him you weren't involved with Emily. But the contact must have sent up a red flag to Wynter."

His deduction made sense. "I want you to dig deeper into Wynter Corp. Check into their bank accounts and expenses."

"Forensic accounting." Dylan nodded. "Will do."

"How much can you find out?" Emily asked. "That information belongs to Wynter Corp. It's protected."

"I've got skills," Dylan said, "and I can hack practically anything. Unlike the feds, I don't have to worry about obtaining the evidence through illegal means because I don't plan to use the data in court. This is purely a fact-finding mission."

She accepted him at his word. "Concentrate on the import-export business. Check inventories against shipping manifests—look for warehouse information."

"I took a peek earlier," Dylan said. "They also handle real estate, restaurants and small businesses."

"For now I'm looking for evidence of smuggling and human trafficking." She bounced to her feet. "I have information that will give you a starting point."

"Cool," Dylan said. "If you give me the flash drive you've got hidden in your necklace, I'll get started."

"How did you know?" She touched her black-and-silver pendant. "Is it obvious?"

"Only to me," he said as he held out his flat palm.

Although Sean didn't speak up and steal his brother's thunder, he had also figured out where she was hiding her flash drive. *Simple logic.* All day long, she'd been touching her pendant, guarding it. What would she want to protect? Her most precious possession was her work; therefore, he guessed she had her documents on a flash drive. And she'd hidden it in chunky jewelry that wasn't her usual style.

Dylan rolled his chair to a computer station with four display screens and three keyboards. Emily followed behind him, eager to learn the magic techniques that allowed Sean's brother to dance across the World Wide

Web like a spider with a ponytail and horn-rimmed glasses.

Long ago Sean had given up trying to understand how Dylan did what he did. The technical aspects of security and investigative work had never interested Sean. He learned more from observing, questioning the people involved and creating a profile of the criminals and the victims. When he'd gone undercover for the FBI, he had to rely on instinct to separate the good guys from the bad. And his gut was good. He was seldom wrong.

He left the sofa and sauntered across the large, open room with high ceilings to the window. It bothered him that John Morelli was in Denver. Dylan's theory of how Wynter got his name had the ring of truth. Tapping the FBI phones was depressingly obvious.

His brother and Emily stared at the screens as though answers would materialize before their eyes. Sean hardly remembered a time when computers weren't a part of life, but he'd never fallen in love with the technology and he hated the way people stumbled around staring at their cell phones. His brother called him a Luddite, and maybe he was. Or maybe he'd made the decision, when they were kids, that computers would be Dylan's thing. Whatever the case, it appeared that Dylan and Emily would be occupied for a while.

Sean announced, "I'm going out to pick up some dinner. Is Chinese okay?"

Barely looking away from the screens, they both murmured agreement.

"Any special requests?"

The response was another mumble.

He went to a file cabinet near the door, unlocked it and took out a Glock 17. He had to pack both of his handguns on the plane and take out the bullets. For the moment, it was quicker to grab the semiautomatic pistol and insert a fresh magazine into the grip. He was almost out the door when Emily ran up behind him and grasped his arm.

"You shouldn't go out there," she said. "Mr. Morelli could be waiting in ambush."

"Mr.?"

"That's what I called him in the interview. He's older, in his forties."

"If he was sneaking around, close enough to show up on Dylan's surveillance, we'd be hearing a buzzer alarm."

She kissed his cheek. "Be careful."

It had been a long time since anybody was worried about his safety. He kind of liked being fussed over.

At the back door, he paused to peer into the trees that bordered the parking lot. There were garages and Dumpsters in the alley behind their office, lots of hiding places if Morelli had staked out the office.

He went down the stairs and got into the rental car to pick up food from Happy Food Chinese restaurant. Then, he backed out into the alley. In less than a mile, he noticed a black sedan following him. Wynter's men had found him. And he'd made it easy. *Damn it, I should have ordered delivery.*

Chapter 8

Emily watched the numbers unfurling across two screens while Dylan used a third screen to enter the forbidden area of the dark web where you could buy or sell anything. Pornographers, killers, perverts and all types of scum hung out on those mysterious, ugly sites.

She looked away. "What's a nice guy like you doing in a place like that?"

"If you want to get the dirt, you can't keep your hands clean."

Even though her investigation was for a worthy cause, she didn't like spying. Hacking broke one of the ethical rules of journalism that said you needed at least two sources for every statement before you could call it a fact. And they had to be credible sources. Some bloggers just fabricated their stories from lies and rumors. She wasn't like that. Not irresponsible. The thought jolted her. *Wow, have I changed!* When she was married to Sean, he'd complained about her lack of responsibility. Now she was saying the same about other people.

She strolled across the room to a window and looked out at the fading glow of sunset reflected on the marble lions outside the renovated mansion across the street. "We shouldn't have let Sean go without backup."

"He can take care of himself," Dylan said. "He took a gun."

And that worried her, too. If he wasn't expecting trouble, why did he make sure he was armed? "We should go after him."

"Call him." Dylan gestured to the old-fashioned-looking phone on the other desk. "Press the button for extension two. That rings through to his cell phone."

"Are you extension number one?"

"No way." He glanced over his shoulder at her. "That number is, and always will be, Mom."

"Sean told me that your parents are still in Denver."

"And my mother would lo-o-o-ve to see you and Sean get back together. Her dream is grandbabies."

"I heard you're dating someone."

"Her name is Jayne. It's a serious relationship." His eyes lit up. "But we aren't talking about babies."

From the sneaky smile on his face, she could tell that the topic of marriage had come up. Little brother Dylan had found a woman who would put up with his computers. She was happy for him.

As she tapped the extension on the office phone, she hoped that she was worrying about nothing. Sean would pick up and tell her he was fine.

From the other side of the desk, she heard his ringtone. Then she saw his cell phone next to the computer screen. He hadn't taken the phone with him.

"Dylan, we have to go." She hung up the phone. "We have to help Sean."

He lifted his hands off the keys and looked up at her. "Is there something about this Morelli person that I don't know about? Is he particularly dangerous?"

Her impression of the man she'd interviewed was that he was a standard midlevel management guy. He'd worn a nice suit without a necktie. His shoes were polished loafers. His best feature was his thick black hair, which was slicked back with a heavy dose of styling gel. When he spoke he did a lot of hemming and hawing, and she had the sense that he wasn't telling her much more than she could learn from reading about Wynter Corp on the internet.

"Not dangerous," she said. "He was the contrary. Quiet, secretive. Morelli is the kind of guy who fades into the woodwork."

"I'm guessing my brother can handle him."

"I hate to say this." But she remembered those horrible moments on the boat when Patrone was killed. "What if Morelli's not alone?"

That possibility lit a fire under Dylan's tail. He was up and out of his computer chair in a few seconds. He motioned for her to follow, and she ran after him. They raced out the front door and onto the wide veranda to an SUV parked at the curb.

Sean would have known right away that he was being followed if it hadn't been the middle of rush hour with the downtown streets clogged and lane changing nearly impossible. He first caught sight of a black sedan when he was only three blocks away from the office. After he doubled back twice, he was dead certain that the innocent-looking compact sedan, probably a rental from the airport, was on his tail.

Weaving through the other cars on Colfax Avenue, his pursuer had to stay close or risk losing Sean in the stop-and-go traffic. A couple of times, the sedan was directly behind Sean's car. At a stoplight, he studied the rearview mirror, trying to figure out if Morelli was by himself or with a partner.

He appeared to be alone.

Emily had described him as being in his forties. That was the only information Sean had. He should have asked for more details, but he didn't want to alarm her. Leaving the office without a plan had been an unnecessary risk. He knew that. So why had he done it? Was he feeling left out while Dylan did his thing with the computers? Jealous of his little brother?

Envy might account for 5 percent of his decision, but mostly he'd wanted time alone to refresh his mind. Ever since he saw Emily, he'd been tense. And when they kissed...

He checked his side mirror. The black sedan was one car back, still following. Dusk was rapidly approaching. Some vehicles had already turned on their headlights. If he was going to confront the man in the sedan, he should make his move. Darkness would limit his options.

Sean didn't necessarily want to hurt Morelli. He wanted to talk to the guy, to have him send a message back to James Wynter that Sean wasn't somebody to mess around with, and he was protecting Emily. The bad guys needed to realize that she wasn't helpless, and—in his role as her bodyguard—he wouldn't hesitate to kick ass.

He set a simple trap. Accelerating and making a few swerving turns, he sped into a large, mostly empty parking lot at the west end of Cherry Creek Mall. Sean fishtailed behind a building, parked and jumped out of the car before the black sedan came around the corner.

His original plan had been to hide behind his car, but a better possibility appeared. Though the parking lot was bare asphalt right now, there had been snow that morning. The plows had cleared the large lot and left the snow in a waist-high pile near a streetlight. Sean dove behind it.

Holding his gun ready, he watched and waited while the black sedan cautiously inched closer and closer. It circled his car, keeping a distance. The sedan parked behind his car, and a man got out. He braced a semiautomatic pistol with both hands.

"Sean Timmons," he shouted. "Get out of the car. I'm not going to hurt you."

"You got that right." Sean came out from behind the snow barrier. His position was excellent, in back of the driver of the sedan. "Drop the gun and raise your arms."

If it came to a shoot-out, he wouldn't hesitate to drop this guy. But he wouldn't take the first shot. The man set his gun on the asphalt, raised his hands and turned. "We need to talk."

Since they were standing in view of a busy street with rush hour traffic streaming past, Sean lowered his gun as he approached the other man. In spite of the gun, this guy didn't seem real threatening. Dressed in a conservative blue sweater with khaki trousers, he wore his hair slicked back. His pale complexion hinted that he spent most of his time indoors.

Sean asked, "Is your name Morelli?"

"John Morelli."

"Are you a hit man, John?"

"Of course not."

"What do you want to say?"

"It's about your ex-wife." He took a step forward and Sean raised his gun, keeping him back. "If you'll let me talk to her, I can explain everything."

He sounded rational, but Sean wasn't convinced. "You could have called her," he pointed out.

"I tried," Morelli said. "I left messages on her answering machine. She's a hard woman to reach, especially since she gave me a fake name."

That much was true. "How did you find out her real name?"

Morelli didn't answer immediately. He exhibited the classic signs of nerves: furrowed brow, the flicker of an eyelid, the thinning of the lips and the clearing of his throat. All these tics and twitches were extremely subtle. Most people wouldn't notice.

But Sean was a pro when it came to questioning scumbags. He knew that whatever Morelli said next was bound to be a lie.

"It's like this," Morelli said. "I saw her on the street and followed her to her house."

"You stalked her?"

Quickly Morelli said, "No, no, it wasn't creepy. I guessed her neighborhood from something she said at our interview."

"Not buying that story."

"Okay, you got me." He tried a self-deprecating gesture that didn't quite work. "I got her fingerprint at our interview and ran it through identification software."

Sean had enough. "Here's what I think. Your boss, James Wynter, used an illegal wiretap, overheard her name. When he pulled up her photo, you recognized the reporter who interviewed you."

Morelli was breathing harder. A dull red color climbed his throat. "I don't know anything about illegal wiretaps, and I'm insulted that you think I would be that sort of person."

As if being a stalker was more reputable? "This is your last chance to be honest, Morelli. Otherwise, I'll turn you in to the feds. They keep an open file on Wynter, and they'll be interested in you."

"Wait!" He lowered his hands and waved them frantically. "There's no need for law enforcement."

"Don't tell me another lie."

"Truth, only truth, I swear."

Sean tested that promise by asking, "Did Wynter send you to Denver?"

"Yes."

"What were you supposed to do?"

"Find your ex-wife. When he said her name was Emily Peterson, I didn't know who he was talking about. I knew her as Sylvia Plath."

Sean stifled a chuckle. Emily's obviously phony alias referenced a famous poet. "What made you think she might come looking for me? Did you miss the 'ex' in front of husband?"

"After I learned that she'd gone on the run, I checked her background on the internet. Your name popped up, and I knew. The first person the girl would look to for help was her macho, ex-FBI husband who runs a security firm."

His story sounded legit. Or maybe Sean just enjoyed being called macho. He liked that he was the guy to call when danger struck. Or was he being conned?

Morelli was turning out to be a puzzle. He readily admitted that he worked for Wynter and he carried a gun, but he looked like a middle-aged man who had just finished a game of billiards in a sunless pool hall. He was less intimidating than a sock puppet.

Sean made a guess. "You don't get out of the office much, do you?"

"Not for a long time." He gave a self-deprecating smile. "I've had both knees replaced."

Scenes from old gangster movies where some poor shmuck was getting his kneecaps broken with a baseball bat flashed through Sean's mind. But he didn't go there. This was the twenty-first century, and criminals were more corporate…more like the man standing before him.

"There's something bothering me," Sean said. "When you called the TST office, you used your own phone."

"So? I wasn't giving anything away. My number's unlisted."

"An easy hack," Sean said. "I might even be able to do it."

"I should've used a burner." The corners of his mouth pulled down. He seemed honestly surprised and upset. *What is going on with this guy?* If Wynter hadn't sent him to wipe out the witness to his son's crime, why was Morelli here?

Sean said, "What were you supposed to do when you found my ex-wife?"

"To warn her."

"About what?"

"If she prints her article from information I gave her, it's going to have several errors. Wynter Corp is planning a significant move in regard to our real estate holdings."

As he spoke, his face showed signs that he was lying. His lip quivered. He even did the classic signal of looking up and to the right. For a thug, Morelli was a terrible liar.

"Seriously," Sean said. "You want me to believe that you rushed out to Denver, tailed my car through rush-hour traffic and pulled a gun so you could talk real estate?"

"Doesn't make sense, does it?"

"Last chance. Tell me the real reason. What do you want from Emily?"

"I want to find out what she knows."

His statement seemed sincere. "Why would you think Emily has information that you don't?"

"She's been researching Wynter Corp for quite a while, and it's possible she stumbled over some internal operations data that would be embarrassing to Mr. Wynter."

"Lose the corporate baloney. What's the problem?"

"Somebody's stealing from us, and we want to know who."

"Now you're talking." Sean believed him. Wynter wouldn't be happy about somebody dipping into his inventories. "Do you really think Emily might have information you missed? Is she that good an investigator?"

"Her first article on Wynter Corp was right on target."

It occurred to Sean that if he pretended that Emily

had valuable information, the hit men wouldn't hurt her. Luckily, he was an excellent liar. "I shouldn't tell you, but she's come up with a working hypothesis. She's figured out what's happening on the inside. If she gets hurt, it all goes public."

"I knew it was an insider." Morelli cleared his throat. "And there's that other matter I need to discuss."

"The murder?"

"She might have imagined seeing something that did not, in fact, happen."

Sean shook his head. "She's sure of what she saw, and she won't be convinced otherwise."

"How much would it take to unconvince her?"

And now Sean had full comprehension. Morelli wasn't here to kill her. He'd come to Denver to seduce her into working for Wynter Corp with cash payoffs and assurances that she was brilliant. Clearly, he didn't know Emily.

It was time to wrap up this encounter. If Sean had still been a fed, he would've taken Morelli into custody and gone through a mountain of paperwork to come up with charges that would be dismissed as soon as Wynter's lawyers got involved. As a bodyguard, he didn't have those responsibilities. His job was to keep Emily safe.

He made a threat assessment. "Are there other Wynter operatives in Denver?"

"No."

But a quick twitch at the corner of his eye told Sean the opposite. "How many?"

For a moment, Morelli sputtered and prevaricated, trying to avoid the truth. Then he admitted, "One other person. He does things differently than I do."

Sean translated. "He's more of a 'shoot-first' type."

"You could say that."

He needed to get Emily out of town before the less subtle hit man caught up with them. He picked up Morelli's pistol, removed the ammo and returned it to him. At the same time, Morelli handed him a business card.

"It's got all my numbers," Morelli said.

"I'll get your message to Emily. If she agrees to talk to you, she'll call. Don't approach her or me again."

They walked away from each other, each returning to his separate rental car. As Sean slid behind the wheel, he wished that he could trust Morelli. It would've been handy to have an inside man at Wynter Corp.

As he drove to the homely, little Chinese restaurant where they always ordered carryout, he checked his rearview mirrors and scanned the traffic. There was no sign of Morelli. He didn't know what the other hit man—the more dangerous thug—would be driving.

At the restaurant, he spotted Dylan and Emily sitting at one of the small tables near the kitchen. He would have been annoyed that she'd left the security of the office and put herself in danger, but this happenstance worked for him.

She stood and faced him. "Next time," she said, "take your damn phone. I was worried."

"Ready to go?" he asked.

Dylan held up a large brown paper bag with streaky grease stains on the side. "It's our usual order."

"Bring it. I get hungry on plane rides."

Emily gaped. "Plane?"

Sean wasn't going to hang around in Denver, waiting for the second hit man to find them. For all he knew, Morelli had already contacted his partner-in-crime. Sean and Emily had to escape. The sooner, the better.

Chapter 9

Emily had no idea how Sean accomplished so much in so little time. It seemed to be a combination of knowing the right people and calling in favors; she couldn't say for sure. Maybe he was magic. In any case, he'd told her that Denver was too dangerous, and within an hour she was on a private jet, ready to take off for San Francisco.

After she'd been whisked to a small airfield south of town, Sean rushed her into an open hangar and got her on board a Gulfstream G200. Her only other experience with private aircraft was a ski trip on a rickety little Cessna, which was no comparison to this posh eight-passenger jet. Sean left her with instructions not to disembark.

She strolled down the strip of russet-brown carpet that bisected the length of the cabin. Closest to the cockpit were four plush taupe leather chairs facing one another. Behind that was a long sofa below the porthole windows on one side and two more chairs on the other. The galley—a half-size refrigerator, cabinet, sink and microwave—was tucked into the rear.

Her stomach growled, and she made a quick search of the kitchenette. There were three different kinds of water in the fridge and the liquor cabinet was well stocked, but the cupboards were almost bare.

At the front of the cabin, she sank into one of the chairs. The cushioned seat and back cradled her, elevating her to a level of comfort that was practically a massage. Still, she didn't relax. A persistent adrenaline rush stoked her nervous energy.

Bouncing to her feet, she paced the length of the aircraft, all the way to the bathroom behind the galley to the closed door that separated the cockpit from the cabin. Sean had left her suitcase, and she wondered if she should change out of the black sweater she'd been wearing since before dawn this morning. A fresh outfit might give her a new perspective, and she needed something to lighten her spirits and ease her tension.

Not that she was complaining about the way Sean had handled the threat from Morelli. He'd done a good job, but she wished that she'd been there. Somehow it felt like the situation was slipping through her fingers. She was losing control.

Or was she overreacting? The trip to San Francisco had originally been her idea, not his. But she had new information and needed to reconsider. Sean should have consulted with her before charging into the breach and arranging for a private jet. She had opinions. This was her investigation. He wasn't the boss. When push came to shove, he was actually her employee.

A sense of dread rose inside her. She'd felt this way before. Frustrated and voiceless, she was reminded of the final, ugly days of their marriage. Until the bitter end, Sean had tried to make all the decisions. He wanted to be the captain who set their course while she was left to swab the decks and polish the hardware. Her only option had been mutiny.

In the past when she'd tried to stop him, she failed more than she succeeded. He was so implacable. And she didn't want to fight. *Make love, not war.* She'd changed. No longer a nineteen-year-old free spirit who tumbled whichever way the wind was blowing, the new Emily was solid, determined and responsible. As soon as she could get Sean alone, she meant to set the record straight.

Dylan stuck his head through the entry hatch. His long hair was out of the ponytail and hanging around his face, making him look like a teenager. "I brought you a brand-new, super-secure computer."

He sat and wiggled his butt. "Nice chair."

"Very." She sat opposite.

Obviously he'd been in this jet before. He knew exactly how to pull out a table from the wall. When it stretched out between them, he set a laptop on it, opened the lid and spun it toward her. "As I've said before, about a hundred times, anything can be hacked. This system has extreme firewalls, but when you're not using it, log off with this code."

He typed in numbers and letters that ran together: 14U24Me.

"One for you two for me," she read.

"Easy to remember." He reached into his backpack. "And here's your new cell phone, complete with camera and large screen. It's loaded with everything that was on your old phone, but this baby is also secure. It bounces your signal all around the world."

She stroked the smooth plastic cover. "I've missed having a phone."

"Yeah, well, don't get tempted to play with this. Keep texting to the bare minimum and don't add a bunch of apps. In the interest of security, keep your calls short. And when you aren't using the phone, log off."

"I thought cell phones could be tracked even when they were off."

"Not this one. Not unless somebody hacks my most recent software innovation, and that's not going to happen for a couple of weeks at least." Digging into his pocket, he produced her flash drive. "You can slip this back into your necklace. I've got a copy."

"While we're gone, will you keep hacking Wynter?"

"You bet."

"You might run comparisons between shipping manifests and inventory, plus sales figures."

He pushed the glasses up on his nose. "Morelli seemed convinced that there was theft. That gives me another angle."

In her research, she hadn't uncovered any evidence that someone was stealing from Wynter. But she hadn't been using the sophisticated hacking tools that Dylan so deftly employed. Part of her wanted to have him teach her; the more ethical part of her conscience held her back. Hacking wasn't a fair way to investigate.

Dylan stood. Before leaving, he gave her a brotherly kiss on the cheek. "I know Sean is supposed to be taking care of you. But keep an eye on him, okay? Don't let him do anything crazy dangerous."

"I'll try."

When Dylan left, she was alone in the cabin. Still seated, she peered through a porthole. Through the open door to her hangar, she could see one of the lighted runways, part of another hangar and several small planes tethered to the tarmac. The control tower was a four-story building with a 360-degree view that reminded her of some of the lighthouses up the coast in Oregon. As she watched, a midsize Cessna taxied to the far end of the airstrip, wheeled around and halted. With a burst of speed, the white jet sped forward and gracefully lifted off. Silhouetted against the night sky, the Cessna's lights soared to the right, toward the dark shadow of the mountains west of the city.

Sean came through the hatch and sat in the chair opposite her, where Dylan had been sitting. As easily as Dylan had pulled down the table, Sean removed that barrier between them. He leaned forward with his elbows resting on his knees.

"Are you okay?" he asked.

His gentleness threw her off guard. She noticed that he hadn't shaved, and dark stubble outlined his jaw. By asking how she was, he'd given her an opening to rationally discuss how she should be kept in the loop. Right now she should assert her needs and desires, let him know she was in charge. *Right now! This moment!*

Instead she stared dumbly at his face, distracted by the perfect symmetry of his features. Why did he have to be so gorgeous?

"Emily?" His eyebrows lifted as though her name were a question. "Emily, tell me."

"When did you find time to change?" He'd discarded his turtleneck for a cotton shirt and a light suede bomber jacket. She couldn't say he looked fresh as a daisy. Sean was much too rugged to be compared to a flower.

"Only took a minute," he said. "Are you—"

"You asked if I was okay." She stumbled over the words. "Okay about what?"

"Going to San Francisco," he said. "We're set to leave in ten minutes. A flight plan has been filed, but this is a private jet. You can change your mind and go any-where."

She wasn't following. "What do you mean?"

"San Francisco is dangerous. There are alternative destinations, like Washington State or heading south to Mexico. We could even go to Hawaii."

Irritated, she pushed herself out of the cozy chair and stalked toward the rear. "I'm not afraid."

"I didn't say you were." He followed her down the aisle.

"But you think I might want to run away." She piv-oted to face him. "Maybe I'd like to take a vacation in Hawaii and lie on the beach. Is that what you want? For me to hide in a safe place while Wynter runs his human trafficking ring and his son gets away with murder."

"It's not about what I want."

"I'm glad you understand." But she almost wished he'd be unreasonable. Making her point was easier when he argued against her. His rational approach meant she had to also be thoughtful.

"You don't have to step into the line of fire," he said. "You could keep researching the crimes on computer. Work with Dylan. There's no need for you to confront Wynter in his lair."

"I've considered that." There were threads of evidence that she needed to be in San Francisco to follow. With Sean to accompany her, she had more access.

"I need an answer on our destination."

"I've got a question for you," she said. "How do you rate a private jet?"

"Don't worry about it."

"I sincerely hope you're not charging my aunt some exorbitant fee."

"This trip is a favor, and it's free," he said. "You'll recognize the pilot from our wedding. David Henley."

She knew the name. "The guy who plays the banjo?"

"Flying planes is his real job."

"Good for him. He couldn't have made much of a living as a banjo picker."

"In addition to this sweet little Gulfstream, he has a Cessna, an old Sabreliner and two helicopters. He freelances for half a dozen or so companies, flying top execs around the country."

The aforementioned David Henley swung through the entry hatch and marched down the aisle toward them. "Emily, my princess. It's been a while."

Though David was an average-looking guy with wavy blond hair, she most certainly remembered him from the wedding. He'd hit on each of her sisters and ended up going home with her former roommate. He tapped Sean on the shoulder. "May I give this princess a hug?"

"Don't ask me," Sean said. "She can speak for herself."

He held his arms wide. "Hug?"

"Don't get too snuggly," she said. "I see that wedding band on your finger."

His arms wrapped around her. "I like to tease the

princesses, but that's as far as it goes. My heart belongs to my queen, my wife."

"My former roommate." She remembered the announcement from a few years ago. "Please give Ginger a hug from me."

"She'll be bummed that she didn't have a chance to get together with you."

She preferred this mature version of David to the horny banjo player. "Thanks for the plane ride."

"I'm sorry you're in so much trouble." He held her by the shoulders and looked into her eyes. "Are we going to San Francisco?"

"Yes, so be sure to wear some flowers in your hair."

"Still cute." He turned toward Sean. "I won't be using you as copilot. This flight is a good opportunity to train the new guy I hired. Now, I've got to run some equipment checks before we take off. Ciao, you two."

While David went forward to the cockpit, she asked Sean, "You know how to fly a plane?"

"David's been teaching me. The helo is more fun." He gestured toward the seats across the aisle from the sofa bench. "Get comfortable. I'll see if he's got any food back here."

In the rush to get to the airfield, they'd forgotten the Chinese food. She couldn't honestly say she had regrets. Fast food from Denver didn't compare with San Francisco's Chinatown, but the remembered aroma tantalized her. Her stomach rumbled again. No doubt, Dylan would munch the chicken fried rice, chop suey, broccoli beef and General Tso's for dinner. With an effort, she managed to pull out the table between the two seats.

Sean didn't have much to put on it: Two small bags of chips and two sparkling waters. "This will have to do."

Not enough to appease her hunger, but it was probably good that she wouldn't be settling down and getting comfortable. Other than being starving, things seemed to be going her way. She wanted to go to San Francisco, and that was where they were headed. If she was smart, this would be a good time to stay quiet. But she wanted to lay down the basics of a plan for *her* investigation, with emphasis on *her*.

She cleared her throat. "I want to talk about what we're going to do when we land."

"Right," he agreed. "I need to make hotel reservations."

"We can stay in my apartment."

"You're joking."

"Not really."

He regarded her with a disbelieving gaze. "Morelli came all the way to Denver to find you. I'm guessing that Wynter's men have found your apartment."

"But they think I'm in Denver."

"These aren't the sort of guys to play cat and mouse with. As soon as they figure out where you really are, they'll be knocking at your door or busting a hole with a battering ram."

She deferred to his expertise. "Make the reservations."

"I like the Pendragon Hotel," he said. "It's near the trolley line and close to Chinatown."

"We're not going on a sightseeing trip."

The copilot boarded the jet, bringing cold cuts and bread for sandwiches. *Food!* She almost kissed him.

While she and Sean slapped together sandwiches, they dropped their discussion of anything important. The sight and smell of fresh-sliced ham and turkey and baby Swiss made her giddy. And the copilot hadn't stinted on condiments, providing an array of mustard, mayo, horseradish and extra-virgin olive oil. Her mouth was watering. Tomatoes, cucumbers, baby bib lettuce and coleslaw.

She sliced a tomato thin and placed it carefully on the ciabatta bread between the mustard and the lettuce. "I suppose we should make something for David and the copilot."

"We should." He glanced in her direction. "But you really don't look like you can wait for one more minute."

"I'm ravenous."

"Get started without me. I'll take food to the cockpit."

"Best offer I've had all day."

The sandwich she'd assembled was almost too big for her mouth, but she tore off a chunk and chomped down on it. The explosion of flavor in her mouth was total ecstasy. As the sandwich slid down her throat, she relished texture, the taste and the nourishment. She took another bite and another.

The last food she'd had was that morning in the mountains, and that felt like a lifetime ago. While she continued to eat, her eyelids closed. She groaned with pleasure.

After a few more bites, she opened her eyes to reach for her water and saw Sean standing behind his chair, looking down at her. He grinned and said, "Sounds like you're enjoying the sandwich. Either that or you've decided to join the Mile High Club all by yourself."

She swallowed a gulp of water. "How do you know I'm not already a member?"

"Are you?"

"No way," she said. "I'm pretty sure it takes two."

"I'd be happy to volunteer."

Standing there, he was devilish handsome with his wide shoulders, his tousled hair, his stubble and his hands, his rugged hands. Too easily, she imagined his gentle caress across her shoulders and down her back. His eyes, when they'd made love, turned the color of dark chocolate, and his gaze could make her melt inside.

She shoved those urges aside and returned her attention to the sandwich. She needed refueling. Before she was full, the Gulfstream taxied onto the runway.

"Don't bite my arm off," Sean said as he scooped up the remains of her sandwich. "The food has to move before takeoff. Or you'll be wearing it."

David opened the door from the cockpit. "Fasten your seat belts."

She buckled up, gripped the arms of her seat and braced herself as the whine of the engines accelerated and a tremor went through the jet. Though she'd actually never been afraid of flying or of heights, she suffered an instinctive twinge in her gut and a shimmer of vertigo when a plane took off or when she stood at the edge of a cliff. Again, she closed her eyes.

Her mind ran through various streams of evidence they'd investigate in San Francisco, ranging from a meeting with the feds to a possible reconnaissance on Wynter's luxury double-decker yacht.

In moments, they were airborne.

Her eyelids opened. She looked at Sean and said the first thing on her mind, "Don't let me forget Paco the Pimp."

"I'm hoping that's a nickname for something else."

"He's a real guy. I met him about a year ago when I was doing an article on preteen hookers." She shuddered. "That was a painful experience, one horrifying story after another. I almost decided to quit journalism and go back to soothing poetry or lyric writing. Paco changed my mind."

"By offering you a job?"

"Oh, he did that…several times. Not that either of us took his offers seriously. Anyway, he reminded me of my obligation to shine a light on the ugly truth in the hope that people would pay attention. And the horror would stop…or at least slow down."

He lowered himself into the seat opposite her and pulled out the table. Instead of returning the last few bites of her sandwich, he placed a bottle of red wine and two plastic glasses on the flat surface. "And why do you need to remember Paco?"

"He's got an ear to the street. He hears all the gossip. And I want to find out if he remembered anything from that night." She hesitated. Maybe she was bringing up a volatile topic. She didn't want Sean to be mad at her. "He might have seen something I missed."

He used a corkscrew to open the wine. "Are you talking about the night of the murder?"

Averting her gaze, she looked through the porthole window. The lights of Denver glittered below them. Ahead was the pitch-dark of the Rocky Mountains. She didn't want to answer.

Chapter 10

Sean was familiar with most of Emily's tactics when it came to arguments. When she didn't answer him back right away, her silence meant she was hiding something. He sank into the plush chair opposite hers. He didn't want to fight. They were on a private jet headed toward one of the most romantic cities in the world, and he hadn't completely ruled out the possibility of inducting her into the Mile High Club.

But he couldn't leave Paco the Pimp hanging. Apparently this Paco had been a passenger on Wynter's deluxe yacht. "You've told me about the night of the murder. You claimed you were at a yacht party. True or false?"

"True."

He poured the wine, a half glass for her and the same for himself. "But you never told me how you got an invite to this insider party. I'm guessing it had something to do with Paco the Pimp. True or false?"

"I don't want to talk about this."

"And I know why," he said. "Your pal Paco was invited to provide a bunch of party girls for the guys on the yacht. And you convinced him to take you along. You went undercover."

"Fine," she snapped. "You're right. I was all dolled up in a sparkly skintight dress, four-inch heels and gobs of heavy makeup."

"A hooker disguise."

"Sleazy except for my long hair. I had it pinned up on top of my head when I went there. I thought it was sophisticated." She sipped her wine. "Paco said I should wear it down. He thought the men would like it."

Imagining her being ogled in a sexy dress made his blood boil. Of course they liked her long, beautiful hair. "What the hell, Emily? You used to believe that hiding your identity was dishonest and unfair."

"You've got no room to talk," she said. "You used to go undercover all the time."

"And you never approved."

"Maybe not."

"And I was trained for it. I have certain traits and abilities that lend themselves to undercover work, namely, I'm good at deception." He downed his wine in two glugs. "You're not like that. You're a lousy liar."

"I've changed. I know when to keep my mouth shut instead of blurting out the truth. I can be circumspect."

"You can't change your basic nature," he said as he poured more wine. "Undercover work is not your thing."

"I pulled it off on Wynter's yacht."

He glared at her. "Not a shining example of a successful mission."

"I made mistakes," she admitted. "Okay, all right, it was gross. Witnessing the murder was the worst, but being pawed by sleazeballs was bad. One of them grabbed me by my hair and kissed me. Another patted my hair like I was a dog. The very next day, I went to the beauty shop and told them to cut it off."

"You're never going to go undercover again, understand?"

"Don't tell me what I can and can't do."

Through clenched teeth, he said, "I'm sorry."

She looked at him as though he'd sprouted petunias from the top of his head. "Did I hear you correctly?"

"You're right. I can't tell you what to do. However, if you decide to go undercover again, I want to know. Give me a chance to show you how to do it without getting yourself killed."

"My turn to apologize," she said. "You're also right. I had no business waltzing onto that yacht without the proper training. The only reason I got out of there in one piece was dumb luck."

He held up his plastic glass to salute her. The wine he'd already inhaled was taking the sharp edge off, but he was still alert enough to realize that something significant had occurred: they hadn't gotten into a fight.

Both of them had been ticked off. They'd danced around the volcano, but neither had erupted. Instead, they'd talked like adults and settled their differences. Maybe she'd matured. Maybe he'd gotten more sensitive. *Whatever!* He'd gladly settle for this fragile truce instead of gut-wrenching hostility.

He didn't want to discuss their successful handling

of the problem for fear that he'd jinx the positive mood. What had they been talking about before takeoff? Oh yeah, the agenda for their time in San Francisco. He wanted to take her to dinner at the Italian restaurant where he proposed.

He gazed toward her. She looked youthful but not too young. Had she changed in the past five years? If he looked closely, he could see fine lines at the corners of her turquoise eyes, and her features seemed sharper, more honed. With her black sweater covering her torso, he could only guess how her body had changed. A vision of her nicely proportioned shoulders, round breasts and slender waist was easy to recall. He hadn't forgotten the constellation of freckles across her back or the tattoo of a cute little rodent above her left breast that she referred to as a "titmouse."

Since he wasn't allowed to touch her without disobeying half a dozen of their weird ground rules, he had to stop thinking like this. Her unapproachable nearness would drive him mad. Back to business, back to the investigation, he said, "Tomorrow, our first appointment should be a meeting with Levine to see if the FBI has any new info."

"But not at the fed office," she reminded him. "Dylan thinks their phones are bugged."

He considered it unlikely that Levine was working with Wynter, but Sean didn't want to take any chances. "I'd rather not let him know where we're staying. We'll meet him for breakfast."

"After that," she said, "we should go to Chinatown. I had a couple of leads there, and I'd like to talk to Doris Liu again. She's the woman who took in Roger Patrone and raised him."

He'd almost forgotten that Patrone was an orphan who had been taken in by a family in Chinatown. "There must have been something remarkable about Patrone when he was a kid. Most residents in Chinatown aren't welcoming to strangers."

"It's been hard for me to ask around," she said. "Patrone's gambling operation—last I heard it was a stud poker game, Texas Hold'em and two blackjack tables—is in the rear of a strip club in the Tenderloin. Even with the attempts at gentrification, I don't blend in."

The Tenderloin had earned its reputation as a high-crime district. He was deeply grateful that she hadn't tried an undercover stint as a stripper. "I'll go there, no problem."

"And I wouldn't mind sneaking onto Wynter's yacht and looking around."

Breaking and entering didn't appeal to him, but he definitely liked the idea of getting out on the water in the bay. San Francisco had many charms, ranging from unique architecture to culture to amazing restaurants. The best, he thought, were the piers and the ocean…the scent of salt water…the whisper of the surf.

She yawned. "Maybe we should go to the docks. I only tried to get in there once, and it didn't go well. The guys who work with shipping containers ignored me, and the supervisors were overly polite, thinking I was sent by management to check up on them."

"What can we learn there?"

"I'm not sure," she said. "It's another avenue."

They were going to be busy. "Tired?"

"A bit," she said.

"You can take off your seat belt and lie on the sofa. It folds out into a bed."

She peeked out the porthole. "How long before we're in San Francisco?"

"A couple of hours." The flight time on commercial airlines was two and a half hours. The Gulfstream took a little longer.

"I wouldn't mind a catnap," she said.

He moved their wineglasses to cup holders beside the chairs, picked up the nearly empty wine bottle and tucked away the table. Before he transformed the sofa into a bed, he opened a storage compartment and took out a thermal blanket and a pillow. Then he dimmed the lights.

After fluffing the pillow, she stood and fidgeted beside the sofa bed. "I feel selfish, taking the only bed. You're as tired as I am."

"Is that an invitation to join you?"

"No," she said softly. "Sorry, I didn't mean to give you that idea."

Her tone sounded regretful. If he pushed, he might be able to change her mind. But now wasn't the right time. He didn't want to rock the boat while they were in a fairly good place. At least they weren't fighting. It was best not to complicate things with sex. *Great sex*, he reminded himself. They'd always had great sex.

"Not tonight," he said, as much to himself as to her. "Lie down. I'm going up to the cockpit."

"With the other cocks?"

"You might say that." He wouldn't, but she would.

No matter how much she claimed to be a responsible, sober adult, there was a goofball just below the surface. That was the Emily that drove him crazy, the Emily he loved.

* * *

While she slept, Sean spent time with his buddy David and the copilot. He loved the night view from the cockpit with stars scattered across the sky. He felt like they were part of the galaxies.

They talked, and he made coffee to counteract the slight inebriation he'd felt. A professional bodyguard shouldn't be drinking on the job, but he couldn't pretend that this was a standard assignment.

If she'd been anyone else, he would have advised them to leave the investigating to the police. And if they refused, he would have terminated the contract. Not a detective, he was well aware that he didn't have the resources that were available to him when he was in the FBI. On the other hand, he had the hacking skills of his brother and none of those pesky restrictions.

Finally, he was peering through the clouds and wispy curtains of fog to see the lights of San Francisco, and he felt a surge. His pulse sped up. His blood pumped harder. This city was the setting for the best time in his life and the absolute, rock-bottom worst. Emily was intrinsic to both.

He went back to the cabin and found her lying on her side, spooning the pillow. As soon as he touched her shoulder, she wakened.

"I'm up," she said, throwing off the blanket.

"Almost there. You need to put on a seat belt."

"Do I have time to splash water on my face?"

"Okay, if you hurry."

While she darted into the bathroom, he verified their arrangements on his phone. They had a suite reserved at the Pendragon Hotel and there should be a rental car waiting at the private airfield. Sean wanted to believe they'd be safe, at least for tonight, but his gut told him to watch for trouble. He put in a call to Dylan at the TST office.

"We're here," Sean announced, purposely not naming the city in case somebody was listening. "Anything to report?"

"Wynter must be taking advantage of his location near Silicon Valley and hiring top-notch programmers. His security is state-of-the-art, truly hard to hack."

Oddly, Dylan sounded happy. Sean asked, "You like the challenge?"

"Oh yeah. Getting through these firewalls will be an accomplishment."

"I'll leave you to it."

"Hang on a sec. I had a phone call from your new BFF, Morelli. He wanted to make an information exchange."

"What did you tell him?"

"I said you'd call him back."

"Thanks, bro."

He disconnected the call. Morelli's business card with all his numbers was burning a hole in his pocket. Though Sean was tempted to make the call, he'd warned Morelli not to contact him. It might seem weak to call back. But it was possible that Morelli had useful information.

Sean set the scrambler on his phone so he couldn't be traced and punched in the numbers for Morelli's cell phone. As soon as the other man answered, he said, "What do you want?"

"Let me talk to Emily."

"You're wasting my time," Sean said. "Talk."

"Tell her that she's not going to be able to sell her

articles to the *BP Reporter* anymore. That's one of the places she published her last article on Wynter."

"Why can't she sell there?"

"A terrible accident happened in their office. The police are saying a leak in the gas main resulted in the fiery explosion that destroyed the building."

"Any deaths or injuries?"

"The editor is in the hospital." Morelli paused for a moment. "It's fortunate that Emily wasn't there."

Chapter 11

Any complacency Emily had been feeling vanished when Sean told her of the explosion. *BP Reporter* was a giveaway newspaper filled with shopping specials and coupons, and the pay for articles was next to nothing. Most writers saw *BP*, which stood for Blog/Print, as a stepping-stone to actual paying assignments. The editor, Jerome Strauss, wasn't a close friend, but she knew him and she felt guilty about his injuries. She was to blame. There wasn't a doubt in her mind that Wynter was behind the supposed "gas leak" detonation.

Refreshed from her catnap and energized by righteous rage, she found it difficult to wait until they got to the Pendragon Hotel to start her inquiries. They'd gained an hour traveling to the West Coast. It was after two o'clock in the morning when they entered the suite. She set up her laptop on a desk in the living room and watched while Sean prowled through the suite with his gun held ready. The floor plan for the suite was open space with the kitchen delineated by a counter and the bedroom separated by a half wall and an arch. Sean was thorough, peering into closets and looking under the bed. When he was apparently satisfied that there were no bad guys lurking, he unpacked some strange equipment. One piece looked like an extension rod for selfies.

"What's that?" she asked.

"An all-purpose sweeper to locate bugs, hidden cameras and the like."

Though she appreciated his attention to detail, she didn't understand why it was needed. "How would anybody know we were coming to this hotel and were assigned to this room?"

"I've stayed here before. And I asked for this room. It's on the top floor, the sixth. Since this is the tallest building on the block, it's hard for anybody with a telescope or a sniper rifle to take aim. There's a nice view when the fog lifts."

"It's a nice hotel," she agreed. The exterior was classic San Francisco architecture, and the furnishings were clean lined, Asian inspired. "Why would there be bugs?"

"I want to be sure we're safe." He started waving his long camera thingy, scanning the room for electronic devices. "Get used to this, Emily. From now on, I'm hyperprotective."

Tempted to make a snarky comment about how vigilance sometimes crossed the line into obsessive-compulsive disorder, she kept her lip zipped. He was the expert, and she needed to rely on his judgment. She sauntered across the room to the counter that separated the kitchenette and climbed onto a stool. "I need to start making phone calls. Which phone should I use?"

"It depends on who you're calling."

"How so?"

He explained, "If you're talking to somebody suspicious who might try to track your location, use the secure phone Dylan gave you. If it's somebody you feel safe with, use a burner. We can load up a burner and pitch it."

He seemed to be thinking of all contingencies. "I want to track down Strauss by calling hospitals."

"Burner," he said as he continued to sweep the room.

She called four hospitals before she found the right one. The only information the on-duty nurse would give her was that Strauss was in "fair" condition, but not allowed to have visitors, especially not visitors from the press.

Relieved but not completely satisfied, she wished she had the type of access the FBI and SFPD had. It didn't seem fair. Law enforcement officers wouldn't be barred from the room, but the press—the very people Strauss worked with every day—had to take a step back.

If Strauss was awake, she'd bet he was planning his coverage on the explosion. The story had fallen into his lap. Would he let her be the one to write about it?

She wasn't his favorite reporter. He knew her as Emily, and she submitted only puff pieces, but the explosion might be a way to integrate her real identity with her secret pseudonym. Strauss already did business with her fake persona; the article about Wynter had been published first by an online news journal that paid for her investigative skills. Strauss had permission for a reprint that cost him nothing.

Maybe she could get Sean to use his influence with Agent Levine to sneak her into the hospital room. She went into the bedroom area behind Japanese-style screens to ask.

There were two full-size beds, and he had taken the one nearer to the archway connecting bedroom and living room. He'd pulled back the spread and collapsed onto the sheets. His shoes were off, but he still wore his jeans and T-shirt. In repose, his features relaxed, and he seemed almost innocent. She crept up beside him and turned off the globe-shaped lamp on the bedside table.

Before she could tiptoe out of the room, his hand shot out and grasped her wrist. His movement was unexpected. She gasped loudly and struggled to pull away from him. He held on more tightly. "Turn it back on."

"I wanted to make it dark so you could sleep."

"Can't see an intruder." He hadn't opened his eyes. "Leave the light on."

She flicked the switch, he released his grasp and she scuttled into the front room with her heart beating fast. He'd startled her, and her fear was close to the surface. If he could spook her so easily, how was she going to fall asleep?

If she stayed up, what could she do? It was too early to make phone calls, and she wanted to talk to Dylan before she used the laptop so she wouldn't accidentally trigger any alarms.

A sigh pushed through her lips. Lying down on the bed was probably a good idea. Getting herself cleaned up was next best.

The huge bathroom was mostly white marble with caramel streaks. Fluffy white towels in varying sizes sat on open shelving that went floor to ceiling. She wasn't really a bathtub person, and the glassed-in shower enticed her.

For a full half hour, Emily indulged herself. Steaming hot water from four different jets sluiced over her body. The sandalwood fragrance of the soap permeated her skin, and she washed her hair with floral-scented shampoo while humming the song about San Francisco and flowers in her hair.

She toweled dry, styled her hair with a blow-dryer and slipped into a sleeveless nightshirt that fell to her knees. Before leaving the bathroom, she turned out the light so she wouldn't disturb Sean.

After she pulled down her covers, she glanced over at his sleeping form. Under the sheets, he stretched out the full length of the bed on his back with his arms folded on his chest. His eyes were closed. He'd stripped off his clothes and appeared to be naked, which had always been his preferred way to sleep.

When they were married, she'd always looked forward to those nights when she was already in bed, not quite asleep and waiting for him. He'd enter the room quietly and slip under the covers, and she'd realize that he was completely naked. She remembered the heat radiating from his big, hard, masculine body, and when he'd pulled her into his arms, she was warmed to the marrow of her bones.

The pattern of hair on his chest reminded her of those days, long ago. Her fingers itched to touch him. She sat on the edge of her bed, silently hoping that he'd open his eyes and ask her to come closer.

Their ground rules started with the obvious: no falling in love, followed by no public display of affection. The complicated part was initiating contact. If he went first, he had to ask. But she was free to pounce on him at any time. *What am I waiting for?*

She shifted position, sitting lightly on his bed and watching him for any sign that he was awake. The steady rise and fall of his chest indicated that he hadn't noticed her nearness. Maybe she'd steal a kiss and return to her own bed.

She leaned down closer. Her heart thumped faster. Her entire body trembled with anticipation. Falling in love with her ex-husband was completely out of the question. If anything happened between them, she couldn't expect it to mean anything. *Really? Am I capable of having sex without love?*

A couple of times in the past, she'd engaged in meaningless sex. The result was never good, hardly worth the effort. Maybe that type of sex would be blah with Sean, but she doubted it. He was too skillful, and he knew exactly which buttons to punch with her. The real question was: Did she dare to open herself up to him, knowing that he'd broken her heart and fearing that he might do it again?

A scary possibility, too scary. She was too much of a coward to take the risk. Exhaling a sigh of sad regret, she pulled away from him, turned her head and stood.

"Emily?"

"Yes."

He was out of the bed, standing beside her. She glided into his embrace, and he positioned her against his naked body. They fit together like yin and yang, like spaghetti and meatballs, like Tarzan and Jane. *Take me, Lord of the Jungle!* She was becoming hysterical. If she was going to avoid sex, she'd better stop him now.

His kiss sent her reeling. With very little effort, he'd caught her.

All logic vanished. The pleasure of his touch erased conscious thought. All she wanted was to savor each sensation. He pressed more firmly against her. She couldn't fight him, didn't want to. *If this is what sex without love feels like, sign me up.*

He gathered the hem of her nightshirt in his hands. Looking down, he read the message on the front. "Promote Literacy. Kiss a Poet."

"I'm just doing my bit to promote education."

"Noble," he said.

In a single gesture, he lifted the nightshirt up and over her head. Underneath, she was as nude as he. By the light of the bedside lamp, her gaze slid appreciatively downward, from his shoulders to the dusting of chest hair to his muscular abs and lower. He was even more flawless than she remembered.

"Hey, lady." He lifted her chin. "My eyes are up here."

"And they're very nice eyes, very dark chocolate and hot. At the moment, however—" she gave him a wicked smile "—I'm more interested in a different part of your body."

He scooped her off her feet and dove with her onto the bed. With great energy, he flung off the covers, plumped pillows and settled her in place before he straddled her hips.

For a moment, she lay motionless below him. She just stared at her magnificent ex-husband. Sex always brought out the poet in her. *He was her knight errant, her Lancelot, a conquering hero who would plunder and ravage her.* Which made her...what? Surely not a helpless maiden; she drove her own destiny. And she most certainly would not lie passively while he had all the fun.

Struggling, she sat up enough to grab his arms and pull him toward her. *A futile effort.* He was in control, and he let her know it by pinning her wrists on either side of her head. He was too strong. She couldn't fight him.

"Relax, Emily." His baritone rumbled through her. "Let me take care of you."

She wriggled. "Maybe you could speed it up."

"I've thought about this for a long time." He dropped a kiss on her forehead. "I want it to last for a very long time."

He hovered over her, balancing on his elbows and his knees. In contrast to his flurry of activity, he slowly lowered himself, seeming to float inches above her. Their lips touched. His chest grazed the tips of her breasts.

She arched her back, desperate to join her flesh with his. He wrestled her down, forcing her to experience each feather touch separately. Shivers of pleasure shot through her, setting off a mad, convulsive reaction that rattled from the ends of her hair to the soles of her feet. She threw her head back against the pillow. Her toes curled.

"Now, Sean. I want you, please."

"Good things are…worth the wait."

His seduction was slow and deliberate, driving her crazy. Her lungs throbbed. She breathed hoarsely, panting and gasping as a wave of pleasure rolled over her. Oh God, she'd missed this! The way he handled her, manipulating her so she felt deeply and passionately. Transformed, she was aware of her own sexuality.

"You're a goddess," he whispered.

And she felt like some kind of superior being who was beautiful, brilliant and powerful. If she could be like this in everyday life, Emily would rule the world.

Somehow, magically, they changed positions and she was on top. She kissed his neck, inhaling his musky scent and tasting the salty flavor of his flesh. She bit down. He was yummy, a full meal.

He nudged her away from his throat. "Did you turn into a vampire or are you just giving me a hickey?"

"I'll be a sultry vampire." She raked her fingers through the hair on his chest. "And you can be a wolf man."

"I like it."

"Me, too."

Sex with Sean was a full-contact sport, engaging mind and body, mostly body, though. He teased and cajoled and fondled and kissed and nibbled.

She'd missed the great sex that only Sean could give her. Not that it was all his doing. She played her part— the role of a goddess—in their crazy, wild affection. And when she reached her earth-shaking climax, she came completely undone, disassembled. It felt like she'd actually left her body and soared to the stratosphere. When she came back to earth, she couldn't wait to do it again.

So they did. Twice more that night.

Chapter 12

The next morning, Sean lifted his eyelids and scanned the open-space suite at the Pendragon Hotel. Yesterday might have been the longest day of his life with more ups and downs than a roller coaster, but he wasn't complaining. The day had turned out great. Sex with Emily was even better than he'd remembered. Their chemistry was incredible. No other woman came close.

He gazed at her, sleeping beside him. She was on her stomach, and the sheet had slipped down, revealing a partial view of her smooth, creamy white bottom. He wanted to see more. Carefully, so he wouldn't wake her, he caught the sheet between two fingers and tugged.

Immediately, she reached back to swat his hand away. She peered through a tangle of hair as she rolled to her side and rearranged the sheet to cover her lovely round breasts. *A bit late for modesty*, he thought, but he said nothing. He wanted another bout of sex, and he was fairly sure she was ready for more of the same.

"Time?" she asked.

He stretched his neck so he could see the decorative clock on the bedside table. The combination of chrome circles and squares showed the time in the upper-left corner.

"Eight forty-six." He looked past the archway into the living room, where faint light appeared around the shades. "The sun's up."

"I thought we were going to run out the door early and have breakfast with Levine."

"It'll have to be brunch. Maybe even lunch." He made a grab for her, but she evaded him. "About last night…"

"Enough said." She climbed out of bed with the sheet wrapped around her. "I'm glad we got that out of the way."

She made wonderful sex sound like a distasteful chore. Surely he'd heard her wrong. "Are you talking about us? You and me? About what happened last night?"

"It was just sex."

"Sure, and Everest is just a mountain. The Lamborghini is just a car."

"The tension was building between us, and we had to relieve it. That's what last night was about." With one hand, she clutched the sheet while the other rubbed the sleep out of her eyes. "I promise you—it's never going to happen again."

She pivoted, squared her shoulders and marched into the bathroom while he sat on the bed, gaping as he watched her hasty retreat. *Never going to happen again?*

He'd be damned if he believed her. She might as well tell the birds not to sing and the fish not to swim. He could not deny his nature, and his inner voice told him to have sex with her as soon and as often as possible.

His number one job, however, was keeping her safe, and meeting with Special Agent Greg Levine was a good place to start. Sean decided not to make the phone call to set the time and the place until he and Emily were near the restaurant; he didn't want Levine to have time to plan ahead.

After they were dressed, he gave her a glance, pretending not to notice how tiny her waist looked in the belted slacks that hugged her bottom. He stared pointedly at her flat ballet shoes. "Do you have sneakers?"

"They don't exactly go with this outfit." She slipped on the matching gray jacket to the pantsuit. "I want to look professional to meet with Levine, and my suitcase is packed with outdoorsy stuff for Colorado."

"You need to wear running shoes. Obvious reasons."

"Okay." She exhaled a little sigh. "Anything else?"

"A hooded sweatshirt?"

"Don't have one with me. I've got several at my apartment. Can we swing past there?"

She wasn't actually disagreeing with him, but her reluctance to follow his instructions was annoying. "Don't you get it? These guys want to kill you. If they recognize you, you're dead."

Her full lips pinched together. "If we can figure out a way to go to my apartment, I have a couple of already-made disguises to go with my pseudonyms. There's a really good one that makes me look like a guy."

Impossible!

He turned away from her and went to the kitchenette to fill his coffee mug again. "Try to find something that makes you look anonymous. Wynter's men might be following Levine."

When she emerged from the bedroom, she threw her arms wide and announced her presence. "Ta-da! Do I look like a punk kid from the city streets?"

Without makeup, her face looked about fourteen. But her jeans were too well fitted. And her Berkeley sweatshirt looked almost new. "Not a street kid," he said. "You look more like a cheerleader."

"Is that anonymous enough?"

"Still too cute. Men will notice you." He motioned for her to come closer. "Give me the sweatshirt."

In one of the kitchen drawers, he found a pair of heavy scissors, which he used to whack off the arms on the sweatshirt and to make a long slit down from the collar. He turned it inside out and tossed it back to her.

"You ruined my sweatshirt," she said as she pulled it over her head. Underneath, she wore a blue blouse with long sleeves. "How's this?"

"Better, but I still can't erase your prettiness." He tilted his head to the side for a different perspective. "Maybe we should cut off the jeans."

"I'd rather not. These cost almost two hundred bucks."

He stalked into the bedroom, dug around in his backpack and took out two baseball caps. The one that was worse for wear, he gave to her. "Whenever you go outside, wear this. It won't change your appearance, but it hides your face."

His clothes were more nondescript than hers; people tended not to notice a guy in jeans, T-shirt and plaid

flannel overshirt. If he stooped his shoulders a bit to disguise his height, he'd fade into almost any background.

They left the hotel shortly after ten o'clock, late
enough that the morning fog had lifted. When he'd been
living in San Francisco, he had a hard time adjusting
to fog. Sunny days in Denver numbered about 245 a
year, and when it was sunny the sky was open and blue.
Sean came to think of the morning fog as the day waking slowly, reticent to leave nighttime dreams behind.

This was the city where he first fell in love with
Emily, and he saw the buildings, neighborhoods and
streets through rose-colored glasses. If last night's sen-
suality had been allowed to grow and flourish, he would
have felt the same today, but she'd squashed his mood.

Behind the wheel of his rental car, he asked, "Is that
North Beach café with the great coffee still there?"

"You mean Henny's," she said. "It's there and the
coffee is still yummy."

The location wasn't particularly convenient to the
FBI offices near Golden Gate Park, but Sean wasn't
planning to go easy on his former coworker. The best
explanation for how Wynter found out about Emily was
that Levine was incompetent enough to get his phone
tapped and not know it. At worst, he was working with
Wynter.

There was street parking outside Henny's Café, a
corner eatery with a fat red hen for a logo. He found a
place halfway down the block and parallel parked. He
ordered her to stay in the car while he did swift reconnaissance inside the café, which was only half-full and
had a good view of the street and an exit into the alley.

Back in the car, he called Levine. The trick to this
phone call would be to keep from mentioning Emily

or Wynter or the possibility that the FBI phones were tapped.

After the initial hello, Sean said, "Long time no see, buddy. Do you remember that case we worked? With the twins who kept spying on each other?"

"Uh-huh, I remember." Levine sounded confused.

"The big thing in that case has been getting more and more common." Sean's reference was to wiretapping, which had been the key to solving the twin case. "Have you ever had a problem like that?"

"What are you getting at?"

"It's probably nothing. I just hope you aren't infected…" *With a bug on your phone.* "Know what I mean?"

"Damn right I do." His confusion was replaced with anger. As a rule, feds don't like having somebody outside the agency tell them that their phones aren't secure. "What about that other matter? The problem with—"

"The Em agenda," Sean said. "Meet me, within the hour, and we'll talk."

After he rattled off the name of the restaurant and the address, he ended the call and turned to Emily, who had been patiently, quietly waiting.

"He'll be here," he said. "We'll wait in the car until he shows up."

"Did you refer to me as the Em agenda?"

"To avoid saying your name."

"Cool, like a code name." She was off and running, chattering on about how she could be a spy. "Just call me Agent Em."

She needed to understand that they weren't playing a fantasy espionage game. The danger was real. But when

Emily followed one of her tangents, she was bright and charming and impossible to resist.

When they were married, it was one of the things he had loved about her. He could sit back and listen to her riff about some oddball topic. She called it free verse; he called it adorable.

"Hold on," he said. "I'm still mad."

"About what?"

"You gave me the brush-off this morning."

"Didn't mean to upset you," she said. "We had an agreement, ground rules. I'm just making sure I don't fall in love with you again."

"There's a difference between sex and love."

"Well, listen to you." Her eyebrows lifted. "Aren't you surprisingly sensitive?"

"I told you I've changed."

"You hardly seem like the same guy who took me to a Forty-Niners game at Levi's Stadium and got in a shouting match that almost came to blows."

"They insulted my Broncos," he said.

"Heaven forbid."

The near fistfight at the football game hadn't been his finest hour, but the undercover work had been eating away at him. He'd needed to let off steam. "I know there were times when I was hard to live with."

"Me, too," she said. "Let's keep it in the past. And never fall in love again."

"As long as we agree that not falling in love doesn't mean we can't have sex."

"That's a deal."

When she held out her hand to shake on the agreement, he yanked her closer and gave her a kiss. He caught her in the middle of a gasp, but her mouth was pliant. Soon she was kissing him back. Emily's recently logical brain might be opposed to sex, but her body hadn't gotten the message. She wanted him as much as he wanted her.

When he turned away and looked out the windshield, he spied Special Agent Greg Levine crossing the street and heading toward Henny's. Walking fast and staring down at the cell phone in his hand, Levine gave off the vibe of a stressed-out businessman and had the wardrobe to match: dark gray suit, blue shirt and necktie tugged loose. His dark blond hair was trimmed in much the same style as Sean's but wasn't as thick. The strands across the front were working hard to cover his forehead.

As Sean escorted Emily up the sidewalk to the café, she asked, "Is there anything I should be careful of saying or not saying? You know, in case Levine isn't on our side."

"Don't mention Hazel. Definitely don't mention that Dylan might hack in to his system." Until they knew otherwise, Sean would treat Levine like an ally instead of an enemy. "First I'm going to pump him to find out how Wynter learned there was a witness. And then how he knew the witness was you."

"I want to ask him what the FBI knows about Patrone's family in Chinatown, the people who took him in when he was a kid."

He nodded. "Anything else?"

"It goes without saying that I want to see if Levine can get me into the hospital to see Strauss."

Inside Henny's, they joined Levine in a cantaloupe-orange leatherette booth at the back. Henny's specialized mostly in breakfast and lunch. The decor was chipper with sunlight filtering through the storefront windows, dozens of cutouts and pictures of chickens and a counter surrounded by swivel stools. A cozy place to wake up, and yet they served alcohol.

Sean did a handshake and half hug with Levine. They'd worked together but never had been close. Since Sean worked undercover, he was seldom in the office; the only agent he cared about was his handler/supervisor, and he knew she'd returned to Quantico. He listened while Levine updated him on other people they knew in common.

The waitress returned to their table with a Bloody Mary for Levine. He must have ordered when he walked in the door. Vodka before noon; not a good sign. Remembering her preference, Sean ordered a cappuccino for Emily. He wanted a double espresso.

"You and Emily," Levine said with a knowing grin. "I always thought you two would get back together."

"We're not together," Emily said. "I hired Sean to act as my bodyguard."

"You're his boss? The one who cracks the whip?" His grin turned into a full-on smirk. "I underestimated you, girl."

"Don't call her girl," Sean said coldly. "And yeah, you didn't give her enough credit. I haven't seen your files, but she's got enough on Wynter for an arrest."

"I'm working on it." Levine swizzled the celery in his glass before he raised it to his lips. "I've got a snitch on the inside."

Sean hadn't expected him to be so forthcoming. As long as Levine was being talkative, he asked, "How did Wynter find out there was a witness to Patrone's murder?"

"The murder was investigated by the SFPD. Patrone was a known associate of Wynter, which put suspicion off Wynter. At first, they investigated Wynter's rivals."

Sean didn't need a history of the crime. "But they came around to the real story. How did that happen?"

Levine couldn't meet his gaze. Dark smudges under his eyes made Sean think he wasn't sleeping well. His chin quivered as he attempted to change the direction of their conversation. "Why do you think my phone is bugged?"

"Simple logic. There's no reason for anybody to connect Emily to me. We haven't seen or talked to each other since the divorce. But you called my office in Denver—"

"I told you," Levine said. "I always thought the two of you would get back together. Hell, you're the reason Emily showed up on our doorstep instead of going to the police. She knew us because of you."

He looked to Emily for confirmation. "Is that true?"

"I thought the FBI would be more careful about keeping my identity secret."

Anger heated Sean's blood. She should have been able to trust the feds, but they'd been sloppy. He glared at Levine. "Did you tell them about Emily?"

"I had to give them something. The cops were off base, asking questions that riled other gangs." His voice held a note of believable desperation. "I said there was a witness and leaked her account of the murder. But I didn't give her name."

Assessing his behavioral cues, Sean deduced that Levine was honestly sorry about the way things had turned out. He'd never meant to put Emily in danger. "I believe you."

"Damn right you do." Levine nodded vigorously. His relief was palpable. "You would have done the same thing."

"I don't think so." Sean didn't allow him to get comfortable. "There are other ways to play a witness, but I'm not here to give you a lesson. You asked why I suspected a wiretap on your phone."

"Right."

"After you called my office, one of Wynter's men made the same contact. How would they know about me if they weren't monitoring your phone?"

Levine took another drink. His Bloody Mary was almost gone, and he ordered another when the waitress brought their coffee drinks. Sean and Emily also ordered breakfast. Levine didn't want food.

While the waitress bustled back to the kitchen, Levine leaned across the table on his elbows and asked, "Did you talk to the guy Wynter sent?"

Sean nodded. "John Morelli."

Levine bolted upright in the booth. It looked like he'd been poked by a cattle prod. "Morelli is my snitch."

Chapter 13

Emily twisted her hands together in her lap as though she could somehow physically hold things together. Nothing made sense anymore. Morelli was her contact but also a snitch, and then he'd pulled a gun on Sean, which made him an enemy. The more Levine talked, the more confounded she felt. Had Morelli been lying to Sean when he said he only wanted to talk to her? He'd said she had information about who was stealing from Wynter. It might be important to go through her notes and figure out what he meant.

While Sean and Levine talked about Morelli, trying to figure out if he could be trusted, she pulled her cap lower on her forehead and slouched down in the booth. How was she ever going to make sense of this tangled mess? Maybe Sean had been right when he suggested leaving town and forgetting all about Wynter and human trafficking. She could retract her witness statement and start her life over.

But she couldn't ignore her conscience, and, somewhere in the back of her mind, she imagined the ghost of the murdered man haunting her. She owed it to him to bring his killer to justice.

She spoke up, "It seems like everybody knows I'm the witness. I should just go to the SFPD."

"Makes sense," Sean said. "And that's ultimately what you'll have to do. But right now we're flying under the radar. Let's take advantage of the moment."

"Where do we start?"

"If we figure out why Patrone was murdered, it takes the focus off you."

Similar ideas had been spinning through her mind, but he pulled it together and made perfect sense. Why was Patrone killed? What was the motive?

After the waitress delivered their breakfast, Emily took a bite of her omelet and looked over at Levine. "You might be able to help us."

"What do you need?"

"More background data on Roger Patrone. I know about the gambling operation in the strip club. And I know the woman who took him into her home is Doris Liu." Emily had visited her once and gotten a big, fat, "No comment" in hostile Cantonese. "Patrone must have had other friends and associates outside Wynter's operation."

"He almost married a woman who owns a tourist shop in Chinatown on Grant. Her name is Liane Zhou. Nobody bothers her because her brother, Mikey Zhou, is said to be a snakehead."

Emily shuddered. The snakeheads were notorious

gangsters who smuggled people into the country. "Does Mikey Zhou work with Wynter's people?"

"Their businesses overlap."

"If you can call crime a business," she said.

"Hell, yes, it's a business."

"A filthy business."

Her own fears and doubts seemed minor in comparison to these larger crimes. Tearing people away from their homes and forcing them into a life of prostitution or slave labor horrified her. According to her research, parents in poverty-stricken villages sometimes sold their children to the snakeheads, thinking their kids might achieve a better life in a different country. Others signed up with the snakeheads to escape persecution at home.

"Human smuggling is a complex job," Levine said as he carefully smoothed the thinning hair across his forehead. "They need ledgers and accounting methods to track how many have been taken and how they're transported. Most often, it's in shipping containers. Then they have to determine how many arrived, how they'll be dispersed and the final payout for delivery. But you know that—don't you, Emily? Isn't that why you were on Wynter's yacht in the first place? You intended to steal his computer records and ledgers."

"So what?" She hadn't actually told him about her plan to download Wynter's personal computer, but it wasn't a stretch for him to figure it out.

"Did you get the download you were looking for?"

She'd failed. After Frankie and the boys had cleared out of the office, she had spent the rest of the night running and hiding. But she didn't want to share that information with Levine. There was something about him that she didn't trust. "The only thing that matters is stopping Wynter. How can we disrupt his business?"

"Cut into his profit," Sean said. "But that won't work as long as there's a market for what he's selling."

"It's slavery," she said. "Twenty-first-century slavery. And it's wrong. How can people justify the buying and selling of human beings?"

"Don't be naive," Levine said. "People argue that prostitutes are a necessary vice. And slave labor keeps production costs down. The freaking founding fathers owned slaves. It took a civil war to change our ideas."

She glanced between Levine and Sean. The FBI agent thought she was a wide-eyed innocent who had no clue about the real world. Her ex-husband had told her dozens of times that she was unrealistic and immature. But those complaints were years ago. Sean was different now.

Looking him straight in the eye, she said, "It's our responsibility as decent human beings to expose these crimes and disrupt this network of evil and depravity."

Levine chuckled. "That sounds like a good lead for one of your articles."

"Sounds like the truth," Sean said.

"Do you really think so?" she asked.

"I've always tried to be a responsible man."

A man she could love. She bit her lower lip. *Don't say it, don't.* After the divorce, she'd wondered how two people who were so unlike each other could be attracted. What had she ever seen in him?

This was her answer. At his core, Sean was decent, trustworthy and, yes, responsible. He was a good man.

She straightened her posture and dug into her breakfast. If she was going to save the world, she needed fuel in her system. Listening with half an ear, she heard Sean and Levine discussing lines of communication that wouldn't compromise Sean's location and would make Wynter think his wiretap at the FBI was still operational.

"Then there's Morelli," Sean said. "Can you use your snitch to feed bad information to Wynter?"

"He wasn't always lying to me," Levine said. He fussed with his hair and finished his second Bloody Mary. "I made a couple of arrests based on intel he gave me."

"You can't trust him," Sean said firmly. "Get that through your head. Morelli isn't your pal."

Emily felt Sean's temperature rising. He was getting angry, and she didn't blame him. Levine was beginning to slur, and his eyelids drooped to half-mast.

Before Sean blew his top, she needed information from Levine. "What can you tell me about Jerome Strauss?"

"The editor of *BP*? He's fine, already out of the hospital."

Good news, finally! She waved her hands. "Yay."

"Strauss is one lucky bastard. He'd fallen asleep at the office and just happened to wake up a few minutes before the bomb—which was on a timer—went off. Strauss was in the bathroom when it exploded. The EMTs found him wandering around with no pants."

"So he wasn't badly hurt?"

"If he'd been in the office near the window, he'd be dead. All he had were some bruises and a minor concussion. Lucky, lucky, lucky."

Or not. Emily enjoyed fairy tales about pots of gold at the end of the rainbow and genies in lamps who granted three wishes, but life wasn't like that. There were few real coincidences. Strauss had escaped, and she was glad but…but also suspicious. He might have been complicit in blowing up his own office.

While she and Sean dug into their food, Levine scooted to the edge of the booth. "I should get back to work," he said. "I can't say it's been great to see you."

"Same here," Sean said.

"If I can be of help, let me know." He gave a wave and whipped out the door, obviously glad to be leaving them behind.

She watched him lurch down the street. He stumbled at the curb. "He's about three months away from getting a toupee."

"I didn't remember him as being so nervous." Sean sopped up the last bit of syrup with his pancake. "The FBI in SF has gone downhill since I left."

She nudged his shoulder. "I'll bet you were the best fed since...who's a famous FBI agent?"

"Eliot Ness."

"The best since him," she said. "Tell me, Nessie, what do we do next?"

"I already talked to Dylan this morning," he said, "but I need to call him again and make sure he's hacking in to Wynter's personal computer, the one he had on the yacht. Levine seemed way too interested in whether you'd managed a download."

She was pleased that she'd picked up the same nosy, untrustworthy attitude. "Something told me I shouldn't share information with him."

"Good instinct, Emily."

"Thanks."

He didn't allow her time to revel in his compliment. "We also need to talk to your friend Jerome Strauss. I'm not buying that coincidental escape from the bomb."

"Me, neither," she said. "But if he knew about the bomb, why would he stay close enough to be injured?"

"His injury makes a good alibi."

So true. The bomb almost killed him; therefore, he didn't set the bomb. She wanted to ask him why. What was his motivation for risking his life? "First we need disguises. Can we please go by my apartment? I'll only take a minute."

"We had this conversation last night."

"And I agreed that we shouldn't stay there. But a quick visit won't be a problem."

"Unless Wynter has men stationed on the street outside, watching to see if you return to your nest."

"They'd never notice me. I have a secret entrance."

Her apartment was on the second floor of a three-story building that mimicked the style of the Victorian "painted ladies" with gingerbread trim in bright blue and dark purple and salmon pink. Following her directions, Sean drove the rental car up the street outside her home.

"Nice," he said. "You've got to be paying a fortune for this place."

"Not as much as you'd think," she said. "One of my former professors at Berkeley owns the property and makes special deals for people she wants to encourage, artists and writers."

"Wouldn't she rather have you writing poetry?"

"She likes that I do investigative journalism. It's her opinion that more women should be involved in hard-boiled reportage." She shrugged. "Otherwise, how will idealism survive?"

"Hard-boiled and idealistic? Those two things seem to contradict, but you make them fit together." He glanced over at her. "You're a dewy-eyed innocent… but edgy. That's what makes you so amazing."

Another compliment? He'd already noticed the cleverness of her gut instincts, and now he liked her attitude. He'd called her amazing. "Turn at the corner and circle around the block so we'll be behind my building."

"Your secret entrance isn't something as simple as a back door, is it?"

"Wait and see."

The secret wasn't all that spectacular. It had been discovered by one of the other women who lived in the building, an artist. She'd been trying to evade a guy who'd given her a ride home. He wanted to come up to her place and wouldn't take no for an answer. She said goodbye and disappeared through the secret entrance.

On the block behind Emily's apartment, she told him to park anywhere on the street. She hadn't noticed anybody hanging around, watching her building. But it was better to be cautious.

As soon as she got inside, she intended to grab as many clothes and shoes as she could. Living out of one suitcase that had been packed for snow country didn't work for her.

She led him along a narrow path between a house and another apartment building. The backyards were strips of green dotted with rock gardens, gazebos and pergolas. People who lived here landscaped like crazy, needing to bring nature into their environment.

Her building had three floors going up and a garden level below. A wide center staircase opened onto the first floor. Underneath, behind a decorative iron fence, was a sidewalk that stretched the length of the building. She hopped over the fence, lowered herself to the sidewalk and ducked so she couldn't be seen from the street. There were three doors on each side for the garden-level apartments. She opened an unmarked seventh door in the middle, directly below and hidden by the staircase leading upward.

She and Sean entered a dark room where rakes and paint cans and outdoor supplies were stored. She turned on the bare lightbulb dangling from the ceiling. "In case somebody saw us, you might want to drag something over to block the door."

He did as she said. "And how do we get out?"

"Over here." She'd found a flashlight, which she turned on when she clicked off the bulb. They went from the outdoor storage room to an indoor janitor's closet with a door that opened onto a hallway in the garden level. She turned off the flashlight and put it back.

The sneaking around had pumped up her excitement. She ran lightly down the hall and up two staircases to her floor. Her apartment was on the northeastern end of the building. She wasn't an artist and therefore didn't care if she had the southern or western light.

As she fitted her key in the lock, she realized that she was excited for Sean to see her place. When they were married, they had enjoyed furnishing their home, choosing colors and styles. For her place, she'd chosen an eclectic style with Scandinavian furniture and an antique lamp and a chandelier. Her office was perfectly, almost obsessively, organized.

The moment she opened the door, she knew something was wrong. Her apartment had been tidy before she left for Colorado. Now it was a total disaster.

Ransacked!

The sofa and coffee table were overturned. Pillows were slashed open and the stuffing pulled out. The television screen was cracked. All the shelves had been emptied.

"No," she whispered.

In her office, the chaos was worse. Papers were wadded up and strewn all across the floor and desktop. Every drawer hung open. All her articles were reduced to rubble. *Why?* What were they doing in here? Were they searching?

Barely conscious of where she was going, she stumbled into the bedroom. If they were searching, there was no need for them to go through her clothing. But her closet had been emptied and the contents of her drawers dumped onto the carpet.

Numbly, she stumbled back to the living room. On the floor at her feet was a framed photo that had hung on the wall, a wedding picture of her and Sean. She was so pretty in her long white gown with her hair spilling down her back all the way to her waist. And he was so handsome and strong. She had always thought the photo captured the true sense of romance. Their marriage didn't work, but they had experienced a great love.

The glass on the front of the photo was shattered.

Sean waved to her, signaled her. "Emily, hurry—we need to get out of here."

She heard heavy footsteps climbing the staircase outside her apartment. Her door crashed open, and she gave a yelp.

It was one of the men she'd seen with Frankie on the yacht when the murder was committed. She knew him from mug shots she'd studied when trying to identify Patrone.

"Barclay."

She knew he was a thug, convicted of assault and acquitted of murder. Not a person she'd want to meet in a dark alley.

Chapter 14

The man who stormed into her apartment didn't turn around. He had his back to Sean, and he paused, staring at Emily.

This would have been an excellent occasion to use a stun gun. Sean didn't want to kill the guy, but Barclay—Emily had called him Barclay—had to be stopped.

"How do you know me?" Barclay demanded.

"I'm a reporter. I know lots of stuff." Emily hurled the framed photo at him. "Get away from me."

When Barclay put up an arm to block the frame, Sean saw the gun in his right hand. In a skilled move, he grasped Barclay's gun hand and applied pressure to the wrist, causing him to drop his weapon.

Barclay, who was quite a bit heavier and at least eight inches shorter than Sean, swung wildly with his left hand. Sean ducked the blow but caught Barclay's left arm, spun him around and tossed him onto the floor on his back. He flipped Barclay to his belly and squatted on the man's back.

Sean glanced up at Emily. "I really need to start carrying handcuffs. This is the second time in as many days that a pair of cuffs would have been useful."

Barclay squirmed below him. "Let me up, damn it. You don't know who you're dealing with."

"I know exactly who you are," Emily said. Her face was red with anger. "You were with Frankie when he shot Patrone."

"How the hell would you know about that?"

"I was there."

"No way." Though Sean had immobilized him, Barclay twisted around, struggling to get free. "Nobody was anywhere near. Nobody saw what happened."

She kept her distance but went down on her knees so she could stare into his eyes. "Three of you dragged Patrone into the office. You took turns slapping him around and calling him a coward, a term that more accurately should have been applied to you three bullies. You threw him in the chair behind the desk. Frankie screwed a silencer onto his gun and shot Patrone in the chest, twice."

Barclay mumbled a string of curses. "This is impossible. We were alone. I swore there was no witness."

"You misspoke," she said.

"Don't matter," he growled. "It's your word against ours."

From his years in the FBI, Sean knew Barclay's assessment was true. A hotshot lawyer could turn everything around and make Emily look like a crackpot. Still, he wished she hadn't blurted out the whole story and confirmed that she was a witness. She would have been safer if there had been doubt. "Emily, pick up his gun please."

Barclay twisted his head to look up at her. "You cut your hair. I wouldn't have recognized you."

But now he would. Now he'd tell the others and they'd know exactly what to look for. Sean bent Barclay's right arm at an unnatural angle. "Why are you coming after her? What do you want from her?"

"You're hurting me."

"That's the idea." But he loosened his hold. If he hoped to get any useful information from this moron, he needed to get him talking, answering simple questions. "Have you got a first name?"

"I don't have to tell you."

Sean cranked up the pressure on his arm. "I like to know who I'm talking to."

"They call me Bulldog."

Sean could see the resemblance in the droopy eyes and jowls. "Do you know Morelli?"

"Yeah, I know him."

"Do you have a partner?"

"I work alone."

Bulldog hesitated just long enough for Sean to doubt him. He twisted the arm. "Your partner, is he waiting in the car?"

"I'm alone, damn you."

Sean decided to take advantage of this moment of cooperation. "You were told to be on the lookout for Ms. Peterson, is that right?"

"Yeah, yeah. Let go of my arm."

Sean wanted to know if Bulldog was responding to an alert that might have come from Levine or if he'd seen them sneak through her secret entrance. "Why did you come into the apartment?"

"I saw you."

"Outside?"

"No," Bulldog said. "There are two cameras in here."

Surely someone else was watching, and Bulldog would have reinforcements in a matter of minutes. They needed to get the hell out of there.

Sean should have guessed. Dylan would have figured out the camera surveillance and also would have known how to disarm the electronics. But Dylan wasn't here. Sean needed to step up his game.

"They told you to look for her," Sean said. "When you found her, what were you supposed to do?"

"Not supposed to kill her. Just to grab her, bring her to Morelli or to Wynter."

"What do they want from her?"

"How the hell would I know?"

Sean thought back to his conversation with Morelli, who had also denied that he meant to hurt Emily. Morelli wanted information about a theft. Why did these guys think she knew something about treachery among smugglers?

Using cord from the blinds, he tied Bulldog's wrists and ankles. He could have called the FBI, but he didn't trust Levine. And they couldn't wait around for the cops; Bulldog's backup would get here first. When he pulled Emily out the door, he was surprised to see that she was dragging an extra-large suitcase.

"What's in there?" he asked.

"I'm not sure. I just grabbed clothes and shoes."

Behind the building, she struggled to push the suitcase through the grass. He took it from her and zipped across the backyards to the sidewalk to their rental car.

Using every evasive driving technique he'd been taught and some he'd invented himself, he maneuvered the rental car through the neighborhoods, up and down the hills of San Francisco on their way back to the Pendragon. Sean was good at getting rid of anyone who might be following. Sometimes he pretended he was being tailed just for the practice.

He seemed to be dusting off many of the skills he'd learned at Quantico and in the field. The martial arts techniques he'd used to take down Bulldog came naturally. And he had a natural talent for interrogation.

Still, he didn't have the answer to several questions: Why did Wynter's men think Emily knew who was stealing from them? Were they being robbed? Was it a rival gang?

It was clear to him that he and Emily needed a different approach to their situation. A strong defense was the first priority, protecting her from thugs like Bulldog who wanted to hurt her. But they also ought to develop an offensive effort, tracking down the details of the crime. He couldn't help thinking that Patrone's murder was somehow connected to the smuggling.

"I don't get it," she said. Her rage had begun to abate, but her color was still high and her eyes flashed like angry beacons. "Why did they tear my home apart? What were they looking for?"

"Evidence," he said. "The research and interviews that went into your articles about Wynter must have hit too close to home. Morelli said he wanted information from you."

"What does that have to do with my personal belongings?"

"Flash drives," he said.

"What about them?"

Her outrage about having her apartment wrecked and her things violated seemed to be clouding her brain function. "Think about it," he said. "You'd store evidence on a flash drive, right?"

"And they were searching for those." She did an eye roll that made her look like a teenager. "As if I'm that stupid? I'd never leave valuable info lying around."

She leaned back against the passenger seat and cast a dark, moody gaze through the windshield. He doubted that she even noticed that they were driving along the Embarcadero where they used to go jogging past the Ferry Building clock tower. They'd stop by the fat palm trees out in front and kiss. She'd have her long hair tamed in braids and would be dressed in layers of many colors with tights and socks and shorts and sweats. He'd called her Raggedy Ann.

Long ago, when they'd been falling in love, the scenery had felt more beautiful. The Bay Bridge spanning to Yerba Buena Island seemed majestic. He came to think of that bridge as the gateway separating him from her apartment in Oakland. When he drove across, he'd tried to leave his FBI undercover identity behind.

After swinging through a few more illogical turns, he doubled back toward Ghirardelli Square. "Do you want to stop for chocolate?"

"No," she said glumly. "Wait a minute. Yes, I want to stop." She threw her hands up. "I don't know."

"Still upset," he said. "You were pretty mad back at your apartment."

"I was."

"It showed in the way you threw that picture at Bulldog. For a minute, I thought I'd need to protect him from you."

She chuckled, but her amusement faded fast. Her tone was completely serious as she said, "I need to be able to protect myself."

"I've been thinking the same thing, but I'd rather not give you a firearm."

"Why not?" She immediately took offense. "I know how to handle a gun."

"Too well," he said. "I'd rather not leave a trail of dead bodies in our wake like a Quentin Tarantino film. I think you should have a stun gun."

"Yes, please."

At the hotel, he used the parking structure to hide their vehicle. In their suite, he ran another sweep for bugs and found nothing alarming. He might be overcautious, but it was better to be too safe than to be too sorry.

He sank down on the sofa. "I wish I'd caught the mini-cameras at your apartment. As soon as we walked in the door and saw the place ransacked, I should have known. Electronics are an easier way to do surveillance than a stakeout."

"No harm done." She flopped down beside him, stretched out her legs and propped her heels against the coffee table.

"Now they know what we look like. You heard what Bulldog said. He must have been working off an old photo of you, didn't even know you'd cut your hair."

"And they have a video of you." She smiled up at him. "Not that it matters. They already had photos of you from our wedding pictures."

"You don't keep those lying around, do you?"

"The picture I threw was from our wedding. We were outside my parents' house by the Russian olive tree."

He was surprised that she'd had their photo matted and framed and hanging on the wall. He'd stuffed his copies of their wedding photos into the bottom of a drawer. He didn't want to be reminded of how happy they'd been. "Why did you keep it?"

"Sentimental reasons," she said. "I like to remember the good stuff, like when you kissed me in the middle of the ceremony, even though you weren't supposed to."

"Couldn't help it," he mumbled. "You were too beautiful."

"What woman doesn't want a memento of the sweetest, loveliest day of her life?"

"I guess men see things differently." He slipped his arm around her shoulders and pulled her closer until she was leaning against him.

"How different?"

"If it's over, move on," he said. "Better to forget when you've lost that loving feeling and it's gone, gone, gone. Whoa, whoa, whoa."

Her chin tilted upward. The shimmer in her lovely eyes was just like their wedding when he couldn't hold back. Sean had to kiss her. He had to taste those warm pink lips and feel the silky softness of her hair as the strands sifted through his fingers.

When he brought her back to the Pendragon, he hadn't planned to sweep her off her feet and into the bedroom, but he couldn't help himself. And she didn't appear to be objecting.

After the kiss subsided, her arms twined around his neck. She burrowed against his chest, and she purred like a feminine, feline motorboat. He rose from the sofa, lifting her, and carried her toward the bed with covers still askew after last night's tryst.

The other bed had barely been touched. The geometrically patterned spread in shades of black, white and gray was tucked under the pillows. He placed her on that bed. Her curvy body made an interesting artistic contrast with the sleek design. He could have studied her for hours in many different poses.

But she wouldn't hold still for that. "Don't we have a lot of other things to do?"

He stretched out beside her. "Nothing that can't wait."

"You haven't forgotten the murder, have you? And our investigation?"

The only detective work he wanted to do was finding out whether she preferred kisses on her neck or love bites on her earlobe. He pinned her on the bed with his leg straddling her lower body and his arm reaching across to hold her wrist. Taking his time, he kissed her thoroughly and deeply.

When he gazed once again into her eyes, her pupils were unfocused. The corners of her mouth lifted in a contented smile. But she didn't offer words of encouragement.

"This is not surrender," she said.

"We're not at war. We both want the same thing."

"Later," she whispered. "I promise."

"Don't say ground rules."

He stole a quick kiss and sprang off the bed. It took a ton of willpower to walk away from her when he so desperately wanted to fall at her knees and beg for her attention. But he managed to reach the kitchenette, where he filled a glass with water and helped himself to an apple from the complimentary fruit basket on the counter.

He was ready to get this crime solved. As soon as he did, she'd promised to give him what he wanted. That was an effective motivation.

She appeared in the archway between the living room and bedroom. "We should start in Chinatown. And don't forget that I want to talk to Jerome Strauss."

They could launch themselves onto the city streets, trying not to be spotted by Wynter's men and hoping they'd stumble over the truth. Or they could take a few minutes to reflect and create a plan. He could use the skills he'd learned at Quantico.

"It'll save time," he said, "if we build profiles. That way, we'll know what we're looking for."

"Profiles? Like you used to do in the FBI?"

"That's right."

She'd always hated his work, and he braced for a storm of hostility. Instead of sneering, she beamed. "Let me get my computer. I want to take notes."

Her reaction was uncharacteristic. He'd expected her to object, to tell him that the feds didn't know how to do anything but lie convincingly. Instead, she hopped onto a stool and set up her laptop on the counter separating the kitchenette from the living room.

When she was plugged in and turned on, she looked up at him. "Go ahead," she said brightly. "I'm ready."

Who are you, and what have you done with my cranky, know-it-all ex-wife? The words were on the tip of his tongue, but he knew better than to blurt them out.

She hated the FBI. While they were married, she'd told him dozens of times that he shouldn't be putting himself in danger, shouldn't be assuming undercover identities and lying to people, shouldn't be taking orders from the heartless feds. On one particularly dismal occasion, she'd told him to choose between her and his work. She would have easily won that contest, but he didn't want her to think she could make demands like that.

Her opinion had changed. And he was glad. "We need two profiles," he said, "one for the victim, Roger Patrone, and another for the person or persons who are stealing from Wynter."

"Frankie Wynter killed Patrone," she said. "What will we learn from the victim's profile?"

"We know *who* killed Patrone, but we don't know *why*. Was Frankie acting alone? Following orders from his father? It could be useful to have the victimology."

"One of the last things Patrone said before he was shot was 'I want to see the kids.' Is that important?"

He nodded. "Who are the kids, and why is he looking for them? It's all important."

While she talked, her fingers danced across the keyboard. "You mentioned profiling the person or persons who might be stealing from Wynter. Why?"

"Once we've identified them, we can use that information as leverage with Morelli and Wynter."

"Got it," she said. "Leverage."

He enjoyed the give-and-take between them. "Solving the crime against the criminals gives us something else to pass on to the FBI."

"If this all works out, we could put Wynter out of business and the person or persons who are stealing from him. We could take down two big, bad birds with one investigation." She hesitated. "It's funny, isn't it? When I look at it this way, I'm not really in danger."

"How do you figure?"

"If I tell Wynter's men what they want to know, they'll owe me a favor. At the very least, they'll call off the chase."

Her starry-eyed, poetic attitude had returned full force. Sean knew this version of Emily; he'd married her. He remembered how she'd tell him—with a completely straight face—that all people were essentially good. She was sweet, innocent and completely misguided.

He gently stroked her cheek. "I guess it's safe to say that investigative reporting hasn't tarnished your sunny outlook."

"But it has," she said. "I'm aware of a dark side. Wynter and his crew have committed heinous crimes. They're terrible people."

"Not people you can trust," he pointed out.

"Oh."

"And what do you think these heinous people will do when they find out what you know? They'll have no further use for Emily Peterson."

"And they'll let me go," she said hopefully.

"They'll kill you."

Chapter 15

Perched on a high stool, Emily folded her arms on the countertop that separated the kitchenette from the living room. She rested her forehead on her arms and stared down her nose at the flecks of silver in the polished black marble surface. She tried to sort through the options. Every logical path led to the same place: her death. There had to be another way. But what? According to Sean, Wynter's men would consider her expendable after she named the person who was stealing from them, which was information she didn't have.

"If I ever figure out who's messing with Wynter," she said, "I can't tell."

"True," Sean said. "But we've got to pretend that you know, starting now."

Crazy complicated! "Why?"

"Information is power. Wynter won't hurt us as long

as we have something he wants, either intelligence or, better yet, evidence."

"But I don't," she said.

"It's okay, as long as he doesn't know that you don't know what he wants to know."

Groaning, she lifted her head and rubbed her forehead as though she could erase the confusion. "I don't get it."

"Think of a poker game," he said. "I know you're familiar with five-card stud because I vividly remember the night you hustled me and three other FBI agents."

She remembered, too. "I won fifty-two dollars and forty-five cents."

"Cute," he said.

"I know."

"Anyway, when it comes to Wynter and the info he wants, we're playing a bluff…until we have the whole thing figured out."

"And then what happens?"

"We pull in the feds, and you go into protective custody."

"Or to Paris," she said. That was another solution. *Why not?* They could forget the whole damn thing and soar off into the sunset. "We could have a nice, long trip. Just you and me."

He still hadn't shaved off his stubble, and his black hair was tousled. He looked rather rakish, like a pirate. She wouldn't mind being looted and plundered by Sean. It wouldn't be like they were married or anything…just a fling.

"Havana," he said, "the trade winds, the tropical heat, the waves lapping against the seawall."

"Let's go right now. I could do articles about Cuba

and see Hemingway's house. We'd lie in the sun and sip mojitos."

But she knew it wasn't possible to toss aside her responsibilities. She needed to take care of the threat from Wynter before he went after her family. Or her friends, she thought of the explosion at *BP Reporter.* She'd tried to call Jerome Strauss, but he didn't answer and she really couldn't leave a text or a number that could be backtracked to her.

"It might take a long time to neutralize the threat," he said. "What if it's never safe for you in San Francisco?"

"I wouldn't mind traveling the world." Living the life of a Gypsy held a certain romantic appeal. "Or I could settle down and live in the mountains with Aunt Hazel. The great thing about freelance writing is that I can do it anywhere. I might even move back to Denver."

"The city's booming," he said.

"I know. You showed me."

Looking up at him, she saw the invitation in his eyes. If she came to Denver, that would be all right with him. And she wouldn't mind, not a bit. She wanted to spend more time with him. Nothing serious, of course.

"Before I forget…" Sean went to his bag. He tucked away the device he'd used to sweep the room and took out a small, metallic flashlight. "This is for you."

"Not sure why I need a flashlight."

"This baby puts out forty-five million volts."

He held it up to illustrate. With the flashlight beam directed at the ceiling, he hit the button. There was a loud crack and a ferocious buzz. Jagged blue electricity arced between two poles at the end. A stun gun!

Eagerly, she reached for it. "I can't imagine why I haven't gotten one of these before."

"When you're testing, only zap for one second or it'll wear itself out. When you're using it for protection, hold the electric end against the subject for four or five seconds while pushing down on the button. That ought to be enough to slow them down."

"What if I wanted to disable an attacker?" Hopping down from the stool, she held the flashlight like a fencing sword and lunged forward. "How long do I press down to do serious damage?"

"Kind of missing the point," he said. "A stun gun or, in this case, a stun flashlight is supposed to momentarily incapacitate an attacker. Much like pepper spray or Mace."

"Does it hurt the attacker more if I press longer?"

"That's right," he said. "And the place on the body where you hit him makes a difference. The chin or the cheek has more impact."

"Or the groin." That was her target. A five-second zap in the groin might be worse than a bullet.

She released the safety, aimed the flashlight beam at the coffeemaker and hit the button for one second. The loud zap and sizzle were extremely satisfying. She glanced at him over her shoulder. "I'd love to try it out on a real live subject."

"Forget it."

She hadn't really thought he'd let her zap him, and she didn't want to hurt him. She hooked the flashlight onto her belt where she could easily detach it if necessary. "Have you got other weapons for me?"

"A canister of pepper spray."

"I'll take it. Then I can attack two-handed. Zap with the flashlight and spritz with the pepper spray."

"A spritz?" He placed a small container on the counter beside her computer. "Enough with the equipment. We can get started by profiling Patrone."

She climbed back up on the stool. "I've already done research on him."

"You told me," he said. "He was thirty-five, never married, lost both parents when he was nine and was raised by a family in Chinatown. Convicted of fraud, he spent three years in jail, which wasn't enough to make him go straight. He runs a small, illegal gambling operation at a strip club near Chinatown. Do you have a picture of him?"

She plugged a flash drive into her laptop and scanned the files until she located Roger Patrone. The photo she had was his booking picture from when he was recently arrested. A pleasant-looking man with wide-set eyes and a flat nose, he had on a suit with the tie neatly in place. His brown hair was combed. Smiling, he looked like he was posing for a corporate ID photo.

"For a guy who's going to spend the night in the slammer, he doesn't seem too upset," she said. "Does that attitude come from cockiness? Thinking he's smarter than the cops?"

"Maybe," Sean said as he squinted at the picture. "Does he strike you as being narcissistic?"

"Not really. To tell the truth, I feel sorry for him. He's kind of a lonely guy. Doesn't have much social life and never married. Apart from Liane Zhou, I couldn't find a girlfriend. I only talked to one woman at the strip club, and she said he was a nice guy, always willing to help her out. In other words, Patrone was a pushover."

"Characteristic of low self-esteem, he's easily manipulated," Sean said. "But why is he smiling in his booking photo?"

"It's a mask," she said. "When life is too awful to

bear, Patrone puts on a mask and pretends that everything is fine."

When she looked over at Sean, he nodded. "Keep going."

"He ignored trouble while it got closer and closer. When he finally took a stand, it got him killed."

"That's a possible scenario," he said. "You're good at reading below the surface."

A thrill went through her. It was comparable to the excitement she experienced when she'd written a fierce and beautiful line of poetry. "Is this profiling?"

"Basically."

"I like it."

"We're using broad strokes," he said. "Our purpose is to create a sketch. Then we'll have an idea of what we should be looking for to fill in the picture."

"Can I try another direction?" she asked.

"Go for it."

"Abandonment issues." She pounced on the words. "His parents left him when he was only nine. And he probably didn't fit in very well with the kids in Chinatown. He didn't know the customs, didn't even speak the language."

"Feelings of abandonment might explain why he joined Wynter. Patrone needed a place to belong, a surrogate family."

"Frankie was like a brother. Patrone trusted him, believed in him," she said. "And Frankie shot him dead."

What had Patrone done to deserve that cruel fate? The Wynter organization was his family, and yet there was something so important that he betrayed them.

Sean echoed her thought. "What motivated Patrone to go against people he considered family?"

"He mentioned seeing the children, which makes me think of human trafficking."

"No doubt," he said. "The theft Morelli mentioned might be about smuggling. Wynter's best profits come from shipping people, mostly women and children, in containers from Asia."

"Someone is stealing these poor souls who have already been stolen." Disgust left a rotten taste in the back of her mouth. "There's got to be a special place in hell for those who traffic in slavery."

"You're passionate about this. I could feel it when I read the series of articles you wrote on the topic."

She was pleased that he'd read the articles, but she wished he hadn't noticed her opinion. "Those were supposed to be straightforward journalism, not opinion pieces."

"You successfully walked that line," he said. "Because I know you, I could hear the rage in your voice that you were trying so hard to suppress. Most people feel the way you do."

"Which is still not an excuse to rant or editorialize," she said. "Anyway, I think we know what was stolen...people."

"Bringing us to our second profile, namely, figuring out who's stealing from Wynter. What are the important points from your research?"

She didn't need to refer to a computer file to remember. "Trafficking is a thirty-two-billion—that's billion with a *b*—dollar business. It's global. Over twelve million people are used in forced labor. Prostitution is over eight times that many. Those are big numbers, right?"

He nodded.

"Less than two thousand cases of human trafficking ended in convictions last year."

She could go on and on, quoting statistics and repeating stories of sorrow and tragedy about twelve-year-old girls turned out on the street to solicit and seven-year-old children working sixteen-hour days in factories.

After a resigned shake of her head, she continued. "Here's the bottom line. Wynter probably imports around a thousand people a year and scoops up three times that many off the streets. His organization has never once been successfully prosecuted for human trafficking. Mostly, this is because the victims are afraid to accuse or testify."

He sat on a stool beside her at the counter. "Much as I hate to be the optimistic one, I'm thinking it's possible that the person who stole from Wynter had a noble motive."

"Free the victims?" She gave a short, humorless laugh. "That's unrealistic, painfully so. The trafficking business runs on fear and brutality. These people are too terrified to escape. They've seen what happens to those who disobey."

When she first dug into the research on Wynter, she'd considered breaking the first rule of journalism about not getting involved with your subject. She'd wanted to sneak down to the piers, wait for a container to arrive and free the people inside. Her fantasy ended there because she didn't know what she'd do with these frightened people. They'd been stolen and dumped in a land where they knew no one and nothing.

"Impossible," she muttered.

"Not really."

"Even with noble motives, it'd be extremely hard to do the right thing."

"Rescuing the victims couldn't be a one-person operation. You'd need transportation, translators, lawyers and more. The FBI would coordinate." He paused to put the pieces together. "I'm sure they aren't involved in anything like this at present. If they had a rescue strategy under way, you can bet that Levine would have bragged to us about it."

Another thought occurred to her. "What if it wasn't a hundred people being stolen from Wynter? What if it was only a handful of kids?"

He jumped on her bandwagon. "A few kids could be separated from the others by an inside man, someone like Patrone."

She built on the theme. "He could have been helping someone else, maybe doing a favor for the woman who raised him. Or it could have been Liane."

She wanted to believe this was what had happened. Patrone had been trying to do a good thing. He didn't die in vain. He was a hero.

"More likely," Sean said, "the human cargo was stolen by a rival gang."

"Who'd dare?" From the little she knew about the gangs in San Francisco, they focused on local crime, small scale. "Wynter is big business, international business."

"So are the snakeheads."

And they were lethal. "Liane's brother is a snakehead."

"Her brother might have used Patrone to get access to the shipments. He could have told them arrival times and locations."

"And Frankie found out."

She shuddered, imagining a terrible scenario with Patrone caught between the brutal thugs who worked for Wynter and the hissing snakeheads.

Which way would he go? Being shot in the chest was a kinder death than what the snakeheads would do to him. She hoped that was a decision she never had to make.

Chapter 16

While tracking down Jerome Strauss, Emily insisted on taking the lead. She was driving when they went down the street where the *BP Reporter*'s offices had been. The storefront windows were blown out, and yellow crime scene tape crossed off the door. The devastation worried her. "If Jerome had been in there, he would have been fried."

In the passenger seat, Sean held up his phone and snapped photos. "I'll send these pictures to Dylan. He might be able to give us a better idea of what kind of bomb was used."

"I'll circle the block again."

She wasn't sure how the attack on Jerome connected to her. He knew her as Emily, a poet who he occasionally published in the *Reporter*. Her journalism was done under a pseudonym. She'd engineered the publication of the Wynter material by Jerome, making sure he got it for free. And they'd discussed the content. But she never claimed authorship.

She thought of Jerome as a friend. Not a close friend or someone she'd trust with deep secrets but somebody she could have a drink with or talk to. She'd hate if anything bad happened to him, and it would be horrible if the bomb had been her fault.

On this leg of their investigation, she and Sean were more prepared for violence. She had her pepper spray spritzer and stun gun. He was packing two handguns, two knives, handcuffs, plastic ties to use as handcuffs, mini-cameras and other electronic devices. Sean was a walking arsenal, not that he looked unusual, not in the least. His equipment fit neatly to his body, like a sexy Mr. Gadget. Under his olive cargo pants and the denim jacket lined with bulletproof material, he wore holsters and sheaths and utility belts.

Her outfit was simple: sneakers and skinny jeans with a loose-fitting blouse under a beige vest with pockets that reminded her of the kind of gear her dad used to wear when he went fishing in the mountains. This vest, however, was constructed of some kind of bulletproof Kevlar. She also wore cat's eye sunglasses and a short, fluffy blond wig to conceal her identity.

Sean's only nod to disguise was slumping and pulling a red John Deere baseball cap low on his forehead. Surprisingly, his change of appearance was effective. The slouchy posture made his toned, muscular body seem loose, sloppy and several inches shorter. He'd assumed this stance immediately; it was a look he'd developed in his years working undercover.

Years ago, she'd hated when he left on one of those

assignments. The danger was 24/7. If he made one little slip, he'd be found out. While the life-threatening aspect of his work had been her number one objection, she'd also hated that he was out of communication with her or anybody else. She'd missed him desperately. He'd been her husband, damn it. His place had been at home, standing by her side. To top it off, when he finally came home, he couldn't tell her what he'd done.

Given those circumstances, she was amazed that their marriage had lasted even as long as it did.

At the crest of a steep hill, she cranked the steering wheel and whipped a sharp left turn while Sean crouched in the passenger seat beside her, watching for a tail.

"Are we okay?" she asked.

"I think so. Are you sure you don't want me to drive?"

"I've got this."

Actually, she wasn't so sure that she could find Jerome's apartment. The only time she'd visited him had been at night, and she'd been angry. She wasn't sure of the location. And she didn't have an address because he was subleasing, and there was somebody else's name above his doorbell.

Also, it was entirely possible that he hadn't returned home after leaving the hospital. "I hope he's all right," she said.

"The docs wouldn't have released him if he wasn't."

It was difficult to imagine Jerome in a hospital bed with his thick beard and uncombed red hair that always made her think of a Viking. "I'm guessing that he wasn't a good patient."

"Are we near his apartment?"

"I think so."

Jerome liked to present himself as a starving author with a hip little publication. Not true. He had a beer belly, and his beard hid a double chin. Not only was he well fed but he lived in a pricey section of Russian Hill with a view of Coit Tower from his bedroom. The word *bedroom* echoed in her mind. She never should have gone into his bedroom.

In her one and only visit, she'd been naive, and he'd had way too much to drink. While showing her the view, he lunged at her. She sidestepped and he collapsed across his bed, unconscious. She left angry. Neither of them had spoken of it.

She recognized the tavern on the corner, a cute little place called the Moscow Mule. "Almost there, it's one block down."

As they approached, Sean scanned the street. "I don't see anybody on stakeout, but I'm not making the same mistake twice. Go ahead and park."

In one of the multitude of pockets in his cargo pants, he found a gray plastic rectangular device about the size of a deck of playing cards. He pulled two antennae from the top.

She parallel parked at the curb. "What's that?"

"It's a jammer. It disrupts electronic signals within a hundred yards."

"Inside Jerome's apartment," she said, "hidden cameras and bugs will be disabled."

He handed her a tiny clear plastic earpiece. "It's a two-way communicator. You can hear me and vice versa."

"But won't this little doohickey be disrupted as well?"

"Yeah," he said with a nod, "but I'll only use the jammer for three minutes while I enter Jerome's place. I'll get him out of there, and deactivate the jammer while I bring him down to the car."

Compared to dodging through the broom closet at her place, this was a high-tech operation. She popped the device in her ear. "I'm ready."

He slipped out the door, barely making a sound.

Turning around in the driver's seat, she watched him as he strode toward the walk-up apartment building, staying in shadows. Though Sean was still doing his slouch and his poorly fitted denim jacket gave him extra girth, he looked good from the back with his wide shoulders and long legs. She was glad to be with him, so glad.

As he entered Jerome's building across the street from where she'd parked, she heard his voice through the ear device. "I'm in," he said. "Which floor?"

"Wow, your voice is crystal clear. Can you hear me?"

"I can hear. Which floor?"

"Jerome is three floors up, high enough to have a view, and his apartment is to the right of the staircase. I can't remember the number, but it's toward the front of the house and—"

A burst of static ended her communication. *Jammer on!*

She looked over her shoulder at the apartment building. If it had been after dark instead of midafternoon, Jerome would have turned his lights on. They would have known right away if he was home or not.

Had three minutes passed? She should have set a timer so she'd know when he'd been gone too long. Not that they'd discussed what she should do if Sean didn't return when he said he would. Her fingers coiled around the flashlight/stun gun. If thugs were hiding out in Jerome's apartment, she might actually have a chance to use it.

The static in her ear abruptly ended. She heard Sean's voice, "Jerome's not here. I'm sure it's his place. He's got stacks of *BP Reporter* lying around."

"What a jerk," she muttered. "He promised to distribute these all over town. They're freebies, after all."

"Great apartment, though. Excellent view."

She saw Sean leave the building and jog to the car. He'd barely closed the door when she offered a suggestion. "We should try the tavern down the block. Jerome goes there a lot."

"No need for an earpiece." He held out his hand, and she gave him the plastic listening device. "Let's go to the Mule."

Sean took over the driving duties and chose his parking place so that if they ran out the back door from the Mule, the rental car would be close at hand for a speedy getaway. He wasn't sure what to expect when they entered through the front door. A tavern named Moscow Mule in the Russian Hill district was a little too cutesy for his taste, and he was glad the Mule turned out to be a regular-looking bar, decorated with neon beer signs on the wall and an array of bottles. Stools lined up in a long row in front of the long, dark wood bar. The only Moscow Mule reference came from the rows of traditional copper mugs on shelves.

Jerome Strauss sat at the bar, finishing off a beer and a plate of French fries. He didn't seem to notice them, and Sean led Emily to a table near the back.

She sat and leaned toward him. "I can't believe he

didn't recognize me. This blond wig isn't a great disguise."

"Maybe your friend Jerome isn't that bright."

When she chuckled, he noticed Jerome's reaction. His back stiffened, and he tilted his head as though that would sharpen his hearing. Sean wasn't surprised. You can change the tone of your voice, but it's nearly impossible to disguise a laugh.

Whatever the reason, Jerome spun around on his bar stool and stared at Emily. His big red beard parted in a grin as he picked up his beer and came toward them.

He squinted at her. "Is that you, Emily?"

"Join us," she said.

He wheeled toward Sean. "And who's this dude? Is he supposed to be your bodyguard?"

"That's right," Sean said as he rose to his full height, towering over Jerome. In case the editor wasn't completely intimidated, Sean brushed his hand against his hip to show his holstered gun. "Ms. Peterson asked you to join us."

"Sure." Jerome toppled into a chair at the table.

Emily gave Sean an amused smile. "Would you like to try a Moscow Mule?"

"Not now," he said for Jerome's benefit. "I'm on duty."

"They're really yummy, made with vodka, ginger beer and lime juice and served in one of those cute copper mugs."

Obviously she'd tasted the drink before. It was a somewhat unusual cocktail, probably not available in many places. Sean had to wonder if she'd spent much time with Jerome in this tavern. The newspaper editor had a definite crush on her.

"I like the blond hair," Jerome said.

Sean suspected that he'd like her whether she was blonde, brunette or bald. But they hadn't come here to encourage their friendship. "You don't seem curious, Mr. Strauss, about why Emily is in disguise and why she needs a bodyguard."

"I can guess." When he leaned forward, Sean noticed his eyes were unfocused. Jerome was half in the bag. He whispered, "To protect you from Wynter."

She fluttered her eyelashes. In the fluffy wig, she managed to pull off an attitude of hapless confusion. "Whatever do you mean? I'm a poet. Why would I have anything to do with a murderous thug like Wynter?"

"You can drop the act," Jerome said. "I've known for a long time that you're Terry Greene, the journalist."

She didn't bother to deny it. "How did you guess?"

"I'm an editor, a wordsmith. I noticed similarities in style. Even your poetic voice reminded me of Greene's prose. You have a way of writing that keeps the passion bubbling just under the surface."

"Uh-huh." Disbelief was written all over her face. The fluffy blonde had been replaced by cynical Emily. "Tell me how you really figured it out."

"I wasn't spying on you. It was an accident." He drained the last of his beer. "I noticed some of the Wynter research on your computer, but don't worry."

Jerome waved to the bartender, pointed to his empty bottle and held up three fingers.

"Don't worry about what?" Emily asked.

"I never told those guys, never, ever." The alcohol was catching up with him. Jerome had trouble balancing on his chair and rested his palms on the table as an anchor.

"What guys?" Emily asked. Her disbelief had turned into concern. "Did someone threaten you? Did they blow up your office?"

"Shhhhh." He waited until three beers were delivered and the bartender returned to his other customers. It was too early for the after-work crowd, but there were a half dozen other people at the bar and at tables.

Emily grasped Jerome's hand. "Tell me."

He raised her fingers to his lips and kissed her knuckles. "A guy came to talk to me. Middle-aged, expensive suit, slicked-back hair, he showed me a business card from Wynter Corp, like it was a regular legit business."

"Morelli," she said. "What did he want?"

"He asked for Terry Greene, and I told him that the Wynter article was just a reprint. He'd have to go to her original publisher." Jerome winced. "I knew it was you that he was after, and that's why I blew up my office."

"What!" She spoke so loudly that everybody in the bar paused to stare. Emily waved to them. "It's okay—nothing to worry about."

"You've got to believe me," Jerome begged. "I'd never tell."

When the murmur of conversation resumed, she glared at him. "You blew up your own office. What the hell were you thinking?"

"I was afraid I might accidentally spill something incriminating, and I didn't want to risk exposing you. Don't you see, Emily? I did it for you."

She surged to her feet and took a long glug of beer. "Please don't do me any more favors."

Sean believed that Jerome was telling the truth, but it wasn't the whole story. Something had scared him enough to make him blow up his office. He was in this bar because he was afraid to go home. And Morelli wasn't all that frightening.

"Who else?" Sean asked. "After Morelli left, who else paid you a visit?"

"I don't know what you're talking about." He lifted the beer bottle to his lips but didn't drink. "I'd never, ever tell. What makes you think there was somebody else?"

His fingers trembled so much he couldn't manage another swig of beer. Though he was half-drunk, Jerome's eyes flickered. He was lying. Sean figured that someone else had been following Morelli, wanting to know what he knew. And the second someone was menacing. "Who was it?"

"Frankie," Emily said. "Was it Frankie Wynter? I feel terrible for putting you in this position. Did he threaten you?"

"I'm the one who should feel bad."

Sean agreed. He figured that Jerome had let vital information slip to the other visitor. It was probably an accident, but Jerome had been terror stricken, numb, and in that state, he'd revealed Emily's true identity. "Was it Frankie? Or someone else?"

"A Chinese guy." Jerome stared down at the tabletop. "A snakehead."

Chapter 17

Sean had been hoping to avoid confrontation with the snakeheads. They descended from gangs in Asia that had roots going back hundreds of years. He'd heard that the word *thug* had been invented to describe the snakeheads that, in ancient days, preyed on caravans. Now they specialized in grabbing people from Asian countries and transporting them around the world to North America, Australia and Europe.

After warning Jerome that he was damn right to be scared if he'd crossed the snakehead, Sean told the half-drunk editor that hiding out in the corner bar wasn't going to save him. He needed to go to the police...even if he'd been stupid enough to blow up his own office.

Then Sean swept Emily away from the bar and into their rental car. The answers to their investigation would be found in Chinatown. Sean was certain of it. But he wasn't sure how to proceed.

Taking extra care to avoid being followed, he made a couple of detours to grab something to eat. San Francisco truly was a town for food lovers. The array of fast food included sushi, fresh chowder, meat from a Brazilian steak house and the best hamburgers on earth. He stocked up and then drove back to the hotel.

As soon as she entered their room, Emily yanked the blond wig off her head and took the carryout bags from him. "I'll set up the food while you do your searching-for-bugs thing."

He placed the jammer on the small round table, pulled up the antennae and turned it on. Sean wasn't taking the smallest chance that they might be overheard. "After we eat, we're going to plan the rest of our time in San Francisco. Then we're out of here."

The corner of her mouth twisted into a scowl. "Do you mind if I ask where?"

"I'm not sure. We're going far, far away from the thugs and Wynter and all the many people who want to kill you."

"I don't understand. I'm such a nice person."

"Speaking of not-so-nice people," he said, "I'd advise you to keep your distance from Jerome. Not only is he crazy enough to set a bomb in his own office but he's a coward."

"What do you mean?"

"I think we have Jerome to thank for making the link between Emily Peterson and your pseudonym."

"But he said…" She paused. "Wasn't he telling the truth?"

"He protested too much about how he'd never tell. I call that a sure sign of a liar."

He swept the room, still finding nothing. Thus far, the hotel had been safe. But how much longer was this luck going to hold? After turning off the jammer, he sat at the table and gazed across at the fine-looking lady who had once been his wife. She liked to set a table, even if they were only eating fast food on paper plates.

Using the chopsticks that came with their order, he picked up a tidbit of sushi. In addition to the California rolls and *sashimi*, he'd ordered fried eel, *unagi*, because it was supposed to increase potency and virility. Not that he believed in that kind of magic…but it couldn't hurt.

"This meal almost makes sense," she said. "We start with the colorful orange-and-green sushi appetizer, then the hamburger and fries main course and finally the doughnuts for dessert."

"Perfect." He wasn't exaggerating. It was an un- proven fact that eight out of ten American men would choose burgers and doughnuts for any given meal.

"And what do we do with the lovely hula Hawaiian pizza? And the meat and salad from the steak house?"

"We might not have another chance to eat for the rest of the day. I say we fill up."

She gave an angry huff. "I've told you a million times about how you can't eat once and expect it to last for hours. It's like fuel—you have to keep burning at a steady level."

"Spicy," he said as he assembled a piece of ginger, *wasabi* and *unagi*. "Eat what you want, and we'll take the rest with us."

"Fine." She raised the burger to her mouth. "Tell me about our next plan."

"First we make a phone call to Dylan and find out how much he's learned from hacking. After that, we go to Chinatown."

"After dark?"

He nodded. "At night, we don't stand out as much. Well, I do because I'm tall, but you can blend right in if you keep your head down. While we're there, we need to visit Doris Liu and Liane Zhou, the girlfriend."

"Whose brother is a snakehead," she reminded him. "Do you think Mikey Zhou was the guy who frightened Jerome?"

"It'd be neat and tidy if he was the one," he said.

"Otherwise, we need to start working another angle."

"I don't think so. If this scenario doesn't pan out, we've got to move on. I'd like to resolve the motive for the murder, but it's too dangerous and too complex for us to solve."

"Is it really? Look at how much I got figured out all by myself."

"That's because you're a skilled and talented investigative journalist."

For a moment, they ate in silence. He enjoyed the stillness of late afternoon when work assignments were winding down and evening plans had not yet gotten under way. The sunlight faded and softened. The streets were calm before rush hour. It was a time for relaxing and reflecting. Though he'd seldom worked at a desk job with nine-to-five hours, his natural rhythm made a shift from work time to evening.

His gaze met hers across the table. She was alert but not too eager. In spite of her mini-lecture about his poor eating habits, she wasn't pushing that agenda. Not like when they were married, and she felt like she had to change him, to whip him into shape.

He didn't miss the nagging, but he wondered why she stopped. It must be that she'd given up on him and decided he wasn't worth all that fuss. He was just a guy she was hanging out with. Technically, he was her employee, not that he planned to charge her or Aunt Hazel for his services. He wouldn't know how to itemize a bill like that. For intimate services, should he charge by the hour or by the client's satisfaction?

"You're smiling," she said. "What are you thinking?"

"I'm imagining you in a waterfall. You're covered in body paint, wild orchids and orange blossoms, and the spray from the waterfall gradually washes you clean."

Her voice was a whisper. "Hey, mister, I'm supposed to be the poetic one."

"We've changed, both of us."

When they'd been married, she never sat still. Nor was she ever silent. He liked this new version of Emily who could be comfortable and relaxed and didn't need to fill the air with chatter.

He wiped his mouth with one of the paper napkins, came around the table and took her hands. "There's one more part to my plan that I didn't mention."

"Let me guess," she said as she stood. "It's the part that takes place in the bedroom."

Hand in hand, they walked into the adjoining room where both beds were messy. He'd hung the "Do Not Disturb" on the door and also requested no maid service at the front desk. He paused at the foot of one of the beds and turned her toward him.

He lifted her chin, gazed into her face. "Nobody ever said it had to be in the bedroom."

"That's a spa shower in the bathroom." A sly smile

curled the ends of her mouth. "I haven't figured out how to use all the spray jets."

"We can learn together."

The bathroom also used an Asian-influenced decorating theme with white tile and black accents. On the double-sink counter, there were three delicate orchids in black vases. The tub was simple and small. The shower was Godzilla. A huge space, enclosed in glass with stripes of frosted glass, the shower had an overhead nozzle the size of a dinner plate. Eight jets protruded from the wall at various heights, and there was a handheld sprayer.

He peeled off his Mr. Gadget outfit and dropped the clothes in a pile with his Glock on top for easy access. Earlier, he'd noticed a special feature in the bathroom: dimmer dials for the lights. Playing around with the overhead and four sconces around the mirrors, he set a cool, sexy mood.

"Do you like this?" he asked.

"It's almost as good as candlelight."

She didn't have nearly as many clothes as he did, but it was taking her longer to get out of them. He was happy to help, reaching behind her back to unhook her bra as she wiggled out of her skinny jeans.

He entered the shower. "I'll get the water started."

As she neatly folded her jeans, she said, "Quite a coincidence, Sean. You have a fantasy about waterfalls, and here we are, stepping into a shower."

"Swear to God, I didn't plan this. But it's not altogether a coincidence. The thought of you, wet and naked, is real good motivation to find a shower."

With the overhead rainfall shower drizzling, he opened the door and took her hand, leading her into the glass enclosure. Her step was delicate, graceful.

The dim light shone on her dusky olive skin and created wonderful, secretive shadows on her inner thighs and beneath her breasts.

When she moved under the spray and tilted her head up, he was captivated. She was everything a woman should be. How had he ever let her slip away from him?

With her back pressed into his chest, he encircled her with his arms and held her while her slick, supple body rubbed against him. The intake and exhale of their breathing mingled with the spatter of droplets in a powerful song without words or tune. Swirling clouds of steam filled the shower.

She turned on the jets and edged closer, letting the water pummel her. "That feels great, like a wet massage."

She moved him around, positioning him so he'd be hit at exactly the right place near the base of his spine. He groaned with pleasure.

They took turns soaping each other, paying particular attention to the sensitive areas and rinsing the fragrant sandalwood lather away. She massaged shampoo into her hair.

"Let me," he said, taking over the job. "I remember when we'd wash your long hair. It hung all the way down to your butt."

"A lot of work," she said.

"I like it better this way. No muss, no fuss."

"Like wham, bam, thank you, ma'am."

"Hey, there, if you're implying that I don't want to take my time, you're dead wrong. With all that hair out of the way, I can devote my attention to other parts of you."

He started by nibbling on her throat and worked his way down her body. Though he wasn't usually a fan of electronic aids, he started using the pulsating, handheld sprayer about halfway down.

The way she shimmied and twitched when aroused drove him crazy. Her excitement fed into his, building and building. One thing was clear: he wasn't going to be able to hold back much longer. On the verge of eruption, he had to get her into the bedroom. In the shower, he wasn't able to manage a condom. For half a second, he wondered if using prevention was necessary. Would it be a mistake to a kid with Emily? He shook his head, sending droplets flying. Now was not the time for such life-changing decisions.

He brought her from the shower to the bed, tangling them both in towels. Condom in place, he entered her. Her body was ready for him, tight and trembling. She was everything to him.

An irresistible surge ripped through him. He felt something more than physical release. More than pleasure, he felt the beginning of something he'd once called love. *Not the same.* He couldn't be in love with her. Those days were over.

He collapsed on the bed beside her. They lay next to each other, staring up at the ceiling, thinking their own private thoughts. Did he love her? He'd give his life for her without a second thought. Was that love? She delighted him in so many ways. *Love?* He was proud of her, of the woman she'd become.

Does it matter? He should let those feelings go. Taking on the biggest gang in the city and the snakeheads, they'd probably be dead before the night was over.

He cleared his throat. "After Chinatown, we've done all the investigating that we can hope to do. Then we leave. We need to put distance between us and the people who want us dead."

"Right."

Reluctantly, he hauled himself up and out of the bed. "I need to make that call to my brother."

Swaddled in the white terrycloth robe provided by the hotel, he went to the desk in the living room and set up his computer equipment to have a face-to-face conversation with Dylan. Through the windows, he noticed that dusk had taken hold and the streetlights were beginning to glow. By the time he was prepared to make contact, Emily had blow-dried her hair and slipped on a nightshirt that left most of her slender, well-toned legs exposed.

She sprawled on the sofa. "Put it on speakerphone."

He took out the earbuds and turned up the volume. Though it was after eight o'clock in Denver, Dylan answered the number that rang through to the office immediately.

"Are you still at work?" Sean asked.

"Of course not. I transferred everything to a laptop, and I'm at my place."

"Turn on your screen and let me see."

"Just a sec."

Sean heard the unmistakable sound of a female voice, and he asked his brother, "Am I interrupting something?"

A slightly breathless female answered, "Hello, Sean. How's San Francisco? It's one of my favorite places. With the cable cars and the fog. Did I mention? This is me, Jayne Shackleford."

She was the neurosurgeon his brother had been dating and was crazy in love with. Sean envied the newness of their relationship. He and Emily would never have that again; they were older and wiser.

"It's a great city." He liked it better when nobody wanted to kill him and Emily. "Put Dylan on."

After a bit of fumbling around, his brother was back

on the line. He turned on his screen so Sean could see into his house and also catch a glimpse of Jayne in a pretty black negligee before she flitted from the room.

"Here's the thing," Dylan said. "I've done a massive hack in to Wynter's accounts, both personal and professional. It took some special, super-complicated skills that I'm not going to explain. I'll take pity on your Luddite soul that barely comprehends email."

"Thanks."

"Is that Emily I see behind you?" Dylan leaned close to the screen and waved. "Hi, Emily."

From her position on the sofa, she waved back, "Right back at you, Dylan."

"You did good. You gathered a ton of info with the research tools at your disposal. But you were missing the key ingredient, namely, James Wynter's personal computer."

"I knew it." She straightened up. "The personal documents are what I was going after on his yacht."

"That's where he kept the real records that didn't synch up with income."

"What does it prove?" Sean asked.

"Somebody's stealing from Wynter," Dylan said. "If I have the codes figured correctly, and I'm sure I do, he lost twelve people last month. They disappeared."

"And there's no way to track them?"

On-screen, Dylan shook his head and rolled his eyes. "What part of disappeared don't you understand? These people—referred to as human cargo—were supposed to arrive at Wynter's warehouse facility. They just didn't show."

Sean took a guess. "Did they come from Asia? Arriving in shipping containers?"

"There was a container. It came up three children short, five-year-olds. All the adult females were accounted for."

And the women would never rat out the kids if they'd somehow found a way to escape. Could those be the children whom Patrone was concerned about?

Sean asked, "What about the other nine?"

"They came on a regular boat. One way Wynter smuggles from Asia is taking his yacht out to sea, picking up the cargo and returning to shore north of San Francisco where he off-loads. Morelli was in charge of the last delivery, which was over six weeks ago."

"When Patrone was killed," Emily said.

"You guessed it," Dylan said. "No human trafficking since then. There's got to be a connection."

"What happened to the nine?" Dylan asked.

"Morelli swore they got onto a truck."

"But they disappeared," Sean said. "You don't happen to know where the yacht off-loads?"

"Medusa Rock, a little town up the coast."

Sean offered his usual brotherly, laconic compliments for a job well done. In contrast, Emily was over the moon, couldn't stop cheering.

"Enough," Dylan told her. "Sean'll get jealous. It's not good to have big brother ticked off."

"He most certainly can be a bear."

Sean growled. "If you two are done, I've got one more question for Dylan. Is Wynter connected with the snake-heads?"

"He's refusing to pay the snakeheads until he gets his hands on the missing twelve. The local gangs are up in arms, inches away from gang warfare."

And Sean and Emily were right in the middle.

Chapter 18

Emily decided against the blond wig for their trip to Chinatown. Instead she tucked her hair behind her ears and put on a baseball cap. She wore high-top sneakers, jeans and a sweatshirt because it was supposed to be chilly tonight. All her curves were hidden. She looked like a boy, especially when she added the khaki bulletproof vest.

Sean regarded her critically. "Do you have a beret?"

"Not with me. I have a knit cap in cranberry red that I packed for the mountains."

"Put it on," he said.

"Really? But the baseball cap is better. I'm trying to pass for a boy."

He slung an arm around her waist, pulled her close and gave her a kiss. "There's too much of the feminine about you. You look like a girl pretending to be a boy, and that attracts attention."

She dug through her suitcase until she found the cap. It covered her ears, smashed her hair down and had a jaunty tassel on top.

"Better," he said.

"Yeah, great. Now I look like a deranged girl."

"When we're on the street," he said, "keep your head down. Don't make eye contact. If they don't notice you, they can't recognize you."

He was more intense than earlier today, and that worried her. "Who do you expect to run into?"

"We're walking into the tiger's maw."

"Very poetic."

"I stole it from you," he said, "from a poem you wrote a long time ago. The description applies. Chinatown is home base for the snakeheads and a familiar place for Wynter's men. I bet they even have a favorite restaurant."

"The Empress Pearl."

When she first started her research, she'd gone there several times to watch Wynter's men and try to overhear what they were talking about. She'd often seen Morelli, but when they finally met for his interview, he didn't recognize her, which made her think that Sean was right about being anonymous and, therefore, forgettable.

She asked, "Are we coming back to the hotel?"

"Sadly no, our suitcases are packed."

"I want to make a phone call from here to Morelli. If he tries a trace, it doesn't matter."

Thoughtfully, he rubbed his hand along his still unshaven jawline. "Why talk to him?"

"At one time, we had a rapport, and maybe that counts for something. I have a question I hope he'll answer."

"You're aware, aren't you, that Morelli is the most likely person to be stealing from Wynter? He has inside information, and he signed off on the nine that went missing."

"I think he's being framed," she said.

"We never did a profile on Morelli," he said. "I see him as a corporate climber, a yes-man scrambling to get ahead. He wouldn't take the initiative in stealing from Wynter, but he might support the double-crosser who took off with the nine."

All this crossing and double-crossing still didn't explain why they were coming after her. Like Bulldog said at her apartment, Wynter wasn't worried about her eyewitness testimony. His expensive attorneys were clever enough to make her look like the crook. If she was about to be framed, she wanted to know why.

She took her last burner phone from her pocket. "I'm making the call."

"And leave the phone behind," he said.

It took a moment to find Morelli's number. He answered quickly, and his voice had a nervous tremor. When she identified herself, he sounded like he was on the verge of tears.

"Emily, I have to meet with you, please. Name the place."

"Actually, John…" She used his given name to put them on a more equal footing. "I was looking for some information. If you help me, I might help you."

"Always the reporter," he said. "Ask me anything."

"According to you and also to Mr. Barclay, aka Bulldog, there's a rumor floating around that I know something about human cargo going missing on shipments from Asia."

"Do you?" He was overeager. If he'd been a puppy, his tail would be wagging to beat the band.

She said, "You first."

"Based on detailed information in your articles about Wynter, I suspected that you had an inside edge. When you talked about our warehouses and distribution, you knew about the supposed warehouse where we stored our human cargo."

"What do you mean 'supposed' warehouse?"

"Don't play dumb with me, Emily. You know it's just a house with mattresses in the basement."

He had it wrong. She had the number of warehouses but not all the addresses. If she'd known where they were keeping the kidnapped people, she would have informed the police.

Morelli continued. "I thought you had inside information, and Bulldog confirmed it."

"Do you always listen to Bulldog?"

"If you didn't want him to talk, you shouldn't have left him tied up in your apartment. It only took ten minutes for somebody to show up and let him go."

"Should we have killed him?"

"Not the point," Morelli said. "He told me that you witnessed the murder from inside the closet in the office."

"That's right." She wasn't sure where this was going but wanted him to keep talking.

"You were in the private office on the yacht...alone with James Wynter's private computer. You were the one who made changes on the deliveries and receipts, trying to cover up the theft."

"I hate to burst your bubble, but everybody on that ship had access."

"Not true. The office was unlocked for a short time only. Only Frankie had a key."

And she'd been unlucky enough to stumble onto the one time when she could get herself in deep trouble. She was done with this conversation. "Here's what I have for you, Morelli. I'm leaving San Francisco and never coming back. I'm gone, so you can quit chasing me. No more threats. Bye-bye."

When she ended the call, she felt an absurd burst of confidence. She dropped the cell phone like a rock star with a microphone. *Emily out.*

After dark, Chinatown overflowed with activity. Sean parked downhill a few blocks, avoiding the well-lit entrance through the Dragon's Gate. They hiked toward the glaring lights, the noise of many people talking in many dialects and the explosion of color. Lucky red predominated. Gold lit up the signs, some written in English and others in Chinese characters. Some of the pagoda rooftops were blue, others neon green.

Sean wasn't a fan of this sensory overload. He ducked under a fringed red lantern as he followed Emily toward the shop owned by Liane Zhou. His gut tensed. This wasn't a good place for them, wasn't safe. He wanted to take care of business and get out of town as quick as possible.

Emily stepped into an alcove beside a postcard kiosk and pulled him closer. "It's at the end of this block. I think the name of the shop is Laughing Duck, something like that. There isn't an English translation, but guess what's in the window."

"Laughing ducks."

"I think you should do the talking. I've already met

Liane, and she was tight-lipped with me. You might encourage her to open up."

The only thing he wanted to ask Liane was if her snakehead brother intended to kill them. If so, Sean meant to retreat. "What did you talk to her about before?"

"I didn't know about the missing human cargo, so I concentrated on Patrone. At that time, he was only missing, and I didn't tell her about the murder."

"And what did she say?" he asked.

"Not much." She scowled. "She might open up if you spoke Chinese. Do you know the language?"

"A little." He'd picked up a few phrases when he was working undercover. Needless to say, the people who taught him weren't Sunday school teachers. In addition to "hello" and "goodbye," he knew dozens of obscene ways to say "jerk," "dumb-ass" and "you suck."

"Liane is easy to recognize. She's five-nine and obviously likes being taller than the people who work for her because she wears high heels."

Glumly, he stared through the window into the fish market next door. A pyramid arrangement went from crabs to eels to prawns to a slithering array of fish. He hunched his shoulders and marched past the ferocious stink that spilled from the shop to the sidewalk. They entered the Laughing Duck, a colorful storefront for tourists with lots of smiling Buddhas, fans painted with cherry blossoms, parasols, pouches and statuettes for every sign of the Chinese zodiac. Since his zodiac animal was the pig, he pretty much disregarded that superstition. Emily was a sheep.

A young woman met them at the front with a wide smile. "Can I help you find anything?"

"Liane Zhou," he said as he entered the shop.

The narrow storefront was misleading. Inside, the shop extended a long way back and displayed more items. He knew from experience that Liane very likely sold illegal knockoffs of purses and shoes and other merchandise that was not meant to be seen by the general public.

Most of these shops had a dark, narrow staircase at the rear that led to second and third floor housing. An entire family, including mom, dad, kids and grandmas, might live in a two-bedroom flat. All sorts of business were conducted from these shady little cubbyholes, ranging from legitimate cleaning and repair services to selling drugs.

Emily's description of Liane was accurate. The tall, slender woman stood behind the glass-top counter near a cash register. She wore a bright blue jacket with a Mandarin collar over silky black pants and stiletto heels. Her sleek black hair was pulled up in a ponytail and fell past her shoulders. Her lips pursed. Her eyes were shuttered.

Hanging on the wall behind her were several very well-made replicas of ancient Chinese swords and shields. He knew enough of history to recognize that the Zhou dynasty was one of the most powerful, long-lived and militaristic. Liane was the daughter of warriors, a warrior herself.

It seemed real unlikely that she'd open up to him… or to anybody else. He decided to start off with a bombshell and see if he could provoke a reaction.

He met her gaze. Sean had been told, more than once, that his eyes were as black as ebony. Hers were darker. In a voice so quiet that not even Emily would overhear, he asked, "Do you want revenge for the murder of Roger Patrone?"

She blinked once. "Yes."

Chapter 19

A fierce hatred was etched into the beautiful features of Liane Zhou. Looking at her across the counter, Sean was convinced that the lady not only wanted revenge but was willing to rip the replica antique Chinese swords off the wall and do the killing herself.

Instinctively, he lifted his hand to his neck, protecting his throat from a fatal slash. He nodded toward the rear of the shop. "We should go somewhere quiet to talk."

Without hesitation, she shouted in Chinese to the young woman running the shop, and then she strode toward the back. When Liane Zhou made up her mind, she took action. It was an admirable trait…and a little bit scary.

Emily had fallen into line, walking behind him, and he wondered if Liane had noticed her. Behind the hanging curtain that separated the front from the back of the shop, Liane rested her hand on the newel post at the foot of a poorly lit staircase and looked directly at Emily. "Good evening, Terry Greene."

"Good evening to you," Emily said. "That's not my real name, you know."

"You are Emily Peterson. You were married to this man."

"I'm sorry I lied to you," Emily said as she pulled the cranberry knit cap off her head. "I thought an investigative reporter needed to go undercover and use an alias. I was wrong."

"How so?"

"There's never a valid reason to lie."

Liane Zhou turned her attention toward him. Her gaze went slowly from head to toe. "You," she said. "You are very…big."

Unsure that was a compliment, he said, "Thank you."

Liane took them to the second floor and unlocked the door to her private sitting room. Compared with the musty clutter in the rest of the building, her rooms were comfortable, warm and spotlessly clean.

When Liane clapped her hands, a heavily made-up woman who was skinny enough to be a fashion model appeared in an archway. Liane gave the order in Chinese, and the wannabe model scurried off.

Liane said, "We will have tea and discuss my revenge."

They sat opposite each other. Liane perched on a rattan throne while the two of them crowded onto a love seat. On the slatted coffee table between them were two magazines and a purple orchid.

Sean said, "You knew Roger Patrone for a long time."

"We arrived in Chinatown at the same time. Roger's parents sold him to Doris Liu."

Sean had never heard this version of the story. He

knew the parents were out of the picture, but he didn't know why. They sold him? Sean mentally underlined abandonment issues in their profile analysis of Patrone.

"He was a boy with special talent," Sean said, taking care not to phrase conversation in questions. He wanted Liane to see him as an equal.

"He was smart." Her voice resonated on a wistful note. "But not always wise."

"A typical male," Emily muttered. "Why did Doris want him so much that she'd pay for him?"

"His English was very good. Written and spoken. And he picked up Chinese quickly, many dialects. He took care of her correspondence."

"It's a little odd," Emily said, "to trust a nine-year-old with that kind of sensitive work."

"Doris preferred using a child. She wanted him to depend on her for his food and shelter. She owned him, and he had no choice but to obey."

"How much?" Emily asked. "I'm curious."

"A thousand dollars. Doris didn't pay. Her boyfriend bought Patrone as a gift. How could that ugly old hag have a man?" She scowled. "Must be witchcraft, *wugu* magic."

The wannabe model brought their tea on a dark blue tray with a mosaic design in gold and silver. She gave a slight bow and left the apartment.

Though they appeared to be alone, Sean didn't trust Liane. Until he felt safer with her, he'd keep the conversation in the past, going over information that wasn't secret and held no current threat. "You didn't live with Doris Liu."

"Only when I chose to," she said. "My parents would never sell me. They were brave and good. In China, we were poor. Life was difficult. But they would not abandon me. They were killed by snakeheads who stole me and my brother."

"I'm sorry," Emily said.

"As am I."

Sean wished he could warn Emily not to blurt the truth. If she confirmed that she'd seen Frankie kill Patrone, there would be little reason for Liane to talk with them.

He sipped his tea and complimented her on the taste and the scent. "You mentioned your brother, Mikey Zhou."

"Do you know him?"

Why would he? Again Sean struggled to remain impassive. "I'm aware of him, but we've never met."

"Agent Levine said you were a good friend. Yet he has not introduced you."

Shocked and amazed, Sean swallowed his tea in a gulp. Levine had told them he had a snitch, and he'd identified that snitch as Morelli. Mikey Zhou, too? Sean's estimation of Special Agent Levine rose significantly. No wonder the guy had been slugging back vodka at breakfast. Levine was playing a dangerous game.

While he sat silently, too surprised to speak, Emily filled the empty air space.

"Greg Levine is an old friend," she said. "He came to our wedding, and we went our separate ways. You know how it is. And then Sean moved back to Colorado after the divorce."

"You made a mistake," Liane said. "You should never have let Sean go."

"Right," Emily said. "Because he's so...big."

Liane inclined her head and leaned forward. "Is it true?"

Emily looked confused. "Is what?"

"Did you witness the murder?"

Sean jumped back into the conversation with both feet. "Your brother is a snakehead. But you said the snakeheads killed your parents and abducted both of you."

"The last wish of my father was for Mikey to protect me. He did what he had to do." She exhaled a weary breath. "I was twelve, and my brother was eight. When the snakeheads took us, I knew my fate. As a virgin, I would fetch a good price for my first time. They would make me a sex worker."

Emily reached across the table and took her hand. "How did Mikey stop them?"

"He sacrificed himself. A handsome child, he could have been adopted. He might have worked as a servant. But he refused. Instead he disfigured himself. He made a long scar across his face. He was damaged goods."

"Did they hurt him?" Emily asked.

"He was beaten but not defeated. He did their bidding with the understanding that I would come to no harm. Mikey labored until he collapsed. He took on every challenge. Ultimately, the snakeheads came to respect him."

"And what happened to you?"

"The expected," she said darkly. "My flower was sold for many thousands but not enough to set me and my brother free. I wore pretty things and worked as a party girl until I was treated badly, ruined. Luckily, I had a head for numbers and learned to help Doris and others in Chinatown with accounts and contracts."

"You and Patrone worked together," Sean said.

"Patrone, my dearest friend, translated and negoti-ated deals with smugglers, local gangs, Wynter Corp and snakeheads. He helped me save until I could open Laughing Duck."

While he was learning to profile, Sean had heard a lot of traumatic life stories. Few were as twisted as the childhood of Liane and Mikey…and Patrone, for that matter. No wonder Mikey Zhou had become a snake-head. And Patrone had been murdered. No doubt, Liane had secrets and crimes of her own.

"I have told my story," she said. "Now Emily must tell me. Who killed my dearest friend?"

Emily glanced at Sean. When he gave her the nod, she cleared her throat and said, "I saw Frankie Wynter and two others drag Patrone into an office on the yacht. Frankie shot him. They threw his body overboard."

Liane bolted to her feet. Her slender fingers clenched into fists at her side, and she spewed an impressive stream of Cantonese curses that Sean recognized from his undercover days.

"I promise," he said as he stood. "We'll bring Frankie Wynter to justice."

"Your justice is not punishment enough. He must die."

Sean was going to pretend that he never heard her threaten Frankie's life. The world would be a better place without the little jerk, but it wasn't his decision. And he wouldn't encourage Liane to take the law into her own hands.

"You're right, Liane." Emily also stood. "It's not fair, and it's not enough pain. But we want to get the person who is truly responsible."

"What do you mean?"

"Frankie pulled the trigger, but he isn't very clever and certainly not much of a leader. He was probably following orders from someone higher up."

"True." Liane spat the word. "Morelli?"

"Or James Wynter himself."

"Wait!" Sean said. "We've got to investigate. We need proof that it's Morelli or Wynter or somebody else."

He glanced from one woman to the other. They couldn't have been more different. Emily had had a charmed childhood and grew up to be a poet and journalist who loved the truth. Liane had suffered; she had to fight to survive. And yet each woman burned with a similar flame. Both were outraged by the murder of Roger Patrone.

"One week," Liane said. "Then I will take my revenge against Frankie Wynter."

Sean couldn't let that happen. He feared that Liane's attack against Wynter would end in gang warfare with the snakeheads.

"We need more information," he said. "What do you know about the human cargo that's gone missing from Wynter's shipments?"

"I help these people," she said simply. "So does Mikey. If you want to speak to him, he is at the club where Patrone worked."

"How do you help them?" Sean asked.

She pivoted and stalked down a narrow hallway. Carefully, she opened the door. Light from the hall spilled across the bed where three beautiful children were sound asleep.

Liane tucked the covers snugly around them and kissed each forehead.

Chapter 20

On the sidewalk outside the strip club where Patrone had run an illegal poker game in the back room, Emily stared at the vertical banner that read, "Girls, Nude, Girls." The evening fog had rolled in, and the neon outlines of shapely women seemed to undulate beside the banner. A barker called out a rapid chatter about how beautiful and how naked these "girls" would be.

"Not exactly subtle," she said as she nudged Sean. "At least it's honest."

"That depends on your definition of beauty. And I'd guess that some of these ladies left girlhood behind many years ago."

"How did you get to be an expert?"

"When I was undercover, I spent a lot of time in dives like this, the places where dreams come to die." He gave her arm a squeeze. "You always wanted to know what I did on my assignments. You pushed, but I couldn't say a damn word. The information I uncovered was FBI classified. And I felt filthy after spending a day at one of these places."

She knew his undercover work had been stressful. One of the reasons she'd pushed was so he could unburden himself. "If you'd explained to me, I would have understood. It had to be hard spending your day with addicts, strippers, pimps and criminals."

"They weren't the worst," he said. "I was. I lied to them. I knew better and didn't try to help."

"I never thought of your work that way."

"But you understand." He gazed down at her, and the glow from the pink neon reflected in his eyes. "You told Liane that you were wrong to lie when you were investigating."

"Maybe we're not so different." Why was she having this relationship epiphany on a sidewalk outside a strip club? "Let's get in there, talk to Mikey and go on our way."

He nodded. "There's not much more we can learn. I'll report to the FBI, sit back and let them do their duty."

She watched the patrons, who shuffled through the door with their heads down, looking neither to the right nor to the left. With her dopey cranberry hat pulled over her ears, she fit right in with this slightly weird, mostly anonymous herd…except for her gender. The few women on this street looked like hookers.

Inside the strip club, she pulled her arms close to her sides and jammed her hands into her pockets. The dim lighting masked the filth. The only other time she'd been here was in daylight, and she'd been appalled by the grime and grit that had accumulated in layers, creating a harsh, dull patina. Years of cigarette smoke and spilled liquor created a stench that mingled with a disgusting human odor. The music for the nude—except for G-string and pasties—girls on the runway blared through tinny speakers. Emily didn't want to think about the germs clinging to the four brass stripper poles.

Long ago, this district, the Tenderloin, had been home to speakeasies, burlesque houses and music clubs. Unlike most of the rest of the city, the Tenderloin had resisted gentrification and remained foul and sleazy.

Fear poked around the edges of her consciousness. Nothing good could happen in a place like this. She moved her stun gun from a clip on her belt to her front pocket so it would be more accessible. And she stuck to Sean like a nervous barnacle as she tried to think of something less squalid than her immediate surroundings.

Liane's life story had touched her. The woman had gone through so much tragedy, from witnessing the murder of her parents to the loss of her "dearest friend." Though she hadn't admitted that Patrone was her lover, it was obvious that she cared deeply about him. And he must have felt the same way about her. He had stolen the three children for her.

After Liane kissed the children, she explained. Patrone had been part of the crew unloading the shipping container. He'd arrived before anyone else because he was supposed to conclude negotiation with the snakeheads. When Patrone saw the kids, his heart had gone out to them. He'd unloaded them from the container and moved them to the trunk of his car. The poor little five-year-olds had been starving and dehydrated, barely able to move. Patrone had taken them to Liane.

This wasn't the first time she'd rescued stolen children and their mothers, protecting them from a life of servitude to women like Doris Liu. Liane fed them and nursed them. The plight of these kids wakened instincts she never thought she had. Though she was unable to bear children, she felt deep maternal stirrings.

Emily hoped that these three children would be Liane's happy ending. According to Emily's calculations, the children arrived shortly before Patrone was murdered. Only six weeks, but Liane loved them as though she'd raised them from birth.

Emily was content to let the story end there. She tugged Sean's sleeve and whispered, "We should go."

"After we check out the poker game," he said. "If Mikey isn't there, we're gone."

"Did Liane call him?"

"She said he'd know we were coming."

Behind a beaded curtain and a closed door, they were escorted into the poker game by the bartender, whom Sean had bribed with a couple of one-hundred-dollar bills. Emily didn't know Chinese, but she could tell from the bartender's tone as he introduced them that she and Sean were being described as rich and stupid, exactly the people you'd want to play poker with.

There were four tables: three for stud poker and one for Texas Hold'em. Emily narrowed her eyes to peer through the thick miasma of cigar and cigarette smoke. Almost every chair at the tables was filled. Most of the patrons were Asian, and there was only one other woman.

Sean guided her to a table and sat her down. He spoke to the others in Chinese, and they laughed. He whispered in her ear, "I said you were my little sister.

They should be nice to you, but not too nice because you like to win."

"Are you leaving me here alone?"

"I'll be close. Don't eat or drink anything."

"Don't worry."

When she felt him move away from her, it took an effort for her to stay in the chair and not chase after him. The dealer looked at her and said something in Chinese. She nodded. Since she knew how the game was played, she could follow the moves of the other players without getting into trouble.

The player sitting directly to her right was an older man with thinning hair and boozy blue eyes. He spoke English and directed one condescending remark after another to her. If she hadn't been so scared, she would have told him off.

Her plan was to be as anonymous as possible. Then she was dealt a beautiful hand: a full house with kings high. Her self-preservation instinct told her to fold the hand and not attract attention to herself. But she really did like to win. She bid carefully, taking advantage of how the others at the table paid her very little regard.

While she was raking in her winnings, she looked around for Sean and spotted him by the far wall, talking to an Asian man with a shaved head. He gave her a little wave, and she felt reassured. He was keeping an eye on her.

She quickly folded the next two hands and then tried a bluff that succeeded. *Really?* Was she really holding her own with these guys? The condescending man on her right gave his seat to another, and she turned to nod. His thick black hair grew in a long Mohawk and hung down his back in a braid. His arms and what she could see of his chest were covered in tattoos. The scar that slashed across his face told her this was Mikey Zhou.

He leaned closer to her. His left hand grazed her right side, and she felt the blade he was holding. "Fold this hand and come with me."

"Yes," she said under her breath. Frantic, she scanned the room. Where had Sean disappeared to? How could he leave her here unprotected?

Though terrified, she managed to keep focus on the game. Lost it but played okay. She rose from the table, picked up her chips and allowed Mikey to escort her toward a dark door at the back of the room. His grip on her arm was tight.

He whispered, "Don't be scared."

Though she wanted to snap a response, her throat was swollen shut by fear. She could barely breathe. The fact that she was moving surprised her because her entire body was numb. She was only aware of one thing: the stun gun in her pocket. Somehow she got her fingers wrapped around it. She got the gun out of her pocket without Mikey noticing.

When he shoved her into a small room filled with boxes and lit by a single overhead bulb, she whirled. Lunging forward, she pressed the gun against his belly. She heard the electricity and felt the vibration.

Mikey shuddered. His eyes bulged, and he went down on his hands and knees.

Before she could move in to zap him again, another man appeared from the shadows and grabbed her arms from behind. He knocked the gun from her hand.

She kept struggling, but couldn't break free. When she tried to kick backward with her legs, he swept her feet out from under her, and she was on her knees with her arms twisted back painfully. She tried to inhale enough air to scream. Could she summon help? Who would come to her aid? Nobody in this club was going to cross Mikey Zhou.

He stood before her and leaned down. His long braid fell over his shoulder. Roughly, he yanked her chin upward so she had to look into his dark eyes. Even with the tattoos and the scar, she saw a resemblance to Liane in the firm set of the jaw.

"Emily," he said. "Special Agent Levine said you would cause trouble."

"Let me go," she said. "I'll leave and you'll never see me again, I promise."

"I will not harm you."

He said something in Chinese to the man who was holding her arms, and he released her. She sat back on her heels. What was going to happen to her? *And where is Sean?*

If Mikey didn't intend to hurt her, why did he grab her? She wasn't out of danger, not by a long shot. "What do you want from me?"

"Wynter has an arrangement with snakeheads. It has been thus for many years. There is disruption. Why?"

"Do you want me to find out?"

Mikey rubbed at the spot where she'd zapped him. "The disruption must end."

Slowly she got to her feet. Common sense told her that only a fool picked a fight with the snakeheads, but she didn't want to lie. The whole reason she was in trouble could be traced to her lies when she'd used an alias and posed as a hooker.

If she told Mikey that she'd help him by finding out who was messing up the smooth-running business of human trafficking, that wouldn't be the truth. She hated that the snakeheads were buying and stealing helpless people from Asia, and she also hated that Wynter Corp distributed the human cargo. Couldn't Mikey see that? After what happened to him and Liane, couldn't he understand?

She inhaled a deep breath, preparing to make her statement. These might be the last words she ever spoke. She wanted to choose them carefully.

The door whipped open, and Sean entered the room. As soon as she recognized him, he was at her side, holding her protectively.

"Are you all right?" he asked her. "Did he hurt you?"

Mikey laughed as he returned her stun gun. "Other way around."

She looked up at Sean. "He wants me to help him. I can't do that. I'm against human trafficking, and if it's interrupted, I'm glad."

"I want peace," Mikey said. "I do not hurt my own people. Explain to her, Sean."

"That might take a while."

She didn't understand what they were talking about, but it was obvious that they'd had prior contact. Did Sean know that Mikey was going to grab her and scare her out of her mind?

Mikey said, "You go now."

Sean whisked her toward the exit door from the small room. When he opened it, she saw the foggy night blowing down an alley.

"Hold on," she said, jamming her heels down. "I need to cash in my chips."

"Not tonight."

As if she'd ever return to this place? Reality hit her

over the head, and she realized that she was lucky to be walking out this door with no major physical injuries.

She went along with Sean as he propelled her around the corner and down two streets to where he'd parked. A misty rain was falling, and she was wet by the time they got to the rental car. As soon as they were inside the car, he started the engine.

"We need to hurry," he said.

"Why?"

"There's another shipment coming in tonight."

She snapped on her seat belt. She had to do whatever she could, anything that would help.

Chapter 21

Mikey the snakehead would not be getting any pats on the back from Sean. After Emily told him how Mikey had mishandled her, Sean was glad she'd zapped him with her stun gun.

"He wasn't supposed to scare you," he said.

"Well, he wasn't Mr. Friendly. When he got close to me, I felt the knife in his hand."

"His comb." Mikey's long braid didn't just happen. He worked on that hair. "A metal comb."

"How was I supposed to know?" she grumbled. "All he had to do was tell me you were waiting for me. And his friend grabbed me. He twisted my arm and forced me down on my knees."

"After you zapped Mikey with a stun gun?"

"Okay, maybe I was aggressive."

"You shot forty-five million volts through him."

She huffed and frowned. "What did he mean about wanting peace?"

"I'll explain."

The fog parted as he drove toward the private marina where the Wynter yacht was moored. It was after midnight. The city wasn't silent but had quieted. Misty rain shrouded the streets.

Though Mikey was a member of the notoriously cruel and violent snakeheads, Sean was inclined to believe him. In his experience, the guys who were the most dangerous were also the most honest, flip sides of the same coin. Besides, Mikey had nothing to gain from lying to Sean.

"Mikey says he's not involved in the actual business of human trafficking. His hands aren't clean, far from it. His job is to take care of snakehead business in San Francisco, buying and selling and extracting payments. His sister's dearest friend, Patrone, helped him negotiate."

"And that's why he knows Levine," she said.

"Right. Mikey's not a snitch. He's more like a local enforcer. He knows that if the snakeheads and Wynter keep losing money, there's going to be a war."

"And we're supposed to stop it?" The tone of her voice underlined her disbelief. "I didn't sign up for this job."

It wasn't fair to drag her any deeper into this quagmire. Until now, she'd been ready to go. Mikey must have scared her, made her realize that she was in actual danger. "You're right."

"Am I?"

"I can turn this car around, hop onto I-80, and we'll be back in Colorado in two days. You'd be safer with your aunt. Better yet, TST Security has a couple of safe house arrangements."

She sat quietly, considering his offer. With a quick swipe, she pulled off the knitted cap, fluffed her hair and tucked it behind her ears. She'd been through a lot in the past few days, and Sean wouldn't blame her if she opted to turn her back on this insanity.

In a small voice, she said, "I started investigating Wynter Corp six months ago, and I've learned a lot. I want to see this through. I want justice for Patrone. And I want the bad guys punished."

Damn, he was proud of her. She'd grown into a fine woman, a fine human being. He was glad she'd chosen to stay involved. If they dragged the FBI into the picture too soon, the investigation could turn messy. Liane might lose the kids and Mikey could be in trouble. If Sean handled the things, the case would be gift wrapped and tied up with a pretty red bow.

At the marina, he parked behind a chain-link fence, grabbed a pair of binoculars and went toward the gate. Security cameras were everywhere. "We can't get much closer. Do you remember where Wynter's yacht was moored?"

"I remember every detail of that night. My red dress and the shoes I could hardly walk in. I remember the other girls, several blondes, a couple of brunettes and some Asian. And I remember Paco the Pimp. He was incredibly helpful. Sure, he charged me a hefty bribe, but he was efficient and kind. Do you think we should talk to him?"

"Save Paco for another story," he said. "Do you remember where you boarded the yacht?"

"Near the end of the pier." When she squinted through the fog, he handed over the binoculars. She fiddled with the adjustments and then lowered the glasses. "I don't see it."

"I was hoping we could catch them before they took off," he said, "but it was a long shot."

"The cargo might be arriving via container ship. We'd have to go to the docks in Oakland to check it out."

A chilly breeze swept across the bay and coiled the fog around them. He wrapped his arm around her shoulder, welcoming the gentle pressure of her body as she leaned against him. She turned, her arm circled his torso and she looked up at him.

Her cheeks were ruddy from the cold. Her eyes sparkled. Before he could stop himself, he said, "I love you."

Her lips parted to respond, but he didn't want words. He kissed her thoroughly, savoring the heat from her mouth and the warmth of her body. She felt good in his embrace, even with several layers of clothes between them.

Saying "I love you" might have been one of the biggest mistakes in his life. He might have sent her reeling backward, frantically trying to get away from his cloying touch. But he wasn't going to take back his statement. He loved her, and that was all there was to it. He'd never really stopped loving her from the first day he saw her.

When he ended the kiss, he didn't give her a chance to speak. "We need to hustle."

"Where are we going?"

"Medusa Rock."

In the car, he immediately called his brother to get the coordinates for the place where Wynter off-loaded cargo. As usual, Dylan was awake. Sean was fairly sure that his genius brother never slept. They discussed a few other electronic devices before Sean ended the call and silence flooded into the car.

After a few miles, she pointed to the device fastened to the dashboard. "Is this the GPS location?"

"That's right."

"Medusa Rock," she said. "Do you think there are a lot of snakes?"

"I don't know. It's a good distance up the coast."

Again, silence.

With a burst of energy, she turned toward him. "We had ground rules, Sean. There's no way you can tell me you love me, no way at all. We had our chance, we had a marriage. When it fell apart, my heart shattered into a million little pieces. I can't go through that again."

"I apologize," he said. "I couldn't stop myself."

"I never thought I'd say this." When she paused, he heard a hiccup that sounded as though she was crying. "You're going to have to practice more self-control."

"Never would have believed it." He tried to put a good face on a bad move. "This time I'm the one who can't keep himself in check. I couldn't stop myself from blurting. What's the deal? Am I turning into a chick?"

"Not possible." She reached across the console and patted his upper thigh. "You're too…big."

When he told her he loved her, she thought she'd explode. The longing she'd been holding inside threatened to erupt in a sky-high burst of lava. And then, to make it worse, he kissed her with one of those perfect, wonderful kisses.

They had both changed massively since the divorce, but she still wasn't ready to risk her heart in another try with Sean. Maybe she'd never be ready. Maybe they were the sort of couple who was meant to meet up every ten years, have great sex and go on their merry way.

While he drove, she kept track of their route on the GPS map. Soon this would be over, and she'd be able to use her phone again. Right now she really wanted to know about the possibility of snakes at Medusa Rock. According to the map, this place was a speck about a hundred miles north along the Pacific Coast Highway from San Francisco.

At their current speed, which was faster than she liked, they'd be there in about an hour. There was almost zero traffic on this road. In daylight when the fog burned off, the view along this highway was spectacular.

"There's a blanket in the backseat," he said. "It might be good for you to get some sleep. If we catch Wynter's men in the act, we'll need to follow them. And probably will switch off driving."

She didn't need much convincing. The spike of adrenaline from her encounter with Mikey had faded, leaving her drained of energy. She snuggled under the blanket. An hour of sleep was better than none.

It seemed like she'd barely closed her eyes when the car jolted to a stop. She sat up in the seat, blinking madly. She grasped Sean's arm. "Are we safe?"

"You're always safe with me." His voice was low and calm with just a touch of humor to let her know he was joking...kind of joking. "We're here."

"I see it." Medusa Rock sat about a hundred yards offshore. Shaped like a skull, it had shrubs and trees across the top that might have resembled snaky hair. "Looks more like Chia pet to me."

The heavy fog from San Francisco had faded to little

more than a mist. The car was parked up on a hill over-looking a small marina where Wynter's party boat was moored. Sean placed the high-power binoculars in her hand, and she held them to her eyes. The running lights on the yacht were off, but there was still enough light to see four men leaning over the railing at the bow and smoking.

"How long have we been here?" she asked.

"Just a few minutes."

"They're waiting for something."

"If they take delivery from another boat," he said, "there's nothing more we can do. But if it's a truck, we'll follow."

She sat up a bit straighter in the passenger seat and fine-tuned the binoculars. The resolution with these glasses was incredible. She could make out faces and features. "Guess who's here."

"I'm pretty sure it's not big daddy James," he said. "Frankie boy?"

"The next best thing." She made a woofing noise. "It's Barclay the Bulldog, the guy who wrecked my apartment."

"It's good to know he doesn't specialize in ransacking."

"The Bulldog is an all-purpose thug." She chuckled as she continued to watch the yacht. "If they drive, we'll be able to see where they make the drop-off."

"We'll coordinate with Levine," he said. "It's not really fair. We do all the work, and that jerk gets all the glory."

"Not necessarily," she said.

She passed the binoculars to him. A fifth man had joined the other four on deck. She'd recognized him right away from his nervous gestures. It was Special Agent Greg Levine.

Chapter 22

Outraged, Sean stared down the hill at the fancy yacht with four thugs and a rat aboard. Levine was a double-crossing bastard who might precipitate a gang war that would tear San Francisco apart. Why hadn't Sean seen the problem before? It should have been obvious to him when he heard that Levine was using both Morelli and Mikey. *Quite a juggling act!* Levine wasn't a charmer and had nothing to offer. Neither of those men had a reason to work with him.

"Maybe," Emily said, "this is a sting."

Sean calmed enough to consider that scenario. On a scale of one to ten, he'd give it a three. Levine wasn't clever enough to set up a sting like this. And Sean hadn't noticed FBI backup in the area. Still, he conceded, "It's possible."

"But not likely," she said.

"Not at all."

They watched for another half hour. The night was beginning to thin as the time neared four o'clock, less than two hours before sunrise. Would Levine dare to drive into San Francisco during morning rush hour? Either he was massively stupid or had balls the size of watermelons.

A midsize orange shipping truck with a green "Trail Blazer" logo rumbled down to the pier. The driver jumped out and trotted around to the back. As soon as he rolled up the rear door, the armed men on the boat herded a ragged group of people who had been belowdecks, waiting in the dark. Sean counted seventeen. Only two men; the rest were women and children. He was glad to see that they also loaded bottles of water and boxes he hoped were food.

"Now what?" she asked.

"We follow," Sean said. "As soon as we figure out his plan, we'll call for backup."

"Why wait?"

"I don't want to waste this opportunity." He was thinking like a cop, not a bodyguard, which probably wasn't a good thing. Undercover cops took risks, while bodyguards played it safe. He promised himself to back down before it got dangerous. "Their destination might lead to another illegal operation."

"Like a sweatshop," she said. "We might be able to track the distribution network for the sex workers."

The orange truck pulled away from the pier with Levine behind the wheel and two armed men in the cab beside him. Staying a careful distance behind so they wouldn't be noticed, Sean followed in the rental car.

The roads leading away from Medusa Rock were

pretty much empty before dawn. As soon as possible, Sean turned off the headlights, figuring that their non-descript sedan would be almost invisible in the pre-dawn light.

The orange truck wasn't headed toward San Francisco. Levine was taking them east. *Where the hell is he going?*

With his assistance, Emily set up a conference call with his brother, who was—surprise, surprise—asleep. It was worth waking him up. If anybody could figure out how to track a moving vehicle, it was Dylan.

"Big orange truck?" His yawn resonated through the phone. "What do you want me to do with it?"

"We're trying to track it," Sean said. "When the sun comes up, in a couple of minutes, the driver of the truck might notice that we're tailing him. I want to drop back…way back."

"That sounds right," Dylan said. "What should I do? Turn you invisible?"

"Wake up, baby brother. I need you to be sharp now—right now."

"I have an idea," Emily said. "Satellite surveillance."

"It's hard to pull off," Dylan said. "If there are any clouds, it blocks the view."

"You could use a drone," she suggested.

"The only drones in the area are probably operated out of Fort Bragg, and I'm not going to hack in to the Department of Defense computers. Stuff like that could get me sent away for a long time."

"There must be something," she said.

"An idea," Dylan said. "Sean, do you have any of those tracking devices I put together a while back?"

"I have the big ones and the teeny-tiny ones."

"Slap a couple of each on the truck when he stops for gas. Turn them on right now, and I'll see if I can activate from here."

While they continued to follow, Sean told Emily where he kept the tracking devices in his luggage. Following his instructions, she checked batteries and made sure they were all working. She activated each.

"Good," Dylan said. "I've got four signals."

Emily chuckled. "You're amazing, Dylan. You can track us all the way from Denver?"

"And I kind of wish I could see what was going on. In the next generation of trackers, I'm adding cameras."

"Where are we?"

"On the road to Sacramento," Dylan said. "According to my maps, there aren't any major intersections on your route."

"But he might be stopping here," Sean said as he dropped back, slowing the rental car and allowing the truck to get almost out of sight. He stretched the tense muscles in his shoulders. He didn't like keeping surveillance in crowded traffic, but these empty roads were equally difficult.

After rummaging around in his backpack, Emily found energy bars and a bottle of water. Both food and drink were welcome. He hadn't slept last night, and the sun was rising.

The orange truck rumbled through Sacramento, still heading east.

Dylan called them back with an alert. "Make sure your car has enough gas. It looks like the route he's taking is Highway 50, otherwise known as the loneliest road in America."

"That's right," Emily said. "I'm reading the road signs. It's Highway 50, and it goes to Ely, Nevada."

"The road's quiet," Sean said, "but not that lonely."

He'd actually driven Highway 50 on one of his trips between San Francisco and his parents' house in Denver. On the stretch across Nevada, there were maybe fifteen towns, some with populations under one hundred.

The good thing about the desolate road was that it wouldn't be difficult to keep track of the orange truck. The negative was that there was nowhere to hide. If he didn't stick the trackers onto the truck soon, he'd never be able to sneak up and do it.

Finally, just outside Ely, the truck made a rest stop. If Levine and the other guards had been decent human beings, they would have made sure the people in the back of the truck were okay. That didn't appear to be part of their plan.

Sean drove up a gravel road behind the gas station and parked on a hillside behind a thicket of juniper and scrub oak. With the tracking devices in his pocket, he started down the hill. Emily caught his arm.

"One kiss," she said.

They made it a quick one.

Emily paced behind the car, stretching her legs after too many hours sitting. She needed to take her turn behind the wheel. Sean was exhausted, and she wanted to help.

Looking for a vantage point, she moved along the edge where the hill dropped off. Behind a clump of sagebrush, she crouched down and lifted the binoculars to watch Sean. He'd found a hiding place behind the gas station, not far from the orange truck.

Her heart beat faster as she realized he was in danger. He had to stay safe, had to stay in one piece. She couldn't bear to lose him again. But that was exactly what was going to happen.

She saw him dart forward and place the tracking devices, and then she lowered the binoculars. Their investigation was wrapping up. Soon, it would be over, and Sean would leave her. If they couldn't be in love, they couldn't be together. He'd be gone.

Behind her right shoulder, she heard the sound of a footstep. Someone was approaching the rental car and being none too subtle about it. She couldn't see him but as soon as she heard him wheezing from the hike up the hill, she knew it was Bulldog.

He whispered her name. "Emily. Are you here, Emily?"

What kind of game is he playing? She still had her stun gun in her pocket and wouldn't hesitate to zap him. But that meant getting close, and she preferred to keep her distance.

Again he called to her. "Come out, Emily. I have a surprise for you."

She ducked down, making sure he couldn't see her.

"Forget you," he said. "I'm outta here."

She heard him walking away and knew he'd take the gravel road rather than scrambling up and down the hillside. She scooted around the shrubs and sagebrush to get a peek at Bulldog and see what he was doing. He jogged down the hill toward the truck. Before reaching the gas station, he paused and looked back toward the rental car.

Incongruously, he held a cell phone in his hand. With his chubby fingers, he punched in a number. The answering ring came from the rental car. That innocent sound was the trigger.

The car exploded in a fierce red-hot ball of fire.

The impact knocked her backward and she sat down hard. Her ears were ringing, and she fell back, lying flat on the dusty earth, staring up at a hazy sky streaked with black smoke from the explosion and licked with flames. The earth below her seemed to tremble with the force of a second explosion. Vaguely she thought it must be the gas tank.

Sprawled out on the ground, she was comfortable in spite of the heat from the flames and the stench of the smoke. Moving to another place might be wise. There was a lot of dry foliage. If it all caught fire, there would be a major blaze. Her grip on consciousness diminished. A soft, peaceful blackness filled her mind.

Sean was with her. He scooped her up and carried her down the hill to the gas station. The orange truck was gone.

In the gas station office, he sat her in a chair and leaned close. "Emily, can you hear me?"

"A little."

"Do you hurt anywhere?"

She stretched and wiggled her arms and legs. Nothing was broken, but she was as stiff and sore as though she'd run a marathon. "I do hurt a little."

"Where?"

"All over." Though wobbly in the knees, she rose to her feet. She grabbed the lapels of his jacket and stared into his face. "I. Love. You."

She wasn't supposed to say that, but she meant it. If he said it back, they'd be on the same page. It would mean they should be married, again. *Say it, Sean.*

"Emily." He kissed the tip of her nose. "You need to sit down."

He guided her back into the chair, brought her cold water and a damp washrag from the restroom. Her hearing was starting to return as she watched the volunteer fire brigade charge past the gas station windows and attack the blaze.

"It was Bulldog," she said to Sean. "He set off a bomb."

"I know."

"How did he know I was with the car?"

He shrugged. "He must have spotted you through binoculars. I was worried that they'd notice us following."

"Did you take care of the plants?"

"Mission accomplished." He ran his thumb across her lips. "You're going to be okay. I want you to stay here. I'll come back for you."

Not a chance. "This is my investigation. You're not going to leave me behind."

He didn't argue with her. As she drank her water and nibbled a sandwich the gas station owner had given her, she was aware of Sean striding around, yakking into his cell phone and making plans. If he had figured out some way to follow Levine, she was coming with him, and she told him so after he loaded her into the back of the local sheriff's car, and they went for a short ride. Had she really said, "I love you"?

As they sat in a pleasant lounge in the Ely airport, Emily's mind began to clear. She was picking up every third or fourth word as Sean buzzed around the room, talking on two phones at once. She figured, from what

Sean was saying, that Dylan was able to track the orange truck. Levine wasn't getting away; he was driving into a trap.

The local sheriff and some of his deputies were in the lounge with her. Law enforcement was involved, and she was glad. She and Sean had taken enough risks. *Like saying I love you?* It was time for somebody else to step up.

Sean sat beside her. "It's almost over."

With all the excitement and confusion swirling around them, she had only one cogent thought. She loved him.

"I can't take it back," she said. "I can't lie."

"You love me," he said.

Not to be outdone, she said, "And you love me right back."

He gently kissed her, and she drifted off into a lovely semiconscious state. Still clinging to her bliss, she boarded a private plane flown by none other than their buddy David Henley. This Cessna wasn't as big or as fancy as the Gulfstream they'd taken to San Francisco, but she liked the ride.

"Sean, where are we going?"

"Aspen."

"Of course."

It made total sense. They'd gone from intense danger in San Francisco—crooked FBI agents, the crime boss's thugs and Chinese snakeheads—to the peaceful, snow-laced Rocky Mountains. She smiled. "I think we should live in Colorado."

"As you wish," he said.

"I also think I'm awake," she said. "Can you give me an explanation?"

"Dylan's tracker worked. Levine and the two idiots drove the truck on Highway 50. The feds and law enforcement are keeping tabs on them. I thought we could join in the chase at Aspen."

"Why Aspen?"

"The timing seemed right," he said. "Ely is about eight hours from Aspen."

It occurred to her that the orange truck could keep rolling all the way across the country, leading a parade of FBI agents and police officers to the Atlantic shoreline.

But that was not to be.

By the time they landed in Aspen, Sean received word that the orange truck had stopped at a ranch in a secluded clearing. The FBI was already closing in.

He turned to her. "Do you want to stay here? I could arrange for your aunt to pick you up."

"I'm coming with you. I won't let you face danger all by yourself…"

"Half the law enforcement in the western United States will be there to protect me."

"But you need me, and I need you."

"I love you, Emily."

"And I'm a reporter." She gave him a hug. "I'm not going to miss out on this exclusive story."

Sean and Emily arrived at the scene in time to see the people in the orange truck go free, as well as dozens of other women and children who had been assembling electronics at this secluded mountain sweatshop.

Greg Levine was arrested, along with the rest of the

men working at the ranch and their leader. The big boss was none other than Frankie Wynter himself.

Three weeks later, when Emily's four-part article was published, she was able to say that Frankie had been charged with the murder of Roger Patrone. Though she knew Patrone was killed because he had saved three children and thwarted Frankie's operation, she managed to write her story without mentioning the kids. Liane Zhou deserved her family.

And so did Emily. Resettling in Denver was easy. She fit very nicely into Sean's house.

On the wall by the fireplace, there were two wedding photos: one from the original wedding and another from the mountain ceremony at Hazelwood.

* * * * *

Cindi Myers enjoys skiing, gardening, cooking, crafting and daydreaming. A lover of small-town life, she lives with her husband and two spoiled dogs in the Colorado mountains.

Visit the Author Profile page
at Harlequin.com for more titles.

SNOWBOUND SUSPICION

Cindi Myers

For D'ann

Chapter 1

"More snow forecast today for most of the state, with highs in the mid to upper thirties. Parts of the state could see accumulations of another foot, on top of already record amounts of snow this past week. Travel advisories remain active and avalanche danger remains high."

Bette Fuller switched off the radio and gripped the steering wheel more tightly. White flakes drifted down from the gray sky like glitter in a snow globe—so pretty unless you were the shaken-up person in the middle of the flurry. To the growing list of things she didn't like she added incessant snow. And driving in the mountains on narrow, two-lane roads with no guard rails and steep drop-offs. Flashing lights up ahead made her tense her whole body as she eased her Ford Focus past the Highway Patrol vehicle parked on the side of the road. The patrolman stood in the road, motioning traffic past what appeared to be a large boulder in the middle of the road. Bette averted her eyes and shuddered.

Cops. She didn't like them, either, and she was headed for a whole house full of them. If Lacy Milligan hadn't been one of her best friends in the whole world, she would have turned the car around and headed straight back to Denver. But Lacy was her friend, and it wasn't every day a friend got married. Not to mention, catering this wedding was a really big deal. Whether she liked it or not, Lacy was something of a celebrity in Colorado, and the press was sure to cover her wedding to Sheriff Travis Walker. The irony of that matchup made the media salivate—Lacy was marrying the man who had been instrumental in sending her to prison for a murder she didn't commit. The sheriff had redeemed himself by working to get Lacy released, resulting in a story the press couldn't get enough of.

This could be the big break Bette needed to really get her catering business on solid footing. What was a little snow compared with the opportunity to help a friend and advance her career? She had faced down tougher situations than this before. She hadn't always made good choices in the past, but she was a different person now. This time she was going to succeed.

Twenty minutes later, she drove the Ford underneath the welded iron arches that proclaimed Walking W Ranch, est. 1942, and wound her way down the plowed drive—five-foot walls of snow on each side of the single snowy lane. The drive ended in a cleared parking area, a short distance from a sprawling log-and-stone ranch house. Bette shut off the engine and let out a long breath. She'd made it. With luck, that drive would be the worst part of the whole two and a half weeks she would be here.

She climbed out of the car and stretched, unkinking muscles that had been tensed for most of the snowy drive. This was some place Lacy's fiancé—or rather, his parents—had. It looked like something out of a movie, or some Western lifestyle magazine. The front door of the house opened and a man stepped out onto the porch—a tall man in a cowboy hat and one of those long, leather coats with the cape about the shoulders. What did they call them? *Dusters*, that was the word.

The man in the duster raised a gloved hand and bounded down the steps and strode toward her through the still-falling snow. Her heart hammered painfully as she took in his broad shoulders and long stride. He might be dressed like a cowboy, but his attitude was all cop. She had been around enough of them the last few years to be able to spot that particular I'm-in-charge demeanor from across the yard.

"You must be Bette. Travis said you were supposed to be here today." The man stopped in front of her and offered his hand.

Tentatively, she extended her own hand, only to have it engulfed by his leather-clad paw. A tremor of a different kind traveled through her as her eyes met his steely blue gaze and she silently cursed. Of all the really inconvenient times for her to be reminded that it had been a very long time since she'd been this close to a good-looking man.

"I'm Cody Rankin," he said. "Travis and his brother are at work and I guess Lacy is in town, though she should be up here later today. Travis's sister, Emily, is around somewhere, but at the moment, looks like it's just you and me."

Oh, joy, Bette thought, though she didn't say the words out loud. Not that Cody Rankin wasn't a perfectly nice—and perfectly gorgeous—specimen of manhood. She just didn't want anything to do with charming men right now. Especially one who wore a badge. "Are you one of Travis's cop friends?" she asked. Better to get that part of the introductions over with.

"I'm a US marshal," he said. "Though I'm on vacation right now." He nodded toward the trunk of the car. "Can I help you with your luggage? Though I'm not sure where the Walkers have you staying—maybe one of the guest cabins."

"I'll leave the suitcases in the car until I find out where they want me," she said. "But I have a cooler that needs to go into the house." Before she had left Denver, she'd stocked up on fondant, meringue powder, good Belgian baking chocolate and a handful of other ingredients she wasn't sure she would be able to find out here in the boonies.

"I'll get it." He waited while she popped the trunk, then reached in and hefted out the heavy cooler as if it weighed no more than a box of paper towels.

"How is it you know Lacy?" he asked as he led the way up the walk.

She was glad she was walking behind him, so that he couldn't see the way she stiffened at the question. Of course, she had expected it. It was the kind of thing people asked at weddings: "How do you know the bride?" She just hadn't had a chance to think of a good answer. "We met when we were cellmates in prison" wasn't the kind of answer that went over well in polite company, even though it was the truth.

"We've been friends a long time," she said.

He opened the door and led the way into a large great room, fire crackling in a woodstove against the back wall, trophy mounts staring down at them from near the log beams overhead. Bette followed Cody through a paneled door into an equally massive kitchen, the marble-topped island in the center of the room as big as a queen-size bed, stainless appliances reflecting the glow of cherry cabinets. He set the cooler in front of a French-door refrigerator and started to open it. "I'll put everything away myself," Bette said, rushing forward. "Thank you."

He straightened. "Okay," he said, then shrugged out of the duster to reveal a snap-button chamois shirt the color of light brown sugar that stretched over impressive shoulders. Well-fitting faded Wranglers and scuffed brown boots completed the outfit. Her gaze shifted to the gun in a holster on his hip. Discreet, but unmistakable. He put a hand to the gun. "I probably don't need this here," he said. "But habits die hard. I'd feel kind of naked without it."

His word choice created a disturbing picture. She turned away, hoping he wouldn't notice her reaction. "How was your drive from Denver?" he asked. "You're lucky you made it through. The pass has been closed."

"I know," she said. "I've been watching for my chance to get here." She leaned back against the kitchen island, arms folded. "The drive wasn't too bad. Are you in the wedding?"

"One of the groomsmen." He reached past her to pluck a grape from a bunch in a bowl on the island and she caught the clean aroma of shaving cream and fabric softener. "I took vacation to come up here early, thinking Travis and I could hang out before he tied the knot—but he's been working overtime on this serial killer case."

"Serial killer? Here?" Eagle Mountain was such a small town, and so remote. What would a serial killer be doing here?

"You didn't know? It's been all over the news."

"I don't pay much attention to the news." She had been too focused on preparing to come here.

"Three women have been murdered so far—one right here on the ranch." He popped a grape in his mouth and crunched down on it. "Be careful if you go anywhere by yourself."

"I'll keep that in mind."

"I'm surprised Lacy didn't mention it to you, but then, maybe she didn't want to frighten you away."

She met his gaze with a hard look of her own. "I don't frighten easily, Marshal Rankin."

"Aw, call me Cody. We're going to be seeing a lot of each other these next two weeks." He popped another grape in his mouth and crunched. "Now that you've arrived, the time here is going to be a lot less dull."

And just what did he mean by that? "I came here to work," she said. Not only had Lacy hired her to cater for the wedding, she was also preparing food for a bridesmaids' tea and the rehearsal dinner.

"If you need a sous chef, I'm your man." He straightened. "Seriously, I'm bored out of my gourd, with Travis working all the time. I'm not used to being this idle. My job is pretty intense, high-energy stuff—pursuing fugitives, most of whom don't want to be caught."

Bette was well aware of what US marshals did—she wasn't likely to ever forget being tackled by one and dragged, handcuffed, into a waiting car. How long into her visit to the ranch before Cody Rankin figured out her history? One phone call to his office was all it would take to get the whole sordid tale. Or he could just ask his friend Travis. Bette assumed Lacy had told her fiancé about her background. Yet he had agreed to let her come to his home and cater his wedding anyway. Now, that was true love.

A door at the opposite end of the room opened, ushering in a blast of cold air and a tall, angular woman wrapped in a blue wool coat. She stopped short upon seeing them. "Marshal Rankin." She nodded to Cody, then her bird-like eyes shifted to Bette. "Who are you?"

"I'm the caterer—Bette Fuller." Bette started around the island toward the woman, but the woman took a step back.

"I'm Rainey," she said. "And I'm in charge of the kitchen here. I told Travis he didn't need to hire a caterer. I'm perfectly capable of providing anything they need in the way of food—I've been doing it for years. But I guess brides these days want to be able to say they've had their wedding 'catered' by a 'chef.'" She sniffed. "Just stay out of my way when it comes to preparing regular meals. I have all the help I need from my son." She looked back over her shoulder. "Doug! Come in here!"

A man Bette judged to be in his late twenties or early thirties, his head engulfed in a fur cap with earflaps, shuffled into the kitchen, half a dozen plastic shopping bags suspended from each hand. He stopped short when he saw Bette. "Hello," he said, his eyes meeting hers, then darting away.

"This is my son, Doug," Rainey said. "He's been to culinary school and plans to open his own restaurant soon, though for the time being he's helping me here at the ranch. The two of us could have provided anything the Walkers need for the wedding."

Well, Bette certainly didn't have to wonder what Rainey thought about her being here. "I'll try to stay out of your way," she said. "I have some things that need to go in the refrigerator." She indicated the cooler.

"Not in here. Put them in the other refrigerator, in the garage." She jerked her head toward a door at the side of the room. "Doug, show her where to put her stuff."

But Doug had disappeared, the back door slamming behind him.

"I'll show you." Cody shrugged back into his duster, then picked up the cooler. "Nice seeing you again, Rainey," he called over his shoulder. "That omelet you made me for breakfast was divine."

Bette said nothing until they were in the garage, in front of an older-model—but still very high-end—refrigerator. She opened the door and surveyed the contents, which appeared to consist mostly of bottles of beer and a large cardboard box labeled Venison Sticks. Cody reached past her and helped himself to one of the sticks, which resembled a very thin frankfurter. "These are excellent," he said, tearing open the wrapper. "Travis's dad makes them, from venison he harvests himself."

Bette nodded and rearranged some of the beer bottles to make room for her chocolate and fondant. "I can see dealing with Rainey is going to be a barrel of laughs."

"Ignore her." Cody held the top of the cooler open for her. "Lacy and Travis want you here, and that's all that matters."

"Oh, I won't let her get to me," Bette said. "I've dealt with worse." Some of the guards at the Denver Women's Correctional Facility would have made Rainey look like a creampuff. She stowed the last of the items in the refrigerator and shut the door. "Are Mr. and Mrs. Walker around? I'd like to find out where I'm staying."

"They headed to Junction while the pass is open," Cody said. "Rainey might know." He looked doubtful.

Bette laughed. "If it was up to her, she'd put me in a horse stall or something." She shut the lid of the cooler. "No, I can wait until Lacy shows up."

She started to pick up the empty cooler, but Cody swiped it from her. She shrugged. If he wanted to tote her belongings for her, let him. It didn't mean she owed him anything.

Instead of heading back into the kitchen, he led the way out of the garage and around to the front of the house. "Okay if I leave the cooler out here?" he asked, indicating a spot on the covered front porch near the door.

"That's fine." She started to open the door but stilled at the sound of a car approaching. A red Jeep zipped into a parking place near the house. The driver's door flew open and Lacy Milligan, her dark hair in short layers around her face and topped by a pink fleece cap with an oversize pom-pom like the tail of a rabbit, her petite frame wrapped in a white puffy coat that reached to the top of her fur-trimmed boots, raced toward them, arms outstretched.

"Bette!" Lacy squealed and grabbed her friend in a

crushing hug. "Oh, it's so good to see you! How have you been? Was the drive from Denver horrible? Oh, let me look at you." She released her hold on Bette and took a step back. "You look fantastic. Oh, I'm so glad you're here."

"You look great yourself," Bette said. She couldn't stop grinning. Just being with Lacy again made her happy.

"I've been trying to make her feel welcome." Cody spoke up from his spot just behind Bette.

"Thank you, Cody," Lacy nodded to him, then turned back to Bette. "I'm sorry I wasn't here when you arrived. With the wedding less than three weeks away things are absolutely crazy. And with the road being closed and Travis working so much—I swear, I'm going to need a vacation when this is over."

She took Bette's arm and ushered her into the house. "I'm going to head over to the stables, if anyone needs me," Cody said, but Bette doubted Lacy heard. She was chattering away about the wedding preparations and the snow and Travis and who knew what else. Bette glanced behind her to watch Cody exit, his duster slung over one arm.

"Leave it to you to make friends with the best-looking single man in the place." Lacy nudged Bette. "It's a good thing you weren't around when I reconnected with Travis. He wouldn't have looked twice at me."

"I'm not interested in catching the eye of any man," Bette said. "That's how I got into so much trouble in the first place, remember?"

Lacy's expression clouded. "You don't hear from Eddie anymore, do you?"

Bette shook her head. "No. And I hope I never do."

Hooking up with Eddie Rialto had been the absolute worst decision she had ever made in her life. "I'm staying happily single from now on."

"Oh, men aren't all bad," Lacy said. "You just have to meet the right one."

"You're in love, so you think everyone else should be, too," Bette said. "That's sweet, but I'm here to work—and to spend time with you and wish you well. That's plenty to keep me occupied."

"And I'm so glad you're here." Lacy took both of Bette's hands in her own and lowered her voice, her expression serious. "Have you met Rainey yet?"

"Oh, yes, I met Rainey."

Lacy winced. "I'm sorry I didn't warn you. She can be a real grouch, but I guess she's worked for the Walker family forever, so I try not to say anything. She wanted to cook for the wedding herself, but thank goodness Travis backed me up when I said I wanted to hire you."

"I really appreciate your giving me this chance." Bette squeezed Lacy's hands, then released them. "But tell me the truth—how many people know about me? How many people know the two of us met in prison?"

"Travis knows, of course. And his parents. I had to tell them. And his brother, Gage, probably knows. I don't think he and Travis have any secrets. But it doesn't matter. They know you served your time and paid for your mistakes, and that you're making a fresh start. They admire you for it, the way I do. And really, what can they say? I was in prison, after all."

"You were innocent," Bette said. "And Travis proved it. You never did the things you were convicted for. But I was guilty. I did help rob a bank."

"You made a mistake and you paid for it," Lacy repeated. "That doesn't mean you're a bad person."

Bette let out a breath, trying to ease the tension in her neck. "I'm glad Travis and his parents were so understanding." She glanced toward the door. "Not everyone would be."

"If you're thinking of Cody, I'm sure he doesn't know," Lacy said. "And Rainey doesn't know, so don't worry about her. Did you meet Doug?"

"We were introduced. He didn't stick around long."

"Just so you know, he has a record, too. He's supposedly reformed, but frankly, he gives me the creeps. Rainey won't hear a word against him, though, so if I were you, I'd have nothing but good things to say about her darling boy. You'll get on her best side that way."

"Does she have a best side?"

Both women laughed. Lacy put her arm around Bette. "We have you staying in one of the guest cabins," she said. "It's adorable, plus you'll have your privacy. Come on, I'll show you. And then I want a nice long visit, so I can hear all about what you've been up to."

Chapter 2

Cody leaned over the stall to run his hand along the rough velvet of the mare's shoulder, and smiled as the animal nuzzled at his shirt pocket. "Sorry, girl, I don't have any treats for you today," he said. He'd have to remember to bring a few horse nuggets or a carrot with him next time he visited the stables.

The mare lost interest and turned away to pull hay from the rack on the wall and Cody sat on the feed bin across from the stall. He inhaled deeply of the oats-and-molasses aroma of sweet feed and the still-green scent of hay, and tried to quiet his racing mind. He'd been spending a lot of time here since coming to the ranch. The stables were a quiet place to think. Or maybe *brood* would be a better word. He wanted to be out there, tracking down and apprehending fugitives, getting bad guys off the streets. Instead, his supervisors

had forced him into taking vacation. One screw-up and
they thought the answer was time off, but they were
wrong. He needed to be back out in the field, proving
to them and to himself that he could still handle the job.

He hadn't minded so much about the forced leave at
first—he'd figured this would be a good chance for him
and Travis to catch up before the wedding. They could
go ice fishing, or maybe elk hunting. Cody could help
with work on the ranch. Instead, Travis was neck-deep
in the hunt for a serial killer, and Cody could do nothing to help. Sure, his friend had taken pity and let him
sit in on a few briefings, but Cody had no jurisdiction
and, really, no experience figuring out who committed
crimes. As a US marshal, his job was to find the suspects after they had been identified.

At least he wouldn't be the only outsider at the ranch
now. Bette Fuller had been a nice surprise. Somehow,
when Travis had talked about the caterer, Cody had pictured an older woman—maybe someone who looked
like Julia Child. Instead, a curvy blonde with the most
amazing blue eyes and a full mouth that smiled with a
hint of a challenge had emerged from the snowstorm
to make life on the ranch a whole lot more interesting.

She hadn't exactly warmed up to Cody. Was Bette so
cool to him because he was a cop, or a man—or both?
Never mind—he liked a challenge, and they had a couple of weeks to get to know each other better. And if
they did hit it off, she was from Denver, and so was he.
This could be the start of a fun friendship.

He stood. Time to head back to the house. Bette and
Lacy should have had enough time to swap girl talk, and
maybe he could find out from Lacy what was up with
Travis. As he exited the stables, the scent of tobacco

smoke drifted to him. He followed the smell around the side of the barn, where he found Doug Whittington, huddled out of the wind, with a half-smoked cigarette. "Hello, Doug," he said.

The young man jumped and made as if to hide the cigarette behind his back. "Too late for that." Cody joined him in the L formed by the stables and the tack room. "I don't care if you smoke—just don't set the barns on fire."

"Don't tell my mother," Doug said, then took another long drag. In his late twenties or early thirties, he had close-cropped brown hair and freckles. Cody had never seen him smile, and probably hadn't exchanged a dozen words with him in the week since he had arrived at the ranch.

Neither man said anything as Doug finished the cigarette. He threw down the butt and ground it into the snow with the heel of his boot. "Who's that girl?" he asked. "The one who showed up today."

"You mean Bette?" Was Doug asking because he was interested in the pretty newcomer? Cody couldn't blame the guy, though he didn't think the sullen cook was the type to catch the eye of someone like Bette. "She's catering the wedding."

"Yeah, but who is she? Where's she from and who decided she should come here?"

"She's from Denver and she's a friend of Lacy's."

"Did you know her in Denver?"

"No. Why did you think that?"

"The two of you seemed friendly, that's all."

Cody laughed. He wouldn't have called his interaction with Bette exactly friendly. "Are you worried she might take your mother's job?" he asked. "I don't think that's her intention at all."

Doug rolled his shoulders. "Just wondering. How long is she going to be here?"

"The wedding is in two and a half weeks, so I imagine she'll be here at least until then."

"Just wondering," he said again, then stuffed his hands in his pockets. "I gotta go."

He shuffled off through the snow, away from the house. He was an odd duck, Cody thought, but then, it took all kinds. He headed back to the house and found Lacy and Bette seated before the fire. "Cody!" Lacy greeted him with her usual enthusiasm. "We wondered where you had gone off to."

"I thought I'd give you two a little time alone to catch up," he said. He took a seat at the end of the sofa on one side of the woodstove, opposite Bette.

"So considerate," Lacy said. "Have you been bored out of your mind up here by yourself? I hope not."

"I'm okay," he said. "How's Travis? Any word on how the case is going?"

Lacy shook her head. "I saw him for a few minutes this afternoon, but you know him—he doesn't like to talk about cases. He did say he'd try to make it home for dinner."

"Being a cop's wife isn't for the faint of heart," Cody said.

"Oh, I know that." Lacy waved off his concern. "But I love Travis as much for what he does as for who he is. I like that he's so committed to doing what's right. If he wasn't, I'd still be sitting in prison."

Cody still marveled that Travis had ended up marrying a woman he had arrested for murder. Three years after her conviction, the sheriff had discovered new evidence that proved Lacy was innocent, and he had thrown himself into seeing that her conviction was vacated. After she was freed, he had enlisted her help to find the real murderer. Talk about an unlikely love story.

"I can't believe there's a serial killer in Eagle Mountain," Bette said. "Lacy, why didn't you tell me?"

"I didn't want to scare you off," Lacy said. "Call me selfish, but it's true." She leaned toward her friend. "You're not scared, are you? You don't need to be. I can't think of anything safer than being here at the ranch, with two lawmen in residence, now that Cody is staying here. And Gage is up here all the time, too."

"I'm not afraid," Bette said. "Though Cody said one of the women was killed here on the ranch."

Lacy frowned. "Well, yes, but that doesn't mean it was someone from here. We were having a scavenger hunt. People were spread out all over the place, so the killer could have sneaked onto the property at any time. But if you make it a point not to go anywhere by yourself, you should be fine."

"I'm happy to accompany you if you need an escort," Cody said, but the offer only earned him a sour look from Bette.

The door from the kitchen opened and Rainey emerged, bearing a large silver tray. Cody rose to help her, but she shrugged him away. "I can get it," she said, as she set the tray on the low table in front of the sofa. "I thought you might like something to snack on before supper."

"Oh, it looks delicious," Lacy said, scooting forward and helping herself to a cheese puff.

Rainey remained tight-lipped. "Have you seen

Doug?" she asked. "He's disappeared and it's time for him to help me with supper."

"I saw him a few minutes ago, out by the stables," Cody said.

"Probably smoking a cigarette," Rainey said. "He does that when he's upset."

Cody stuffed a sausage roll into his mouth, using it as an excuse not to comment.

"I can help you if you like," Bette said. She started to stand. "Just tell me what you want me to do."

"I can manage fine on my own," Rainey said. "I've been doing it for years. I'm sure you're the reason Doug is staying away. You've upset him."

"What have I done to upset him?" Bette asked, but Rainey was already walking away, back to the kitchen.

"I'm sorry she's being so rude to you," Lacy said. "I can talk to Mr. and Mrs. Walker if you like. I'm sure they would speak to her."

"No, don't say anything. I don't want to cause trouble." She stood. "I think what I'd like to do is freshen up before dinner. And I want to check out that cute cabin where you've put me. I didn't see much when we dropped off my luggage."

Cody stood. "Let me walk you out. My cabin isn't far and I should probably clean up before dinner, too."

"I don't think that's really necessary," she said.

"Humor me," he said, lifting her coat off the pegs by the door.

"Let him go with you," Lacy said. "I mean, you're probably perfectly fine, but until Travis catches this killer, it probably doesn't hurt to be overly cautious."

If looks could kill, Cody thought Lacy might have been at least injured by the glare Bette sent her, but she allowed Cody to help her into her coat, and she stalked out the door in front of him.

Cody followed, not trying to catch up with her, more amused than insulted. He half suspected Lacy of doing a little matchmaking, trying to throw the two of them together, but it probably didn't hurt for the women to be a little more careful until the murderer was caught.

Bette had been assigned the first in a row of four log guest cabins arranged alongside the creek, past the horse barns. Cody's cabin was next to hers, the other two reserved for wedding guests due to arrive later. Someone—one of the ranch hands, probably—had shoveled the stone walkway leading to the cabin, which, if it was like Cody's, consisted of a single large room and attached bathroom, and a small covered porch with a single chair and small table.

The sun had set, casting the world around them in gray twilight, but a light shone over the door of Bette's cabin. She stopped at the bottom of the steps leading up onto the porch. Cody halted behind her. "What is it?" he asked, then followed her gaze to the door. There, in bright red paint, someone had scrawled the words *Go Home!*

Once she was over the initial shock of seeing the message on her door, Bette was more angry than frightened. "I guess we know what Doug Whittington was up to when his mother couldn't find him," she said, starting up the steps, her key in her hand.

"Don't touch the door." Cody took her hand as she was reaching for the knob.

She glared at him. "What? You think you're going to find fingerprints? And then what? I don't think a nasty message is exactly a major crime." She pulled out of his grasp, inserted her key in the lock and shoved open the door. Not waiting to be asked, Cody followed her in—not that that surprised her. He was in full-on cop mode, on the case. Except there was no case.

"You don't know that Doug did this," he said.

"Unless his mother took a break from preparing dinner and ran out here with a can of red paint, my money is on Doug. No one else here is so anxious for me to leave." She looked around the room, but clearly nothing had been disturbed. Her unopened suitcases stood by the bed, which was still neatly made, a blue-and-yellow patchwork quilt draped across it.

"I'll talk to him," Cody said.

"No." She grabbed his wrist, squeezing hard, making sure she had his full attention. "Don't say anything. The best way to deal with this kind of harassment is to ignore it."

He set his jaw in a stubborn line and his eyes met hers—denim-blue eyes a woman could get lost in. Clearly, he wasn't a man who ignored anything. "If I tell him to lay off hassling you or he'll have to deal with me, I think he'll stop," he said.

"Your job is not to protect me," she said. "I'm perfectly capable of looking after myself."

He took a step toward her, so that the front of his duster almost brushed against her puffy coat. He was breathing hard, and she realized she was, too. She was torn between wanting to slap him and wanting to grab his shoulders and pull him down to her in a kiss. Her hormones were jumping up and down, shouting, "Big, sexy man—must have," trying hard to drown out her brain, which was pleading that she had more sense than this.

Cody's gaze shifted to her lips and she wondered if he was thinking the same thing—a dangerous thought that had her releasing her hold on him and stepping back, until she bumped into the bed. "You need to leave," she said, her brain momentarily getting the upper hand.

"Yeah, I probably do." He stepped back also, though his eyes remained locked to hers. "Just promise me if anything else happens—something more than annoying messages—you'll call for me. My cabin is next door." He nodded to his right.

"Sure." She hugged her coat more tightly around her body. "But nothing is going to happen. This is kid stuff."

"What are you going to do about the door?"

"I'll find something to clean the message off the door before anyone sees it."

"Or you could show it to the Walkers and let them know what's going on."

"No. I don't want to do anything to upset them. They've got enough on their hands, between the wedding and this whole serial killer thing. I mean, it can't be that easy, having two sons out hunting a murderer."

Cody wanted to argue—she could practically see the words building up in his head. She braced herself to reply, but instead, he turned and took hold of the doorknob. "Have it your way. But remember—I'm right next door if you need me."

He left and she dropped onto the bed, struggling to control her racing heart. Great. He was next door. Entirely too close for comfort. He had no idea, but Cody Rankin was a lot more dangerous to Bette's well-being than Rainey and her son.

Chapter 3

Bette couldn't decide if the dinner of roast beef, potatoes au gratin, green beans almandine and homemade rolls was designed to impress her with Rainey's prowess in the kitchen, or if it was simply the way the Walker family ate every evening. Add in the gleaming oak table, polished silver and dishes she guessed were hand painted, and the place screamed laid-back luxury. "Everything is so delicious," she said, determined to give credit where credit was due.

"I wish Travis and Gage could have been here," Mrs. Walker said, as she passed the dish of potatoes.

"They said they were sorry to miss eating with us, but they think they have a break in the case," Lacy said.

"I hope that means they're close to catching the murderer," Mrs. Walker said.

"And without another woman dying," Mr. Walker said.

Silence descended on the table, broken only by the clink of ice in glasses and the scrape of forks on china.

"Not the most cheerful topic of conversation," Travis's sister, Emily, said, slicing into her roast.

"One of the hazards of living with law enforcement," Cody said. "Lacy will get used to it."

"Oh, I am," Lacy said. "I think it's interesting, actually."

Mrs. Walker turned to Bette. "I hope you're finding the cabin comfortable."

"Oh, yes," Bette said. "It's beautiful. I'm going to really enjoy staying there."

"Well, if you need anything, just let me know," Mrs. Walker said.

"Maybe some more cleaner." Seated next to her, Cody whispered the words under his breath. Bette kicked him in the shin. She had refused his offer to help scrub the painted message off the front door, but it was true she had used most of a bottle of cleaner and probably ruined a bath towel cleaning everything up. Someone looking closely would probably still be able to see the shadow of the words, but tomorrow she planned to make a wreath or something to hang on the door to cover them up. She had gotten to be pretty crafty, all those years behind bars.

"If I wasn't staying here, you could have had my room," Lacy said. "Though you'll probably appreciate the privacy of the cabin."

"I thought you had a place in town," Bette said. She remembered Lacy's excitement over the apartment she had rented from a friend.

"I do, but Travis persuaded me that I should stay here until the wedding."

"He didn't like the idea of you living alone while this killer is on the loose," Mrs. Walker said. "And I don't blame him."

"It's very sweet of you to take me in," Lacy said. "My room is very nice."

"We thought about putting you in one of the cabins," Mr. Walker said. "But we didn't want to make it too easy for Travis to sneak off to see you. It's good for young men to have a challenge."

Lacy blushed bright pink, while the rest of the table burst into laughter.

The door from the kitchen opened and Rainey entered. "Does anyone need anything?" she asked, surveying the table.

"Everything is delicious," Bette said. "I'll have to get your recipe for the roast—it's so well-seasoned."

"I don't give out my recipes," Rainey said.

Bette kept a smile on her face. She wasn't going to let this old bat get her down.

"My favorite is the potatoes," Cody said.

"Doug made those," Rainey said.

"So I guess he made it back in time to help you with the cooking after all," Cody said.

"I told you, he was just out smoking." She turned on her heels and left them.

"I'm afraid Rainey's feelings are a little hurt that Travis and Lacy didn't ask her to cater the wedding," Mrs. Walker said. "I tried to explain we didn't want to burden her with so much work—and that it meant a lot to Lacy to have her friend do the job. I'm sure she'll calm down soon. In the meantime, I hope you won't let her bother you, Bette."

"Of course not." Bette took a sip of her water, aware

of Cody watching her. Honestly, did he have to sit right
next to her? She couldn't make a move without being
aware of him. When he reached past her for the rolls,
his arm brushed hers and a tremor shuddered through
her. So annoying. Tomorrow, she'd suggest she trade
places at dinner with Lacy or Emily. Or maybe she
could stick Travis next to his friend.

"What's next on the wedding agenda?" Emily asked.

"The bridesmaids' tea is Saturday," Lacy said. "Now
that Bette is here, we can finish planning that."

"It sounds very formal," Cody said.

"It's just a chance for us to dress up and eat lots of
fancy finger food," Lacy said. "I wanted something different from a bar crawl."

"There aren't many bars to crawl to in Eagle Mountain," Emily said.

"That's not going to stop the men." Lacy looked
down the table to Cody. "Gage told me he's planning
to kidnap Travis and force him to attend his bachelor
party Saturday night."

"If the roads stay open, he's booked a hotel in Junction," Cody said. "If not, we'll make do with Moe's
Pub."

"I'm rooting for Moe's," Lacy said. "There's no
way they can get into trouble there, with half the town
watching them."

Rainey returned and began clearing the table.
"Where's Doug?" Cody asked. "Doesn't he usually
help you with that?"

"He wasn't feeling well," Rainey said. "I sent him
to lie down."

"Let me help." Bette stood and began gathering the
plates on her side of the table.

"There's no need for that," Rainey said. "I can manage on my own."

"I want to help," Bette said.

Cody stood and began collecting dishes also. "I'll help, too," he said.

The two of them followed Rainey into the kitchen. "Put the dishes in the sink and then go sit down," Rainey directed. "I don't like a lot of other people in my kitchen while I'm trying to work."

"I'm the same way," Bette said. "You know just where everything is and how you want to do things, and it's annoying to have to keep stopping and telling other people what to do."

Rainey glared at her, but Bette kept smiling.

"I don't think your plan to win her over with flattery and kindness is going to work," Cody whispered as they made their way back to the table.

"Maybe I'm not trying to win her over," Bette said. "Maybe I'm trying to drive her crazy. Crabby people hate it when their enemies are nice to them."

A few moments later, Rainey entered the dining room, carrying a large apple pie and a carton of vanilla ice cream. She set them in the center of the table. "You can serve yourselves," she said.

"None for me." Lacy stood. "I have a wedding dress to fit into."

"Thank goodness, I don't." Bette picked up the knife and prepared to cut into the pie. "Who wants ice cream?"

Mrs. Walker declined, but everyone else wanted dessert. Bette dished up the pie, while Cody took charge of the ice cream. When everyone was served, Bette sat back and took a bite.

"What do you think?" Cody asked.

"It's very good." She took a small spoonful of ice cream. "A little sweeter than I like, and a dash more of cloves would have been a good addition—but very good."

Lacy, who had left the room, returned, phone in hand. "I just had a text from Adelaide Kinkaid." She glanced at Bette. "She's Travis's office manager."

"Is something wrong with Gage or Travis?" White-faced, Mrs. Walker half rose from her chair.

"They're both fine," Emily said. She studied her phone screen. "Adelaide says they've made an arrest in the Ice Cold Killer case."

"The Ice Cold Killer?" Bette asked.

"That's what they're calling the serial killer," Emily said. "Apparently, he leaves behind little cards—like business cards—that say 'ice cold.'"

"Who did they arrest?" Mrs. Walker asked, settling into her chair once more.

"I texted back that question," Lacy said.

The phone pinged and Lacy swiped the screen. Her eyes widened. "She says they arrested Ken Rutledge."

"Who is Ken Rutledge?" Cody asked.

"He's a schoolteacher," Lacy said. "He lives in the other half of the duplex where Kelly Farrow—the first murder victim—lived."

"So he's the serial killer?" Emily asked.

Lacy shook her head. "Adelaide doesn't say. She just says Travis arrested Ken and Gage and Dwight are driving him to the lockup in Junction tonight."

"Well, she can't say, can she?" Emily asked. "But if Travis arrested him—and he's really connected with the case—then he must be the murderer."

"This whole situation has been horrible," Mrs. Walker said. "But I hope it's over now."

"I do, too," Emily said. "In any case, I know I'll sleep better tonight, knowing a killer is behind bars."

"Speaking of sleeping…" Bette pushed back her chair. "I'm going to say good-night now. I still have to unpack, and I've had a very long day."

"The drive from Denver is enough to wear anyone out," Mrs. Walker said.

"I'll walk you to your cabin." Cody stood also.

"I don't need an escort," Bette said.

She could see in his eyes that he wanted to protest, but she didn't give him a chance. She hurried to hug Lacy, said good-night to the others and quickly made her way to the front door. To her relief, Cody didn't follow.

As she took the shoveled path toward the cabins, she told herself she really didn't have to run away from Cody Rankin. He was just another man, and she was a strong enough woman to resist his attractions.

Maybe she should go ahead and tell him she had a record. As a cop who devoted his life to putting away people like her, that information was sure to make him keep his distance.

Cody waited up with the Walkers until Travis came home. The Rayford County sheriff looked as sharp-pressed and alert as always, though Cody recognized the fatigue in his eyes.

"Well?" he asked, once Travis had shed his coat and kissed Lacy.

"Well what?" Travis asked, his arm around Lacy.

"Is Ken Rutledge the Ice Cold Killer?" Lacy asked.

"Probably not—though we're still tracing his movements around the time of all the murders."

"If he's not the killer, why did you arrest him?" Mrs. Walker asked.

"He attacked Darcy Marsh."

"Darcy is a local veterinarian," Emily told Cody. "She and Kelly Farrow were business partners."

"But you don't think he's the serial killer?" Mrs. Walker asked.

"We're not ruling that out completely." Travis moved past them, toward the fire. "I really can't talk about the case—except I'm wondering how you all already know about the arrest."

"Adelaide texted me," Emily said.

"Of course she did." Travis settled onto the sofa.

"She wanted me to know you were all right," Emily said. "And it's not as if something like that is going to stay a secret very long. I imagine most of the town knows about it by now."

"I imagine they do," Travis said, without anger.

"Did you have anything to eat?" Mrs. Walker asked.

Travis shook his head. "I'll get something in a minute. Right now, I just want to rest and warm up."

"What's the weather like?" Mr. Walker took a seat across from his son.

"It's snowing again. I told Gage and Dwight to hurry to get the evidence we collected to Junction. If one of the avalanche chutes on Dixon Pass lets loose, they'll have to close the road again."

"You'll be in big trouble if two of your officers get trapped on the other side of the pass," Cody said. "You might even have to deputize me."

"Only as a last resort," Travis said. He didn't smile, but Cody caught the glint of humor in his eye.

"Bette arrived this afternoon," Lacy said. "She's in the first guest cabin. Poor woman was exhausted from the drive." She squeezed Travis's arm. "I can't wait for you to meet her."

"I'm looking forward to it," Travis said, though he didn't sound very enthusiastic. In fact, to Cody's ears, his friend sounded like a man who was telling his fiancée what she wanted to hear, not what he necessarily felt.

Rainey appeared, carrying a tray, which she set on the coffee table in front of Travis. "I've been keeping this warm for you," she said. "Eat it now before it gets cold." Before he could reply, she had turned and fled.

"I see Rainey is in one of her moods tonight," he said. He leaned forward and picked up a fork.

"Her nose is out of joint because Bette is here," Lacy said. "But honestly, Bette is the nicest person in the world. If anyone can win over Rainey, she can."

"She doesn't have to win her over," Travis said. "She just has to ignore her and cater the wedding."

"Oh, Bette will do a good job," Lacy said. "A wonderful job. And she really appreciates us giving her this chance. It means a lot to her."

"Happy to help." Travis focused his attention on his plate. "I'm starving."

Mr. and Mrs. Walker said good-night, as did Emily, leaving Lacy and Cody alone with Travis. He was wondering if he should leave the couple to themselves when Travis said, "It would make it easy on everyone if Ken Rutledge turns out to be our killer. But I really don't think he is."

"What happened tonight?" Cody asked. "That is, if you think you can talk about it."

"I can talk about it to you." He turned to look at Lacy.

"You know I won't say anything to anyone," she said. "And this is your life. I have to be a part of it."

Travis nodded and looked thoughtful as he chewed, then swallowed. "Someone has been harassing Darcy since Kelly was killed," he said. "Someone ran her off the road, and someone attacked her and Highway Patrolman Ryder Stewart while they were skiing yesterday. Apparently, Rutledge was trying to frighten Darcy into turning to him for help. I think he saw his opportunity when Kelly and Christy O'Brien were murdered, but he went too far."

"You say he attacked Darcy again tonight?" Lacy asked.

"He kidnapped her. Ryder spotted the damaged snowmobile at Ken's duplex and figured out he was the man who had attacked him and Darcy. He found them at Darcy's house and rescued her."

"Why do you think he didn't kill the other women?" Cody asked.

"He has alibis for two of the killings. Pretty solid ones. And while he was willing to admit everything he had done to Darcy, he's adamant that he didn't have anything to do with the murders. We'll see." He pushed his empty plate away and stretched his arms over his head. "I need a shower and bed," he said.

Cody stood. "Good night. See you in the morning."

After the warmth of the fire, the cold hit him like a slap. He hurried along the path to the cabins, his breath fogging in front of his face, snow squeaking under his boots. As he neared the first cabin in the row—Bette's cabin—movement on the little porch caught his eye. He stopped and stared at the dark shape near the door of the cabin. He moved off the path and took shelter behind a tree. The shape on the porch didn't flee or move toward him—maybe it hadn't seen him coming.

No lights showed behind the cabin's drawn blinds. Bette was probably asleep, unaware that someone was outside her door—and clearly up to no good. Stealthily, using the cover of the trees, Cody moved closer to the cabin. The shape on the porch shifted slightly but didn't leave its position by the door. The shadow wasn't tall enough to be someone standing—Cody thought the man was crouching by the door, perhaps trying to jimmy the lock.

Reaching the end of the porch, Cody didn't hesitate. He made a flying leap and tackled the lurker, forcing him to the ground.

"Let go of me, you creep." An elbow thrust hard into his ribs, followed by nails raked across his face. "Get off of me!" The voice—definitely not a man's—demanded.

Cody couldn't get off fast enough. The beam of a flashlight blinded him. "Cody Rankin!" Bette said. "What do you think you're doing?"

Chapter 4

Cody held up a hand to shield his eyes and took another step back from an enraged Bette. "I saw someone on the porch and thought they were trying to break into your cabin," he said.

"I couldn't sleep and I was sitting out here, enjoying the moonlight." She gathered what appeared to be the quilt from her bed around her. A knit hat covered most of her blond hair, and thick gloves on her hands had probably prevented her from doing more damage to his face.

"It's zero degrees out," he said. "Who sits outside in that kind of weather?"

"It's not bad if you're wrapped up," she said.

He was feeling more foolish by the minute. "I'm sorry," he said. "I didn't hurt you, did I?"

She lowered the light so that it was no longer shining in his eyes. "You scared me half to death, but I'm not hurt. What about you?"

He rubbed his side. "My ribs are going to be sore for a few days, I think."

"Serves you right. Who appointed you my personal protector, anyway?"

"I was on my way back to my cabin and I saw someone lurking on your porch. Someone I didn't think should be there. And protecting people is what I do."

"No, you pursue them."

"I pursue bad guys as a way of protecting law-abiding citizens," he countered.

"Well, you can stop pursuing me."

He started to argue that he wasn't pursuing her, but he was tired of standing out here in the freezing cold. "I'm going to bed," he said, and limped past her.

"You are hurt!" She touched his shoulder, stopping him.

"I've dealt with worse."

"Sure you have, tough guy." She wrapped both hands around his biceps. "Come inside and let me have a look. You might have broken ribs."

He let her lead him into her cabin. Inside, warmth wrapped around him like a cocoon. He sank into the single armchair while she went around turning on lights. She dropped the quilt back onto the bed and divested herself of hat and gloves, revealing herself dressed in knit leggings and a long sweater that clung to every curve. "Take off your jacket and pull up your shirt so I can check your ribs," she said.

He took off the jacket, then took off the shirt, as well. When she turned toward him again he was standing beside the chair, naked from the waist up, and enjoying seeing her flustered. "I didn't tell you to get undressed," she said, avoiding his gaze.

"It's easier this way." He held his arms out to his sides, wincing only a little from the effort.

She moved closer and, after a brief hesitation, felt gently along his rib cage, where a faint bruise was already starting to show. Now it was his turn to be unsettled, the silken touch of her hand sending a jolt of desire straight to his groin. He shifted, trying to get comfortable in an impossibly uncomfortable situation.

She looked up, her eyes soft with concern. "I'm sorry. Did that hurt?"

"No." He took a step back. It was either that or pull her into his arms and kiss her until she was as hot and breathless as he felt. Or until she punched him in the mouth for presuming too much. He reached for his shirt. "I'll be fine," he said. "A little sore, but I guess that's no more than I deserve." He turned away, trying to hide his arousal. "I'll just use your bathroom, then say good-night."

In the bathroom, he splashed cold water on his face and practiced deep breathing until he had himself under control. Unfortunately, every breath pulled in the soft, feminine scent of Bette's perfume, which did little to lessen his arousal. For whatever reason, Bette Fuller checked every box on his list. His head could tell him to play it cool and keep his distance, but his body was determined to go full-on caveman.

He looked around for a towel on which to dry his hands and wipe his face. Finding none, he opened the cabinet beneath the sink. He spotted a stack of hand towels, but as he reached for one, his hand knocked against something. Crouching and peering into the cabinet, he spotted a paintbrush—and a can of red paint.

The same crimson color that had been used to paint the warning message on her cabin door.

Bette paced while Cody was in the bathroom, trying desperately to cool down and calm herself and act like a sensible woman instead of some sex-starved maniac. The sight of Cody Rankin, all six-pack abs and muscular chest, was one that would haunt her dreams—and her fantasies—for no doubt years to come. She wouldn't have been surprised if she had seared her fingers touching him—he was that hot.

And she was in so much trouble if she even thought about fulfilling the fantasies he inspired. She had lost her head over a man like this before, and he had come close to ruining her life. She didn't put Cody in the same category as Eddie, but he had the same potential to distract her from her goals and make her act recklessly.

The door to the bathroom opened and he emerged—fully dressed and looking grim. Obviously, she had injured him worse than she thought. She straightened. She wasn't going to feel remorse over that. He deserved a little pain for tackling her like that.

She expected him to head for the door, but instead, he sat in the chair again. "Tell me a little more about yourself," he said. "How, exactly, do you know Lacy?"

She frowned. She was tired, it was late and this was no time for a get-to-know-all-about-each-other conversation. Then again, she had been looking for a way to put some distance between herself and this sexy cop. The truth was sure to do that.

She sat on the end of the bed and pulled one end of

the quilt across her lap. "We were cellmates in prison." She kept her head up, defiant. She wasn't proud of what she'd done, but she wasn't going to deny it, either.

He blinked. Clearly, he hadn't expected that one. She waited, then he asked the question she had known would come next. "What were you doing in prison?" he asked.

"Ten years for robbing the bank where I worked as a teller," she said. "Though I was paroled early because I was such a model prisoner."

His eyes narrowed. "So you admit you're guilty."

"Oh, yes. There were five of us—four of us were caught. I was the person on the inside. It was the stupidest thing I ever did and I don't intend to so much as jaywalk from here on out."

"You robbed a bank," he repeated.

"The man I was living with at the time was the one who waved a gun around and demanded the money—I only silenced the alarm and let him out the back door. That made me just as guilty, of course."

"Why did you do it?"

"Because I was stupid. Over a man." She stood. "That's a mistake I won't make again, either."

"Does Travis know about this?"

"Of course he does. And his parents. I wouldn't ask them to invite me into their home without being honest about my past. I appreciate the chance they're giving me to start over. Their trust really means a lot."

He rose also and stood looming over her—still sexy, but also menacing. She had to force herself to stand firm and not shrink under his cold gaze. "I hope their trust isn't misplaced," he said.

"It isn't," she said, licking her suddenly dry lips.

The lines around his eyes tightened. "Just know, I'm going to be keeping an eye on you," he said.

Delivered in another tone of voice, the words might have been a sexy come-on. But Bette heard only warning behind the words—the words of a cop to a suspect. Though she had achieved her goal of putting emotional distance between herself and Cody, her success left a heaviness in her heart. She supposed part of her had hoped Cody Rankin would be different—able to forgive, even if he couldn't forget.

Cody lay awake for several hours that night, trying to make sense of that paint can and brush under the sink in the bathroom of Bette's cabin. Surely she would have mentioned finding them there when she pulled out the cleaner and towels to clean the paint off the door.

But she wouldn't have mentioned them if she had known all along the paint was there—known because she had put it there herself, and used it to paint that message. But why? So that he would see it and feel protective?

No—that wasn't her game. She definitely didn't like him hovering too close. And she hadn't put the message there in order to make a fuss with the Walkers—she had refused to mention the incident, and had made him promise not to, either.

But he couldn't assume her motives were those of most law-abiding people, he reminded himself. She had a record. She had admitted to the bank robbery with scarcely a trace of shame. Oh, she had made all the right noises about having learned her lesson and intending to go straight, but how many times had he heard that kind of talk before? Just because she had big blue eyes and a sweet, sincere manner—and a body that made it difficult for him to think straight—didn't mean they shouldn't all be on their guard around her. If she was concocting some scam to cheat his friend or his friend's family, she was going to have Cody to deal with—and he'd make sure her punishment was swift and sure.

On this disturbing thought, he fell asleep, and woke at dawn, stiff and sore. After a hot shower, he walked up to the ranch house, thankful that he didn't run into Bette. He found Travis alone in the dining room, eating breakfast. "Where is everyone?" Cody asked, helping himself to coffee from a pot on the sideboard.

"We're the early birds," Travis said.

Cody sat, moving gingerly still.

"What's up with you?" Travis asked. "You take a fall or something yesterday?"

"Something like that." Cody changed the subject. "What do you know about your caterer, Bette Fuller?" he asked.

Travis frowned. "Why do you ask?"

"She told me she and Lacy were cellmates—that she served time for bank robbery. She admitted it outright."

"Lacy says she was led astray by her boyfriend, a longtime felon named Edward Rialto."

"Do you believe that?"

"It happens." Travis spread jam on a slice of toast. "And I did check on her—she didn't have so much as a traffic ticket before the robbery."

"She said they caught all but one of the people involved in the robbery," Cody said.

"That's right. The getaway driver evaded capture," Travis said. "Apparently, the car he was driving struck and killed a pedestrian while the gang was fleeing from the bank. He's wanted for vehicular manslaughter as well as bank robbery. The others refused to identify him."

"Including Bette?" Continued loyalty to her "gang" didn't sound good to him.

"She said she had only seen him once, for a few minutes, that they hadn't been introduced and she couldn't identify him."

"Convenient." Cody scooped up a forkful of eggs. "I know I don't have to tell you to be careful, but I'm going to play the role of concerned friend and tell you anyway."

Travis set down his coffee cup and studied Cody. "What's wrong? Has Bette done something, or said something, that's disturbed you?"

Cody thought about mentioning the can of paint and the message on Bette's door, then thought better of it. He had no real proof Bette had put the message there herself, and no motive for her to have done so. Right now, Travis and his parents had accepted having a convicted felon catering the wedding. Cody had no grounds for upsetting them. "No, I just wanted to know more about her. What are you up to this morning?" he asked.

"I'm going to stay here this morning, catching up on paperwork. Gage texted me late last night—he and Dwight made it back to town about two in the morning. I've got two other deputies on duty, and I'll go into the office about noon."

"Do you have other suspects for the murders?"

"Not really." Travis pushed back his empty plate and held his coffee mug in both hands. "There are a few possibilities, but no one who lines up for everyone. The only connection the women have is that they were all in their twenties or thirties, and they all lived here in Eagle Mountain." He pushed back his chair. "There's still a lot to sift through. We'll find him."

"Let me know if there's anything I can do to help."

"Sure. What are your plans for the day?"

"I thought I'd go ice fishing, over on Lake Spooner."

"Sounds good. If you catch enough, maybe we can have a fish fry. There's a bunch of fishing gear in the tack room, if you want to borrow any. I think there's even an ice auger in there." He pushed back his chair. "I'd better get to work. Talk to you later."

At breakfast her first morning at the ranch, Bette waited anxiously for Cody to appear. Not that she was looking forward to seeing him again after their tense parting the night before, but since he was the only person who knew about the message that had been painted on the door of her cabin, he was the only one she could confide in now.

This morning, while getting ready for a shower, she had retrieved a towel and washcloth from beneath the bathroom sink and been startled to discover a paintbrush and a can of red paint. She had even cried out, as if she had encountered a snake under there. She was positive the paint hadn't been there earlier, and she wasn't sure what to do about it now. She hated the idea that someone had come into her cabin while she wasn't there, but she didn't know if she should say anything to the Walkers. Cody might not be her friend, but he might have some idea about what she should do.

"Good morning!" Lacy greeted Bette with a hug and walked with her to the breakfast table, where Mr. and Mrs. Walker and Emily were eating.

"Good morning," Mrs. Walker said. "I hope you slept well."

"I was fine," Bette said. No sense revealing she had lain awake for hours, fretting and furious about Cody Rankin. In the cold light of day, it seemed foolish to waste any time thinking about a man like that.

"Glad to hear it." Mrs. Walker smiled. "I know you and Lacy are working on plans for the tea this morning. You're welcome to anything in the house you need in the way of furniture or decorations or ingredients. Just help yourself."

"Thanks," Bette said. "That's very generous."

Mr. Walker checked his watch, then pushed back his chair. "We'd better be going," he said to his wife.

She laid her napkin beside her chair and stood. "We'll see you girls later."

"I have to go, too," Emily said. "I have a conference call."

"I thought you were off school for winter break," Lacy said.

"I am. But research projects don't stop just because school isn't in session. I need to meet by phone with my colleagues about a research grant."

"Emily is an economics graduate student at Colorado State University," Lacy said when she and Bette were alone.

"How is school going for you?" Bette asked as she added cream to her coffee. She recalled her friend had used part of the wrongful conviction settlement money she had received from the state to finance her education.

"I'm only just starting out, but I'm loving it so far," Lacy said. "I'm really looking forward to being a teacher."

Travis joined Bette and Lacy as the women were finishing up their breakfast. Bette had seen pictures of the sheriff before—his efforts to clear Lacy's name, and their subsequent engagement, had made the pages of the Denver paper. But in person he was both more handsome, and more forbidding, than she had imagined. Certainly he welcomed her warmly enough, but it was clear he was tired, and probably distracted by his case.

"You're up early," Lacy said, after the introductions had been exchanged and Travis informed them that he had already had breakfast. "You've been working some long hours lately."

"I'm going to stay around here this morning and catch up on some paperwork," he said. "There are too many interruptions at the office."

"Good idea," Lacy said. "Have you seen Cody this morning? He wasn't at breakfast with everyone else."

"He said something about going ice fishing," Travis said.

Or maybe he's avoiding me, Bette thought. But the marshal didn't strike her as a man who avoided much of anything.

Cody finished his breakfast, then collected his coat and his car keys and headed to the tack room. No sign of Doug Whittington stealing a cigarette this morning. He found the fishing gear and selected what he'd need and loaded it into the RAV4 he used as his personal vehicle.

The day was sunny, though bitingly cold, the sky free of clouds and a blindingly bright blue. The road to the lake had been plowed, only a thin layer of snow left in place. Dark evergreens crowded close to the side of the narrow track in a wall that looked almost impenetrable. He passed a pair of cross-country skiers and waved, then turned onto the narrower Forest Service track that led to the lake. This road hadn't seen a plow, but enough traffic to the lake and backcountry ski trails had packed it down so that Cody's RAV4 had little trouble navigating.

Just before he reached the lake, he spotted a silver Hyundai pulled to the side of the road ahead. He passed it slowly. It appeared to be empty, but this was a funny place to park. The snow around the vehicle was churned up, as if several people had been walking around it. He drove on, but something about the vehicle nagged at him, so he decided to go back.

He parked across the road and about fifty yards away from the Hyundai and walked slowly toward it, keeping to the center of the road until he was even with the driver's side door. Then he approached cautiously and peered inside.

A woman stared up at him from the passenger seat, as dead and lifeless as a store mannequin.

Chapter 5

After breakfast, Lacy and Bette moved to the sun-room, just off the main room, to plan the bridesmaids' tea to be held that Saturday. Windows on three sides sent sunlight streaming over plank-wood floors and an overstuffed sofa and two chairs in a faded floral print. Despite the bitter cold outside, the room felt warm and inviting. Bette brought along her planner, menu suggestions, pictures of possible table settings and a notebook for jotting down ideas, and spread these over the massive coffee table.

"You're so organized," Lacy said as she flipped through the pictures of place settings and centerpieces. "I'm very impressed."

"I want to do as professional a job for you as I'd do for anyone," Bette said. "It's very hard to start a new business when you don't have a lot of experience to show. That's why I really appreciate you and Travis giving me this chance."

"I promise to post lots of glowing reviews everywhere—and to recommend you to everyone I know," Lacy said. She put her hand over Bette's. "But I'm not doing this out of the kindness of my heart. I'm doing it because I want a great caterer for my wedding, and I know that's you."

"How do you know?" Bette asked. "The only things I've catered on my own are a couple of birthday parties and a bridal shower. And you weren't there for either one of them."

"But I've eaten your cooking," Lacy said. "And it's wonderful."

Bette couldn't keep back a snort of laughter. "You ate things I cooked in the prison kitchen." Once the warden learned that Bette had culinary training—she had been attending culinary school at night and working weekends for a caterer when she was arrested—he'd seen to it that she was moved to the kitchen. "That's not a great compliment."

"Your food was so much better than anything else they served," Lacy said. "I knew if you could work magic in that setting, you'd be fabulous when let loose on your own."

"I've been doing a lot of practicing since my release," Bette said. She was a good cook, and she had a gift for making occasions special. All she needed was a chance to prove herself—and Lacy and Travis were giving her that chance. She angled one of her notebooks so Lacy could see it. "Here are some menu ideas. If you want a traditional high tea, you'll want scones, with jam and clotted cream, fancy tea sandwiches and a variety of little cakes—maybe petit fours. Those always look so elegant. I could do chocolate-dipped strawberries, if I can get the berries, and there are lots of sandwich choices."

"It all looks wonderful," Lacy said, scanning the lists of dishes and their descriptions.

"How many people will be at the tea?" Bette asked.

"Let's see." Lacy sat back and began counting on her fingers. "There's my mother and Travis's mom, and my maid of honor, Brenda. She's married to one of Travis's deputies, Dwight Prentice. A second marriage, so it was a small ceremony, at Dwight's family's ranch over Thanksgiving. You haven't met her, but she's a dear, dear person."

She held up a fourth finger. "Then there's Maya Renfro—Gage's wife. She kept her maiden name. They had a quick ceremony, too—they ran off to Vegas one weekend without telling anyone. And she'll be bringing her niece, Casey, who is five. Casey is my flower girl, and she's so excited about it. So Casey makes five."

She held up a sixth finger. "Travis's sister, Emily, is one of my bridesmaids, of course." A seventh finger went up. "And last but not least, Paige Riddell. She used to run a bed-and-breakfast here in town, but after it burned down she decided to move to Denver. Her brother and her boyfriend live there—he's a DEA agent. I guess that's all—seven adults, if you include me, and one child."

"A lot of cops in the wedding party," Bette said.

Lacy laughed. "Yes, can you believe it? But I've found out when you hang out with one cop, a lot of his friends are cops, so that becomes part of your life."

"Besides Cody and I assume Gage, who are Travis's groomsmen?" Bette asked.

"There's Ryder Stewart—he's with the state highway patrol. And Nate Hall. He's with Parks and Wildlife."

"A park ranger?" Bette asked.

"Not exactly—a wildlife officer. I guess that's what they call game wardens these days."

So, lots of men with guns who were used to being in charge. "No chance of anyone getting out of line with so many law enforcement officers at the wedding," Bette said.

"When I first got out of prison, it made me nervous to be around so many men in uniform," Lacy said. "But it doesn't bother me now. Travis's friends are all really nice."

"You were innocent and they all know it," Bette said. "They can't look at me the same way."

"Don't say that!" Lacy squeezed Bette's hand again. "Travis was happy to have you here."

"Travis wanted to please you. And maybe, because of his experience with you, he's a little more forgiving than some. Not everyone feels that way." She thought of the cold expression in Cody's eyes last night.

"Has someone said something to upset you?" Lacy asked. "What is it?"

"I told Cody Rankin last night about my record," Bette said. "He wanted to know how I knew you and I figured I might as well come out with the truth. It would be easy enough for him to find out."

"How did he take the news?" Lacy asked.

"About like I expected. He's suspicious, wondering if I'm up to something. He doesn't trust me."

"He doesn't know you," Lacy said.

"I don't care if he doesn't like me," Bette said. "As long as he doesn't hassle me."

Lacy regarded her friend kindly. "I know it can be very hard to start over on the outside when you have a record," she said. "But it will get easier, you'll see. Your business will be a success, and while you might have to tell employers about your conviction, there's nothing that says your new clients ever have to know. In a few years you'll look back on your time behind bars as something awful that happened to someone else."

"Maybe." She picked up her pen. "Now tell me which sandwiches you want for your party, and which of these petit fours and cookies you want to serve. I'd suggest three types of sandwiches, three varieties of cookies and one petit four, or two cookies, strawberries and a petit four, or—"

"Enough!" Lacy held up her hands in surrender. "Too many choices." She scanned the lists again. "Why don't you tell me your favorites and we'll go from there?"

Thirty minutes later, they had a menu plan and a decor scheme. They decided to hold the tea in this sunroom and in addition to tea, they'd have champagne cocktails. The decor would be "winter wonderland," with lots of snowflakes and lace and little fascinators for everyone to wear in their hair in lieu of hats. "This is going to be so much fun," Lacy said.

She left to keep a hair appointment, and Bette headed for the kitchen, to see what ingredients were available, and what she would need to buy. List in hand, she pushed open the door to the kitchen. Rainey leaned against the counter, a cup of coffee in hand, a frown on her face. She straightened when Bette entered. "What do you want?"

"I'm making the refreshments for Lacy's bridesmaids' tea this Saturday." Bette walked to the refrigerator and swung open the door. "I wanted to see what ingredients were already on hand, so I'll know what to buy."

"Don't think you're going to go raiding my kitchen for what you need," Rainey said. "If you need anything, go buy it."

"I can certainly do that." Bette closed the refrigerator. Mrs. Walker had told her to help herself to flour, butter, sugar and anything else she needed, but Bette wasn't going to fight this battle. And she could understand that, if Rainey had purchased supplies with the intent to make certain meals, it could throw a wrench in her plans if Bette came along and used up all the butter in baked goods, for instance. Later today, she'd go into town and shop, and store everything either in her cabin, or in the garage refrigerator.

The back door opened and Doug slouched in. He looked different this morning, a hoodie pulled over his head, shoulders slumped. Rainey stared at him. "What do you think you're doing, coming in here looking like that?" she asked. "You haven't even shaved."

Doug rubbed his chin, the scratchy sound setting Bette's teeth on edge. "I thought I'd grow a beard," he said.

"I won't have one in my kitchen," Rainey said. "They're nasty."

Bette decided she had heard enough and retreated to the living room. She chose a chair by the fire and began to make a long shopping list. She hoped she could find fresh strawberries in Eagle Mountain in January. Real clotted cream was probably out of the question, but she could make her own.

The sound of boot heels on the hardwood floor behind her startled her, and she looked up to see Travis, in full uniform, crossing to the door. So much for sticking around the house to do paperwork.

He noticed her sitting by the fire. "Hello, Bette," he said. "Did Lacy abandon you?"

"She went to get her hair done. But I have plenty to keep me occupied, seeing to the tea this Saturday."

He nodded and slipped into his heavy black leather coat, with a shearling collar. He looked troubled. "Is everything all right?" Bette asked. Maybe he was going into work early because something had happened.

He frowned, as if unsure whether to say anything to her or not. "They've found another body," he said, after a moment. He opened the door. "I have to go."

He left, the door shutting softly behind him. Bette sagged back in her chair and stared at the flames dancing in the woodstove. Another body. Another victim of the Ice Cold Killer. The knowledge made her sick, and a little frozen inside.

Chapter 6

Cody stood with Travis and wildlife officer Nate Harris on the side of the road, as two EMTs carefully removed the woman's body from the Hyundai. Nate, a tall blond native of Eagle Mountain and another of Travis's groomsmen, had been patrolling in the area when the call went out requesting assistance. The men stood hunched against the cold, hands shoved into the pockets of their coats. "I was in this area yesterday and this car wasn't here," Nate said. "In fact, mine were the only tracks on this road then."

"I passed a couple of cross-country skiers on the county road," Cody said. "This road had obviously been driven on—I assumed by other fishermen headed to and from the lake."

"There's better fishing on Lake Monroe," Nate said. "This one doesn't get that much use."

The medical examiner, a portly man dressed in cam-ouflaged snow boots that came almost to his knees, an ankle-length duster and a wool cap with ear flaps, stood to one side, chin tucked to his chest as he watched a crew of EMTs remove the body from the vehicle. Travis had introduced him as Butch Collins, a retired local doctor who filled the role of county medical examiner. When the ambulance doors had shut, Butch moved over to join the three lawmen. "You know, when I took this job, they told me if I had to go out on one call a month for an unattended death, that would be a local record," he said. "This murderer seems determined to keep me busy."

"Any estimate on the time of death?" Travis asked him.

"I'd say she was killed last night," Butch said. "Maybe in the lab I can get a better idea, but she had been there long enough for the tissues to freeze."

"The low was minus nine last night," Nate said.

Butch nodded. "This looks the same as the others to me."

"Hands and feet bound with duct tape, throat slit," Travis said.

"Did you find one of the killer's calling cards?" Cody asked.

Travis took an evidence pouch from his coat pocket and held it so that Cody could see the white, business-card-sized rectangle of cardboard, with the block-print words ICE COLD. "It was tucked in her coat pocket," Travis said, stowing the evidence pouch back into his jacket.

Nate looked up and down the narrow road, snow-shrouded evergreens crowding in close on each side.

"Not much traffic out here this time of year," he said. "The road dead-ends at the lake. There aren't any houses or campgrounds along the way. Fishermen use it, sometimes skiers, but no one would be out here after dark in the winter. No reason to be."

"So what was she doing out here?" Cody asked.

"Maybe she wasn't here," Travis said. "Maybe the killer drove her here."

"And walked out?" Cody asked.

"Or was driven out," Nate said. He turned to Travis. "Didn't you tell me once that you think the killer might have an accomplice—or rather, there are two men working to kill together?"

"That seems the most likely scenario to me," Travis said. "Two men working together would have an easier time subduing the women and killing them quickly. Several times the bodies have been found in remote places, which points to someone transporting them there, then leaving in another vehicle."

"Is it twice as hard to find a pair of killers?" Cody asked. "Or twice as easy? You'd think there would be more evidence with two people. More clues."

"You'd think," Travis said.

"Tell me about the other killings," Cody said. "Were the circumstances of those similar to this?"

"Similar," Travis said. "Kelly Farrow was the first— a local vet. A really vivacious, pretty woman. She had only been in Eagle Mountain four months. A highway patrolman found her car up on Dixon Pass—Ryder Stewart. I think you've met him before. He's in the wedding, too."

"I remembered Ryder," Cody said. "Was the car like this—on the side of the road?"

"It had been buried by an avalanche and Kelly's body was inside. That night, the second woman was killed. Christy O'Brien. She had actually driven the wrecker that pulled Kelly's vehicle out of the snowbank."

"Did the killer know about that connection?"

"I don't know. The third woman, Fiona Winslow, died four days later, on my family's ranch," Travis continued. "We were having a scavenger hunt. She and Ken Rutledge—the man we arrested yesterday—were partnered for the hunt. They had a disagreement and she decided to leave him and join some girlfriends who were hunting as a team. She never made it."

"Rutledge couldn't have killed this woman," Cody said. "Not if he's in jail."

"He's still there," Travis said. "I already double-checked."

"Having someone killed on the ranch hits close to home," Cody said. "Do you think that was intentional?"

"Maybe. Leaving those cards is a way of taunting law enforcement. So would a killing right under my nose, so to speak."

"Who else was at the party?"

"Lots of people. There were a couple of college guys who came to town to rock climb and got trapped by the storm. They knew Emily from school and she invited them out. They were top on my suspect list, but I saw them yesterday at the gas station and they said they were headed back to Denver."

"Worth checking that," Cody said.

"Oh, I will."

Cody studied the draped figure on the gurney. "So this is the fourth victim."

"I was hoping the killer or killers took advantage

of the break in the weather and left town," Travis said. "But I guess we couldn't be so lucky."

The license plate on the car had been issued in Denver—the prefix told Cody that much. "Who was she?" he asked.

Travis consulted a small notebook. "Lauren Grenado," he said. "Her license information has an address in Denver. We found paperwork in the car that seems to indicate she's staying at a condo here in town."

"Is she married? Have kids?" Cody asked.

"The paperwork lists the rental in the name of Adam Grenado. I'm guessing that's her husband. We need to check at the condo and find out."

"I don't envy you that job," Cody said.

"I was hoping you'd come with me," Travis said. "I've called Dwight to stay here and finish processing the scene."

"I'll stay, too," Nate said.

"Then will you come with me?" Travis asked Cody.

Cody didn't hesitate. His friend needed backup, and Cody was more than qualified for the role. "Sure, I'll come."

Travis exchanged a few words with Gage, then signaled that Cody should follow him. They drove around the barriers and headed into town. Travis was on the phone for most of the drive—probably giving instructions to his deputies, and maybe checking in with Lacy. Cody wanted to call his own office, to find out what was going on—what he was missing during his forced time off. But he doubted anyone would tell him anything, and he might have to endure another lecture about how he needed to get his head clear and de-stress. No one seemed to realize how stressful it was to be out of the action so long.

Travis signaled a turn onto a road that skirted town and passed the high school. Three teenagers with snow shovels labored to clear the walkway in front of the school. Travis slowed and rolled down his window. Cody followed suit. "How's it going, boys?" Travis called.

"It's going okay." The tallest of the three spoke, a blond in an expensive down jacket and mirrored sunglasses. The other two boys looked up, their expressions unreadable.

"Keep up the good work," Travis said, and drove away.

Cody parked behind Travis on the street in front of a row of cedar-sided condos, probably purpose-built to rent to summer residents and winter tourists. He joined Travis beside his SUV. "Those boys back at the school," Cody said. "Community service?"

"Yeah. They were involved in a series of pranks that got out of hand. They were near the place where the second murder occurred and I was hoping they might have seen something that could help us, but they say no." He consulted his notebook. "Lauren Grenado was in 2B."

They climbed the stairs to the second floor and knocked on the door labeled B. Beyond the door came the sounds of a television, then someone's approach. The young man who opened the door wore a T-shirt and sweats, his light brown hair uncombed and the shadow of a beard across his jaw. He blinked at them, a little bleary-eyed. "Yes?"

"Adam Grenado?" Travis asked.

"Yeah." He squinted, as if trying to bring them into better focus. "Is something wrong?"

"We need to talk to you for a few minutes. It would be better if we came in."

"Oh, okay. Sure." He opened the door wider and Cody and Travis filed past. Adam rushed forward to sweep a pile of jackets off a chair and pick a blanket up off the floor. The room smelled of stale food. Adam grabbed the remote and muted the television. "What's going on? Is this about Lauren?"

"What about Lauren?" Travis asked. Cody sat back. He saw his role as an observer. He'd let Travis do all the talking.

Adam sank onto the sofa. "She left yesterday," he said. "We had a fight. I guess we got pretty loud. If some of the neighbors complained…" He let the words trail away and shook his head.

"Where was she going?" Travis asked.

"She said she was going out for a drive—that she needed to think."

"You'd had a fight?"

"A disagreement. I wanted to take some money her folks gave us for Christmas and buy a boat, but she didn't think we should do that."

"Where is she now?"

"I don't know. She isn't answering her phone." He picked up a cell phone from the end table beside the sofa and studied the screen. "When she didn't come back last night I tried calling and texting—after a while I'd decided she must have gone back to Denver. She did that to me once before—left me stranded without a vehicle."

"So you haven't been worried about her?"

"A little. But mostly I'm angry. Like I said, she's

pulled this kind of thing before—she can be very impulsive."

"What did you do last night when she didn't come back?" Travis asked.

"I got drunk and went to bed." He shrugged. "I'm not proud of it, but that's the truth. Why? What's with all these questions?" The first sign of fear shadowed his eyes. "Is something wrong? Has Lauren been in some kind of accident or something?"

"I'm sorry to have to inform you that your wife is dead, Mr. Grenado."

He stared at them, eyes gone glassy. "No." He shook his head. "No. She can't be dead. She was fine when she left here last night."

"She apparently died last night. Marshal Rankin found her this morning, in her car on a remote Forest Service road." He nodded to Cody.

Adam shook his head. "No. That can't be. How did she die? Was there an accident?"

"No," Travis said. "She was murdered."

The echo of the word hung in the air, stark and ugly.

Adam stared at them a few seconds more, then buried his head in his hands and began to weep, great, racking sobs that shook his body. Travis and Cody waited a moment, then Travis said. "Mr. Grenado, we need you to pull yourself together so you can help us find who did this."

He nodded, and after a visible struggle, sat upright, though his voice broke when he spoke. "Who would do something like this?"

"What did you do after your wife left here last night?" Travis asked. "Did you follow her?"

"No. I stayed here." His eyes widened. "You don't

think I—I would never hurt Lauren. I loved her. Sure, we had had a fight, but we did that sometimes. It didn't mean anything."

"So you were here all night?"

"Yes. I told you."

"Is there anyone who can prove you were here all night?" Travis asked.

"No. I mean, I guess you could ask folks in the other condos if they saw me leave. But I don't have a car. Lauren has it."

"Do you know anyone else who might want to hurt her?" Travis asked. "Have you noticed anyone suspicious hanging around the condo, or following you while you were out?"

"No. Nothing like that. Lauren didn't have any enemies." He scrubbed his hand across his face. "Is this that serial killer? I thought I heard something about a serial killer. Did he kill my wife?"

"What do you know about the serial killer?" Travis asked.

"Not much. We're on vacation, so we haven't been following the news. But we were in a restaurant the other night and someone said something about this guy who had killed three women around here." He frowned. "He had a funny name—you know, how the press always tags these guys with nicknames. Like people would forget them if they didn't have a catchy handle."

"The Ice Cold Killer," Travis said.

"That was it. Did he kill my wife?"

"We don't know, Mr. Grenado," Travis said. "Do you know of any reason your wife would have been out on a deserted Forest Service road last night? Would she have gone there to meet a friend, maybe?"

"No. Lauren didn't know anyone here."

"Why did you come to Eagle Mountain?" Travis asked.

"We wanted a getaway, somewhere in the mountains. And the rates are good this time of year."

"What have you been doing while you're in town?"

"Just, you know—relaxing. We went out to eat. We rented snowmobiles and took them out one day." He shrugged. "We were just hanging out."

"And you didn't see anyone suspicious or encounter anyone who made you nervous?"

"No." His face crumpled again. "What am I going to do?"

"Do you have a family member you can call to come help you?" Travis asked.

He nodded. "My brother. He lives in Denver, but I know he'll come."

Travis stood. "I can send someone from my office to wait with you until he comes."

"No." He rose also. "I'll be okay. Am I supposed to do something else, about my car and about…about Lauren's body?"

"Someone from my office will call you later today with that information." Travis handed him a business card. "If you have any questions, or you think of anything else that might help us, call me."

"Okay. I will."

Travis waited until he and Cody were at the curb again before he spoke. "What do you think?" he asked.

"He's really grieving and logistically, I don't see how he could have done it." Cody glanced around the parking lot. "You'll verify he and his wife only had one vehicle here. And then there's that business card."

"Information about that card has been in the paper."

"So you're thinking this could be a copycat killing?"

"It could be, but I don't think so." Travis looked back toward the building. "I think Lauren Grenado went out alone at night and the killer saw her and took the opportunity to kill her, then drove her to that remote location, thinking it would be a while before anyone found her."

The burden of these killings showed on Travis's face. Cody knew he took each death personally. "I've asked the Colorado Bureau of Investigations to send some help," Travis said. "Now that the road is open, someone should be able to get through."

Cody nodded. "You've been hung out on your own until now. It's a lot for a small department to handle."

"Still, it's my county. There aren't that many people here—I should have been able to handle it."

Cautioning Travis not to be so hard on himself wouldn't do any good. He was wired to take responsibility—it was one of the things that made him a good sheriff. "Tell me what I can do to help," Cody said.

"Right now I need you to go back to the ranch and let everyone there know what's going on. Tell the women especially to be on their guard. They probably shouldn't drive anywhere alone. I already talked to Lacy."

"All right. But if there's anything else, you know I'm here."

Travis stared down the quiet street, snow mounded on the sides of the road, no sign of activity in the surrounding homes. If not for the knowledge of what had happened near here, it would be an idyllic scene of winter peace. "The killer is here, too," Travis said. "And I need to find out where, before he kills again."

Chapter 7

The town of Eagle Mountain might have been a village in the mountains of Switzerland or Austria—Victorian buildings lining narrow streets in a valley below snow-capped peaks. Glittery snowflake decorations adorned light posts along the town's main streets, and storefronts advertised winter sales. Bette guided her car slowly through town, struck by the jarring discordance of such horrible violence taking place in such a peaceful setting.

It hadn't taken long for news of the latest murder to spread through town. As Bette guided her grocery cart down the aisles of Eagle Mountain Grocery, she overheard customers discussing the murder, speculating on the identity of the latest victim and the motives of the killer. Most people seemed to think the woman who was killed was a visitor to town, since no one knew of any local who was unaccounted for.

Weather and news that the highway remained open were the next most popular topics of conversation, though some people were of the opinion that the town's reprieve wouldn't last. "Those avalanche chutes above the pass are full to bursting and all this sunshine is making them more unstable," one woman said to a friend as they perused the selections in the dairy case. "I'm stocking up while I can, before the snowslides start and they have to close the road again."

Bette selected several pounds of butter and two cartons of cream, then steered her cart toward the center aisles. As she had feared, good strawberries weren't to be had this time of year in the mountains, so she had switched her menu to chocolate-covered dried fruit. She was trying to decide between apricots and cherries when an attractive woman with streaked blond hair approached. "Excuse me, but are you Bette Fuller, the caterer?"

"Yes," Bette said, cautious in spite of the woman's friendliness.

"I'm Brenda Prentice." The woman offered her hand. "I'm Lacy's maid of honor. It's so good to meet you. Lacy has told me so much about you."

How much? Bette wondered. Did Brenda's friendliness mean she didn't know about Bette's past—or that she knew and had decided to give her the benefit of the doubt? Bette hoped it was the latter, but she knew better than to expect that. "It's good to meet you, too," she said, shaking Brenda's hand.

"It was so kind of you to come all this way to cook for the wedding," Brenda said. "I know it means a lot to Lacy."

"I was happy to do it." In her opinion, Lacy was the one who was being kind.

"I'm looking forward to the tea this weekend,"

Brenda said. "Such a clever idea to do that instead of a girls' night out at a bar."

"It was all Lacy's idea," Bette said. "But it should be a really fun party. Lacy said you're married to one of Travis's deputies."

"That's right. Dwight Prentice. We went to high school together, but it wasn't until after my husband died that we connected again."

"Lacy mentioned you're a newlywed."

"Yes. She still hasn't forgiven me for cheating her out of being a bridesmaid in a big, fancy wedding." She shifted the package of salad she carried to her other hand. "I'd better get back to work. I only swung by to grab something for lunch. See you on Saturday."

"It was good to meet you."

Bette took her time completing her shopping. Brenda had been very nice—exactly the sort of woman she would have pictured as one of Lacy's best friends. If Bette and Lacy hadn't been thrown together in prison, she doubted they would have ever made a connection at all. Lacy came from a conventional family in a small town. She had always been loved and protected and, even after she had been convicted of murder, her family and friends had stood by her.

Bette was a city girl from a broken home. She had been on her own since she was seventeen, and had never had much support from anyone. It didn't take a psychologist to see that was why she had fallen so hard for Eddie. He had not only promised to love and protect her, he had made her believe he couldn't do anything without her by his side. When he told her of his dream of opening a garage, she had believed every word, because she had always wanted to open her own catering business. When he proposed robbing the bank where she worked to get the money to make those dreams come true, she had hesitated only a few hours before he made her believe it was the right thing to do.

She had had years since then to regret her decision, and to see how Eddie had manipulated her. He had never had any intention of opening a garage, and the people he had introduced to her as friends of his who wanted to help had only been criminals like him, out for their share of the take. All Eddie's flattery and lovemaking had been a lie. He had singled her out for attention because she worked at the bank, and he recognized her as someone he could manipulate.

It was a good thing for her the police had caught the robbers. If her arrest hadn't halted her brief criminal career, there was no telling where she would have ended up. Now, thanks to Lacy and people like her, she at least had a chance to live her dream.

She paid for her purchases and loaded them into her car, then drove slowly through town. She had no desire to live in a sleepy place like Eagle Mountain, but she could enjoy visiting here. She hoped she would have the chance to come back in the summer or fall and explore the surrounding mountains more.

Reluctantly, she turned the car and headed back toward the ranch. She didn't look forward to the inevitable confrontation with Rainey when she went to unload the groceries she had purchased. She wasn't anxious to see Cody again, either, though she needed to talk to him about the paint she had found in the bathroom. And she needed to come up with a way to keep intruders out of her cabin.

Her mind full of these thoughts, she didn't notice the

vehicle coming up behind her until it was on her bumper. The dark SUV raced up behind her, the insistent blare of the horn shattering the peace of the quiet countryside. Alarmed, Bette steered her car as far over to the side of the road as she could safely go. The vehicle surged up beside her and she took her foot off the gas, anxious for it to pass. Instead, the car stopped in the road, and the driver got out. She had an impression of black—black pants, black gloves, black coat with the hood pulled up to hide the driver's face. As he raced around the car toward her, she pressed down on the gas, determined to drive away, but the tires spun in the soft snow. The man, whose face she still couldn't see, beat his hands on her closed window. Bette groped for her phone, to call for help. Then the window shattered. A large rock hit the side of her head, then the door opened and the man dragged her out, into the snow.

Snow had started falling again by the time Cody headed back toward the Walker ranch. Flakes whirled toward his windshield in a mesmerizing onslaught and his SUV plowed through already-forming drifts across the road.

So much for his fishing trip. Maybe he'd try again in a day or two, and this time, he'd ask Bette to go with him. It would give him a chance to question her about the paint and about her intentions toward the Walkers, without an audience to overhear.

He didn't see the car on the side of the road until he was almost on it. Snow drifted over the vehicle, which listed in the ditch like a boat taking on water. He braked hard and turned on his wipers in an attempt to clear the snow from his windshield. No movement in the other car, but the vehicle looked familiar. With a jolt, he realized it looked like Bette's Ford.

He punched the button to turn on his emergency flashers and stopped in the road, then bailed out of his RAV4 and trudged down into the ditch and around the car. The driver's side door was open, snow sifting over the upholstery. A large rock rested in the driver's seat. Cody stared at it, trying to make sense of the sight. Fields and woods lined this stretch of road, not rocky cliffs. For that rock to get there, someone must have thrown it.

And where was Bette? Had she gotten her car stuck in the ditch and decided to walk to the ranch for help? But that didn't explain the rock.

"Bette!"

The silence swallowed his shout. He stepped back, intending to set out to look for her. His foot struck something soft and yielding.

Something that groaned.

Bette lay in the ditch, snow sifting over her still body. Cody knelt beside her and felt for a pulse at her neck. Relief flooded him when he found the steady beat and felt the warmth of her skin. "Bette, wake up." He tapped her cheek with the back of his hand.

She groaned and rolled her head away from him.

He pulled out his phone and called 911. "There's been an accident on County Road Seven," he said. "About a mile from the Walking W Ranch. A woman is unconscious."

The dispatcher promised to send an ambulance and a sheriff's deputy. Cody pocketed the phone and examined Bette more closely. Blood oozed from a jagged cut over her left temple, but he could find no other injuries. She groaned again. Cody squeezed her hand. "Bette, it's me, Cody. You're going to be okay."

Her eyes fluttered, snow caught in her lashes. "What happened?" She stared at him, her gaze unfocused, tense with pain.

"I don't know," he said. "I found you here, in the ditch beside your car. You must have been on your way back to the ranch."

She moaned and tried to sit up, but he pressed her gently back down. "The ambulance is on its way," he said. "Don't try to move."

"I'm cold," she said.

Of course she was cold—lying in the snow. Cody stripped off his coat and laid it over her. "The ambulance will be here soon," he said, hoping the words were true.

"What happened?" she asked again.

"Something hit your head. I think a rock. What do you remember?"

She closed her eyes. "I can't remember. I was at the store, talking to a nice woman—Brenda. I bought some butter and cream." She shook her head, wincing. "I can't remember."

"It's okay. Don't worry about it."

"My head hurts."

"I know. It will be all right soon."

She didn't try to talk after that. Had she passed out again? Should he try to wake her? Her hand in his was so cold, a chill he could feel even through his gloves. He gathered her other hand between his palms and chafed them both gently. Her nails were short and she wore no rings—maybe jewelry got in the way of cooking. She had long, slender fingers and delicate wrists. He pressed her palms to his cheek—the skin was like satin and smelled faintly of roses.

She moaned again, and he quickly lowered her hands

and tucked them beneath the coat he had draped over her. It didn't feel right, to be studying her this closely while she was unaware. Where was that ambulance?

"Cody?" she asked.

"I'm right here."

"Did you come to arrest me?"

He stiffened. "Arrest you for what?"

"That's what you do, isn't it? You arrest people."

She stared at him, but he had the sense she wasn't really seeing him. "Only if they've broken the law," he said. "Have you broken the law?"

"That doesn't matter, does it?" she said. "You think I'm bad, and I'll never be able to make you believe I'm good." She closed her eyes again.

"Bette?"

She didn't answer, only moaned and shook her head.

The distant wail of the ambulance broke the winter silence. Cody stood and trudged out of the ditch, into the road to flag it down. It parked in the road behind his RAV4 and a middle-aged man and a slightly younger woman climbed out. "Emmett Baxter," the man introduced himself as and shook Cody's hand. "This is Joan Anderson." He indicated the woman, who was taking a large plastic tote from the rear of the ambulance. "What have we got?"

"I'm not sure." Cody led the way around the car. "She's got a head injury."

They knelt in the snow, one on each side of Bette, and opened the medical tote. Cody moved to the bumper of Bette's car, trying to get a sense of what had happened here. He could barely make out the tracks where her car had left the road and gone into the ditch. He wasn't trained in assessing traffic accidents, but he couldn't see any skid marks—no churned earth or deep ruts to indicate she had skidded off the road. Yet surely she wouldn't have deliberately driven into the ditch.

He moved to the front of the car. Except for the broken driver's side window, the vehicle appeared undamaged, though the snow might be hiding some ding or scrape that would tell a different story. Had someone sideswiped her and driven away? Had someone stopped after she had gone into the ditch and, instead of helping her, had thrown the rock through the window and dragged her out of the vehicle? The idea sent a chill through him that had nothing to do with the temperature.

Emmett stood and Cody walked back to join him. Bette was sitting up now, a bandage over the cut on her head. "How are you feeling?" Cody asked.

"I've been better, but I'll live." She looked more alert, though still in pain.

"Do you remember anything more about what happened?" Cody asked.

"No. It's all…just a blank."

"Short-term memory loss isn't uncommon with a head injury," Joan said. "Or with any kind of trauma, really."

"Will my memory come back?" Bette asked.

"Maybe. Maybe not," Joan said. "I wouldn't worry too much unless you start noticing bigger gaps."

"We can take her to the clinic in town, but they can't get her to the hospital," Emmett said. "Dixon Pass is closed again. Chute number nine let loose about half an hour ago. It'll be twenty-four hours, at least, before the road opens. More, if it keeps snowing."

"I want to go to the ranch," Bette said.

"I can take her," Cody said. "There are plenty of people who can look after her there."

"What about my car?" Bette asked.

"We'll get a wrecker, or maybe one of the ranch trucks, to pull it out later," Cody said.

"I'll need my purse and the groceries I bought."

"I'll get them." Emmett moved toward the vehicle, but stopped short when he saw the broken window and the rock. "What happened here?"

He started to reach in for the rock, but Cody caught his arm. "Don't touch anything," he said.

"What, you think someone did this deliberately?" Emmett asked.

"I don't know. But don't touch it. Just get her purse off the passenger seat." He scanned the interior. "The groceries must be in the trunk."

He took the keys from the ignition and pressed the button to unlock the trunk. He and Emmett were retrieving the grocery bags when a black-and-white sheriff's department vehicle parked behind the ambulance and Travis Walker got out. "I heard the call on the scanner, figured I'd better see what was up," he said. He looked over as Bette, leaning on Joan, came around the front of her car. Cody read the relief on his face and realized the sheriff had been worried the victim might be his fiancée, Lacy. "What happened?" Travis asked.

Bette shook her head. "I'm not sure," she said.

"The head injury is hampering her memory of the events," Joan said. She steered Bette over to Cody's vehicle and helped her into the passenger seat.

Travis walked around to the side of Bette's car, where Emmett was packing up the last of the medical supplies. "Looks like someone broke the window with that big rock in the driver's seat," Emmett said. "She must have been sitting in the seat at the time and the rock hit her on the side of the head."

Travis studied the broken window and the rock. "Where is this somebody now?" he asked.

"Bette was the only one here when I showed up," Cody said. "I didn't pass any other cars after I turned on the county road."

"Neither did I," Travis said. "And there aren't any houses between here and the ranch." He looked at Bette again. "She really doesn't remember anything?"

"She says not. It's a pretty nasty gash on the side of her head—she was unconscious when I got here."

"Good thing you showed up when you did," Travis said. "She might have frozen to death before anyone found her."

Cody had been trying not to think of that. "I need to get her to the ranch," he said. "But someone should take a closer look at the car."

"I'll take care of that," Travis said. "The snow is going to make finding tracks almost impossible, but I'll do what I can."

"Thanks."

He returned to the RAV4 and started it up, then turned the heater to high. "You doing okay?" he asked Bette.

"I'll be fine." She stared out the window, not looking at him.

What had she meant, when she had said he thought she was bad? It wasn't true. She made it sound as if he passed judgment on everyone he met, putting them into categories—bad and good. If he did do that, he wouldn't know where she belonged. She had a bad past, and he couldn't say he entirely trusted her, but it wasn't fair for her to say he had made up his mind about her.

When they reached the house, no one else seemed to be around. Cody helped Bette out of the car, his grip firm, yet gentle. "I'll be fine," she said, pulling away from him. "I'll just go to my cabin and lie down for a while." She tried to turn away but almost lost her balance.

"I think you'd better come into the main house for a little while," he said. He put his arm around her. "Let me help. You don't want to fall and bust open your head again."

She gave in and let him help her into the house. He settled her into a chair near the fire. "Thank you for your coat," she said, returning it to him.

He hung the coat on a peg by the door, then returned to sit beside her. "How are you feeling?" he asked.

"I wish people would quit asking me that."

"You'd better get used to it. How are you feeling?"

"I have a pretty bad headache," she admitted.

"Do you remember any more about what happened?" he asked.

"No." Her eyes met his, her expression troubled. "I'm sorry, I can't."

"There's no need to apologize."

"Hello, I didn't hear you come in." Emily came in from the other room, smiling, but her smile vanished when she noticed the bandage on Bette's head. "What happened to you?" she asked.

"I'm not sure." Bette touched the bandage gingerly. "Cody found me on the side of the road, in a ditch."

"Cody! What's going on? Did you call Travis?"

"He's still on the scene. Bette has a head injury—

maybe a mild concussion. She can't remember anything. I thought it would be a good idea for her to stay where someone can be with her until we're sure she's okay."

Emily sat beside Bette and took her hand. "You need to see a doctor."

"I called for an ambulance and the paramedics treated her," Cody said. "They couldn't take her to the hospital because an avalanche has closed the pass again."

"I didn't want to go to the hospital, anyway," Bette said. "I'm sure I'll be fine, once I get a little rest. I just wish I could remember what happened. The last thing I remember, I was in the grocery store. I met Brenda— such a nice woman."

"But how did you hit your head?" Emily looked to Cody. "You say you found her in a ditch?"

"Her car was in the ditch and she was lying in the snow beside the car," he said. "The driver's side window was busted out, and a big rock sat in the driver's seat. The rock probably hit her in the head when it went through the window."

"A rock?" Bette stared at him. "But how did it get there? I mean, I always see the road signs that say watch for falling rocks, but I never dreamed one could come through the window like that."

"This wasn't a falling rock," Cody said. "It happened in an area of open fields and woods. There isn't any place near there that a rock could have fallen from."

"Are you saying someone *threw* the rock at her?" Emily asked.

"We don't know," Cody said.

"Who would do something like that?" Emily asked.

He didn't see any point in trying to answer that question. "You might fix her some tea or something," he said. "She was lying in the snow who knows how long and she's probably still chilled."

"I'm sitting right here," Bette said. "If I want tea, I can get it myself."

"I'll get it." Emily stood. "I could use a cup myself."

She left them. Bette glared up at Cody. "Don't you have something to do?" she asked.

"I'm doing it."

"I don't like you hovering over me."

He leaned toward her and lowered his voice. "Want to tell me about the red paint I saw in your bathroom last night?" he asked. He hadn't planned to question her about the paint right now, but why not take advantage of the opportunity?

She gasped. "What were you doing snooping around in my bathroom?"

"I was looking for a towel and I saw the paint and a brush. The same color paint that was used to write that message on your door."

"Why didn't you say something to me about it then?"

"Why didn't you say something to me?"

"Because I didn't know it was there—not until this morning." She clutched at his arm. "I swear that paint wasn't there before last night. Someone—probably the same person who put that message on the door—must have come in while I was out and put it there."

"How did they get in? You locked your door, didn't you?"

"Of course I did, but mine might not be the only key."

"I'll ask the Walkers if there's another key."

"Don't." She drew back. "And don't look at me that way."

"What way?"

"As if you think I'm guilty of something."

"If you're not guilty of something, why don't you want me talking to the Walkers?"

"Because I don't want to worry them over something so stupid. It was just a childish message painted on my door."

"But who wrote it, and why?"

"My guess is someone who doesn't want me here. Someone who wants me to, as the message said, go home."

"I guess Rainey is at the top of that list. And maybe Doug."

"Probably. But it doesn't matter. I'm not going to leave, and there's no sense making a fuss. That's probably what they want. When they realize I'm going to ignore them, they'll have to give up."

"I'd think the Walkers would want to know if one of their employees is harassing a guest," Cody said.

"They have enough to worry about right now, with the wedding and the snowstorms and the serial killer," Bette said. "I can look after myself. Promise you won't say anything to them."

"All right. I won't say anything."

"Won't say anything about what?" Emily returned, carrying a loaded tray.

Cody stood and relieved her of the tray. He handed one of the steaming mugs on it to Bette and took one for himself. "I asked Cody not to say anything to Rainey and Doug about my injury," Bette said. "I don't want Rainey using it as an excuse to push me out of her kitchen."

"She's bound to hear about it from someone." Emily

settled next to Bette with the third mug of tea. "And she's not going to push you out of the kitchen. We won't let her."

"Still, it would be better if you just don't mention me to her," Bette said.

The door opened and Travis came in, followed by Lacy. "Come sit by the fire," Emily said. "The two of you must be frozen."

The couple shed their coats, then Lacy sank into a chair across from Bette. Travis remained standing. "I was on my way home when I saw Travis on the side of the road, with your car," Lacy said. "He told me what happened. How are you feeling?"

"I'm fine." She looked up at Travis. "Did you find anything to tell us what happened?"

"Have you remembered anything that happened?" Travis asked.

"I'm sorry, no. I'm trying to remember but…" She shook her head. "I don't even recall leaving the grocery store and getting into my car."

"I'm having your car towed to the station so we can take a better look at it there," Travis said. "If you need to borrow one of the ranch vehicles in the meantime, just ask my mom or dad. They'll be happy to lend you whatever you need."

"I shouldn't need to go anywhere for a few days, at least," Bette said. "I stocked up on supplies today. By the way, I need to bring them inside and put them away."

"I'll take care of that in a minute," Cody said.

"There's something else you should know." Travis took an evidence pouch from the pocket of his coat. "We found this in the ditch near the car."

Bette took the packet from him and frowned at the contents. "Duct tape?"

A chill went through Cody. The Ice Cold Killer had used duct tape to bind the hands and feet of his victims.

"Did you have any duct tape in your car that might have fallen out when you got out?" Travis asked.

"No," Bette said. "It's not something I've ever owned."

He tucked the evidence pouch back into his pocket. "I need to get this over to the station. I just stopped by to see how you were doing."

"I'm going to be fine," Bette said. "Thank you."

"I'll get those groceries out of the car," Cody said. He followed Travis out the door. On the front porch, the two friends stopped. "Did you find any of the killer's calling cards?" he asked.

"No," Travis said. "Just this roll of duct tape. It looks brand-new. I'm not even sure any tape has been used off the roll."

"Maybe the killer ran out and needed more."

"There are only a couple of places in town that stock the stuff," Travis said. "I'll be checking with them." He shoved his hands in his coat pockets. "It's snowing pretty hard, but I got out of the cruiser several times and walked the roadside on the way back to the ranch. I didn't see any signs where a vehicle might have turned off the road—no tracks or depressions in the snow or broken plants or anything."

"Cars don't vanish into thin air," Cody said.

"They don't," Travis agreed. "If whoever attacked Bette didn't turn off and he didn't turn back, that means it came here, to the ranch. And it means he's still here."

Chapter 8

The idea that Bette's attacker could be here at the ranch put Cody on high alert. "What do you need me to do?" he asked.

"I need you to help me search the ranch," Travis said. "We'll check all the outbuildings and anywhere someone could possibly stash a vehicle."

"Sure. Do you suspect someone at the ranch—an employee or somebody else?"

"Right now, I suspect pretty much everyone."

Cody retrieved Bette's groceries from his RAV4 and stashed them in the garage refrigerator, then he and Travis set out across the ranch.

"If this was the Ice Cold Killer, he's getting pretty reckless," Cody said as he and Travis made their way toward the stables.

"He killed Fiona Winslow in the middle of a party,"

Travis said. "Anyone could have come upon him at any time. I think that's part of the thrill for him."

"What are we looking for, specifically?" Cody asked, as they stopped behind a trio of vehicles parked near the stables. All three were covered with snow—in one case the vehicle, an older-model sedan, was almost buried in a drift.

"I'm looking for anything that looks like it's been driven in the last two hours," Travis said.

"It's been well over an hour," Cody said. "The engine probably won't be warm."

"No, but we should be able to tell if it isn't covered with snow. We can rule out your car, mine and Lacy's, but anything else we find, we'll take a very close look at the driver."

For the next two hours, they trudged through the snow, knee-deep in places. They peered into sheds and walked up narrow tracks that led into the woods. What few vehicles they spotted had clearly not been moved since the snow started. Travis questioned a few ranch hands, but all denied seeing any strange vehicles—or even any familiar ones. "Not much call to go out in a storm like this," one man said. "Especially with Dixon Pass closed."

By the time they made it back to the house, the sun was setting, and Cody's fingers and toes ached with cold. "Let's check around back here and we'll call it a night," Travis said, leading the way around the side of the house.

"The killer really has nerve if he's stashing his car this close to the house," Cody said, but he trudged along behind his friend, toward the back door, and the beckoning warmth of the kitchen. They had almost reached that warmth when Travis stopped. "What is it?" Cody asked. He followed his friend's gaze toward the shadows at the edge of the glow from the light shining through the kitchen window. He could just make out the bumper of a car.

He followed Travis over to the car and the sheriff played the beam of his flashlight over the windshield and hood. A scant half inch of snow coated the vehicle, compared with the much thicker coatings they had found on the other ranch vehicles. Travis directed the light to the ground around the car. "Does it look like there's less snow behind the back wheels to you?" he asked.

"That's harder to tell," Cody said. "Maybe. Whose vehicle is this?"

"It belongs to Rainey." He switched off the flashlight. "Let's see what she has to say."

"I'm going to be fine," Bette said, struggling to keep all trace of annoyance out of her voice. Lacy and Emily meant well, fussing over her like two mother hens, but she was beginning to feel a little smothered. They had plied her with tea, ibuprofen, blankets and offers of chicken soup and a hot water bottle, and they didn't want to let her out of their sight, even to go to the bathroom. She pushed aside the blankets and pillows and stood. "I'm going to go check on the groceries Cody put away, and then I'm going out to my cabin. I'm going to take a shower and go to bed early, get a good night's sleep and I'm sure I'll be fine in the morning."

"Shouldn't someone check on you during the night?" Lacy asked. "I mean, aren't you supposed to wake up someone with a head injury periodically, so they don't go into a coma or something?"

"If anyone wakes me up out of a sound sleep I can't be held responsible for the consequences," Bette said.

"You can't blame us for being worried about you," Lacy said.

"I know," Bette said. "And you're being really sweet, but I'll be fine. I'm feeling much better now. I hardly even have a headache." Not exactly true—her head still hurt a lot. But she wasn't going to let on about it or they would insist on taking turns waking her up all night to make sure she didn't die. And if they did that, the only lives that would be at risk would be theirs.

Lacy and Emily exchanged looks. Bette was sure they were going to argue with her. Before they got the chance, she headed for the kitchen.

Rainey looked up from the pot she was stirring on the stove. "What do you want?" she asked. "I'm in the middle of fixing dinner."

"I don't need anything from you," Bette said. "I'm just going through to the garage."

Once safely in the garage, she switched on the light and pulled open the door to the refrigerator. As she had expected, Cody had shoved both bags full of groceries on top of the cases of beer, not bothering to sort out what required refrigeration and what didn't. Sighing, she pulled out the bags and took out the dried fruit and several other items that didn't need to be kept cold. She would store these in her cabin until she needed them. She wouldn't give Rainey an excuse to complain that Bette's supplies were taking up space in her pantry.

She closed the refrigerator, hooked the bag of gro-

ceries to take to her cabin over one wrist and returned
to the kitchen—and almost collided with Cody.

He reached out to steady her. "What were you doing
in the garage?" he asked.

"I needed some things from the refrigerator." She
looked past him, to where Travis stood with Rainey.
Neither of them looked happy about something. Travis
was scowling and Rainey was hunched, arms folded
tightly across her chest.

Rainey glanced at Bette, then looked back to the
sheriff. "I always park my car back there," she said. "I
don't see what business it is of yours. If your parents
have a problem with it, they can tell me themselves."

"I don't care where you park, Rainey," Travis said. "I
asked you when the last time you moved the car was."

"Why do you need to know that?" she asked.

"Just answer the question, please."

"Yesterday," she said. "I ran some errands in town
and it's been parked there ever since."

"Are you sure?" Travis asked.

"Of course I'm sure," she said. "What is all this
about?"

"I noticed there isn't much snow on the car," Travis
said. "Not as much as you'd expect if it had been sitting
there over twenty-four hours."

Rainey hunched her shoulders more. "Doug cleaned
it off for me. I don't like letting snow pile up on it too
high. Then it's that much more trouble to clean off. So
he swept it off for me."

"When was this?" Travis asked.

"I don't know. Sometime after lunch."

"Where is Doug?" Travis looked around the kitchen.
"Shouldn't he be helping you with supper?"

"He wasn't feeling well, so I sent him to his room to lie down. I think he might be coming down with the flu or something."

"I'll need to talk to him," Travis said.

"Why? He hasn't done anything wrong."

"Then there won't be any problem with him answering some questions for me."

"What kind of questions?" Rainey demanded.

"He's a grown man," Travis said. "I think he can speak for himself."

Rainey uncrossed her arms and whirled to face him. "Do you think that badge gives you the right to pick on him?" she shouted. "Just because that woman lied about him in court and he had to go to prison, you think you can blame anything that happens around here on him. When you've invited someone else into your home who is so much worse. You ought to be ashamed of yourself, Travis Walker."

"Rainey." His voice carried a sharp edge of warning.

Bette shrank back, half hiding behind Cody as Rainey turned on her. "She's the one you ought to be questioning," she said, pointing to Bette. "She robbed a bank, and she's probably planning to rob you all blind as soon as you turn your backs."

Rage fogged Bette's vision. How dare this woman accuse her of wanting to harm people who had been so kind to her. If anyone had dared to say something like that to her in prison, she would have lit into them then and there. Fighting meant losing privileges, maybe even having time added to your sentence. But that was better than losing face. If some of those cons learned they could take advantage of you, they would make your time behind bars a living hell.

This isn't prison, she reminded herself. This was a respectable home, and Bette was here to do a job. She wouldn't let this spiteful woman take that from her. So she held her head up and forced herself to move into the middle of the room. "The sheriff knows I'm happy to answer any questions he has," she said, finding and holding Rainey's gaze. "Now, if you don't mind, I'm going to say good-night. It's been a trying day."

She was halfway across the yard, cold wind freezing the tears that streamed down her face, when Cody caught up with her. "Hey," he said, taking hold of her arm.

"Leave me alone," she said, wrenching away from him.

"I'm going to walk you to your cabin," he said, falling into step beside her.

"I didn't ask you to be my bodyguard," she said.

"No. But someone has threatened you twice in the last two days—and this morning you might have been killed. I'm not going to ignore that, even if you are."

She didn't know what to say to that, so they walked without speaking the rest of the way to her cabin, their footsteps crunching on the snow. "No messages on the door," he said as they climbed the steps to the little porch. "That's good."

"Everything looks fine." She faced him, key in her hand. "All right, you saw me here, you can go now."

"Not until we make sure everything inside is all right." He took the key from her and inserted it into the lock.

She followed him into the room. Everything looked as she had left it. "Everything's fine," she said. *Just— go*, she thought.

But he didn't leave. "I'm sorry about what happened back there, in the kitchen," he said. "But it was all on Rainey. Travis will see that, too. She was upset about him questioning her, so she tried to create a distraction."

Bette sat on the side of the bed. "What was all that about the car?" she asked. "Why was Travis questioning her?"

"We were looking for the car driven by whoever attacked you," he said. "Neither of us passed another vehicle between the turnoff for the country road and your car. If your attacker didn't travel that way, the only other direction he could have gone was toward the ranch. When we looked at cars on the ranch, Rainey's was the only one we found that looked as if it had been cleared of snow in the last few hours."

"Rainey hates me, but forcing me off the road and attacking me with a rock?" Bette shook her head. "She doesn't strike me as the type. She'd rather spit in my soup, or spread rumors behind my back—or announce to everyone that I'm a bank robber and I can't be trusted." That moment in the kitchen when everyone had turned to look at her still stung.

"What about Doug?" Cody asked. "Do you think he was the one who attacked you?"

"I don't know." She curled her hands into fists. "I honestly don't remember anything from the time I was standing in the grocery story with Brenda, until I woke up with you shaking me. It's frightening, having a chunk of your life just missing that way."

"But you can't say Doug wasn't the one who hurt you?"

"No. I guess Doug could have done it, but why?"

"He has a record," Cody said. "He served time for beating up his girlfriend. He put her in the hospital."

"Not exactly a comforting thought, but I can't see why he'd want to hurt me," Bette said. "We haven't said more than half a dozen words to each other since I got here."

"He could have hurt you out of some misguided attempt to protect his mother," Cody said.

"Oh, please!" Bette grabbed a pillow and hugged it to her stomach. "I know Rainey resents my getting to cater the wedding, but it's not like she's out of a job. She's still doing what she's done for years, doing the cooking for the ranch. After the wedding I'll be gone and she'll still be here. That isn't a good reason to physically hurt someone. The petty harassment—sure, maybe she'll make me miserable enough and I'll leave. But violence?" She shook her head. "It's not worth the risk of getting caught."

"Is there someone else who might be a threat to you, then?"

"Who? I know it's a cliché for someone to say she doesn't have enemies, but honestly, I don't."

"What about your ex? The one who talked you into robbing the bank?"

"He's still in prison."

"Do you know that for sure?"

She frowned. When she had first been released, she had been almost obsessive about keeping tabs on Eddie. Lately, that obsession had faded. "The last time I checked was six months ago, but yes, he was still serving his sentence."

"A lot of cons have connections outside prison—people who are loyal to them who will do things for them, like check up on an old girlfriend to make sure she doesn't say something she shouldn't."

"But he's in prison. Nothing I say can hurt him worse," she said.

"There was one member of the gang who was never caught," Cody said.

"So you did check up on me."

His expression remained cool. "Are you really surprised?"

"No. I guess I'd have been more surprised if you hadn't. So yes, the guy who drove the getaway car was never caught."

"You didn't testify against him." A statement, not a question. Oh, yeah, he had gotten all the details, hadn't he?

"I didn't know anything to testify," she said. "I saw him for a few minutes exactly once, and I don't remember anything about him."

"Does your ex know that?"

"Yes. He was the one who made sure I knew as little as possible. He said it was for my protection, but it worked both ways. The less I knew, the less I could testify to."

"All right, so you don't know who the getaway driver is—but he probably knows you. Maybe he's come after you to shut you up."

"That's pretty far-fetched." She held up her hand and began counting off the reasons. "One—how does he know I'm in Eagle Mountain? Two—when did he get here? There was only, what, a two-day window when the pass was open so he could follow me here. And three—and this is the biggest reason I think you're wrong—it's been nine years since that robbery. What are the chances that he's still out there walking around? He probably committed other crimes and is locked up for one of them."

"Maybe he was like you—a dupe for your ex. The near miss scared him into going straight."

"In which case, why would he throw all that away to shut me up?"

"If you identify him, you ruin his life. He might have a good job now, a wife and a family. Those things are worth taking risks for."

"But this is a crazy risk. And really foolish. Because I don't know anything."

"All right," he said. "But until we find out who's behind these threats, I'm going to be keeping a closer eye on you than you may like."

"Why? Why do you even care?"

"Let's just say it gives me something to do. I can only take so much shoveling snow and chopping firewood."

"What are you doing here at the ranch anyway?" she asked.

"I'm one of the groomsmen."

"Yeah, but the wedding is two weeks away. Why are you here so early?"

He studied her for a long moment, silent.

"It's a simple question," she said.

"But it doesn't have a simple answer." He stared at the floor, then let out a long, slow breath. "I told you before I'm on vacation, but that's just the polite word for it. Actually, it was more of a forced leave."

"What happened?" she asked. "Did you screw up? Shoot someone you shouldn't have?"

He winced, and she wanted to take the words back. "I'm sorry," she said. "I shouldn't have assumed."

"It's okay. I'd rather you said what you were thinking than try to tiptoe around my feelings. I've had enough of that."

She waited for him to say more. The silence stretched, until she became aware of the gentle sigh of his breath and the brush of the denim of his jeans when he shifted in the chair. "I was on a job," he said finally, his voice low and tight, as if he was forcing out the words. "Routine stuff—pursuing a fugitive with a warrant. The guy was wanted for sexually molesting his ten-year-old niece. Nice, upstanding citizen—a banker. A girls' soccer coach, so there was a question of whether other girls were involved. Basically, I thought he was scum, but I would never have let him know that. I did my job—tracked him down at a friend's cabin where he had gone in a pretty feeble attempt to hide from the cops. I gave him my usual spiel of how he should come with me quietly."

He closed his eyes, and she sensed he was replaying the scene in his head. "He had a gun. He was waving it around. One of those cases you hate, because the way he was holding the gun, I could tell he wasn't really going to shoot me. He was trying to commit what we call suicide by cop. But I wasn't going to let that happen."

He opened his eyes again. "It's a matter of pride for me that when I go after someone, I bring them back alive ninety-nine percent of the time. I knew I could handle this guy. I wasn't in a hurry. I had all the time in a world to talk him off the ledge, get him to put the gun down. There are rules for handling these kinds of things and I knew how to follow them to reach a good outcome."

He fell silent again, the lines around his eyes so deep,

the hunch of his shoulders that of a man in pain. "What happened?" she whispered.

He licked his lips. "He didn't know the rules. I was right that he didn't want to shoot me. Instead, he shot himself. Put the barrel of the gun in his mouth and pulled the trigger. He was looking me right in the eye when he did it."

She put a hand to her mouth to stifle the cry she couldn't keep back.

Cody shook his head, like a boxer shaking off a blow to the chin. "It rattles you, something like that. But I knew I could deal. I told my boss the best thing for it was to get back out in the field, but he didn't see it that way. He ordered me to take time off—to get out in nature, to see a counselor if I needed. But not to come back on the job until February."

"So you came here."

"I couldn't just sit around my apartment. And Travis is a great guy for giving you perspective. You might not see it, but the man is beyond calm in a crisis. I figured he and I could hang out, go fishing, I could work on the ranch. But he's tied up chasing a killer, and I'm going crazy." His eyes met hers again. "That's where you come in."

"So I'm going to be your distraction."

"Oh, you're a distraction all right."

He stood and moved toward her. There was nothing subtle about his stance, or the look in his eye. She felt that look like a bottle rocket straight to the middle of her chest, the heat of the explosion radiating down through her middle to pool between her legs. Something pulsed between them, and her gaze shifted from the almost painful fire in his eyes to his lips, the bottom one a little fuller than the upper, the black shadow of whiskers above the upper lip.

He took the pillow from her and tossed it aside, then pulled her up to face him, one hand at her waist, the other beside her left breast as his lips crushed hers. She returned the fierceness of that caress, kissing him as if her next breath depended on it, opening her mouth and tangling her tongue with his, wanting—insisting—on having all of him, right this minute.

It was a long time before he dragged his head up, breaking contact and staring into her eyes with a look that was equal parts desperation and defiance. "If you want me to leave now, I'll go," he said, his voice a rough growl that scraped across her nerves. "But you'd better be sure it's what you want."

"What do you want?" she asked. It wasn't a question so much as a dare.

"I think you know that." His lips closed over hers again and she surged up, her whole body bowing toward him, her hands clutching his biceps, fingers digging into his taut muscles. He grasped her hips and ground against her, leaving no doubt of his desire.

Her need for him thrilled and frightened her. Some small voice in the back of her mind said she was being too reckless. It was too soon. She hardly knew this man. He—

She told the voice to shut up and grabbed the hem of the fleece pullover he wore and shoved it upward. Then they were tearing at each other's clothes with an urgency that would have destroyed less sturdy garments.

She pulled him down to the bed on top of her, then he rolled until she was straddling him. She laughed at the heady feeling. "What's so funny?" he asked.

"Haven't you ever laughed simply because something felt so good?" she asked.

"I don't know. If I ever did, it's been a while."

"Then I'll have to see if I can change that." She slid down his body and took him in her mouth, surprising a gasp from him. He caressed and kneaded her shoulders as her mouth worked on him, then he dragged her back up to meet his mouth with hers. "Let's not end this too soon," he said, with some effort. His gaze searched hers. "Are you sure you're up to this? I forgot you had a pretty hard blow to the head."

"I read an article once that said sex was better than painkillers for getting rid of a headache," she said.

The slow, sexy smile he gave her could have melted chocolate. "Then I'll do my best to make you forget the pain," he said. It was his turn to surprise her, as his skillful fingers delved and fondled. When he began licking first one breast, then another, she squirmed against him. "Do you like that?" he asked.

"No, I hate it. Can't you tell?"

In answer, he drew the tip of one breast into his mouth, while his fingers moved more deftly.

Her climax rocketed through her, fierce and freeing. She collapsed against him and he held her—rather tenderly, she thought, which made her blink back foolish tears. She propped herself up on her elbows and met his gaze. "It's, um, been a while," she said, almost sheepishly.

"I'm a very lucky man," he said. He flipped her over on her back and moved between her legs.

She grasped his shoulder. "Wait."

His eyes met hers, and she saw the moment he recognized the problem. "We don't have any protection," he said.

"Hmm. Then we'll have to work around that."

She started to slide down the bed, but he pressed her back against the pillows. "Wait a minute," he said, and got up.

He disappeared into the bathroom and returned seconds later, a gold foil packet held aloft. "Where did that come from?" she asked.

"The medicine cabinets in these cabins are fully stocked," he said. "The Walkers think of everything for their guests' comfort."

"I didn't see those before," she said.

"You weren't looking." He parted her knees and knelt between them. "I was."

She wanted to ask him what he meant by that but was distracted by the sight of him sheathing himself. And then he was moving into her, and she didn't want to think about anything for a while. She only wanted to lose herself in the sensation of being filled and surrounded and uplifted by this man.

Such a wonderful feeling.

And a dangerous one. But she didn't want to think about the danger now. She'd have all kinds of time for thinking later.

Chapter 9

Bette untangled herself from the bedcovers the next morning, aching in body and mind. Her head hurt and her muscles ached, but worse than that, her emotions felt bruised. Cody had stayed long into the night, making love with such tenderness and ferocity, before slipping away some time very early this morning. What was it about him that made her want to be so reckless? He had given her probably the best night of her life, but this morning she was no more certain about where she stood with him than she had been at this time yesterday.

She dressed and emerged from the cabin into a world frosted in white. Sunlight sparkled on the drifts of snow that covered everything, transforming woodpiles and old machinery into glittering confections. The air was so sharp and clean it hurt to breathe. She felt energized with every inhalation. She found Emily, Lacy, Travis and

Cody in the dining room, digging into an egg-and-ham casserole that smelled mouthwatering. "How are you feeling this morning?" Lacy asked. "Does your head hurt?"

"Only a little. I feel fine." A little beat up, perhaps, emotionally and physically, though for long moments last night she had forgotten all about her headache, or anything else. But all the closeness and compatibility that had come so naturally last night in the intimacy of her cabin felt a lot shakier and out of reach here in the real world. She poured coffee, avoiding looking at Cody, though she was as aware of him as if he were the only person in the room.

"I'm so glad," Lacy said. "I had to make myself not go out there in the middle of the night, just to make sure you were okay."

Bette was glad she had her back to the table as she served herself from the buffet. Her cheeks burned with the memory of what Lacy might have found if she had decided to visit the cabin last night. "I'm glad you restrained yourself," she said. "I was fine." Though *fine* was a poor word to describe what she had been feeling last night—*elated*, *transported*, even *awed* would have been better choices.

"I have something fun for all of us to look forward to," Emily said. "Gage and I have decided we should have an old-fashioned sleigh ride to take advantage of the snow. Dad agreed we could use the old sleighs that are in the barn—he and Mom are out there now, checking the harness."

"When did you and Gage decide this?" Travis asked.

"Yesterday. He telephoned the ranch, wanting to talk to you, but you were in the kitchen with Rainey, so he and I got to talking. Casey has been begging to go on a sleigh ride ever since he showed her that album of family pictures that Mom gave him. We figured with all this snow, now is the perfect time."

"When is the sleigh ride?" Travis asked.

"Tonight, after supper," Emily said. "We'll hook up both sleighs and ride over to the little line shack in the south pasture. We can have hot chocolate and maybe s'mores." She nudged him. "Don't look so stern—it will only be for a few hours, and it will be a nice break from all the tension. We've all been feeling it, you know— not just you."

"It sounds like fun," Lacy said. "Romantic."

"Very romantic," Emily agreed. "We'll have lots of fur robes and blankets for snuggling under, and Gage promised to bring a flask of peppermint schnapps for spiking the hot cocoa."

"That sounds like Gage," Travis said drily.

"Oh, you're going to enjoy it," Emily said.

"I wouldn't dream of disobeying orders." Travis kept a straight face, but Bette didn't miss the sly look he sent Lacy across the table.

Lacy sat up straighter, her cheeks only slightly pink. "It does sound like lots of fun. I'll be looking forward to it. In the meantime, I have a Skype meeting with the wedding planner this morning." She looked around the table. "What are the rest of you doing today?"

"I'm working here for a while, then heading to the office," Travis said.

Cody made no comment, eyes focused on his plate. Bette had the strong impression he was pretending not to have heard Lacy's question—when, really, he didn't want to answer it. "I'm a little concerned about how a couple of my recipes will turn out at this altitude," she said. "I thought I'd make some test batches, in case I need to tweak things."

"I've talked to Rainey," Travis said. "She shouldn't give you any trouble."

"Thank you." Bette settled in the chair across from the sheriff. He really had been so kind to her—Lacy was lucky to have found a man who was so perfect for her. "If they turn out well, we can use them for more refreshments for tonight."

"Any idea when the road might reopen?" Cody asked.

Travis shook his head. "They'll be working this morning to clear the avalanche chutes."

"What does that involve, exactly?" Bette asked.

"They use dynamite, or sometimes a grenade launcher, to explode the snow out of the chutes and create a slide—an intentional avalanche," Travis said. "All the snow ends up on the highway and they have to haul it off. There are twenty-four chutes in that section of highway, so clearing them can take several days. And there's more snow in the forecast."

"Why don't they build another road?" Bette asked. "It's crazy to have a whole town full of people who can't go anywhere every time it snows."

"The road usually only closes for a few hours, maybe half a day, at a time," Lacy said. "Some winters it doesn't close at all. This winter is just particularly bad."

"There's nowhere to put another road," Travis said. "Not without spending hundreds of millions of dollars to blast through mountains. And it would probably be subject to avalanches, too. The people here are used to it. They know how to cope." He slid back his chair and stood. "I need to get to work."

The rest of them finished breakfast and left the table

one by one, until Bette was the only person left. She lingered over coffee, wanting to give Rainey time to finish the dishes and clear out. She wasn't afraid to confront the cook, but it would be easier on everyone if she didn't have to.

About ten o'clock, she retrieved the ingredients she needed from her cabin and returned to the kitchen, relieved to find it empty. She pinned up her hair, then slipped her apron over her head, some of the tension draining from her body as she did so. She smiled to herself as she began assembling the tools and ingredients she needed. This was the best therapy. So many times, when her life had felt out of control, she had found solace in the kitchen. Mixing, kneading, stirring, basting—here she was ruler of her own domain, a magician who had the power to conjure beautiful things from simple ingredients.

She went into the garage to get the cream and butter she needed for the tea cakes. She found the butter immediately, but where was the cream? She moved items around and even looked to see if somehow the carton had slipped behind the cases of beer. But the cream simply wasn't there. She shut the door, confused. Had the cream been left behind when Cody transferred the groceries from her car to his? No—she was sure it had been there last night when she rearranged everything.

She returned to the kitchen and began opening doors and searching everywhere for the missing cream. She was being silly—there was no reason the carton would have ended up anywhere in these cabinets. But she couldn't shake the compulsion to look.

And then she found it, sitting on a middle shelf in the kitchen's walk-in pantry, next to a jar of roasted peppers. The carton was warm in her hand, and before she even opened it, she knew it would be spoiled. Disgusted, she dumped the contents in the sink, rinsed the carton and tossed it in the recycling bin. She knew she hadn't put the cream in the pantry, which meant someone else had—probably Rainey or Doug.

A shadow passed in front of the window. She looked out and spotted Doug, shoulders hunched, hood pulled over his head. She grabbed a coat from a peg by the back door and shoved her feet into a pair of women's snow boots—no doubt Rainey's. Let her complain about Bette borrowing her coat and boots and she'd get more than an earful in return.

She found Doug huddled next to a tall stack of split firewood, cupping his hand around a cigarette to light it. "Doug!" she called.

He jumped and almost dropped his cigarette. "What do you want?" he asked, half turning away from her.

"Someone took a quart of cream from the garage refrigerator and put it in the pantry to spoil," she said. "Did you or your mother do that?"

He blew out a stream of smoke, which hung in the cold air between them. "You probably did it yourself. I heard you got hit in the head. It probably made you loopy."

She took a step closer; he moved a step back. "What do you know about that? Did you hit me in the head?"

"Why would I do that? I never laid eyes on you before you showed up here."

"So why do you and your mother hate me?" The answer to that question was behind all this, wasn't it? "It's not like I'm trying to take your jobs," she continued. "I'm just catering the wedding of a friend. Then I'm going to go back to Denver and you'll probably never see me again."

"You should just go back now." He flicked ash into the snow.

"You're the one who painted that message on my door, aren't you?" she asked.

"I don't know what you're talking about. I just think it would be a lot less trouble for everyone if you went home now."

"Since the pass is closed, that's impossible. But why do you care if I'm here or not?"

"Who said I cared?" He dropped the cigarette on the snow and ground it out with the heel of his boot. "If you've got a beef with my mom, take it up with her."

"I'll do that. Where is she?"

"She went to her room to lie down. Said she had a migraine. You won't get anywhere talking to her right now." He left, moving along the edge of the woodpile and staying as far from her as possible, keeping his head down.

Bette stared after him. What was up with this guy? He wouldn't even look at her.

She returned to the kitchen and shed the coat and boots. She'd make do without the cream today and go into town tomorrow to buy more. For the moment, she would leave Rainey alone. She wouldn't get anywhere if the woman really did have a migraine. Instead, she would focus on baking, and getting ready for the brides-maids' tea. Those were things she could control, in a world where so much was out of her hands.

Cody walked by the kitchen, refusing to give in to the temptation to go in and talk to Bette. He could hear her in there, opening and closing doors, rattling bowls and pots. He imagined her, focused on her work, the scents of vanilla and cinnamon clinging to her, mingling with her own sweet essence, the memory of which made him hard.

He hadn't gone to her cabin last night intending to take her to bed, but he wasn't sorry he had. She got to him. He hadn't talked to anyone about what had happened on his last assignment—not even the shrink his bosses had made him see—before last night. He had been certain that he didn't need to talk about it. Talking didn't do anything but pull the scab off the wound.

But telling Bette had been easy somehow. Once he had made up his mind to talk to her, he had *wanted* her to know. He didn't feel the need for barriers with her. He couldn't say that about many other people. Last night had been powerful, but he wasn't sure what it meant for the future.

Hell, he didn't know if he even had a future. He might as well admit that, if only to himself. He didn't know if he would have a job waiting for him when he reported back to the US Marshals Service in February. He had heard rumors of budget cuts and restructuring for months now. An officer they saw as "damaged" would be first in line to be let go.

He needed to work—to prove he could still do the only job he had ever really wanted. With this in mind, he knocked on the door of Travis's home office, half of a suite of rooms he occupied on the ground floor, just off the kitchen. "Come in," the sheriff called.

Dressed in his sheriff's department uniform, as if at any minute he might be called out, Travis sat behind a scarred wooden desk in a small, cluttered room that resembled, in many ways, the cramped space he had claimed at the sheriff's department in Eagle Mountain. Cody stepped in and closed the door behind him and Travis looked up from a laptop computer, but said nothing.

"What can I do to help?" Cody asked.

Travis pushed the laptop to one side. "Aren't you supposed to be on leave?" he asked. Cody had told his friend some—but not all—of what had happened.

"I'm not an invalid," Cody said. "I need something to do and you need help. Deputize me or something." He sank into a cowhide-covered armchair across from the desk. "Besides, with the pass closed, you're not going to be able to call in help from the state. I'm the best you've got."

"Then I'd better not turn down your offer," Travis said.

"So what can I do? Is there someone you want me to interview? Something you need researched?"

"You've spent more time with Bette than I have—what's your feel for her?"

Cody had an immediate, intense image of heated, satiny skin sliding beneath his fingers. He kept his face stony, betraying nothing, hoping Travis wouldn't notice how tightly he gripped the arms of the chair. "What do you mean?" he asked.

"Is she really reformed?"

"She seems serious about her catering duties, and I haven't found any evidence of wrongdoing." He didn't see any need to mention his suspicions about the painted message on her door. As evidence of a crime, it was pretty weak, especially since she'd refused to say anything about it to the Walkers.

"There's a *but* at the end of that sentence," Travis said. "But what?"

"But she has a record. And bank robbery is a pretty

serious crime." He couldn't forget that, no matter what else he thought about her.

Travis nodded.

"Why are you asking me about her?" Cody asked. "Do you know something about her I don't?"

Travis sat back, hands clasped over his stomach. "Have you considered the possibility that no one attacked her?"

"What do you mean? Someone threw that rock and hit her in the head."

"She could have driven the car into the ditch, then gotten out, picked up the rock and thrown it through the window herself. We didn't find any blood in the car."

Cody frowned. What Travis described was certainly possible. "Why go to all that trouble?" he asked. "And it doesn't explain the head injury."

"We only have her word for it that it was a bad enough injury to cause memory loss," Travis said. "The EMTs weren't able to x-ray her, or perform any other tests. The cut didn't require stitches. Maybe she bashed her own head."

Would Bette do something like that? Then again, was it any more far-fetched than his suspicions that she had painted those words on her door? Some sick people worked to call attention to themselves, even if it meant hurting themselves. "Again—why?" he asked.

"I don't know." Travis frowned. "I'm not saying that's what happened. I'm just trying to look at all the possibilities."

"Then why not focus on the most likely scenario— that she was attacked by the Ice Cold Killer and something scared him off?"

"What scared him off?" Travis asked.

"Maybe my arrival."

"You didn't see a car. We never found a car or any sign of one."

"Did you talk to Doug Whittington?" Cody asked. "He could have driven his mother's car."

"I talked to him," Travis said. "He said he was sleeping in his room all afternoon. His mother vouches for him."

"I think Rainey would lie to protect her son," Cody said.

"Maybe. But I can't find anyone who remembers the car not being parked near the kitchen yesterday, or anyone who saw Doug in Rainey's car. Rainey's story about having him brush the snow off her vehicle so it wouldn't pile up is plausible."

"Then maybe it was someone else," Cody said. "There was a big time gap between when I found Bette and when we started looking for a vehicle. Time enough for someone to hide a vehicle where we couldn't find it. And we were hampered by the snow. This Ice Cold Killer has done a good job of eluding detection so far."

"This doesn't fit the pattern of his other victims," Travis said. "They were subdued and bound fairly quickly, especially in the case of Fiona Winslow. Yet he didn't even have time to get any tape off the roll we found. And the whole deal with the broken window and the rock—it's sloppy. It doesn't feel like the same man."

"Maybe he felt rushed. Maybe he's getting desperate."

"There are too many *maybes* with this case."

"What do you think we should do?" Cody asked.

"Nothing right now. But keep your eyes open. Let me know if you notice anything suspicious."

"I will." He didn't need an excuse to watch Bette closer, but Travis had just given him a reason to take the job even more seriously.

Chapter 10

"Oh, it's lovely weather," Lacy sang as she stepped out onto the front porch, arm in arm with Travis.

"For a sleigh ride together with you!" Bette joined in. The sleighs stood ready in the drive—old-fashioned wagon boxes with curved sides, painted bright red and hung with silver bells that glinted in the light from the lanterns hung at the four corners of the sleighs. The horses—two teams comprising four big draft horses hitched to each sleigh, their manes and tails combed and braided—stood between the shafts of the sleighs, their harness also hung with bells, which rang out with every shake of their heads or stamp of their hooves.

"Right this way." Gage, a red scarf wound around his neck above the collar of his shearling jacket, ushered the group toward the sleighs. "Find a seat on one of the benches in the sleighs," he instructed. "There are plenty of blankets for keeping warm, and a few buffalo robes, too."

Bette hopped up onto the wooden crate that served as a step into the sleigh. Someone reached up to steady her and she glanced back to see Cody, his hand at her back. "Where did you come from?" she asked. She had looked for him when she had first stepped onto the porch and hadn't seen him anywhere.

"I'm sticking close." He joined her in the sleigh and took her arm to pull her to the bench at the very back.

She opened her mouth to protest that she didn't necessarily want to ride next to him, but who was she kidding? The thought of snuggling under a buffalo robe with this man made the prospect of this evening even more pleasant. He slid in next to her and pulled the heavy covering over them. Bette sank her gloved fingers into the thick, black fur of the robe, smiling at the sensation of softness and warmth.

"You're in a good mood tonight," Cody said.

"Baking always puts me in a good mood," she said.

"All kinds of lines come to mind about cooking something up with you," he said. "But for now, I'll resist."

"You'd better." But she took his hand underneath the robe.

"More coming aboard!" Gage declared, and assisted a petite young woman, the tips of her dark hair dyed a bright blue, into the sleigh, followed by a little girl dressed all in pink, from the pom-pom of the knit hat pulled over her blond braids to the toes of her snow boots.

"That must be Gage's wife, Maya, and her niece, Casey," Bette whispered to Cody.

"I think you're right," he said.

The little girl's fingers flew, and Bette realized she was using sign language. Gage responded in kind, and said, "I've got a seat saved for us right up front so you can see the horses." He settled her on the front bench between himself and Maya, and tucked a blanket securely around her.

In addition to Gage and his family, Bette's sleigh contained Mr. and Mrs. Walker. Lacy and Travis rode with Dwight and Brenda Prentice and Emily in the sleigh ahead of them. Though only a few days ago the presence of so many law enforcement officers would have made Bette uncomfortable, she was more at ease with them now. She could even admit their presence tonight made her feel a little more secure.

A ranch hand, swathed in a long leather duster, climbed aboard to take the reins of their sleigh. "Giddy up!" he called, and with a jolt, they surged forward, then glided smoothly over the snow. Casey laughed and clapped her hands and Bette felt like joining in. There was something magical about floating over the snow on a cold night, the stars overhead like diamond dust, so bright and sharp that if she reached up she feared she might cut herself.

"There you go, smiling again." Cody leaned close and spoke in a low voice. "Makes me suspect you're up to something."

"I'm always up to something." She watched him out of the corner of her eye. "I thought you knew that."

He let go of her hand, but only to slide along her hip, his fingers coming to rest between her thighs. "So am I," he said.

She looked away, lifting her face to the rush of icy air

across her cheeks, aware of the strong beat of her pulse in time to the jingle of the sleigh bells, of the skitter of sensation across her skin as Cody languidly rubbed his thumb up and down the seam of her jeans. For so many years in prison she had kept herself numb, pretending feelings like these didn't exist. If you didn't let yourself feel, then you couldn't hurt. Pretending that avoiding emotion made her stronger was a habit she had carried into life after she was freed. How quickly Cody had proved that belief to be a lie!

"Oh, it's lovely weather!" Emily sang out, and the others joined in to sing "Sleigh Ride"—slightly off key, but with great gusto. Cody's voice, a tuneful baritone, mingled with Bette's clear alto, and she thought how well they sounded together.

Almost too soon, the sleighs stopped before a flat-roofed log cabin, the windows outlined with white lights. A cowboy came out to meet them, and everyone piled out of the sleighs and trooped into the cabin, which glowed with the warmth of a wood fire and half a dozen lit oil lamps.

Two cowboys passed out tin cups, then came around the room with kettles of hot chocolate and ladled the hot drink into the cups. Another man served platters of the tea cakes and cream puffs Bette had made that afternoon.

The young woman with the blue hair approached with the little girl. "I'm Maya," she said, offering a hand. "And this is Casey."

Casey held out one of the cream puffs and signed with her free hand. "She says she really likes the cream puff," Maya said. "I told her you made them."

"I did." Bette smiled at the little girl. "Tell her I'm glad she likes them."

"And you must be Cody." Maya turned to the man beside Bette. "Gage has told me about you and I know you've been staying at the ranch, I just haven't made it up there since you arrived."

"I'm pleased to meet the woman who could put up with Gage," Cody said.

"Don't say that." Gage joined them. "I'm the underdog in my own house now. These two team up on me all the time."

"Excuse me if I don't feel sorry for you," Cody said, grinning at Maya.

"That's a beautiful ring," Bette said, nodding to the silver band on the third finger of Maya's left hand. "May I see?"

Maya held out her hand. The filigree band sparkled with brilliant pink and blue stones. "I wanted sometime simple, so Gage had it made. All the materials are from Colorado. The stones are Colorado rhodochrosite and aquamarine."

"It's gorgeous," Bette said.

"You should see the rings Travis and Lacy picked out," Maya said. "Gage and I went with them to pick them up."

"Sometimes my brother has good taste," Gage said. "Or maybe I should say Lacy has good taste."

"If you're saying something about me, it had better be good," Lacy said, as she pushed in between Gage and Cody, Travis right behind her.

"I was just telling them about your wedding rings," Maya said. "How beautiful they are."

"I'm really happy with them." Lacy looked at Travis. "You should show them to them when we get back to the ranch house."

Travis's brow furrowed. "Isn't that bad luck?" he asked. "To see the rings before the wedding?"

"That's the wedding gown," Lacy said. "And I want them to see them."

"All right," Travis said.

Emily joined them. "Everyone having a good time?" she asked.

"We are," Bette said. "This was a great idea."

"It was mine," Gage said.

Emily punched him. "It was not. It was mine."

"It was your idea to have a party," he said. "I suggested the sleighs."

"All right, I guess I'll give you that."

His expression sobered. "It's good to have a night off…from everything else."

A shiver ran up Bette's spine. For a little while, she had forgotten about the killer who was preying on women in the area. She imagined the thought of him seldom left Gage's and Travis's minds.

Maya slipped her arm into Gage's. "No work talk," she said. "We agreed."

"That's right." He raised his arms over his head and began clapping. Everyone turned to look at him. "Finish up the snacks, people," he said. "Part two of the evening's festivities are about to begin."

"What are we going to do now?" Bette asked, handing her cup to the man who came to collect it.

"Party games," Emily said. "You have your choice of cornhole or bowling." She held up a small beanbag and a plastic bowling pin.

Groans rose from around the room. "Don't be sticks

in the mud," Emily said. "This will be fun." She began dividing them into teams. Bette found herself assigned as one of the cornhole players. The object was to pitch a small beanbag into a hole on a slanted board set up at the other end of the room. Cody was nowhere to be seen. *Coward*, she thought, as she hurled her first beanbag toward the game board, only to have it land in the floor only halfway to the target.

"I'm horrible at this!" she complained a few minutes later, after her third miss in a row. She gladly relinquished her beanbag to the next person in line and looked around for some avenue of escape.

Cody had emerged from hiding. He grabbed her hand and pulled her toward the door, where he helped her into her coat and slipped on his own. "Where are we going?" she asked.

"Just to get some fresh air." He glanced back toward the game players. "Unless you're dying for another turn at cornhole."

"No!" She zipped up the coat and slipped her hands into her gloves.

Outside, the first blast of icy air made her catch her breath and made her wonder at the wisdom of being out here. But when Cody set off around the side of the cabin, she hurried to catch up with his long strides. "Where are we going?" she asked. "It's freezing."

"I brought you out here to get warmed up."

"Cody, that sentence doesn't even make sense."

"Oh, no?" He pulled her to him and lowered his lips to hers.

She returned the kiss, slipping her arms inside his open coat and around his back. She loved that he was taller than her, but not too tall—exactly the right height for kissing. "Are you warm yet?" he asked, smiling down at her.

"I don't know." She wiggled against him. "Maybe you should try again."

He kissed her again, and she willingly lost herself in the bliss of that moment, floating on a mix of desire and contentment and anticipation.

A burst of noise several minutes later made them jump apart. Cody glanced over her shoulder toward the front of the cabin, where light spilled onto the snow from the open front door. "I think everyone's getting ready to leave," he said.

"I guess we'd better go with them," she said.

"Or we could let them leave behind us and spend the night here by ourselves," he said.

"Right. But I didn't see a bed in that cabin, did you?" she said. "And the few chairs I spotted didn't look that comfortable."

"Home it is, then."

They loaded into the sleigh and Cody put his arm around Bette as they settled onto the back bench. She leaned her head on his shoulder and closed her eyes, half drowsing in his warmth and the magic of the moment. She wanted to sear times like this in her memory, stamping them over recollections of darker times in her life, when such bliss had seemed utterly unreachable— happiness so far from her grasp she couldn't even fantasize about it. Her life was so different now, and she never wanted to take even one moment for granted.

Back at the ranch house, everyone gathered in the great room, saying their goodbyes. "Don't go yet," Lacy said. "I promised to show you the rings. Travis, would you get them right quick?"

The sheriff headed out of the room and Lacy turned back to her guests. "We found this jeweler in Cheyenne who does these incredible Western designs—mostly belt buckles and things like that, but he does wedding rings, too. We had them made from the gold from melting down my grandmother's wedding ring and rings from both Travis's grandparents."

Travis rejoined them, but empty-handed. His face wore a pinched expression. "What's wrong?" Lacy clutched his arm. "Where are the rings?"

"I had them in the top drawer of my dresser," he said. "They're gone."

Travis's announcement shifted the mood in the room. Everyone fell silent, looking at each other. Cody looked, too, examining the faces of those around him. Did anyone seem unsurprised by this news? Did anyone look guilty?

Lacy, white-faced but trying to maintain her composure, clutched Travis's arm. "Maybe they fell behind the dresser," she said. "Or you accidentally put them in another drawer."

Travis shook his head. "They were there this morning when I got dressed. Now they're gone."

"You mean someone came in and stole them?" Travis's mother stared at her son.

"I don't know, Mom," he said. "I don't know what else could have happened."

"It couldn't have been any of us," Maya said. "We were all together at the sleigh ride."

"It might have happened earlier today," Travis said. "The last time I saw the rings was this morning."

"This house is full of cops," Emily said. "You ought to be able to figure out who did it." She turned to the others. "In the meantime, the rest of you should go on home. Thank you for coming."

She and Lacy helped usher people out the door. Maya took Casey and Brenda with her, and Gage promised to catch a ride home later with Dwight. Then the law enforcement contingent—Travis, Gage, Dwight and Cody—gathered in a corner of the room. "I think you can rule out family," Dwight said. "Your mother and father and Emily, and, of course, Lacy wouldn't have any reason to take the rings."

"Maya and Brenda only came to the sleigh ride," Gage said. "They're out."

"All the employees have been with the family a long time," Travis said. "I'm not saying one of them didn't do it, but I can't think why."

"Doug Whittington hasn't been here that long, has he?" Cody asked.

"He has a record," Dwight said. "Though not for theft."

"There's someone else here who has a record," Gage said. "For robbery."

A chill ran through Cody. "I don't think Bette—"

"You don't know she wouldn't," Gage said. "None of us really know much about her. And she was working in the kitchen all day—right next to Travis's rooms."

Cody nodded. Gage was right. He couldn't let his personal feelings for Bette cloud the fact that on paper, at least, she looked like the ideal suspect. "How do you want to handle this?" he asked.

"I'll talk to Doug first," Travis said. "I think just you and me. He knows both of us, so that may put him more at ease."

"Do you want Dwight and me to talk to Bette?" Gage asked.

"Wait," Travis said. "Let's see what we hear from Doug first."

They found Doug and Rainey in the kitchen, washing cups and plates brought over from the cabin. Rainey turned when Travis and Cody entered the kitchen, but Doug remained hunched over the sink. "What can I do for you two?" she asked.

"We wanted to talk to Doug for a bit," Travis said. He crossed the room and opened the back door. "It won't take long."

Rainey dried her hands and started to remove her apron. "Just Doug," Cody said, and looked hard at the young man. It was a look that had induced many a suspect to be more cooperative, and it worked on Doug, as well. The young man tossed his dish towel on the drain board and followed Travis out the door, Cody close behind.

Outside, the cold bit through Cody's fleece pullover and jeans, and he noticed Doug was already shivering. Maybe that was part of Travis's plan. Instead of sweating the truth out of Doug, he planned to freeze it out of him. "What do you want?" Doug asked.

"Have you been in my room today?" Travis asked.

Doug blinked. "Your room? You mean your bedroom? Here?"

"Yes. Have you been there?"

Doug shook his head. "No. I never go in that part of the house. I mean, why would I?"

"Have you seen a couple of rings I had in there?" Travis continued. "Gold wedding rings."

"No. I told you, I don't go in there. I keep to the kitchen and the dining room and my room. Mom was real clear about that when I moved here."

"Have you seen anyone else in or near Travis's room?" Cody asked.

"Is something missing?" Doug asked. "Is that why you're asking all these questions?"

"Have you seen anyone near Travis's room?" Cody asked again.

He hesitated, then said. "I think I saw that Bette woman. Not in your room, but in the hall just outside of it."

He was lying. Everything in his manner—the shifting eyes, the defensive hunch of the shoulders, as if he was expecting a blow, told Cody his words were a lie. Did Travis see it?

"What time was this?" Travis asked.

"I don't know. This afternoon. She was supposed to be in the kitchen, baking. Mom had told me to stay out of her way. So I thought it was strange she was in the hall in that part of the house."

"Where were you when you saw her?" Cody asked.

Another long pause. "I was just, you know, crossing the great room. I thought I might have left my gloves in there."

"Why would you have left your gloves in there if you never go in there?" Cody asked.

Doug flushed. "I didn't say I never go in there."

"Thank you, Doug. You can go back in now."

The young man left them. As soon as the door closed behind him, Cody turned to Travis. "He's lying," he said.

"Maybe." Travis turned and walked around the side of the house.

"Where are you going?" Cody asked, hurrying after him.

"Let's talk to Bette."

The light over the door to her cabin was lit, and Bette opened the door within seconds of Travis's knock. She was very pale, her lips in a tight line, and she wouldn't meet Cody's gaze. "Come in," she said. "I've been expecting you."

The two men filed in. Bette sat on the edge of the bed—just as she had last night. Cody took the same chair he had used last night, too, while Travis remained standing. "We're asking everyone what they know about the missing rings," the sheriff began.

"You asked Doug," she said. "Now you're asking me. That's not everyone. Just the people with prison records."

Travis didn't react to this accusation. "Do you know anything about the missing rings?" he asked.

"No. I'm not a thief. The bank job—that was one time. And it was stupid. Something I'll regret the rest of my life. But it doesn't matter to you how many times I say I'm sorry, does it? People like you are going to blame me for the rest of my life." Her voice broke on the last words, and Cody had to curl his fingers into his palms to keep from reaching for her. He pushed away the emotion here, freezing it out. Bette wasn't his lover right now—she was a suspect.

"Someone said they saw you near my room this afternoon," Travis said.

"Who said that?" she asked. "Rainey or Doug? They both hate me. They'd say anything to get me into trouble."

"Why do they hate you?" Travis said. "You didn't know them before you came here, did you?"

"No," she said. "Lacy said Rainey was upset that she wasn't chosen to cater the wedding, so maybe this is all part of that resentment. Some people are like that, building grudges into rage."

"I've known Rainey a long time," Travis said. "She gets upset at people, but she's not a liar."

Bette said nothing, merely stared at him.

"Were you in my room at any time today?" Travis asked.

"No," she said. "I've never been in your room. And I didn't take the rings. I didn't even know about the rings."

"Lacy didn't mention them to you when the two of you were talking about the wedding?" he asked.

"No," she said. "I mean, I assumed there would be rings, but we never discussed them."

"Beyond their monetary value, they have a great deal of sentimental value," Travis said. "Especially to Lacy."

"I know. But I didn't take them. I wouldn't do something like that. I would certainly never hurt the person who is my best friend in the world."

"Do you know anyone else who might have taken them?" Travis asked. "Have you seen anyone suspicious in the house?"

"No. I'm sorry, I don't."

Travis glanced around the cabin. "Do you mind if we take a look?"

"You want to search my cabin?" She stood, face flushed, eyes bright with tears. "You mistrust me that much?" This last question was directed at Cody.

"You don't have to submit to a search," Cody said. "But doing so is the quickest way to establish your innocence."

"Oh, sure, because you couldn't just believe me or anything simple like that." She threw up her hands. "Go ahead. Rifle through my belongings. You won't find a ring."

The look she gave him made Cody feel black inside. Whatever the two of them might have started last night, it had ended now. He turned away, to Travis. "Where do you want to start?"

Chapter 11

They found the rings in Bette's cosmetic case, the box wrapped in a piece of tissue and stuffed beneath tubes of lipstick, mascara and eyeliner. When Travis showed it to her, she went so white Cody poised to catch her, thinking she might faint.

She shook her head. "No." She covered her mouth but couldn't hold back a sob. "I swear on my mother's grave, I don't know how that got there." She looked at Cody. "You believe me, don't you?"

His throat hurt as he tried to get the words out that she needed to hear—that yes, he believed her. Of course he knew she wouldn't take the rings.

But he had spent years training to believe what was right before his eyes. He dealt daily in evidence and rules of law based on hard facts, not emotions.

So, though his heart wanted him to say the words, it couldn't overrule his head.

Travis slipped the ring box into his pocket. "Are you going to arrest me?" Bette asked.

"As long as the pass is closed, you can't go anywhere," Travis said. "I don't want to upset Lacy, so for now we'll leave this, while I investigate further."

She sank to the bed again, face buried in her hands. As Cody followed Travis out of the cabin, her sobs hit him like blows. He didn't even feel the cold as they walked toward the house, but when Travis stopped on the porch and turned to him, Cody said, "If that was the right thing to do, why do I feel so awful?"

"Do you think she took the rings?" Travis asked.

"It doesn't matter what I think," Cody said. "We have a witness who said he saw her outside your room this afternoon, and we have the rings in her possession."

"And we have her record."

"Yeah. And we have her record."

Travis pulled out the ring box and looked at it. "I don't think she was faking her shock when we found the ring box."

"Maybe she thought she'd hidden it too well," Cody said.

"It was a lousy hiding place," Travis said. "And she could have put up more of a fuss about us searching. She's been in the system, so she knows her rights. She could have insisted we get a warrant. But she didn't."

"She's right that Doug and Rainey resent her," Cody said.

He nodded. "But if she didn't take the rings, how did someone get into her room?"

"Is there more than one key to those cabins?"

"Yes. There are at least two—maybe three," Travis said.

"Do a lot of people know where they're kept?"

"They're in my dad's office," Travis said. "But it isn't locked. Anyone could get in there."

"This isn't the first time someone may have been in Bette's cabin while she wasn't there," Cody said.

"Oh?"

Cody glanced at the cabin door. "Can we go inside to discuss this? I'm freezing out here."

Travis blinked. Cody thought his friend probably hadn't even noticed the cold until now. "Sure. We'll go into my office."

"Travis!" Lacy called from her seat by the fire when he and Cody entered. He waved her off and led the way across the room to his office.

Cody sank into the cowhide-covered chair and let the warmth of the room wash over him. Travis sat behind the desk. "Bette thinks someone has been in her cabin before?" he asked. "Why didn't she say anything to me or my parents or Lacy about this? How do you know about it?"

"She didn't want to upset your family," Cody said. "She felt they had enough to worry about, what with the upcoming wedding and a serial killer running around. Also, I think she didn't want to call attention to herself or get any kind of reputation as a complainer or a troublemaker. She didn't tell me that, but that's the impression I get."

"That answers part of my question," Travis said. "When did someone go into Bette's cabin, and how do you know about it and I don't?"

"It happened the first night she was here," Cody said.

"I walked her to her cabin—mine is the one next to hers. Someone had painted the words *Go Home* in red paint on her door. She washed it off before anyone else could see, and she made me promise not to tell anyone."

"That's still outside her cabin," Travis said. "You said someone was inside."

"I'm getting to that," he said. "The next night I walked her back again, and this time, I went inside. While I was there, I used the bathroom, and when I opened the cabinet to get a towel to dry my hands, I saw a can of red paint and a brush there."

Travis waited, a skeptical look on his face. "I didn't say anything about it to her," Cody said. "I even played with the idea that Bette had painted the door herself, but I couldn't figure out why she would do something like that. If it was a ploy to call attention to herself, it failed, because I was the only one who saw."

He shifted in the chair. "Later—after her accident, when we were talking—I asked her about it and she said she hadn't seen the can of paint in the cabinet until she was getting ready to take a shower the next morning. She thinks someone was in her cabin while she was out—someone who had a key."

Travis considered this. "So that same someone could have taken the rings and planted them in Bette's cabin, knowing she would be a suspect in the theft, because of her past."

"Right," Cody said. "Except who would do that, and why? Would Doug and Rainey really go to so much trouble to get rid of her? Would they take such personal risk just so they could cater your wedding? It doesn't make sense."

"No. Is there anyone else who might want to get rid of Bette?"

"Whoever attacked her on the road," Cody said.

"If that's the case, her attacker wasn't the Ice Cold Killer," Travis said.

"Did your investigation of Lauren Grenado's murder turn up any new evidence?" Cody asked, grateful for a momentary shift of focus.

"Nothing so far." Travis sat back, the chair creaking underneath his weight. "The business cards are generic cardstock available at pretty much any office supply or craft store and online. The printer is a laser printer—we don't have the expertise to determine a particular brand. The duct tape, again, is a brand that is sold by the millions in hardware stores and home improvement centers. We checked with the stores here in town that sell it, but their records haven't turned up anyone suspicious making a purchase. We've turned up some hairs and fibers from the vehicles, but we're still waiting on test results from the ones we were able to get to the lab before the road closed. No fingerprints. No DNA. No other physical evidence to speak of."

"Is this killer that skilled, or just that lucky?" Cody asked.

"Maybe both," Travis said. "I'm still hanging on to my theory that we're looking for two people, not one. The speed of the crimes points to that. It takes time to subdue and secure a conscious victim and, except for Fiona, the evidence points to the women being conscious until they're killed. Fiona was hit on the head with a rock, but that may be because it was the most public of the killings, and therefore necessitated silencing her immediately."

"And no suspects?" Cody asked.

"There are always suspects," Travis said. "I have a couple I want to interview again tomorrow, if you want to come with me."

"Yes." Cody sat up straighter. He had been dying to have more of a role in the case.

"I'd be interested in getting your perspective on these guys," Travis said.

"What are you going to do about Bette?" Cody asked.

"You two are friends," Travis said. "Talk to her. Feel her out on this theory that someone planted the ring. See if she can come up with possibilities."

"I'll talk to her," Cody said. Though he doubted the friendship they had been building could ever be repaired after tonight. She thought he had betrayed her.

Part of him thought that, too.

"I think it would be better if I didn't cater your wedding," Bette said to Lacy as she pulled her aside after breakfast the next morning. She had lain awake half the night agonizing over what she should do. Travis was willing to let her walk around free for now, but his accusations had cast a pall over what was supposed to be a happy occasion.

"What are you talking about?" Lacy stared at her, confusion filling her hazel eyes.

"After what happened last night, I don't think it would be right for me to have a role in the wedding." Bette twisted her hands together, determined to remain businesslike and not upset her friend more than she had to. "Travis doesn't trust me and I would never, ever want to come between you two."

"What are you talking about, silly?" Lacy took Bette's hand and pulled her down onto the sofa beside her. The two were alone in the great room. "What makes you think Travis doesn't trust you?"

"He thinks I stole your wedding rings."

Lacy's eyes widened. "He does not!" Lacy put her arm around her friend. "He found the rings last night," she said. "He'd misplaced them, that's all."

Bette couldn't look at her friend. Travis must have told Lacy that lie to protect her. He certainly hadn't done it to save Bette.

"I don't want anyone else catering my wedding," Lacy said. "Besides, you've worked so hard already. Those cream puffs and tea cakes you made yesterday were divine, by the way. I know people don't come to weddings for the food, but my guests are going to be blown away by your dishes. Besides, where do you think I'd get a caterer this close to the wedding?"

"Rainey and Doug could do it."

Lacy snorted. "Please! If I wanted to serve steak and potatoes and apple pie, they'd do a fine job. But I don't want that."

"Travis would probably like it," Bette said.

"He'd love it. But he'll like your food, too. He's not as hidebound as he comes across sometimes."

Last night in her cabin, the sheriff had been as unbending as steel. Obviously, Lacy knew another side of him.

"Come on," Lacy said, patting Bette's back. "You need to get away from the ranch for a while. Let's go to town and poke around in some of the cute shops and have lunch."

"All right," Bette said. "While we're there, I need to stop by the store and get some more cream."

"Didn't you just buy some?" Lacy asked. Before Bette could reply, she laughed. "I probably shouldn't have eaten so many of those cream puffs last night—cream puffs, indeed. They'll probably go straight to my hips. Let me get my purse and we'll go right now. I'll meet you by the car."

Bette trudged through the snow to her cabin, torn over what to do next. She had thought to spare her friend pain by resigning from the catering job and quietly fading away. She could find some place in town to stay until the pass opened again. She would have to let Travis know her new address, of course. Otherwise, he might think she was trying to leave town to escape charges.

Was he going to press charges? Should she try to find a lawyer to represent her? The idea dragged at her like a lead coat. She had thought she was past ever having to deal with lawyers and courts and prison again. Yet here she was, being sucked right back into that life. Maybe the real reason so many people returned to prison wasn't that they went back to a life of crime, but because everyone around them assumed they were guilty whenever anything bad happened.

She tried to push these worries aside and focus on having a good time with Lacy. As her friend drove, she chattered happily about the upcoming bridesmaids' tea, the wedding, honeymoon plans and all the things that should capture a bride's attention. Bette listened and nodded and faked enthusiasm. Whatever happened, she was determined it wouldn't spoil Lacy's happiness. She believed Travis wanted that, too, which meant he would do what he could to avoid making a big scene. For now, she would try to be thankful for that small consideration.

Eagle Mountain, with its beautiful setting and access to hiking, skiing, Jeeping and other outdoor activities, catered to tourists. The town's main street was lined with shops selling everything from antiques to climbing equipment to T-shirts. Bette and Lacy spent the morning admiring the clothing in the boutiques and the decorative items in gift shops. Bette even purchased a ceramic chicken designed to hold a recipe card or ingredients list in its beak. She hoped after she left here the item would remind her of her friend—and not the sad way they had parted.

As they headed into the Cake Walk Café for lunch, Lacy hugged Bette. "I'm so glad you could be here for my wedding," she said. "You are one of the dearest people in the world to me. I don't know if I would have survived those years in prison without you."

Bette returned the hug, struggling for composure. "You would have survived," she said. "You're a lot tougher than you look."

Inside, they took a table by the window, looking out onto the town's main street. Tall berms of snow formed a wall on each side of the pavement, and long icicles hung from the eaves, the sun highlighting intricate ice crystals. Under happier circumstances, the effect would have been magical.

After they had ordered, Bette said, "I always knew you were innocent of the charges against you."

"How did you know?" Lacy asked.

"The man who died—your boss?"

"Andy Stenson."

"He was stabbed, right?"

Lacy nodded.

"I couldn't see you doing that—ever," Bette said.

"You're just not that type. You don't have a hair-trigger temper. You don't get frustrated easily. If you didn't like your boss, you would quit and find another job. You wouldn't kill him."

"No, I wouldn't."

Bette picked up the paper cover from the straw in her glass and began tying it in knots. "I don't mean to bring up a painful subject," she said. "But what Travis did to you—accusing you of murder and sending you to prison—it was so awful."

"Yes."

"You used to talk about how much you hated him. And now it's easy to see how much you love him. What happened to change that?"

Lacy traced a line of condensation down the side of her water glass with one finger. "I guess I learned to see past my anger to Travis himself," she said. "To the kind of man he really is. He arrested me not because he disliked me personally, but because he believed at the time that it was the right thing to do. A man had been killed and he believed the man's family—his widow, Brenda—deserved justice. That's not just an abstract term to Travis. He really believes in it. Which is why, when he found evidence that proved I was innocent, he did everything in his power to see that I was released, and the real killer apprehended."

The tender expression on Lacy's face when she spoke of her fiancé made Bette feel teary again. Or maybe that was just her general state of mind today. She touched her friend's hand. "You're a very lucky woman."

Lacy nodded. "I am."

Bette frowned. "Did you say the murdered man's widow was Brenda? Is that Dwight's wife?"

Lacy nodded. "Brenda Prentice was Brenda Stenson. It's kind of crazy, all the connections. But that's part of life in a small town."

"And she never held her husband's death against you?" Bette asked.

"I don't think so." Lacy squeezed her hand. "Forgiveness is a really powerful thing."

After lunch, they headed to the grocery store to buy the cream Bette needed. As they headed up an aisle from the dairy section toward the cash registers, they had to squeeze past a tall gray-haired man, his shoulders hunched. He turned to look at them and Bette gasped and stepped back.

The man grinned. "Hello, Bette," he said. "Somebody told me you were here in town. Small world, isn't it?"

Bette grabbed Lacy's hand and pulled her toward the cash register. She all but threw her money at the startled clerk and hurried out of the store.

Lacy caught up with her in the parking lot. "What was all that about?" she asked, a little breathless.

"Let's just go." Bette tugged at the handle of the locked passenger door on Lacy's car.

"All right." Lacy unlocked the car and slid into the driver's seat.

Bette leaned back against the seat, trying to control her breathing. She watched the exit of the store to see if the man followed them out, but he did not.

"Who was that back there in the store?" Lacy asked as she turned onto Main Street. "Why did he frighten you?"

"I knew him as Carl. Just Carl. No last name." She

shook her head. "He was a friend of Eddie's. He was one of the bank robbers."

"Oh," Lacy said, the one syllable full of understanding. "What is he doing in Eagle Mountain?"

"I don't know."

Lacy pulled the car to the curb and stopped. "I guess I understand why seeing him would have been a surprise, but why are you so terrified? I mean, you're trembling."

Bette clenched her hands in her lap. "I guess I—he was a really good friend of Eddie's. I thought, maybe Eddie sent him after me."

"Why would Eddie do that?" Lacy asked.

"Eddie threatened to kill me if I told the police anything about the robbery and any of the people in it," Bette said. "Of course, I testified at my trial about what I knew. Everyone but the getaway driver had already been arrested and the police had more than enough evidence to convict them. Nothing I said added to that. But Eddie might not have seen it that way."

Lacy turned off the car and unbuckled her seat belt. "We need to tell Travis this right away," she said. "That man may be the one who attacked you the other day."

Bette looked over and realized they were parked in front of the sheriff's department. The last person she wanted to see right now was Travis Walker. But Lacy was right. Carl might be the key to the whole crazy mess she was in.

Chapter 12

"Tell me about these guys we're going to talk to," Cody said as he rode with Travis toward town. All the coffee he'd drunk at breakfast in an attempt to be more alert after a sleepless night had left him wired and jittery. He welcomed this expedition to interview two suspects as a distraction from thoughts of Bette.

"Alex Woodruff and Tim Dawson," Travis said. "They're undergraduates at Colorado State University, where Emily is doing her graduate studies. She knows them casually. Their story is that they came up here to ice climb and got stranded when the road closed earlier this month. They're staying at a vacation cabin that belongs to Tim's aunt."

"Does their story check out?" Cody asked.

"I didn't have any luck getting in touch with the aunt,

but the cabin is registered to her. They are students and they do climb."

"Why are they suspects in the murders?" Cody asked.

"They can't account for their whereabouts when the first two women—Kelly Farrow and Christy O'Brien—were killed. They were at the ranch the day Fiona Winslow died. I want to ask them what they were up to the night Lauren Grenado was murdered."

"There are two of them and you think two men are responsible for the murders," Cody said.

"I don't have enough evidence to get a warrant to search their property, or to request hair and DNA samples to look for a match to what we've got," Travis said. "All I can do is keep a close eye on them."

The cabin where the students were staying was outside town, on a snow-packed Forest Service road. When Travis pulled up to the square log building with a rusting metal roof, it was clear the driveway hadn't been plowed since the last storm. The windows of the house were dark and no vehicle sat under the attached carport. "Looks like no one's been home in a while," Cody said.

"Let's take a look."

Crossing to the house meant post-holing through thigh-deep snow. Cody followed Travis, instinctively taking up position behind and to the right of him, one hand on his Glock. The house might look deserted, but someone inside could be watching their approach, ready to ambush them when they got closer.

But no gunfire or other noise greeted them as they stepped onto the porch. The shades were drawn over the windows and the door locked. Cody looked around. Snow had settled and crusted over the firewood pile and an old bucket that sat overturned near the carport. "I don't think anything here has been disturbed in a while," he said.

"They must have gone back to Fort Collins when the road opened up." Travis turned away and headed back toward his SUV. "I'll contact the university and the police in Fort Collins and double-check with them."

Back in the SUV, Travis put the vehicle in gear and turned back toward town. "Depending on when they left town, they couldn't have killed Lauren Grenado," he said.

"That place looks like it's been empty more than a couple of days," Cody said.

Travis nodded. "On one hand, it's good to rule out innocent men."

"On the other, it bites not having a good suspect for the murders," Cody said.

"I need to stop by the office, if you don't mind hanging out there awhile," Travis said.

"No problem." Cody stretched. "I'm desperate enough for work I'll even fill out reports for you."

As they approached the sheriff's department, Travis said, "That looks like Lacy's car parked out front."

"What did she say when you told her about the rings?" Cody asked.

"I didn't." Travis sighed. "I knew it would upset her terribly if I told her about Bette, so I pretended I had found the rings in another drawer. I don't like to lie to her, but I couldn't think what else to do."

"You don't know that Bette took the rings."

"I don't. And maybe because of what happened with Lacy—that wrongful conviction—I'm more inclined than most to give a person the benefit of the doubt.

There are a lot of things about what happened last night that don't quite fit."

He drove around behind the station and parked, then he and Cody entered through a back door. Adelaide met them in the hallway. "Sheriff, Lacy and—"

"Thanks, Addy. I saw Lacy's car out front. I assume she's in my office." He moved past the older woman. Cody nodded to Adelaide, and followed Travis into his office.

He stopped short when he saw not only Lacy, but Bette, seated in front of Travis's desk. Both women looked upset about something.

Travis moved behind his desk. "Close the door," he said to Cody, then turned to Lacy. "What's wrong? Has something happened?"

Lacy looked to Bette. She pressed her lips together, as if debating whether to speak, then said, "I saw a man in the grocery store just now—one of the other bank robbers. It…it frightened me. I don't know why he's here."

"What this man's name?" Travis asked.

"Carl. I just know him as Carl."

Travis turned to his laptop. As he typed, Cody watched Bette, willing her to look at him. But she kept her head down, staring at her clasped hands in her lap.

"Carl Wayland," Travis said after a moment. "He was released from the Englewood Federal Correctional Facility six months ago. This was his second conviction for armed robbery, and he has a record of a few other lesser crimes—auto theft, one count of menacing. He took a plea bargain in the bank robbery case, thus the lighter sentence."

"What is he doing in Eagle Mountain?" Lacy asked.

"What do you think, Bette?" Travis asked.

Bette shook her head. "I don't know."

"Did he recognize you also?" Travis asked. "How did he behave?"

"Oh, he recognized me. He smiled and said someone had told him I was here." She looked ill. "I don't know, it just struck me as if…as if he had been looking for me."

"Do you think he's the person who attacked you on the road?" Cody asked.

"I don't know. I still can't remember anything about that attack."

"Did he say anything else?" Travis asked. "How long he's been in town, where he was staying—anything?"

"No. I didn't give him a chance to say anything else. I just left."

"Have you been in touch with him, or with anyone else who was part of that robbery, at any time since your release?" Travis asked.

"No! I don't want anything to do with any of them."

"Have any of them tried to contact you? Any phone calls? Letters? Other encounters?"

"No. Never."

Travis angled the computer toward the women to show a mug shot of a man in his fifties with thinning gray hair and a wispy gray goatee. "Does he still look like this?" he asked.

"Yes," they chorused.

"He was wearing a black leather jacket," Lacy said. "And jeans."

Travis swiveled the computer back around. "I'll find him and try to learn what he's doing here."

Lacy took Bette's hand. "Come on," she said. "Let's go back to the ranch. Travis will take care of this now."

Bette rose and the two women left the office. When they were gone, Travis looked up from the laptop again. "What do you think?" he asked Cody.

"I think Bette is terrified of this man. And I think she's telling the truth."

"I think so, too." He stood. "Come on. Let's go see if we can find Carl."

"He's not going to admit it if he is after Bette."

"No. But we might be able to warn him off. A con with a record like his might think twice about going after a woman who's under the protection of a couple of cops."

"I like the way you think." He followed Travis back outside, the image of Bette's terrified white face haunting him. In all the time they had been in the office together, she had never once looked at him. It was as if he no longer existed for her. That hurt worse than if she had stabbed him in the heart.

When Bette and Lacy returned from town, Lacy insisted on going over the seating list for the wedding reception, as well as reviewing the menu for both the reception and the bridesmaids' tea. Bette knew her friend was trying to distract her from her worries, and she was grateful for the attempt, but nothing could make her forget for long the shock of seeing Carl standing in the aisle in the grocery store in Eagle Mountain.

What was he doing here, unless he had somehow followed her? A man like Carl wouldn't have any business in a small town like Eagle Mountain. She kept going over and over the events of the day she had been attacked. Had Carl been in the grocery store that day, too? Had he followed her back to the ranch?

But if Carl was targeting her, why would he do so? The bank robbery had occurred almost nine years ago. Bette had been out of prison eight months. If Eddie had been serious about exacting revenge for her testimony at his trial, surely he would have acted long before now.

Still, it seemed too much of a coincidence that Carl should be in Eagle Mountain, just when so many bad things had happened to her. Had Carl stolen Lacy's and Travis's wedding rings and hidden them in her cabin? She shook her head. That didn't make sense, either. Carl would have kept the rings for himself. From what she remembered, he had a taste for theft. He had even bragged about things he had stolen, the way other men might boast about their times in a marathon or deals they had closed at work. Then again, theft was Carl's work. As far as Bette knew, he had never held a legitimate job—something he had in common with Eddie, though she hadn't realized it at the time.

She was still pondering all this when Travis and Cody returned to the ranch. Everyone else had finished supper, so the two men ate the food Rainey had saved for them and recounted their afternoon's work. "We tracked Carl to the motel in town," Travis said. "But by the time we got there, he had checked out."

"He registered under the name of Charlie Fergusen and paid cash," Cody said. "But the clerk recognized him when we showed her his photograph."

"She says he checked in two days ago," Travis said. "Shortly after the road closed. He said he was passing through and got stranded."

Bette's heart sank. "If he's not at the motel, where is he?" she asked.

"Is the road open again?" Lacy asked.

"Nope." Travis finished the last bite of roast beef. "Which means he found somewhere else to stay. Maybe he heard we were looking for him."

"Or he figured since Bette and Lacy saw him, it was time to hide out," Cody said.

"Every one of my deputies has his description and photograph and will be watching for him," Travis said. "So do all the ranch hands. He won't get near the ranch without us knowing."

"Thank you," Bette said. "I… I don't know what to say. If I brought this trouble to you and your family—"

"You didn't do anything wrong," Travis said. "If this man intends to cause trouble, that's on him." His eyes met hers. "You're my guest and my wife's friend. I'm going to make sure you're protected. I'm sorry if I didn't make that clear before."

Bette read the determination and sincerity in his eyes and in that moment thought she knew what Lacy saw in this serious, quiet lawman. She nodded and turned away, aware as she did so of Cody watching her, just as he had watched her in Travis's office. He was serious and quiet, too, but harder for her to interpret than the sheriff. How could he have made such passionate love to her one night, and stood by saying nothing while Travis accused her of taking those rings? Whatever feelings he had for her, they weren't enough to overcome his suspicions—or his desire to look good in front of his friend. He wasn't that different from Eddie, really—the kind of man who would always put his own best interests ahead of any woman.

Chapter 13

Bette returned to her cabin after breakfast the next morning, and found Cody waiting on the front porch.

He rose from the chair where he had been sitting. "I wanted to talk to you," he said.

She did not want to talk to him. What could she possibly say to him? When he refused to defend her to Travis, she had known what people meant when they talked about a broken heart. It had felt that way, that night in her cabin, a great, tearing pain in her chest.

"You shouldn't be here," she said. "I don't have anything to say—" She stopped, the incongruity of his presence here hitting her. "How did you get in here?" she asked. "I locked the door when I went to breakfast."

He held up a key, identical to the one in her hand. "There are at least three of them for every cabin," he said. "In a box in the drawer of Mr. Walker's desk, where anyone can help himself."

She shut the door behind her and sat on the side of the bed, while he once more took the chair she had almost begun to think of as his. "Why do they have so many keys?" she asked.

"When they built the cabins, they had the idea to rent them out to tourists—sort of a cowboy guest ranch," he said. "They had multiple keys made so that they could give out more than one if, say, a couple stayed in a cabin, and in case someone lost a key."

"How did you find out about the keys?"

"I asked Travis. And I told him about the paint on your door and the paint you found in the bathroom. I know you didn't want me to say anything about that, but I wanted him to know it was possible someone got into your cabin—using a spare key—and planted those rings there."

She eyed him warily. Cody had actually defended her? And Travis had listened? "Did he believe you?"

"He was open to the possibility."

Do you believe me? But she had too much pride to ask the question. "So I know how you got in," she said. "What are you doing here?"

"I came to ask you to go ice fishing with me."

She definitely hadn't seen that one coming. "Ice fishing?"

"Yes. There's a lake on Forest Service land near here that Nate Hall assures me has good fishing. We can use one of the snowmobiles to get there." He actually looked excited about the idea.

"Why would I want to go ice fishing?" she asked. "With you?"

"It's a beautiful day. And I don't want to go fishing by myself."

"Then ask Travis or one of the ranch hands to go with you." She folded her arms across her chest. "Or is this your idea of keeping an eye on me—trailing after me like you trail after one of the fugitives you intend to apprehend?"

He flinched, but she couldn't feel very victorious about the hit. Sitting here with him, in such familiar postures, made her ache for what they had had between them. How perverse was it that she could hate him—and at the same time want to jump his body? She stood. "You need to leave."

He stood also, but instead of moving toward the door, he moved toward her. "Look," he said. "I'm sorry about the other night. You don't want to hear it, but I am."

"You didn't even try to defend me!" She couldn't keep the words back, or the venom behind them. "You stood there while he accused me of a horrible betrayal of my best friend, and you wouldn't even look at me. And you helped him paw through my things, as if I was some common criminal—because that's all that I am to you."

"Bette, no." He took her by the arms. She tried to pull away, but he held on, gentle, yet unyielding. "Look at me," he said.

She looked, and was surprised to see pain in his eyes. "I'm a cop," he said. "It's what I do. What I've trained to do for years. That night, I wasn't here as your lover, I was here as a cop. I had to put aside emotion and consider the evidence as dispassionately as possible."

"So I didn't matter at all—only the evidence."

"That's what I've been taught." He slid his hands

down, until they encircled her wrists, his touch burning into her. "But I learned something important that night."

She couldn't help it, he mesmerized her. This must be what the mouse felt before it was swallowed by the viper. "What did you learn?"

"That I'm not the stone-cold, by-the-book cop I always thought I was. You do matter. And it didn't make any difference what my brain told me when I looked at the evidence, my heart shouted something different. That's why I told Travis about the paint, and went looking for the key."

She wanted to believe him, more than she had ever wanted to believe anyone. Her gaze shifted to his lips, and she leaned in closer, wanting to feel their touch, to taste him, to breathe him in and…

She pulled away. "I don't know if I can trust you," she said.

"I understand that. But come fishing with me today anyway."

"Why?"

"Because you're smart. And I'm smart, too. And I think the two of us can figure this out. Whoever put those rings in your cabin wanted to get you into trouble. I figure if we spend some time away from the ranch and all the tension here, just the two of us doing something mindless like fishing, it might come to us how and why they did it—and maybe even who."

He released her wrists and stepped back. "The Walkers are having a new lock put on your cabin today," he said. "With only one key, which they'll give to you. It would be a good idea if you got away for a few hours so they can do the work."

"So I guess I might as well come with you," she said.

"But just so you know—fish are the only thing you're going to catch today."

The lines around his eyes tightened, and she wondered if he was trying not to laugh at her. "Understood."

Apparently, ice fishing required donning a pair of thick insulated coveralls and round-toed insulated rubber boots that made prison uniforms look like high fashion, and a helmet that weighed as much as a Thanksgiving turkey. "Are we going fishing or visiting the moon?" Bette asked when she was thus dressed.

"You don't want to get cold, do you?" Cody asked.

"Why would anyone want to do anything where you have to dress like this?" she asked, as she climbed onto the back of the snowmobile he had parked in front of her cabin.

"Because it's fun."

"Standing around a hole in the ice waiting for a fish to get hungry enough to eat a worm does not sound like my idea of fun," she said.

"Sure it is." He climbed on the snowmobile in front of her and punched the button to start the engine. It roared to life, shaking every part of her. "Hang on!" he shouted over the rumbling noise, then they shot forward.

She clung to him, her heart in her throat, but after a few hundred yards she began to relax a little and enjoy the sensation of racing over the snow. Cody whooped and steered the machine through the trees, which sped by in a blur of white and green. They roared up an incline, then plunged across an iced-over creek. It was like riding a motorcycle, only better, since they didn't have to follow a road. They could pick any path they liked over the deep snow, though she realized after a while that Cody was following orange markers blazed on the trees.

Half an hour or so later, he slowed the machine. He gestured toward a frozen lake in the distance, the ice a blue mirror reflecting the surrounding evergreens. After a few minutes, the lake disappeared from view. Cody halted the snowmobile in a clearing. Bette's ears rang in the sudden silence. They climbed off the snowmobile and removed their helmets. "You know how they say getting there is half the fun?" she asked.

"Yeah," he said.

"I think in this case, it was all the fun." She grinned. "That was a blast."

"You've never been on a snowmobile before?"

"No."

"Then after we're done fishing I'll take you the long way home."

"I want to drive," she said.

"No." He pocketed the keys. "You just told me you've never even been on one of these things before."

"I'm a quick learner. Besides, how hard could it be? They rent them to tourists."

He opened a compartment on the back of the snowmobile and took out some disassembled fishing poles, a tackle box, two plastic buckets and what looked like an oversize drill. He fitted the sections of the poles together, handed the poles and tackle to her, then shouldered the drill and picked up the buckets. "What is that thing on your shoulder?" she asked.

"Ice auger. We just have to hike through those trees and up that little rise to reach the lakeshore." He strode toward the trees and she tromped through the snow after him. As the woods thinned, the lake came into view once more, heavy snow on its shore giving way to thick ice. Out on the ice, Cody lowered the auger. "As soon as I drill a hole with this, we can fish," he said.

"Excuse me if I don't stand around watching," she said. She returned to shore and began following a trail around the edge. Hoofprints in the snow showed where deer had walked along the edge of the lake, perhaps searching for open water to drink. She couldn't see the snowmobile from here, which made her feel all the more isolated. When she had gone some ways, she turned and looked back toward Cody. He was attacking the ice with the auger, all his concentration on the task.

I'm a cop. It's what I do. What did that mean—to be a cop? If someone had asked her that question a year ago, when she was still in prison, she would have said cops went after people who committed crimes—and a lot of people who didn't. She would have pointed out that cops too often locked someone up because it was easy to make a case against them, and that they were more interested in cadging free doughnuts from the coffee shop than finding out the truth.

There were still some cops like that, she believed. But there was another kind, too. Travis had worked hard to get to the truth and free Lacy, long before she fell in love with him. His brother, Gage, seemed to be a man who tried to do what was right.

Then there was Cody—who had refrained from killing a desperate man, only to have that man commit suicide right in front of him. The pain she had seen in his eyes when he had told her that story, and the pain she recognized when he had apologized to her, had been real, mirroring her own hurt. She believed he was trying to see past the evidence and his training to her innocence. But was that going to be enough?

He set aside the auger, then spotted her and motioned her to come back to him. She retraced her steps around the pond and out onto the ice. He handed her a fishing pole, then turned one of the buckets upside down and set it beside the hole. "Make yourself comfortable and drop your line in," he said.

She sat on the bucket and plopped the end of the weighted line into the water, where it sank out of sight. Cody sat on the other bucket beside her. "Isn't this fun?" she said, heavy on the sarcasm.

"It's a beautiful day," Cody said. "We're out in the fresh air, we might catch some fish for supper and we're alone."

Right. Alone at last. "Then let's talk about who stole those wedding rings and put them in my cabin," she said.

"Almost anyone at the ranch could have taken the key from Mr. Walker's desk and let himself into your cabin," Cody said. "Just as many people had access to Travis's bedroom, where he kept the rings."

"It would be easier on everyone if the thief wasn't someone on the ranch, but an outsider," Bette said. Another reason suspicion had focused on her.

"Someone like Carl Wayland," Cody said.

"Yes, but I don't see how Carl—or Charlie, or whatever name he's going by these days—could have slipped into the house unnoticed, taken the key and the wedding rings and stashed them in my cabin," she said. "There are always too many people around. Besides, why carry out such a complicated plot to implicate me?"

"I agree," Cody said. "I still think Doug or Rainey is

the most likely candidate for that, though I can't think why. Even given that they're jealous of you, or want to cater the wedding themselves, that kind of behavior doesn't make sense. They risk too much for too little gain."

"I agree," Bette said.

"Is there someone else who wants you away from the ranch, but is being more subtle about it?" Cody asked. "Do you have an ex-lover among the ranch hands? Or someone you double-crossed in prison who wants to get back at you? Are you the long-lost daughter of the duke who has come to claim her birthright and the family fortune?"

She laughed. "I guess those theories made as much sense as anything I can come up with."

His expression grew more serious. "Let's put aside the ring theft for a while. What about the person who attacked you with the big rock on your way home from town? Still no memory of that?"

"No. I'm wondering if I should try being hypnotized or something. I can't remember anything."

"But it could have been Carl?"

"Yes," she said. "That attack strikes me as more his style."

"Why would he want to hurt you?"

"He was friends with Eddie. Eddie swore he'd kill me if I gave the police any information about the gang or the robbery."

"So you think maybe Eddie sent him here to make good on his threat?" Cody asked.

She shifted the fishing pole in her hand. "I don't know. That doesn't make a lot of sense to me, either. By the time the police arrested me, they already had everyone but the getaway driver, and I didn't know anything about him. Nothing I told the police made things worse for Eddie. I never talked to him again after the day of the robbery, but he could have easily gotten a message to me if he wanted to threaten me again or remind me of his promise. I've been out of prison eight months and nothing has happened to make me feel like I'm in danger."

"Until you showed up here." He sat forward on his bucket. "I think I got a bite."

A few seconds later, he was scooping a large trout into a net and depositing it on the ice between them. "Dinner," he said, and grinned at her.

While he took care of the fish and rebaited his hook, she thought about Carl. "When I saw Carl in the grocery store, he didn't seem surprised to see me," she said. "Maybe that's because he did come to Eagle Mountain to look for me."

"Was a lot of money taken in that robbery?" Cody asked. "Maybe Carl thinks Eddie gave the loot to you and he wants his share."

She shook her head. "The bank got all the money back. The police caught Eddie and the others before they even had a chance to divide it up."

"Why didn't they catch the driver?" Cody asked.

"I guess he wasn't at the apartment the afternoon the police showed up. I really don't know, since I wasn't there, either. They arrested me later, after they learned of my relationship with Eddie. They already knew someone had shut off the alarm system and left the back door unlocked." She hung her head. "You don't know how many times I've regretted doing those things.

I knew they were wrong, but Eddie had persuaded me the ends justified the means. I was so stupid."

"You paid for your mistake," he said.

"I did." She gripped the fishing pole tighter. "I've worked really hard to build a new life for myself, and I wouldn't risk throwing all that away by stealing a couple of wedding rings—especially rings that belong to a woman who's done everything she could to help me."

"I believe you," Cody said.

She stared at him. "You're willing to overlook the evidence and take my word for it?"

"I'm not overlooking the evidence," he said. "The rings were hidden in an obvious location. You're not that dumb. If you had taken them, you would have locked them in your suitcase or tucked them under the eaves or, I don't know, sewn them into your bra. You wouldn't have put them where we could find them so easily."

"Maybe I believed you wouldn't look," she said.

"You let us search your cabin without a warrant. Even an innocent person might not have done that. Again—you're not stupid."

"Thank you. I think."

"I convinced the Walkers not to tell anyone about the new lock on your cabin," he said. "They're going to leave the spare keys in the desk, just like before, and Travis is setting up a hidden video camera in the office, focused on the desk. If anyone comes to take the key again, we'll catch them."

"Then I hope they do come," Bette said. She cleared her throat. "And thank you. You're going to a lot of trouble to clear my name. Travis, too, I guess."

"We want to catch the right person," he said. "The worst thing that can happen, as a law enforcement officer, is to find out you helped put an innocent person behind bars. It makes you doubt everything about yourself and the job."

"I guess I never thought about that," she said. "I only saw things from the point of view of the innocent person—someone like Lacy."

"Sometimes cops are victims of their own zeal to close a case," he said. "Or we get fooled by the evidence. It can happen easier than you think."

"Has it ever happened to you?"

"No. And knowing it can happen makes me more careful." His eyes met hers. "I don't want you to be my first mistake."

She looked away, warmed by his words, but too unsure to speak. She wanted to believe Cody had her best interests at heart, but she had learned the hard way that her hormones could overrule good sense. She didn't want to make the same mistake again.

She cleared her throat and turned to him. "Why a cop?" she asked. "I mean, why would you want a job that puts you in contact with so many dangerous, unpleasant people?"

"Why did you want to be a caterer?"

"Because I like to cook, I like parties and it's something I'm really good at."

"It's sort of the same thing with me." He pulled up his line and checked the hook, then lowered it into the water again. "I started out wanting to be a lawyer. I liked the idea of putting away criminals, and television shows and books make it seem really glamorous. By the time I graduated and started prepping to take the bar exam, I'd figured out it was a lot duller than most people know. Then I met a guy who worked for the US

Marshals Service and he told me they were hiring, and that with my law degree, I'd have one up on a lot of candidates. I decided to apply, maybe do the job for a couple of years before I took the bar exam." He shrugged. "I got hooked and never looked back."

"Do you ever think about doing anything else— maybe taking the bar?" she asked.

He hesitated before answering. "I never used to," he said. "Now... I don't know. Maybe someday. I guess seeing somebody blow his brains out right in front of you gives you a different perspective on the job."

She put her hand on his arm and kept it there. "I guess law enforcement needs people like you," she said. "But you'd probably make a good lawyer, too."

"The path we choose when we're young doesn't have to be the one we stay on our whole lives." His eyes met hers, and she had the sense of seeing the real man, with no defensive screens. "People can change."

He was telling her he believed she had changed, and her heart felt too big for her chest as the idea sank in. This hard-nosed cop was telling her that—maybe—he was learning to see past the mistakes she had made.

Maybe even into a future where a woman like her and a man like him might be together.

By the time the sun began sinking behind the trees, Cody and Bette had caught five good-sized fish. He cleaned them and packed them in snow in one of the buckets, then they gathered their gear and headed back toward the snowmobile.

They were still a few dozen yards from the machine when Cody halted, frowning. Bette set down the tackle box and followed his gaze toward the snowmobile. "What is it?" she asked.

He shook his head and started forward again. Twenty yards farther on, Cody stopped again and set down the auger and the bucket of fish. He motioned for Bette to stay back and he approached the snowmobile.

The snow around the machine had been churned up. The snowmobile's hood lay in the snow a few feet beyond them, and Bette could see wires sticking up out of the engine compartment. Cody carefully circled the machine, then scanned the area around them. "What's wrong?" Bette called when she could bear the tension of his silence no more.

"Someone's wrecked it," he said. "On purpose." He gestured toward the dangling wires. "They've cut the wiring harness."

"What are we going to do?" she asked.

He pulled out his phone and took photographs of the damage, and of the ground around the snowmobile. "No service," he said, checking the screen. "We'll have to walk back."

She looked past the snowmobile, at the faint track they had made getting to this place. "How far is it?" she asked.

"About five miles." He moved the bucket of fish and the auger closer to the snowmobile, and took the poles and tackle from her to add to the pile. "Come on," he said. "We'd better get started if we want to make it back before dark."

Chapter 14

The trek back to the ranch was brutal, post-holing through snow up past the knees. They hadn't traveled half a mile before Cody was sweating inside the thick insulated coverall, and the rubber boots that were fine for snowmobiling and fishing felt as if they weighed ten pounds each. Bette was having a hard time, too, though she didn't utter a word of complaint. He tried to break trail for her, but that didn't make the going much easier.

He had remembered to grab a water bottle from the snowmobile, and he stopped after what he judged to be the first mile and handed it to her. She drank deeply and returned it to him. "How do you know we're headed in the right direction?" she asked.

"I'm following our path here, and the blazes on the trees." He indicated the orange plastic diamonds affixed to tree trunks at regular intervals.

She nodded. "So, is this just another prank to annoy me—like the message on my door?"

"The lake is on National Forest land," Cody said. "It's possible someone came along and decided to mess with the snowmobile—malicious mischief."

"Why didn't we see them—or hear them?"

"I think they parked in the woods and walked in," Cody said. "We were out of sight over the hill, and the sound wouldn't necessarily have carried that far. They wouldn't have had to make a lot of noise."

"Maybe I'm being paranoid, but I think this was directed at me," she said. "It kind of fits with a pattern of harassment."

"Would Carl do something like this?"

"I have no idea. Maybe. I didn't know the man. I didn't want to know him."

"When Travis finds him, he can follow up on his alibi for this afternoon."

"If he finds him," she said.

He stashed the water bottle in one of the pockets of his coat. "Come on. Let's keep walking." But before he could take even another step forward, something whistled past his ear, followed by the distinctive popping sound of weapons fire.

"Get down!" He shoved Bette into the snow and threw himself on top of her, as bullets continued to strike around them. "Into the trees," he said and shoved her forward. Scrambling in the deep snow, they headed for a stand of fir, fifty yards to their left, away from the direction of the shots. They moved clumsily through the thick snow, clawing their way toward cover as bullets continued to rain down. Cody tried to keep himself between Bette and the shooter, staying low to present a smaller target and moving erratically when possible. They had almost reached cover when the impact of a bullet propelled him forward. Burning pain radiated from his shoulder as he fell, but he kept moving, crawling after Bette, into the trees. They lay at the base of one of the evergreens, gasping.

Grimacing, Cody raised up enough to unzip his coverall and draw his Glock, though the movement cost him. His right shoulder felt as if someone had rammed a hot poker through it, and he could feel blood dripping down his back.

"You're hurt!" Bette stared at his shoulder, her face almost as white as the surrounding snow.

He sat back against the tree, keeping his weight on his good side, and closed his eyes a moment, gearing up for what he knew he'd have to do next.

Bette crawled up beside him. "Let me see," she said.

He angled his body so that she could look. "I think the bullet is still in there," he said. "How much blood is there?"

"Not as much as I would have thought," she said. "It's more seeping than gushing. That's good, I think."

He nodded. It was good—as long as the bullet hadn't nicked some internal artery. But he didn't think so. "How are you at first aid?" he asked.

"I can put a Band-Aid on a boo-boo," she said. "I think this requires more than that."

"If I was the kind of man who carried a clean white handkerchief everywhere, we could use it as a bandage," he said.

She studied the wound again. "I guess what we're looking for is something clean that can soak up the blood and protect the wound from dirt, right?"

"Right."

"Then I have something." She turned her back to him and unzipped her coveralls. A few deft movements later, she pulled out her bra and dangled it in front of his face. "It's padded and it's mostly cotton. And it's clean."

He choked back a laugh. "You're amazing, you know that?"

"I'm practical. It's not the same thing. Now turn around."

He grit his teeth and cried out only once as she doused the wound with the rest of the water from their bottle, then twisted and wrapped the bra into an awkward bandage. "It looks ridiculous, but I think it will serve our purposes," she said. "Now what?"

"Now we try to find a way out of here," he said. The gunfire had stopped, leaving the area silent—the unnatural silence after violence has intruded.

Bette followed his gaze to the open area they had just crossed. "He was waiting for us," she said in a ragged whisper. "Watching us. He let us get away from the snowmobile, out in the open, and when we stopped, he tried to kill us."

"It looks that way." Cody checked his gun to make sure it was loaded—it was always loaded, but this gave him something to do with his hands, since whoever had put them in this situation wasn't close enough to strangle.

Bette closed her eyes, then opened them again. "This is crazy. I just need to find Carl and ask him what he wants. That's what I should have done in the grocery store that day, instead of running away."

"Maybe this isn't Carl," Cody said.

She stared at him. "You don't think it's Doug? Or Rainey?"

"Maybe it's the Ice Cold Killer."

"He's a serial killer. He ambushes women and cuts their throats."

"He didn't cut your throat," Cody said. "You're unfinished business." The more he thought about it, the more it made sense to him. Yes, the attack on Bette hadn't been the killer's usual style, but that might be a sign that he was getting desperate. Coming unhinged. Considering that it took a kind of mental imbalance to become a serial killer in the first place, was it so far-fetched to think that could progress into an obsession with one particular woman? "Maybe he's been waiting for another chance and thought this was it."

"So what do we do now?" she asked. "Lie here and wait for him to come after us?"

"I think we wait and see what he does next."

"I am not going to lie here and let him pick us off like shooting fish in a barrel," she said. She started to rise but wasn't to her feet yet when a bullet hit the tree trunk above her head, sending bark flying.

With a yelp, she flattened herself on the ground once more. "Okay, I guess that was stupid," she muttered.

Cody studied the landscape beyond this stand of trees. A small rise, slightly above and to the left, would provide good cover for the shooter. "I think he's in the rocks up there," he said, indicating the spot. "I don't think he can see us here, but he probably knows he hit me. He's waiting to see what we do next."

"Can you shoot him from here?" she asked.

"No. He's using a rifle. My handgun isn't going to do us any good unless he gets closer." He nudged her.

"Let's start moving back, deeper into the woods. He won't be able to get a clear shot at us, and he may have to expose himself to come after us."

They crawled backward twenty, then thirty feet, to the banks of a frozen creek that wound through the trees. Cody moved awkwardly, trying and failing to protect his wounded shoulder, so that by the time they reached the creek, he was dizzy from pain. When he could speak, he said, "If we move along this creek, we'll be headed toward the ranch, but we'll still have cover."

"It's going to take all night to get back to the ranch, crawling on our hands and knees," she said. "And you need a doctor."

Cody didn't tell her they probably didn't have all night. A killer who had followed them to the lake, sabotaged their snowmobile, then waited patiently for them to provide clear targets wasn't going to stop his pursuit now. All Cody could do was try to make the task more difficult for him. Keeping in the shelter of the trunk of a large fir, he rose to his knees, then stood. All remained silent. "Come on. It will be easier walking."

They moved alongside the creek, climbing over snowbanks and skirting deadfall. No one fired on them, but Cody had the sensation that they were still being watched. Was the shooter waiting for them to emerge into the open again?

And then they were almost out of cover, the woods giving way to a broad meadow, snow like icing over a sheet cake. He stopped ten yards from the last tree. "We can't cross that," Bette whispered.

Cody scanned the surroundings, looking for the shooter's vantage point. He saw half a dozen possibilities. He needed to draw the man out, make him show his hand. He had no chance if he didn't know where the shots would come from. But Bette was right—stepping into that open field would be suicide.

"When we don't come back for supper, someone from the ranch will come looking for us," Bette said. "They knew we were coming here to fish."

It was anyone's guess how long that would take. By himself, Cody might have hazarded more direct action, but he couldn't risk Bette. "Then I guess we wait," he said.

He made himself as comfortable as possible—which wasn't very comfortable, his back to a tree, the gun in his right hand, trying to ignore the throbbing pain in his left shoulder and arm. Bette sat beside him, one hand on his thigh. She kept glancing at his injured shoulder. "What?" he asked, the tenth time she looked.

"The blood is seeping through," she said.

"I hope it wasn't your favorite bra," he said.

"If you'd ever had to wear one, you'd know there is no such thing," she said.

"I think I can speak for most men when I say you never have to wear one on our account."

A twig snapped, and they both sat up straighter. His hand tightened on the Glock.

"Maybe it's just a deer," she whispered.

A bullet thudded into a tree five feet in front of them. "Last time I checked, deer didn't carry rifles," Cody said, as he urged her to the ground. He peered around the trunk of the tree. Was that movement there, behind those rocks? He fired, and shards of rock flew from a boulder at the front of the grouping, followed by a volley of gunfire in their direction.

He flattened himself on the ground over Bette. "You're crushing me," she said, her face in the dirt.

"Better flattened than dead."

"And people say chivalry is dead."

"If I could get a little closer, I'd have a better chance of hitting him," he said.

She clutched his arm. "No. He'll kill you."

"Not if I'm careful."

"No," she said again. "Don't leave me."

"I won't." He realized he couldn't. If the gunman did kill him, she'd be left helpless. The shooter fired sporadically for the next ten minutes, with Cody returning fire. Then the hammer clicked onto an empty cylinder. He sagged to the ground behind the tree again and tried to move his left hand toward the spare ammo clip on his belt. It was impossible.

"What are you doing?" Bette asked.

"I need you to get the ammo clip off my belt," he said.

She fumbled a little, but managed to unfasten the clip. "Aren't you Mr. Prepared?" she said.

"Aren't you glad I am?"

"Oh, I am." She levered herself up and kissed him, hard. "I'm very glad."

The roar of an engine—more than one engine, Cody decided—broke the stillness that had followed the last volley of gunfire. Headlights swept the edge of the forest. Breaking twigs and muffled steps announced the shooter's retreat. Cody waited, heart pounding painfully. Beside him, Bette breathed raggedly.

"Cody! It's Travis! Are you okay?"

"In here!" Bette stood and waved, then moved toward their voices. Cody closed his eyes and sagged against the tree. They were safe. For now, anyway.

Chapter 15

"Travis, I've never been so glad to see anyone in my life." Bette grabbed the sheriff by the arm and dragged him toward the tree where she and Cody had been sheltering. "Cody's hurt. He needs a doctor right away."

"What happened?" Mr. Walker strode up behind his son.

"Someone sabotaged our snowmobile, so we had to walk out," Bette said. "Then they started shooting at us. They hit Cody." They had reached the tree.

Travis knelt beside Cody. "Hey."

Cody scowled at him. "Hey yourself. About time you got here."

"Bette said somebody shot you."

"Rifle shot. It didn't bleed too much."

"Let me take a look." He helped Cody sit forward,

and he shined the light on the bloodstained bandage. He frowned. "What is that you've got on there?" he asked.

"A padded bra," Bette said, her tone daring him to say something about it.

"Any idea who was doing the shooting?" Travis asked.

"Never got a look at him," Cody said. "He fired on us first in the open, then followed us in here. He had us pinned down while he was shooting from behind those rocks." He gestured toward the shooter's location. "I kept him from getting any closer, then you scared him off."

"I need you to wait here while I take a look," Travis said.

"I'm not going anywhere."

Mr. Walker stayed with them while Travis went to investigate the rock outcropping. "When you didn't show up for supper, we figured your snowmobile might have broken down," Mr. Walker said.

"Someone cut the wiring harness," Cody said. "It shouldn't be too hard to fix."

"I'm not too worried about that machine right now, son," Mr. Walker said. He turned to Bette. "How about you? Are you okay?"

"I am now," she said. "You arrived just in time."

The approaching beam of Travis's flashlight signaled his return. "I didn't find much," he said. "Some impressions in the snow. We'll come back in the morning and take a better look. It's getting too dark to track anybody right now."

"Whoever it was is probably long gone," Cody said.

Travis handed his father the flashlight and moved to Cody's other side. "Can you walk?" he asked.

"I can walk," Cody said. With Travis's help, he staggered up. Bette followed, Mr. Walker bringing up the rear. Travis helped Cody onto his snowmobile, then Bette climbed on behind his dad.

The return trip to the ranch had none of the joy of the morning's journey. Bette held on to Mr. Walker, teeth chattering as icy wind buffeted her, her gaze fixed on the dark shadow of Cody's back on the snowmobile just ahead.

As they neared the ranch, Travis slowed. "We've got a phone signal now," Mr. Walker called over his shoulder. "He's phoning ahead for help."

Fifteen minutes later, they arrived at the ranch house, where a small crowd waited to greet them. "An ambulance is on the way," Travis said. "Let's get inside, where it's warm."

Bette climbed off the snowmobile, stiff with cold. She tried to move toward Cody, but Lacy put her arm around her and steered her toward the house. "You're half-frozen," she said. "Come in here by the fire."

"Cody—" Bette looked over her shoulder.

"I've got Cody," Travis said. "Go inside."

Too worn out to argue, Bette let Lacy lead her into the house and help her out of the bulky helmet, coveralls and boots. She sighed with relief as Lacy tucked her under a blanket in a chair by the fire. A few second later, Cody came in, leaning on Travis's arm. But he balked at sitting on the sofa. "I'm not going to bleed on your furniture," he said.

Mr. Walker brought a chair from the dining table and Cody lowered himself gingerly into it. His face was gray, tight with pain. Bette hurt, looking at him, but she couldn't tear her eyes away. She couldn't forget the way he had lain on top of her, protecting her body with his own. "Where is the ambulance?" she asked.

"It's coming," Lacy said.

"What happened?" Emily asked. "Travis didn't give a lot of details when he called."

"Someone wrecked the snowmobile, then started shooting at us," Cody said. "He had us pinned down behind a tree when the cavalry arrived and scared him off."

"Who would do something like that?" Emily asked.

"If I knew the answer to that, I sure wouldn't be sitting here right now," Cody said.

The strident wail of the ambulance stopped all conversation. Mr. Walker went outside to direct them and moments later two paramedics came in and began examining Cody.

Lacy handed Bette a mug and pulled a chair closer to her. "Are you okay?" she asked. "No wounds or frostbite or anything that needs seeing to?"

"No, I'm fine." She sipped the mug, which turned out to be hot chocolate, heavily laced with peppermint schnapps. Soothing warmth spread through her.

"That must have been terrifying," Lacy said.

"Yes." The fear still hadn't left her. They both might have been killed. No. She couldn't think about that. They were safe. They were going to be okay.

Cody let out a sharp cry and she had to set the mug on the table beside her, her hands shook so violently. Then the paramedics helped him onto a waiting stretcher and draped blankets over him.

Travis came and bent over Bette. "They're taking him to the clinic in town to have the bullet removed," he said. "I'm going to go with him. Is there anything else you can tell me about the guy who shot at you?"

She shook her head. "We never saw him. Cody said he had a rifle. He followed us for a while. I think he was waiting for us to come out into the open again, then he came in after us. I don't know who he is, I swear."

"Doug and Rainey both served supper tonight," Travis said. "So it wasn't them. We're still trying to find Carl Wayland."

"Call us after Cody comes out of surgery," Lacy said.

"I will." He kissed her goodbye and left.

"Drink your chocolate," Lacy said. "I'll bring you something to eat."

"I don't think I could eat," Bette said.

"Then I'll bring it and you can pick at it."

After she left, Bette leaned back in the chair and closed her eyes. She had thought the events of the afternoon would replay in her head but instead the image that came to her was of Cody, bringing up that first fish and giving her a look of triumph—the kind of look friends would share.

The kind of look she thought she would like to see over and over again. For the rest of her life.

Cody called the sheriff's department the next morning just after eight. Adelaide answered and when Cody said he wanted to speak to the sheriff, she informed him that Travis was still at the ranch, probably eating breakfast. "He was out on a call very late last night," she said.

"I know," said Cody. "I was that call."

"Marshal Rankin, is that you?" Adelaide asked. "How are you doing?"

"I'm sore and grumpy and don't intend to stay in this clinic one minute longer than necessary."

"I don't know what you expect the sheriff to do about that."

"I want him to come get me and take me back to the ranch. But since he's not there—Adelaide, everyone knows you really run that department. Can't you send a deputy over to get me?"

"This is a sheriff's department, not a taxi service."

"I'm an officer of the law, so consider it an inter-agency favor." No response. He resorted to begging. "Please, Adelaide. They don't even make decent coffee in this place and I had to threaten the nurse to get her to bring me my clothes."

"I'll see what I can do."

Ten minutes later, Gage walked into the clinic. He grinned when he saw Cody, who was sitting on the edge of the narrow clinic bed, his shoulder swathed in bandages. "I figured your shirt was trashed, so I brought you this." He held out a Rayford County Sheriff sweatshirt. "Size extra-large, so it should fit over those bandages."

"Thanks." Cody stood and began struggling into the shirt. Gage moved over to help him. "Let's get out of here," Cody said, when he was dressed.

When they were in the cruiser, Gage handed him a large cup of coffee. "Adelaide sent this," he said.

"Bless her." He popped the lid and drank deeply.

"She said you were a real bear on the phone. Want to tell me why?"

"Oh, I don't know. Having a divot taken out of my shoulder and trying to sleep in that clinic on that narrow bed, and nobody telling me anything about what is going on—I think that would put anyone in a bad mood."

"Normally we send gunshot victims to the hospital in Junction," Gage said. "The clinic isn't really set up for surgery. And from what I hear, you were lucky. The bullet just missed shattering your shoulder blade."

Cody grunted and drank more coffee. He began to feel more human. "How is Bette?" he asked.

Gage glanced at him. "Was she shot, too?"

"No. I just… I just wondered how she's doing."

"I haven't heard. You can ask her yourself when you get to the ranch. I called and let Travis know you were coming."

"Any sign of Carl Wayland?"

"Nope. But unless he hiked out, he's still here. Last avalanche on the pass took out a bunch of power lines—poles and line strung all over the highway, under about ten feet of packed snow and rock. It's going to take a while to fix that mess."

Another grunt from Cody. That seemed to be the best he could do at the moment. His shoulder hurt like the devil, but he had refused the pain meds the doctor had prescribed, not wanting to fog his brain. He had lain awake in the early morning hours, replaying everything that happened yesterday. But no matter how many times he went over the puzzle, he couldn't find the missing pieces. That, more than anything, had put him in a bad mood.

At the ranch, Travis came out to meet him, followed by Bette and Lacy. Cody refused Travis's offer of assistance and got out of the car under his own power. He caught Bette's eye and nodded. He was all right. And he was going to make things all right for her.

"Should you be out of the hospital?" Lacy asked.

"There is no hospital," he said. He moved past her. "I can mend here as well as anywhere."

"You look like you're in pain," Bette said, coming alongside him.

"So do you," he said. "What's your excuse?" He winked, to let her know there was no heat behind the words, no matter how gruff they may have sounded. That earned him a smile.

"I'd better get back to work," Gage said. "And I've got a bachelor party to see to."

"I don't think now is a good time for that," Travis said. "We should put it off."

"Moe is closing down the whole pub for us," Gage said. "It won't kill you to take a few hours to say goodbye to single life with your friends."

"Neither you nor Dwight had a bachelor party," Travis said.

"Right. So we're really looking forward to yours. It's too late for you to back out now."

"Besides, you have to get out of the house so we women can have our party," Lacy said.

Gage glanced at Cody. "If you feel up to it, you're still welcome to come," he said. "Since you probably can't drink, you can be our designated driver."

"I'll let you know," Cody said.

When Gage had gone, Travis joined Cody by the fire. "Dad and I went out to the lake again at first light," he said. "We were able to follow tracks we think were the shooter's to that rock outcropping, back to where it looks like he parked a snowmobile. But then we lost him."

"What about your wrecked snowmobile?"

"Dad doesn't think it'll be too hard to fix. We brought home the fish you caught—frozen solid in that bucket."

"Guess we'll take a rain check on that fish fry," Cody said. He pulled a plastic bag from his pocket. "I brought you something."

Travis studied the smashed piece of metal. "The bullet they took out of you?"

"They got a few bone fragments, too, but I didn't think they qualified as evidence." He nodded to the bag. "It's pretty distorted, but you can tell it's a .225 round."

"Maybe it will help, if we ever find anybody to pin this on." He pocketed the bag. "What does the doctor say about your shoulder?"

"I didn't smash my shoulder blade. I didn't slice an artery and bleed out—which I already kind of figured. Didn't tear any major ligaments. Chipped some bone, damaged some muscle. I need physical therapy and for the rest of my life I'll know when a snowstorm is on its way." He blew out a breath. "Two months off work, at least. Maybe three."

"That bites."

"Yeah, well. Maybe I'll take up a hobby."

"I have to go," Travis said. "I'm determined to track down Carl Wayland today."

"I hope you do."

Travis started to walk away, then turned back. "About this party tonight. You really don't have to come."

"Are you kidding? I wouldn't miss it for the world."

Bette spent the rest of Saturday morning in the kitchen, preparing the food for the tea that evening, glad to have something to keep her busy. She was pulling a sheet of petit fours out of the oven when Rainey came in. Bette braced herself for some criticism or complaint. "What are you making?" Rainey asked.

The question surprised Bette. Rainey sounded genuinely interested. "These are petit fours for Lacy's bridesmaids' tea," she said. "They don't look like much right now, but they will after I decorate them."

"I guess those girls really go for that fancy food," Rainey said. "I never learned how to do all that. All I know is plain cooking."

"Every meal I've had here has been excellent," Bette said, truthfully. "I imagine you make exactly the kinds of meals the family loves."

"Oh, yeah. Cowboys like plain food that'll stay with them when they're working all day," Rainey said. "Still, it might be nice to know how to do fancy stuff."

"You could learn," Bette said. "You already know how to cook, so it wouldn't take you any time at all to pick up a few new techniques. I could even show you if you like."

"Maybe. Though I don't know if I'd have time. They keep me pretty busy around here."

"I imagine you were glad to have your son come and help you," Bette said.

"I was. Except…"

"Except what?"

"He hasn't been all that much help since you came." She gave Bette a sideways look. "I was hoping you could tell me why."

"What do you mean?" Bette asked.

"It took me a while to figure it out, but it finally come to me—Doug is afraid of you. That's why he avoids you so much."

"Afraid of me?" She stripped off her oven mitts and faced Rainey. "Why would he be afraid of me?"

"I was hoping you could tell me."

Ah. Maybe this explained Rainey's uncharacteristic friendliness. "What makes you think Doug is afraid of me?"

"Just the way he acts. I know my boy. What I can't figure out is why."

"I don't know what to tell you," Bette said. "I haven't done anything to him, I promise. I mean, what could I do?"

"Well, he's always had some strange ideas," Rainey said. "But he's a good boy. He's made some bad choices, but he's promised me he's going to do better."

"Then I hope he will," Bette said. The timer dinged and she pulled the last tray of petit fours out of the oven. "These need to cool before I decorate them. The oven is all yours if you need it to prepare lunch."

"Oh, I made a stew and sandwiches," Rainey said. "We'll be fine."

"I think I'll go see if Lacy needs any help with the decorations for tonight," Bette said. She still wasn't that comfortable with the older woman.

She was crossing the living room when Cody hailed her. "Bette!"

She turned to find him moving toward her. He still wore the sweatshirt over one arm, leaving the other arm free. "Can you help me with something in my cabin?" he asked. "It's supposed to be a surprise for Travis, so I can't really tell Lacy or his folks."

"I'd like to," she said. "But I was going to see if Lacy needed any help with the decorations for her party."

"Emily is helping her," he said. "It sounded to me like they have everything under control."

"All right." She was curious to know this big secret of his.

They collected their coats and crossed to Cody's cabin, which was the twin of Bette's. The only real difference was a large stuffed cow that occupied the chair beside the small table. It was easily three feet long and two feet tall. "Where did you get this?" she asked, hefting the brown-and-white plush beast.

"Gage got it somewhere," Cody said. He slipped out of his coat, then helped her with hers. "This was all his idea—it's a gag gift, for the party tonight."

"You aren't going to the bachelor party, are you?" she said.

"Why not? I can suffer there as well as I can here, and at least there I'll have distractions."

She scowled at him.

"You're cute when you're disgusted with me," he said.

She launched the cow at him. He caught it by one hind leg, grinning. She couldn't help but grin back. "What am I supposed to help you with?" she asked.

He set the cow on the table and picked up a set of deer antlers. "We have to tie these to the cow's head."

"Why?"

"According to Gage, when Travis was twelve, his father and his uncle took him on his first deer hunt. Travis was so nervous and excited he ended up shooting a neighbor's cow. He spent all summer working to pay for that beef."

"Travis did that?" She had a hard time imagining the

straight-arrow sheriff ever coloring outside the lines, even as a kid.

"Gage swears it's true."

"And, of course, his brother never let him forget it," she said.

"Of course." Cody picked up a spool of brown ribbon. "I bought this. I figured we could use it to tie on the antlers—but that's kind of hard to do one-handed. And you probably tie a better bow than I do, anyway."

"I ought to tie a bow around your neck," she said, as she took the spool from him.

"Why? Because I led you into an ambush?"

"No! Do you really think I blame you?"

All the teasing and laughter had left his eyes. "I'm trained to track people. I ought to know when someone is tracking me."

"You had no reason to believe anyone would follow us," she said. "Much less attack us. It was a fishing trip. And I was having a good time until the shooting started."

"Me, too." He reached out with his uninjured arm and pulled her closer, then kissed her. She sank into that kiss, the tension of the past few days easing. She had missed this—she had missed him.

He raised his head and looked into her eyes. "Do you know what one of my favorite memories of yesterday is?"

"What?"

"When you sacrificed your bra to bandage my wounds."

She laughed. "You would say that."

He shaped his hand to her breast, a mock look of

disappointment pulling down the corners of his mouth. "You're wearing a bra now."

"I have more than one."

"I'll buy you a new one." He slid his hand around to her back and deftly undid the clasp. "Something low-cut. With lace."

"I might have guessed." The last word came out in a rush of breath as he pulled down the neck of her sweater to expose the tops of her breasts. He began kissing his way along them. "Cody, what are you doing?" she gasped.

"This." He pulled the sweater lower, and dragged his tongue across her nipple. "And this." He addressed the other breast.

"But, um, you're wounded," she said.

"Not where it counts." He unzipped her jeans.

"I'm worried I'm going to hurt you," she said.

"Sex is a great pain reliever," he said. "I think you told me that once."

He was definitely making it hard for her to think straight. Then again, what did she need to think about? She wanted him, and she was more than relieved to be with him again. Making love seemed right. Healing. She slid both hands under the sweatshirt he wore, skimming the taut muscles of his stomach and over his chest. "Let me help you undress."

"Best idea you've had in five minutes."

She helped him out of his clothing, with a minimum amount of pain on his part, and multiple apologies on her part. "Maybe we shouldn't do this," she said, after she managed to get the sweatshirt off over his head.

"We definitely should," he said, and slipped his hand inside her panties to persuade her.

"All right, we should," she agreed, a little breathless. She moved toward the bed, then stopped. "Should you lie down, or should I?" What would hurt less for him?

"I have an idea." He grasped her hips and backed her toward the bed, which, like the one in Bette's room, was an old-fashioned iron-framed model that sat high off the floor. With her sitting on the edge of the bed and him standing, they lined up perfectly.

"Oh." She wrapped her legs around his hips. "Good idea."

He leaned over and reached for the condom packet on the bedside table. "I see now you didn't really want help with that cow," she said. "You planned to seduce me." She took the packet from him and tore it open.

"I still need help with the cow." He kissed the side of her neck. "Later."

She took the condom from the packet and reached for him. "Allow me."

"There are…definitely…some advantages…to being one-handed," he breathed as she rolled on the condom. Then he wrapped his arm around her and drew her to him, kissing her fiercely.

The man knew how to kiss—deftly setting every nerve on fire with the pressure of his lips or the sweep of his tongue. She reveled in the feel of him in her arms, tracing the line of his spine with her fingers, cupping his firm ass. She let out a sigh when he slid into her, and opened her eyes to stare into his as he began to move. She grasped his hips and met him stroke for stroke, watching as passion etched deeper lines on his face and darkened his eyes. Then he raised her legs, tilting her back slightly, and her breathing grew ragged and her vision blurred. She was dimly aware of the bed knocking against the wall, and her own rising cries as a powerful climax shook her. Cody gripped her more tightly and drove harder, until he came with a shout.

They fell back together on the bed. Bette rolled over and he slid up beside her. "Careful of your shoulder," she cautioned.

"What shoulder?" he breathed.

They lay, not speaking, for a long time. She trailed her fingers through his hair, eyes half-closed. "Did you ever think you'd be involved with a former bank robber?" she asked.

"No." He lifted his head to look at her. "Did you ever think you'd take a US marshal as your lover?"

"Never."

"What's going to happen to us?" he asked.

"Someone is trying to hurt me—maybe kill me," she said. "This isn't a great time to talk about the future."

"Call me an optimist," he said. "I think it is."

"Since when is any lawman an optimist?"

"Since I met you." He kissed her cheek. "You have me believing all kinds of improbable things."

Improbable. That's exactly what they were. Yet here they lay, together, and in spite of the fact that her life might be in danger and she didn't know what she should do next, she was happier than she had ever been.

Chapter 16

"I can't believe how beautiful everything turned out." Emily stepped back and admired the array of white-clothed tables, each with a centerpiece of white lilies and silver plumes. The buffet table featured similar arrangements, as well as carved-crystal snowflakes and drifts of glittery fake snow.

"Most of the decorations were Lacy's idea," Bette said. "I stuck to what I know best—food."

"And what food." Emily lifted the plastic wrap off a tray of silver-and-white-frosted petit fours. "They look so good—you don't mind if I take just one, do you?"

"Go ahead," Bette said. "But just one."

Grinning, Emily chose a petit fours and bit it in half. The delight on her face transformed into a grimace. She spit out the cake, choking.

"What is it?" Bette asked. "What's wrong?"

"The cake!" Emily stared at the mangled pastry in her napkin. "I don't mean to criticize but—did you taste these?"

"No. I mean, I did taste the batter, and I sampled the frosting—they were fine."

"This one wasn't fine."

Bette pulled another cake from the tray and bit into it. The bitterness brought tears to her eyes. She spit it out and looked around for water, but there was none. "Someone has done something to my petit fours!" she wailed. She scanned the buffet table. The finger sandwiches and cream puffs were still in the refrigerator. She wouldn't put them out until after the guests arrived. But the scones, chocolate-dipped apricots and hazelnut shortbread were already arranged on the table, covered with plastic wrap. "We'd better taste everything," she said. "The refrigerated food, too."

Looking doubtful, Emily followed Bette down the table. They sampled cakes and scones and cookies, and by the time they reached the end of the table, Emily was smiling again. "Everything else is delicious," she said.

Bette remembered Rainey's interest in the petit fours, and how she had left the cook alone in the kitchen with the cakes while she went to Cody's cabin. She turned and raced toward the kitchen, Emily in pursuit. "Where are you going?" Emily called.

Bette burst into the kitchen. Rainey looked up from the dishes she was washing. "Is something wrong?" she asked.

"You know what's wrong." Bette crowded the other woman against the sink. "What did you put in my petit fours?"

Rainey's eyes widened in fear. "What are you talking about? I didn't touch your petit fours."

"I left you alone with them and you put something in them," Bette said. "You wanted to embarrass me in front of Lacy and her guests, so you ruined them."

Rainey leaned away from her. "I swear I didn't."

"Taste this!" Bette shoved a cake at the older woman.

Hesitantly, Rainey took the cake and put it in her mouth. She immediately made a face and spit it out. "That's horrible! It tastes like pine cleaner."

"Bette." Emily tugged on Bette's arm. "I think Rainey is telling the truth. Why would she doctor your cakes that way?"

"If she didn't do it, her son did." Bette glared at the cook. "Has Doug been in here this afternoon?"

Rainey hesitated. "He helped me with lunch," she said after a pause.

"Did you see him messing with the cakes?" Bette asked.

"No. I swear I didn't." She swallowed. "He asked me about them, and I told them they were petit fours for the party tonight, and that you were coming back later to frost them."

"Was he ever alone in the kitchen after that?" Bette asked.

Rainey looked panicked. "Maybe," she said. "But why would he ruin your beautiful cakes? And try to ruin Lacy's party? He likes Lacy."

"But he doesn't like me," Bette said. "And you said he's afraid of me. He would like me to leave here."

Rainey hung her head. "He was in here alone while I cleared the table. When I came back, he was acting funny. He left before we had even finished the washing. He told me he had something he needed to do."

"Where is he now?" Emily asked.

"In his room, I guess," Rainey said.

"We'd better talk to him," Bette said.

Rainey led the way up a set of back stairs, to a room at the rear of the house. She knocked on the door, but there was no answer. "Doug?" she called. "Doug, it's Mom. Please open the door."

Silence. Rainey frowned. "I can't think why he's not answering."

"Is the door locked?" Bette asked.

Rainey tried the knob. It wouldn't turn.

"We'll have to wait until he comes back or wakes up," Emily said.

"No we don't." Rainey reached up and took a cotter key from atop the door frame. "All the doors around here unlock this way."

"I always forget about those," Emily said.

Rainey slipped the angled bit of metal into the hole beneath the doorknob and they heard the lock pop.

Doug's room was dark and crowded, the blinds drawn and items piled on the floor, the bed and every flat surface—clothing, shoes, magazines, video games—and on a bookshelf by the door, a bottle of pine cleaner and a syringe. Bette stared at the items. "He must have injected the cakes with this," she said. "He could have even done it after I iced them. If he used just a little bit you wouldn't even be able to tell what he had done by looking."

Behind her, Rainey began to weep. "Why would he do something so horrible?" she sobbed. "Why would he ruin your beautiful cakes?"

The woman's distress moved Bette. She was angry about the ruined petit fours, but Rainey was devastated. "I don't blame you," she said. "Doug is responsible for his own actions."

"What are you going to do about the party?" Rainey asked.

"We have plenty of other food," Emily said. "I'm betting the sandwiches and cream puffs are all right."

"But the cakes—you have to have cake at a party," Rainey said. She sniffed and wiped her eyes. "I can help you make more. I'll do whatever you need me to do."

Bette considered the offer. "We don't have time to make more petit fours."

"We could make cupcakes," Rainey said. "They don't take long, and you could decorate them all fancy."

Bette nodded. "Cupcakes are a good idea." Not as impressive as petit fours, maybe, but the women would like them. She patted Rainey's arm. "Come on. Let's get to work. We have just enough time before Lacy's guests arrive."

"Surprised to see you here, Cody," Dwight said as he entered Moe's Pub that evening and spotted the marshal at the end of the bar with Travis and Gage. "How are you feeling?"

"About like you'd expect someone to feel who's been shot and carved up." Cody wrapped his hand around a glass of iced tea. He would have preferred a stiff whiskey, but before leaving the ranch he had reluctantly taken one of the pain pills the doctor had prescribed and he knew better than to mix narcotics and alcohol.

"You could have stayed back at the ranch," Travis said.

"He didn't want to miss seeing you attempt to cut loose and enjoy yourself," Gage said.

Travis looked as if he wanted to cut something, all

right. Or someone. "What's the plan for this evening?" he asked.

"I wanted to hire dancing girls, but you nixed that idea," Gage said.

"There are no dancing girls in Eagle Mountain," Dwight said. "What's plan B?"

"Plan B is to buy the groom a beer." He signaled to Moe, who was behind the bar. He slid over a pint and Gage handed it to Travis. "Then we have a little gift for you."

Cody and Bette had eventually gotten around to attaching the antlers to the stuffed cow—they poked out of the top of the shopping bag he handed to Travis. The sheriff set aside the pint glass and accepted the bag with the stoicism of a man who has resigned himself to eating a live worm. He pulled the cow out of the bag and his cheeks pinked. The rest of the men, who had already heard the story behind the gift, guffawed. "You never got a trophy from your first deer hunt," Gage said. "So we thought you deserved one now."

"You can hang it over the fireplace," one of the groomsmen, Ryder Stewart, said.

"Very funny." Travis set the cow aside and stood. "How about a game of pool?"

Someone put money in the jukebox, and most of the men teamed up to play pool at the two tables at the back of the room. Cody remained at the end of the bar, sipping tea and wondering if he would have been better off staying home. Gage slid onto the stool next to Cody. "You should have been the one to have a bachelor party," Cody said. "You would have enjoyed it more."

"Oh, Travis is having a good time." They watched as the sheriff bent over the pool table and lined up his cue. "He's a shark and this lets him show off his skills, plus I'm going to make sure he drinks more than he should. He needs to forget about this serial killer business for a while."

"Is he getting a lot of pressure from the town to solve the crime?"

"Eagle Mountain's new mayor thinks Travis hung the moon—but he doesn't need to apply any pressure. My brother is good at doing that himself."

"It's a tough case," Cody said.

"It is. We can't catch a break, and meanwhile, this guy goes around murdering more women." He set down his beer. "This conversation is too depressing. We need to talk about something else."

"Such as?"

"Such as—what's up with you and that pretty blonde caterer?"

"Bette."

"Yeah. Bette." Gage gave him the look of a cop interrogating a suspect. "Travis said you went to bat for her pretty hard over those stolen rings. You don't think she took them."

"Travis doesn't, either," Cody said. "Not really."

"Travis said she was pretty upset about you getting shot," Gage said.

"The guy was shooting at her, too. That would upset anybody."

"She was the first person you asked about when I picked you up this morning."

Cody sipped his tea. "Why are you interested in my personal life?"

"I'm a nosy guy. It's a good quality for a cop."

"Go nose into someone else's life."

Gage stood. "Maybe I will."

The door to the bar opened and a man stepped in. He scanned the room, taking in the half a dozen men playing pool and the two at the bar. A tall man with hunched shoulders, he had a few wisps of gray hair about his balding head and a ragged gray goatee. Moe moved from behind the bar. "This is a private party," he said. "Didn't you see the sign on the door?"

"It's okay, Moe." Cody put up his hand. He motioned to the newcomer. "Come on in. I'll buy you a drink."

The man hesitated, but apparently the prospect of a free drink won him over. He shambled to the bar and took the stool a few down from Cody. Moe had just served him a beer when Travis and Gage joined them. Travis slid onto the stool beside the man. "Hello, Carl," he said.

The man flinched. "Are you talking to me?"

"Carl Wayland, right?" Travis asked.

"I don't know anybody by that name." He turned his attention to his drink.

"How about Charlie Fergusen?"

"I'd better go." The man stood, but Gage put a hand on his shoulder. "Stay a minute and talk to us."

Carl looked around. All the men had gathered at the bar now. Dwight and Ryder still carried pool cues. "What is this?" he demanded. "Can't a man come in out of the cold and have a drink?"

"What are you doing in Eagle Mountain, Carl?" Travis asked, his tone genial.

"None of your business."

"Where are you staying since you checked out of the Eagle Mountain Inn?" Cody asked.

"Again—none of your business." He hunched over the bar and sipped his beer.

"Where were you yesterday afternoon?" Travis asked. "From, say, three o'clock until seven?"

Carl remained silent.

"What about Wednesday morning?" Cody asked. "Where were you then?"

Carl shoved back from the bar. "I gotta get out of here. It stinks too much of cop in this place."

He moved past Travis and Gage, but Cody blocked his exit. "Bette Fuller doesn't want to see you," he said. "If you come anywhere near her, I'll have you back in jail, charged with harassment."

Carl grinned, showing a broken incisor. "Bette is an old friend," he said. "A real nice girl. When you see her, you tell her I said hello." He pushed past Cody and out the door. Cody started to follow, but Travis held him back.

"I just want to get a look at his car," Cody said.

"Dwight is taking care of that," Travis said. "He's going to follow him and see where he's staying."

Of course Travis would have thought of that. Cody sat on the bar stool again.

Travis's phone rang. He answered it, turning slightly away from Cody and speaking low. Then he pocketed the phone and looked around the room. "Gage!"

Every head in the room swiveled toward the sheriff. There was no mistaking the urgency in his voice. Gage came over. "What's up?" he asked.

Travis voice was rough with strain. "There's been another woman killed," he said. "They found her in her car near the high school."

"To Lacy!" Maya held a glass of champagne aloft in a toast. "A wonderful friend who is going to be a beautiful bride, my future sister-in-law and a woman who knows how to throw a great party!"

"To Lacy!" the others echoed.

"Speech! Speech!" someone called.

Cheeks flushed with happiness—and maybe a little from the champagne—Lacy stood. "Thank you all so much for coming tonight," she said. "It's been so special for me to get to spend this time with all my favorite women in the world." She spread her arms wide, as if to give them all a hug, and they clapped.

Lacy gestured to the one vacant place at the tables. "I'm so sorry Paige wasn't able to be here. Everyone keep your fingers crossed that the highway opens again before the wedding."

"I ate her share of the refreshments," Emily said, to more laughter.

"Wasn't the food fantastic?" Lacy said. She held up her champagne glass. "I want to propose a toast to my friend Bette, who made this scrumptious feast."

"Thanks to Rainey, too," Bette said. "She helped a lot with the cupcakes." Together, Rainey and Bette had baked carrot cake and devil's food cupcakes, decorated with cream cheese or buttercream frosting, and decorated with hand-piped snowflakes.

"And now I have something else for you all," Lacy said. She beckoned to Bette, who came forward and began handing out little white boxes tied with silver ribbon. "These are just little thank-yous to all of you for being in my wedding. I appreciate each of you so much."

A beaming Casey held aloft the little crystal snowflake on a silver chain that Lacy had chosen for her.

The other women oohed and aahed over the jewelry they received while Bette rearranged the refreshment table, consolidating the food so it looked less picked-over, and removing empty trays and platters. There wasn't that much left, a sign that the women had enjoyed everything. Fortunately, the petit fours were the only casualty of Doug's tampering.

"Bette, come up here," Lacy said.

Bette turned, surprised. Lacy had retrieved a white gift bag from somewhere. "I have something for you, too," she said. "You didn't think I'd leave you out, did you?"

Feeling a little self-conscious, Bette walked over and accepted the gift bag. "Open it!" Emily called.

The bag contained a large box wrapped in silver paper. Bette lifted the lid of the box and gasped. "Lacy!" She lifted out a pristine chef's smock, her name in dark blue lettering on the left breast pocket. Beneath this was a pair of checked chef's pants. Tears stung Bette's eyes as she stroked the fabric.

"I remembered you saying how one day you wanted a real chef's outfit," Lacy said.

Yes, Bette had said that. But these items, the cut and quality of them, had been out of Bette's reach when she had so many other expenses associated with starting her catering business. "They're beautiful," she said.

The friends hugged, then retreated to the kitchen with the boxes. "That's a really nice gift," Rainey said, admiring the chef's coat. "You'll look real professional in them." She nodded toward the party. "Travis found himself a really nice young woman. I wasn't too sure at first, but then it goes to show I can be inclined to misjudge."

"I think we all do that," Bette said. She had misjudged Rainey, mistaking her insecurity for animosity and her concern for her son as involvement in his wrongdoing.

"Doug still hasn't come home," Rainey said. "It's

not like him to be away so long. I guess he knows he's in big trouble over those petit fours."

"I had to tell Lacy what happened," Bette said. "And I'm sure she'll tell Travis. It's up to them what happens next."

Rainey nodded. "I wanted him here because I wanted to keep him out of trouble," she said. "I thought away from the city, he'd have less temptation. And this would be a good job to have on his résumé. I guess you know how it is—when you have a blot on your record, people never want to look past it. They don't even give you a chance."

"I know." Lacy had given Bette a chance—her wedding planner had already talked to Bette about catering another wedding for a client in Denver, and with a few more jobs like that, and good references, she would be on her way.

"The problem is, a young man who's used to the city life gets bored here in the country," Rainey continued. "There's not enough for him to do. And it's always been hard for Doug to make friends. He told me recently he ran into someone he knew from Denver, who was visiting Eagle Mountain, and that seemed to cheer him up. But I worry, you know? Maybe if his father had stayed around to be a good influence on him he would have had an easier time of it. Or if I'd stayed in Denver to keep a closer eye on him, but as soon as he was out of school, he was anxious to be out on his own, and the opportunity came to take this job with the Walkers—I didn't feel I could pass it up. They've been so good to me—I hope they don't blame me for what he's done."

"I'm sure they won't." Bette squeezed the older woman's arm. "I'll make sure they know you didn't have any part in this," she said.

Rainey sniffed and turned away. "They're still talking and eating in there," she said. "You have time to put your gift in your cabin. You don't want those nice things getting dirty. And really, I can handle cleaning up after them myself. I'll box up the leftovers and we can deal with the rest in the morning."

"Thanks. But I shouldn't be gone long." Bette grabbed her coat from the pegs by the back door and stepped outside. The moon was almost full and provided plenty of light for the walk to her cabin. The old snow crunched underfoot, but new flakes were beginning to fall, like a sifting of powdered sugar over an already-iced cake.

She reached the cabin and shifted the box to one arm so she could dig out her key. The new one the Walkers had given her when they changed the locks was attached to a key chain with a rabbit's foot—maybe they hoped this key would be luckier for her than the last one. She grabbed hold of the key chain and started to pull it out when a strong arm wrapped around her neck and dragged her back. She dropped the bag that contained the chef's outfit, the contents spilling across the welcome mat in front of her door. She tried to shout, but the arm around her neck tightened. "Hello again, Bette," a familiar voice growled in her ear. "Or should I say, goodbye."

Chapter 17

Anita Allbritton was a short, plump woman of about forty, with strawberry blond hair and round, tortoise-shell glasses. She taught business technology and computer science at the high school, and worked summers at the local Humane Society thrift store. She drove a burnt-orange Toyota Yaris, and was discovered in the front seat of this vehicle in the high school parking lot by a parent who was picking up his son from a sleepover.

"I recognized Anita's car and thought it was odd it was parked way out on the edge of the lot like that," the very agitated man told Travis and Cody, who had insisted on coming with the sheriff to the scene. "I stopped to see if there was any kind of note or obvious sign of trouble." He swallowed, struggling for composure. "I couldn't believe when I looked inside and saw... saw..." He shook his head, unable to go on.

What he had seen was Anita Allbritton laid across the front seat of her vehicle, her throat cut and her wrists and ankles bound with duct tape. Travis had found the Ice Cold Killer's card in the ashtray of the car, and a bloodstain beside a dumpster behind the school that he thought indicated the kill site. The car itself was clean of evidence.

"It almost looks like it was just vacuumed," Gage said, studying the vehicle's gray carpeting. "Do you think he did that—took the time to vacuum it out?"

"Maybe." Travis looked around the lot. "There are no lights this far out. No games or other activities tonight. Not a lot of traffic on the road. The killer may have felt he could take his time, be more careful. It was just chance that the parents decided to meet here to pick up the kids from that birthday sleepover. Just chance that the dad drove over to take a look."

"You don't think he's the killer?" Gage asked.

Travis shook his head. "He had his two children in the car with him. We'll confirm the time he left his house with his wife, but I'm pretty sure it will check out." The man had been devastated by the discovery, and had vomited on the edge of the parking lot. Fortunately, by the time Travis questioned him, he had pulled himself together and was anxious to get his children away from there.

Deputy Jamie Douglass, an attractive young woman with long dark hair worn in a bun beneath the regulation Stetson, joined them. "I talked with the Delaneys," she said. "They're the parents who met Mr. Karnack here to drop off his son, Colin. They didn't even notice the car parked over here. They live on the other side of town. They chose the high school as a good place to meet because it's halfway between the two homes."

Travis surveyed the area. The school was flanked on three sides by empty pasture. Across the street the school district's bus barn and maintenance sheds were deserted. "There's a neighborhood behind the bus barn," Travis said. "Start knocking on doors over there. Maybe someone was driving by here and saw something."

"Yes, sir." Jamie shoved her hands into the pockets of her Sherpa-lined leather jacket. "I'm sorry I had to break up your bachelor party with something like this," she said.

"You weren't interrupting anything," Travis said. "Whenever I'm not working on this case, I'm thinking about it—and dreading the next call about a dead woman." He looked at the Yaris. "It was only a matter of time. We aren't even managing to slow him down."

"Maybe we'll catch a break this time and someone saw something," Jamie said. "I'll get right on it."

"What can I do to help?" Cody asked, when she was gone.

"Go back to the ranch," Travis said. "Tell the women at Lacy's party to spend the night there. We have plenty of room. I don't want any of them out driving around tonight. And I'll feel a lot better if there's at least one cop there with them."

"Of course." Cody hesitated, then said, "Don't let this eat at you. You're doing everything you can to catch this guy—he's just not giving you anything to work with."

Travis studied the toes of his boots. "They tell you in the academy not to take the job personally. Maybe that works in the city, but in a small town like Eagle Mountain, everything is personal. I knew almost every one of these victims—some better than others, but they're all my responsibility. I wasn't just hired by the town—the citizens of this county elected me to do a job. There's no way to do that job except by taking it personally."

"It's why you're good at it," Cody said.

Travis swore—something Cody had never heard him do. "I'm not good at it right now," he said. "If I was, I would have caught this guy—or guys—by now."

There was no sense arguing about it, Cody thought. In Travis's position, he would feel the same way. Though he could have told Travis that sense of responsibility wasn't limited to small-town cops. As much as Cody had tried to deny it in the weeks since it had happened, he felt responsible for the man who had killed himself in front of him. The man might be the worst kind of criminal—one who preyed on young children. But Cody's job had been to bring him to justice. When the guy pulled the trigger on that gun, he had cheated his victims and their families of that justice. He had prevented Cody from doing his job.

The drive to the ranch on the narrow mountain road seemed to take forever. Snow was falling again, and the cold seeped through Cody's clothes and the layer of bandages to his wound, until he felt like a giant was gripping him with strong fingers and squeezing, hard. The pain pill he had taken before the party had long since worn off. All he could do was grit his teeth and clench the steering wheel with one hand and keep pushing forward.

At the ranch, the women were gathered in the living room, donning coats and exchanging hugs. They stopped talking when Cody walked in and turned to look at him. "Cody, you're white as a sheet," Mrs. Walker exclaimed. "Come sit down before you fall down."

He shook his head. "Ladies, I have some news," he said. He looked for Bette in the crowd but didn't find her. She was probably in the kitchen, cleaning up after the party. "I'm afraid there's been another murder, a teacher from the school."

"Who?" It was Maya who spoke. She pushed her way to the front of the group. "Cody, please tell me," she said. "You're talking about one of my coworkers."

"Anita Allbritton." He looked at them sternly. "That information doesn't leave this room. The sheriff hasn't had time to notify her family."

"Poor Anita," Maya moaned. "How horrible."

"Travis wants you all to stay here tonight," he said. "We'd feel better if you weren't out on the roads tonight."

"Of course," Mrs. Walker said. "We have plenty of room."

"It'll be like a slumber party," Lacy said. "We'll find night things for you to wear—and we still have a couple of bottles of champagne and more food."

They moved away from the door, removing coats and talking all at once about this latest turn of events. A group clustered about Maya, asking about Anita, while Emily and Brenda conferred with Lacy and Mrs. Walker about sleeping arrangements. Cody interrupted them. "Where's Bette?" he asked.

"In the kitchen, probably," Lacy said. She smiled. "The party turned out so wonderful. It was a real triumph."

"I'll let her know what's going on," he said and made his way to the kitchen.

Rainey was alone in the room, arranging leftover sandwiches in plastic storage containers. She looked up at his arrival. "Hello," she said. "What can I do for you?"

"Is Bette here?" he asked.

"No, she isn't. She left a little while ago to put something away in her cabin and she hasn't come back yet. I told her I didn't mind cleaning up after the party and I guess she decided to take me up on the offer."

"That doesn't sound like her, leaving you to do the work," Cody said.

"Well, no, it doesn't. But maybe she was tired. She worked really hard today." She yawned. "So did I."

"I'll stop by her cabin and check on her," Cody said. He moved past her to the back door, quickening his pace as he stepped into the snow. He told himself the latest murder had raised his anxiety level, but he couldn't shake the sense that something was really wrong. By the time he could see the row of cabins ahead, he had broken into a painful jog, every movement jarring his injured shoulder.

The scene didn't look right. Something was scattered across the porch of Bette's cabin. He bounded up the steps and stared at the gift bag, a box wrapped in torn silver paper, and what looked like a top and a pair of pants spilling across the doormat. A gift? But what was it doing here?

He stepped over the items and pounded on the door. "Bette! Bette, it's me, Cody!"

He pressed his ear to the door but heard nothing inside. He tried the knob, but the door was locked—and Bette was the only one with a key to the new lock.

He forced himself to step back, to slow down and examine the scene objectively—to think like the cop he was. He studied the items strewn across the door-mat. They hadn't been placed—they had been dropped. Bette had been standing here in front of the door, maybe searching for her key, and something had made her drop the package. Surprise? Fear?

He retraced his path to the steps and studied the snow illuminated in the moonlight. The snow here was churned up, then dug into grooves. A struggle, then someone being dragged backward, the person's heels digging in. Heart pounding, he followed the marks until they stopped, beside the track from a vehicle.

He squatted down and studied the impressions, still fairly clear despite a light dusting of snow. Deep tread on wide tires. But not car or truck tires. They were too close together. They were tractor tires—or no, tires of one of the utility vehicles used around the ranch for everything from hauling hay to plowing snow to herd-ing cattle.

That meant that whoever took Bette was probably still on the ranch. Cody pulled out his phone and called Travis. "I'm here at the ranch and Bette is missing," he told the sheriff. "Looks like someone grabbed her on the front porch of her cabin. I found the tracks of what looks like a utility vehicle. I'm going to follow them."

"Wait for me," Travis said. "I can be there in thirty minutes."

"I don't have time to wait," Cody said. "The snow is covering the tracks fast." And he didn't know what whoever took her planned to do with Bette. He might already be too late. "Where is Carl? Is Dwight still with him?"

"Dwight followed him to a rental out of town, then he returned to help process the scene at the high school."

Carl could have hurt Bette. "I have to go after them now," Cody said.

"Get one of the ranch hands to go with you," Travis said. "Or more than one."

"I don't have time to go looking for people," he said. "Besides, it's Saturday night. They might not even be here. They're probably in town, or visiting family or friends."

Snow was falling harder. "I have to go," he said. "You can track me when you get here." He ended the call and stowed his phone, then pulled his coat more tightly around him and set off across the snow, following the line of treads that led over the pasture.

Bette lay on the floor of the old cabin where the sleighing party had gathered. Was that really only two days ago? Duct tape tightly bound her hands and feet, and a bone-deep chill had seeped in, so that her teeth kept chattering—or maybe that was just fear.

Carl sat on an upturned section of log across from her. "I bet you never thought you'd see me again," he said. He chuckled, a sound like an accordion with a hole in the bellows. "Get it, 'Bette'?"

"Why are you doing this, Carl?" she asked. "What did I ever do to you?"

"Oh, it's nothing personal, sweetheart. I'm just doing a favor for an old friend. He needs you out of the way before you open your big mouth."

"You mean Eddie." She'd known it, hadn't she? As

much as she told herself she had nothing to worry about, that Eddie wouldn't waste any more time on her, she'd been fooling herself.

"Eddie?" Carl laughed again. "Not him. He's dead."

"Dead?"

"Yeah. Got knifed in an alley one night just a couple weeks after he got out." Carl shrugged. "Guess he crossed the wrong guy."

"I don't understand," she said. "If you're not doing this for Eddie…"

"You don't think I have more than one friend?"

Stamping footsteps on the porch interrupted him. The door opened and Doug Whittington came in, brushing snow off the shoulders of his coat. "We could have picked a better night for this," he said.

"Doug, what are you doing?" Bette asked.

He scowled at her. "What do you think we're doing? We're going to slit your throat, stick you in your car and drive you out to some deserted road. By the time the cops find you, Carl and I will be safely tucked in our beds—innocent lambs who don't know anything about what happened to you."

"You're the Ice Cold Killer?" She hated the way her voice shook on the words.

"No!" Doug shook his head. "But that's who the cops will think did you." He felt around in his pockets and handed Carl a small white card. "This is why I was late. I had to wait until the coast was clear so I could sneak into the Walkers' home office and print this."

Carl showed Bette the card, which read "Ice Cold." "It's genius, right?" he said.

"It's a stupid catering job!" she said. "That's not worth killing me over."

He walked over to her and stood looking down. "You really don't know who I am, do you?" he asked. He picked up one of the kerosene lanterns and held it closer to his face. "Sure I don't look familiar?"

She stared, recognition washing over her like a bucket of cold water. "You drove the getaway car," she whispered.

"Bingo." He set the lantern down. "I couldn't have you telling the police that, could I? They don't just want me for my part in the bank robbery—they want to hang me for the murder of that pedestrian. It wasn't my fault the dope walked out in front of me!"

"But I didn't remember it was you!" she said. "I couldn't have told the police anything."

"You'd have figured it out soon enough," Doug said. "I couldn't keep avoiding you all the time. Not with my mom nagging me about helping her more in the kitchen, and you always popping in and out of there. It's your own fault we're having to take such drastic measures, you know."

"What do you mean?" she asked.

"I tried to warn you off," he said. "I left that message on your door—I even hit you in the head with that rock. I thought you'd believe you'd narrowly escaped being the Ice Cold Killer's next victim and you'd want to get out of Dodge, wedding or no wedding."

"You stole the wedding rings and planted them in my room," she said.

He frowned. "I thought the sheriff would carry you off to jail and that would be the last we saw of you. It was really tempting to keep those rings for myself, but I figured that was working a little too close to home. But then that marshal had to stick his nose in things and I finally accepted that I wasn't going to scare you off. I was going to have to do something more drastic."

"That's where I come in," Carl said. "A job like this works better with two people."

"So he called you to come out and help kill me," she said.

"Not exactly," Carl said. "I actually looked him up. I wanted to see about doing another job together. He told me about his problem with you and I offered to help him out."

"Which one of you tampered with the snowmobile and shot at Cody and me?" she asked.

"That was me," Carl said. "I should have just picked you off while you were sitting out there on the ice, but I wanted to make it a little more fun. I almost had you, too. A few more minutes and the marshal was bound to run out of ammo, then I would have closed in for the kill." He frowned. "Too bad I didn't finish off the marshal when I had the chance. I would have liked to have taken out a fed."

Bette looked at Doug. "You're being stupid," she said. "You'll never get away with this."

"Who are you calling stupid? I'm the only one involved in that bank job that didn't get caught. I've been walking around free while you did eight years. Besides, Travis and his buddies think I'm just some jealous punk. They think poisoning your fancy cakes is as malicious as I get." He reached down and took her arm. "Come on. We need to go."

He lifted her by the arms, while Carl hefted her legs. They carried her out to the utility vehicle and dumped her in the bed. She had to lie with her knees to her chin to fit. "This snow is perfect," Carl said. "It will cover up our tracks. Did you get her car keys?"

"I got them," Doug said. "I had to break the back window to get in. The key I had for the door to her cabin doesn't work anymore. They must have changed the locks after the business with the rings."

"I told you that was never going to work," Carl said. "You should have just kept the rings for yourself. That gold is worth a lot these days. We could have melted it down and no one would ever know."

"Yeah, well, it's too late now." Doug climbed in beside him. "Let's get this over with."

Carl started the vehicle and it jolted forward. Bette tried to sit up. If she could lean out over the back, maybe she could fall out.

And then what? It wasn't as if she could run away, or even crawl, trussed up as she was. She closed her eyes and tried to pray. Surely someone from the ranch house had missed her by now—Lacy, or even Rainey. What time would Cody and the others return from Travis's party? Probably not until late. Too late for her.

"What the—!" The vehicle skidded sharply to the right as gunshots sounded. Bette flattened herself to the bed of the cargo area, flinching as a bullet thudded into the side of the vehicle.

"It's that marshal!" Doug shouted. He—or maybe Carl, Bette couldn't be sure—returned fire.

"Come on!" Doug shouted. "He's on foot. He can't catch up with us."

"I'm going as fast as I can," Carl said. "It's not that easy in this snow."

Another bullet struck the vehicle, this time hitting the tailgate, inches from Bette's curled legs. She had to let Cody know she was in here, before he accidentally shot her.

Grunting with the effort, she sat up, praying Cody

would see her. She looked back and spotted him, pounding after the utility vehicle, his gun in his uninjured hand. But he was no longer firing. He had seen her; she was sure of it.

The vehicle jounced over rough ground, throwing her back against the tailgate. One of the men fired at Cody, but the shot was wild. She wondered if they were even aiming—if it was possible to aim in the wildly careening vehicle.

She jolted against the tailgate again, and one side of the latch popped. Sitting up again, she braced herself against the side of cargo bed and slammed both feet into the other end of the latch. It gave way and, afraid of losing her nerve if she waited, she rolled out of the vehicle.

She hit the ground hard, but the thick snow provided some cushion. She forced herself to keep rolling, despite the pain of every movement, trying to put as much distance between herself and her two captors as possible.

Cody stopped her, dropping to his knees beside her. "I'm here," he gasped, trying to catch his breath.

She lay still, tears freezing on her cheeks. "What are they doing?" she asked.

"They're coming back."

"They'll kill us," she said.

"No." He crouched in front of her and fired toward the approaching vehicle. They returned the fire, but as before, their shots went wild. Cody kept firing, a rapid burst of staccato reports. Bette closed her eyes and waited—for what, she wasn't sure.

And then she realized the sound of the utility vehicle's motor was fading. And Cody had stopped shooting. "They're running away," he said.

He holstered his weapon, then found a knife and

began cutting away the layers of tape around her wrists and ankles. He helped her sit up, rubbing her hands between his own to restore her circulation. She cupped his face and kissed him. They held each other for a long moment, neither of them speaking.

"Come on," he said finally. "Let's get out of here before we freeze to death." He stood and helped her to her feet, then, leaning on each other, they started walking toward the ranch house.

Travis and Gage met them when they were halfway home, pulling up on snowmobiles. "Carl Wayland and Doug Whittington are in one of the ranch utility vehicles," Cody said. "I'm pretty sure I wounded both of them. They had kidnapped Bette and they tried to kill both of us."

"They were going to kill me and make it look like another murder by the Ice Cold Killer," Bette said. "Doug even printed up a business card on your home office printer."

"We need to go after them," Travis said. "Can you make it back to the ranch house?"

"Go," Cody said. "We'll be fine."

By the time they reached the house, Bette was shaking with cold and Cody's breath hissed through his teeth with each step. The man had just gotten out of the hospital this morning—how had he even found the strength to come after her?

The women who had attended the party descended on them with blankets and steaming mugs of cocoa and hot water bottles, then Lacy shooed them all away. "Don't bombard them with questions," she said. "Let them catch their breaths."

Bette and Cody huddled together on the sofa. When

Bette had finally stopped shaking, she asked, "Do you think Travis and Gage will find Carl and Doug?"

"They'll find them," he said.

"Doug admitted he wrote that message on my door," she said. "And he stole the rings and planted them in my room. And he was the one who attacked me that day on the road. Carl was the one who tampered with the snowmobile and shot at us."

Cody sipped his cocoa. "Why did they go after you?" he asked.

"Doug was the getaway driver in the robbery. The one who killed that pedestrian. I didn't recognize him, but he had never let me get a really good look at him. Once I saw him in good light, I realized who he was. He was afraid I'd turn him in and he'd go to prison for robbery and for killing that man."

"Where does Carl come in?"

"He came to town to ask Doug to do a job with him. I think he meant another robbery. Doug told him about me and they decided they needed to get rid of me. Permanently."

She laced her fingers in his. "Thanks to you, that didn't happen."

He turned to look at her. "I think I'm going to have to take you into protective custody," he said.

Her heart skipped a beat. "What are you talking about?"

He brought their linked hands to his lips, kissing her knuckles. "One of my jobs as a US marshal is witness protection," he said. "I think I need to put you under my protection. Permanently."

She caught her breath. "You're going to have to speak plainer than that, Marshal."

"I'm asking you to marry me," he said. "I love you and tonight I learned that I don't really want to live without you."

She thought of him, facing down that vehicle racing toward him, bullets flying. He had done that to protect her. To protect what they had found together. "Can a US marshal marry someone with a criminal record?" she asked.

"I don't care if they can or not," he said. "I want to marry you. If you'll have me."

"I'll have you." She kissed his cheek. "But your job—"

"I'm on leave for at least three months, with my injured shoulder. And since I've come here, I've been thinking. Maybe it's time for a change."

"What will you do if you're not a marshal?"

"I have a law degree. All I have to do is pass the bar and I can study for that while I recuperate. What would you think of being married to an attorney?"

"Defense or prosecution?"

"Prosecution. I can leave law enforcement, but I can't leave putting away criminals."

"Fair enough."

He squeezed her hand. "So your answer is yes?"

"Yes. I'll marry you." She kissed him, then couldn't stop smiling. "You know, I have a fabulous recipe for wedding cake."

"I can't wait to taste it."

"By the time we caught up with Carl and Doug, they were ready to surrender," Travis said over breakfast the next morning. "They had wrecked the ute and were both freezing, and bleeding pretty heavily." He glanced at

Cody, who sat across from Travis at the table, next to Bette. "You hit Doug once and Carl twice. None of the shots were serious, though Carl has a broken arm. I've got two deputies guarding them at the clinic. As soon as the doctor will release them, we'll lock them up in our holding cell until we can transfer them to Junction."

"We found that business card on Doug," Gage said. "Too bad we couldn't get them for the Ice Cold murders, too."

"They couldn't have done those murders," Travis said. "Carl was talking to us at Moe's when Anita was killed. He was in Denver when Kelly and Christi died, and Doug was here at the ranch."

"How is Rainey taking the news about Doug?" Lacy asked.

"She's stoic," Travis said. "Blaming herself, I think."

"I imagine she's heartbroken," Bette said. "He's really all she has. She told me she raised him pretty much on her own after his father deserted them."

"I'm glad he's gone," Lacy said. "Poisoning those cakes was downright creepy, and then when I learned all he did to you—well, it was horrible."

"We caught him on camera taking the spare key to the old lock on your cabin yesterday afternoon," Travis said. "And we have the gun Carl used when he shot at you two. We shouldn't have any trouble sending both of them to prison for a long time, on multiple counts."

"Any news on Anita's murder?" Cody asked.

"No." Travis poked at his eggs with a fork, his expression glum. "All we can do is keep looking."

"You'll find the killer," Lacy said. "If anyone can, you will."

"Spoken like a loving bride," Bette said.

"Of course." She looked at each of them in turn. "I'm not being callous, but in spite of this killer, we have a wedding to prepare for," she said. "In the midst of so much tragedy, it's especially important to hold on to the joyous occasions."

Bette lifted her glass of orange juice. "Here, here," she said.

Lacy's smile grew sly. "I hear you have some joyous news of your own," she said.

Bette looked at Cody, who cleared his throat. "Bette and I are going to be married," he said.

"Congratulations," Travis said. "Though it's no surprise."

"No?" Cody asked.

"I figured you were pretty much gone after that first day." He glanced at Lacy. "I know the signs from personal experience."

"We haven't set the date yet," Bette said. "It will be after we're settled again in Denver, but you'll all be invited to the wedding, I promise."

"If I were you, I'd wait until that shoulder heals," Gage said. "Be a shame to have to deal with that on your honeymoon."

"I don't know about that." Bette rubbed Cody's uninjured shoulder. "This way, I have the upper hand. Not a position I've ever been in with a US marshal."

"Watch yourself," Cody said. "Even with one hand tied behind my back—so to speak—I can get the best of you."

"I don't know about that," Lacy said. "It looks to me as if Bette has pulled off one last heist."

Cody's eyes narrowed. "Oh?"

Lacy laughed. "Yeah, you goof. Clearly, she's stolen your heart."

Everyone around the table groaned, but Cody's eyes met Bette's, and she thought she could never get tired of looking into those depths, figuring out what made this man tick. "Guilty as charged," she said. Lacy was right. In spite of all the tragedy around them, it was important to celebrate the things in life worth hanging on to. Like the kind of love that gave you infinite second chances.

* * * * *

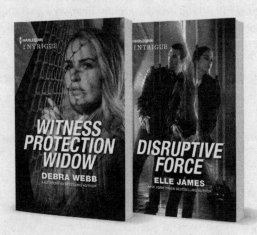

His hands cupped her face. She blinked up at him.

"They buried me," she said, fighting the emotion trying to take over at the thought of never seeing him again.

Anger flashed in his blue eyes, and his jaw muscles clenched. "They better never touch you again. We can make an excuse to get you out of here. Say one of your family members is sick and you had to go."

"They'll see it as weakness," she reminded him. "It'll hurt the case."

He thumbed a loose tendril of hair off her face.

"I don't care, Ree," he said with an overwhelming intensity that became its own physical presence. "I can't lose you."

Those words hit her with the force of a tsunami.

Neither of them could predict what would happen next. Neither could guarantee this case wouldn't go south. Neither could guarantee they would both walk away in one piece.

"Let's take ourselves off the case together," she said, knowing full well he wouldn't take her up on the offer but suggesting it anyway.

Quint didn't respond. When she pulled back and looked into his eyes, she understood why. A storm brewed behind those sapphire-blues, crystalizing them, sending fiery streaks to contrast against the whites. Those babies were the equivalent of a raging wildfire that would be impossible to put out or contain. People said eyes were the window to the soul. In Quint's case, they seemed the window to his heart.

He pressed his forehead against hers and took in an audible breath. When he exhaled, it was like he was releasing all his pent-up frustration and fear. In that moment, she understood the gravity of what he'd been going through while she'd been gone. Kidnapped. For all he knew, left for dead.

So she didn't speak, either. Instead, she leaned into their connection, a connection that tethered them as an electrical current ran through her to him and back. For a split second, it was impossible to determine where he ended and she began.

Don't miss
Mission Honeymoon *by Barb Han,*
available August 2022 wherever
Harlequin Intrigue books and ebooks are sold.

Harlequin.com